THE BORGIA MISTRESS

A Novel

SARA POOLE

ST. MARTIN'S GRIFFIN
NEW YORK

This is a work of fiction. All of the characters, organizations, and events portrayed in this novel are either products of the author's imagination or are used fictitiously.

www.stmartins.com

Library of Congress Cataloging-in-Publication Data

Poole, Sara, 1951–
The Borgia mistress : a novel / Sara Poole.—1st ed.
p. cm.
ISBN 978-1-250-02352-0 (hardcover)
ISBN 978-0-312-60985-6 (trade paperback)
ISBN 978-1-250-01092-6 (e-book)
1. Alexander VI, Pope, 1431–1503—Fiction. 2. Borgia, Cesare, 1476?–1507—Fiction. 3. Borgia family—Fiction. 4. Women poisoners—Fiction. 5. Family secrets—Fiction. 6. Conspiracies—Fiction. 7. Church and state—Fiction. 8. Renaissance—Italy—Rome—Fiction. I. Title.
PS3569.E42 B677 2012
813'.54—dc22 2012007569

First Edition: May 2012

10 9 8 7 6 5 4 3 2 1

THE BORGIA MISTRESS

Prologue

Montségur, France

March 1244

Hélène! Where are you?" The woman's voice carried over the rough stone walls and across the barren ground at the center of the fortress high atop the rocky crag. Several people turned to look at her, but she ignored them and hurried on. "Hélène!"

"Here, Maman!" The child emerging from the low entrance to one of the many caves that dotted the crag was weighed down by a bucket of water drawn from the cistern hidden within. Small and thin for her seven years, she wore layers of ragged wool that failed to keep out the chill wind. Even so, she smiled at sight of her mother.

"Look," the child said, drawing from beneath her cloak the heel of a small loaf of bread. "Perfecta Jeanine gave it to me for helping to pull up the water."

"We will find a little broth for you to dip it in," her mother said. "But first we must get inside."

As she spoke, shouts echoed from the slope below the fortress. The mother seized her child's hand and ran. Several others within sight did the same, but a few men and women remained where they were out in the open, not moving. Their faces serene, they prayed quietly.

A large round boulder flew through the air and struck an outer wall of the fortress. Almost at once, several more followed. One broke apart as it hit the ground. A large fragment struck a praying woman. Her head whipped back as blood flew from the gash in her skull. She fell and did not get up.

The child, Hélène, tried to hold on to the bucket as she ran, but her mother wrenched it from her and threw it to the side. Together they dove into the shelter of a basement just as another boulder landed nearby. The bombardment continued without surcease for more than an hour. Peering outside, the child saw several more people who had not sought shelter being struck and killed. The sight terrified her.

Her mother gathered her close, holding her daughter's head against her breast and stroking her hair gently.

"Do not be afraid, *ma petite*. You know they are among the Perfect Ones. Death carries no sting for them. They embrace it, assured that they will be free forever from the cycle of rebirth into this world of evil. Instead, they will follow the path of light into the eternal realm of the true God of Goodness."

She drew back a little, smiling down at the child. "We must be happy for them."

"What about Father? Is he going to die?" The thought of

her father being crushed by the flying stones made her want to cry, but she knew that she must not. He was among the *perfecti,* destined for the light. He and the others like him had brought them all to the fortress on the top of the crag months before when the bad men sent by the Pope of Satan had come to their homes in the village below. Ever since, the evil ones had been advancing up the slope of the mountain, coming closer each day with their siege engines and their deadly bombardment. In recent days, the boulders had begun to fall into the fortress itself. Soon the last of the stone walls would be shattered, and then there would be nothing left to protect them except their faith.

"Why doesn't the God of Goodness stop them?" the child asked. "If we pray harder, maybe He will—"

"Hush, Hélène. You know that only the God of Evil rules in this world. He has trapped the light of our souls in these bodies, but we can still free ourselves from Him. Your father and all the Perfect Ones show us the way."

The child nodded, for she trusted her father and loved her mother; but even so, she remained afraid. Long after she should have been asleep that night, she lay awake listening to the low murmur of their voices. Much that they said she did not understand. But she was aware when her mother cried out and began to weep.

In the morning, her mother woke her with a smile that did not reach her eyes. "I have wonderful news," she said. "Your father told me last night that I have been found worthy. Later today, he will perform the rite of *consolamentum* and I will be raised among the Perfect Ones."

Terror flared in the child. Her mother would be like the people crushed beneath the stones. She would go into the light. "Do not leave me behind!"

Just then, her father appeared at the door of the small room they shared. He frowned at his daughter. "You are old enough to know better. Live your life in accordance with our ways and you, too, will be redeemed from this world of evil; if not in this lifetime, then in another."

The thought of being born again and again into the world of evil without the comfort of her mother was more than Hélène could bear. Wrenching sobs broke from her. When her mother would have gone to her, her father pulled her mother away and took her from the room. The child was left alone with her terror.

Hours passed without either of her parents' returning. When her tears were exhausted, Hélène climbed out of the basement and stood for a moment looking out over the valley far below. Dimly she remembered coming to it when she was very small, finding delight in the sparkling streams and lush forests that were filled with birds and flowers in season. For a while, life had been good. But now the shadows cast by the crag and the steep cliffs below made it impossible for her to see the village where they had lived. Perhaps that was just as well. The evil ones were there now; in the thousands, it was said. Soon they would be in the fortress itself.

Her stomach, even shrunken as it was since rations had been cut yet again, rumbled. She thought of trying to find food, but the bombardment could start again at any moment and she was afraid to be caught in the open. As she hesitated, she saw the Perfect Ones, numbering in the several hundred, all going together into the underground chamber where they often met. Left behind were the simple *credenti*—believers—followers of the faith yet not true members of it until they could attain perfection. Gathering her courage, Hélène darted forward and crossed the open space. She pressed herself tightly against a wall and remained still until her heartbeat returned to normal. Only then did she creep forward, listening intently.

Curiosity drove her; that and the hope that she would see her mother at the moment of her transformation into a *perfecta*. It was the greatest wish of all those who belonged to the one true faith to be raised to the state in which escape from this world could be attained. But she was too late. Her mother was in the chamber, but she already wore the dark blue robe of a Perfect One. Her hands were clasped at her waist and her face appeared blank, yet her eyes were red-rimmed.

A man, also enrobed, was passing among the assembly. He held a small, plain bowl covered by a length of linen. Each person he stopped before reached beneath the linen to select a smooth rounded pebble. Most of the stones were white, but a few were black. Hélène's mother reached her hand into the bowl. When she withdrew it, she was holding a white stone. Her father was among the last to draw a stone. His was black.

"It is done, then," he said. "Let us rejoice for those who go on ahead, in the certain knowledge that we will all meet again in the light."

The assembly murmured in agreement. Many began to pray. More than a few appeared to the child's eyes as though they had been transported, their spirits no longer fully attached to this world. She looked to her mother but could not catch sight of her, swallowed up as she was by all the others.

But later, when the Perfect Ones had emerged from the chamber, it was announced that all, *credenti* and *perfecti* together, would share a special meal. Food was brought out such as the child had not seen in months. Although dairy and meat were strictly forbidden, there were dried fruits and fish, nuts, vegetables, and wonderful bread. The child ate until her stomach could hold no more. In the aftermath of the feast, she could hardly keep her eyes open; but she was determined to do so. Though her mother had remained with the Perfect Ones, the child could see her from time to time. She still looked as if she had been crying.

It was dark when the meal ended and families withdrew to their own quarters. Hélène went at once to her pallet on the floor, but her father called her back. He had kept his cloak on and he was holding a small cloth bundle.

"Embrace your mother," he said. "When you meet again, you will both be in the light."

The child stiffened and held back, afraid of the meaning behind his words. But her mother came forward and, taking her gently by the shoulders, looked deeply into her eyes.

"Do not be afraid," she said. "The choice has been made and I rejoice in it. Live your life well, and we will be reunited again soon." Her gaze shifted to the man waiting with some impatience near the door. "Be kind to your father and obey him. He has agreed to remain here while almost all the rest of us go into the light."

"Let me go, too, Maman!" the child cried. "I am not afraid!

Even if I have to come back into this world again, let me go with you now. Please!"

A low murmur of anguish came from her mother. She pressed her lips together, but it was too late. The father had heard.

"Enough," he said as he stepped forward. "The others are waiting. We must go." Looking to his wife, he directed, "Fulfill the teachings of our faith. Show the followers of Satan that we are beyond all fear and dread. Strike at their souls with the strength of our conviction."

Mutely, the woman nodded, but Hélène wondered if she had heard. Her eyes were focused on her daughter even as the father took the child's hand and led her out of the small room. She looked back frantically, clinging to her mother's gaze all the way across the fortress to the far side above the cliffs.

Only a few people were gathered there; the other Perfect Ones whom Hélène had seen choose black stones and several *credenti,* who appeared anxious and fearful. Almost half were children like her.

"Come, then," her father said and led the way down into a chamber that gave way to one of the caves that honeycombed the crag. From there, they went on through a narrow passage where the air was so chill and damp that Hélène began to shiver uncontrollably. When they came out at last, they were at the foot of the crag on the far side opposite the village.

"We shelter in the forest tonight," her father said as he led them toward it. "Tomorrow, we bear witness."

Hélène slept for a few hours on a bed of pine needles, but what rest she found was fractured by images of her mother alone on the crag. No, not alone; she was among the Perfect Ones, and soon she would go into the light. Perhaps the God of Goodness Himself would descend to claim His faithful. Choirs of angels would sing, and the evil ones below would fall to their knees in terror. The thought of witnessing such a miracle eased the pain in the child's heart a little but still, she missed her mother.

Before mid-morning, her father gathered them all together and led the way through the forest to a small rocky terrace that overlooked the village. There they hid themselves, able to see without being seen.

"Do not make a sound," he cautioned. "Remember, we are here to bear witness."

For an hour or more, nothing seemed to happen. Hélène tried to distract herself from the cold and from her own fear by looking out over the armed encampment that had replaced the village. The banner of the Pope of Satan flew, surrounded by the emblems of those who did his bidding. She had never seen so many people in one place. There had to be thousands. The ground beneath them was churned to frozen mud, devoid of a single blade of grass. Almost all the trees had been cut down to build the immense siege engines on the slope leading up toward the fortress. Tents sprouted everywhere, but in the center of the village a space had been cleared of everything save for an immense wooden cage, the purpose of which she could not imagine.

The sun was high in the winter sky when a sudden silence fell over the encampment. All eyes turned toward the top of the crag. Hélène's breath caught when she saw the lines of

Perfect Ones, all garbed in blue, descending toward the army of Satan. Distantly, she could hear that they were singing. One by one, as they reached the center of the village, each stepped unhesitantly into the wooden cage.

When they were all inside, the doors were closed and bound with iron chains. A man high up on a noble steed shouted an order. Other men ran forward, piling kindling around the cage. Hélène heard a low mewing sound and realized that it was coming from her. Her father placed a hand on her shoulder.

"Do not look away," he said. "It is your duty to see all and remember."

She obeyed not because she wished to but because she could not move. Her eyes, searching frantically, found her mother pressed against the back of the cage, looking out in their direction. Hidden as they were, Hélène did not think her mother could see her. Hot tears poured down her cheeks. She opened her mouth to cry out, but no sound emerged.

Men came forward with torches, which they set to the base of the cage. A priest of the evil ones made the sign of the cross. A great roar of approval went up from the assembled army. Black smoke spiraled into the sky. The fire caught quickly. Soon red fingers of flame were running up the front of the cage and over the top. The robe of one of the *perfecti* caught fire, followed quickly by another and another. And still they sang.

Hélène closed her eyes, only to open them a moment later in response to the pressure of her father's hands on her shoulders.

In a thick, gruff voice, he said, "As you love your mother, bear witness."

She did as he said, not looking away again even as the fire ran down the back of the cage and her mother's robe caught. She watched as the flames engulfed her, as she twisted and writhed, as her arms reached out through the bars of the cage as though to embrace her daughter one last time.

Hélène watched until there was nothing left save smoldering ash and the cry of the wind around the empty crag.

When it was done, her father spoke to her and all the others, who stood, their faces streaked with tears and their lips bitten bloody where they had held back their cries.

"By their sacrifice, the Perfect Ones have proven the power of our faith and the rightness of our God," he said. "As we dwell in this world of evil, never forget that." He took Hélène's hand in his and held it firmly. "Teach your children that they may teach theirs. The time of reckoning will come. And when it does, the Cathars will be prepared."

The wind dried the child's tears. The anguish within her hardened into resolve alloyed with hatred. She kept the faith, she remembered, and she taught her children.

As they taught theirs down to the present day.

1

Rome

October 1493

"Donna Francesca . . ."

I was in the Campo dei Fiore, walking toward Rocco's shop. There was something important that I needed to tell him.

"Lady . . ."

I quickened my pace, avoiding the pushcarts and passersby, the piles of manure and the importuning peddlers, afraid I would be too late.

"Wake up!"

I really had to . . . it was important . . .

The street in front of me dissolved. I blinked in the sudden glare of light piercing the cocoon of my curtained bed. Portia, holding up a lamp, grasped me by the shoulder and shook me.

"For pity's sake—" I squinted, trying without effect to cling to the dream.

"Condottieri are here," the *portiere* said. "*His* condottieri. They say you must come."

"They say—what?"

"You must come. They wanted me to let them in, but I said I would wake you myself. Even so, they are right outside. They won't wait for long."

Despite the coolness of early autumn, I slept naked. A film of sweat shone on my skin. The nightmare had come as usual, leaving its mark on me.

"I'll kill him, I swear I will."

The dwarf chuckled. She jumped down from the stool, found a robe of finely woven Egyptian cotton dyed a saffron hue, and held it out.

"No, you won't. He'll charm you as he always does and you'll forgive him."

Slipping my arms into the sleeves of the robe, I winced. "How can the sharpest-eyed *portiere* in all of Rome be such a romantic?"

Portia shrugged. "What can I say? He tips well."

I started to laugh, coughed instead, caught myself, and strode out of the bedchamber, through the salon filled with my books and the apparatus I used in my investigations, all feeding the rumors about me. The robe billowed around my legs, gold mined from the crushed stigmas of Andalusia crocuses. I went quickly between light and shadow, pausing in neither. A cat, perversely white in violation of hallowed superstition, followed in my wake. The door to the apartment stood open. Beyond, I could see helmeted soldiers in shining breastplates pacing anxiously.

Their leader saw me coming and stiffened, as he damn well should have, given the circumstances.

"Donna," he said and sketched a quick bow. "A thousand apologies, but I thought it best . . . That is, I wasn't certain if you would . . ."

"Where is he?"

The captain hesitated, but he could not lie. Not to me. One of the benefits of my having a reputation as dark as the Styx.

"At a taverna in the Trastevere. He's not . . . in good shape."

I sighed and arched my neck, still struggling to wake fully. A thought occurred to me. "It's Sunday, isn't it?"

"It is, donna, unfortunately. We don't have much time."

"Wait here."

I went back into the apartment. Portia, the only name by which I knew the *portiere*, was laying out clothes for me. As her eye for such things was much better than my own, I did not protest. Instead, I said, "Remind me to change the lock on the door. Either that, or just give me your key."

She grinned and shook her head. "What good would either do, donna? The locksmith would be in the pay of the landlord and I'd have a new key before the day was out. Besides, who would look after things for you if you have to go away?"

I pulled a shift over my head, muffling my voice. "Why would I go away?"

Portia shrugged. "I'm only saying . . . it could happen."

"What have you heard?" For surely the *portiere* had heard something. She always did.

"It's not very nice in the city right now. Too much rain, the

Tiber flooding, rumors of plague. Certain people might think this was a good time to visit the countryside."

"Oh, God." Manure, pigs, bucolic romps, too much open space. I hated the countryside.

"Just get him to the chapel," the *portiere* advised. "That will spare us all a lot of trouble."

My name is Francesca Giordano, daughter of the late Giovanni Giordano, who served ten years as poisoner to the House of Borgia and was murdered for his pains. To acquire the means to avenge him, I poisoned the man chosen to take his place. Fortunately, Cardinal Rodrigo Borgia, as he was then, saw past my offense to perceive my usefulness. At his behest, I set out to kill the man I believed at the time to have ordered my father's murder. Only God knows if Pope Innocent VIII died by my hand. What is certain is that his demise opened the way for Borgia to become pope.

Recoil from me if you will, but know this: No one feared the darkness of my nature more than I. Had I been able to recast myself into an ordinary woman—a wife and mother, perhaps—I would have done so in an instant, though it require me to walk through the fires of Hell. Or so I liked to believe. Saint Augustine, while still a young man wallowing in debauchery, prayed to God to make him chaste—but not yet. My own aspirations may have owed at least some of their appeal to the unlikelihood of their achievement any time soon. I was as I was, may God forgive me.

I was then twenty-one, brown-haired, brown-eyed, and, although slender, possessed of a womanly figure. I say this without pride, for in the parade of my sins, vanity brought up the rear. Working in a man's profession as I did, my appearance discomfited more than a few. That suited me well enough, for while they were preoccupied with thoughts of either burning or bedding me—not excluding both—I did not hesitate to act.

The taverna was on one of the little *corsie* that ran off the Campo dei Fiore. When the marketplace was bustling, as it usually was, the place would be easy to miss. But in the hours before dawn, the light and sound spilling from its narrow door made it impossible to overlook.

A burly guard stood outside to deter the pickpockets who preyed on drunken young noblemen too busy slumming to notice that they were being robbed. He took one look at the approaching condottieri and vanished down a nearby alley.

"If you wish us to go in first, donna . . . ," the captain said.

I ignored him, pushed open the door, and stepped inside. The smell hit me at once—raw wine, sweat, roasted meat, smoke. I inhaled deeply. *Ah, Roma.* The looming threat of the countryside flitted through my mind, but I repressed it.

A lout cross-eyed with drink saw me first and reached out to grasp my waist. I eluded him easily and pressed on. The greater part of the din was coming from a large table toward the back behind half-closed curtains where a bevy of mostly naked young women clustered, vying for the attentions of the male guests.

A burst of deep laughter . . . a girlish shriek . . . a snatch of ribald song . . .

I pushed past a nubile young thing wearing only diaphanous harem pants, elbowed another even more scantily clad, and came at last within sight of the reason why I had been rousted out of bed in the wee hours of the morning.

Lolling back in his chair, a goblet in one hand and a rounded breast in the other, the son of His Holiness Pope Alexander VI appeared to be in high good humor. A blonde—to whom the breast belonged—straddled his lap, while a completely nude brunette posed on the table in front of him, her legs spread invitingly.

Cesare raised a brow, though whether in interest or amusement I could not say. His dark hair with a slight reddish cast was loose and brushed his shoulders. In features, he resembled his mother—the redoubtable Vannozza dei Cattanei—far more than he did his father, having her long, high-bridged nose and large, almond-shaped eyes. He had been in the sun even more than usual and was deeply tanned. In public he generally wore the expected raiment of a high-born young man, but that night he was dressed for comfort in a loose shirt and breeches.

He bent forward, whispered something in the ear of the blonde that made her shriek with feigned shock, and called for more wine.

"*Vino! Molto vino* for everyone!"

"Cesare."

He blinked once, twice. A moment passed, another. He let

go of the girl's breast, set the goblet on the table, and sighed deeply.

"*Ai, mio,* he sent you."

"Of course he did," I said. "Whom did you think he would send?"

A murmur went around. The whisper of my name. The brunette paled, pressed her legs together, and fled. So, too, did most of the crowd. Scrambling off her perch, the blonde fell. For a moment, her smooth rump was high in the air before she picked herself up and followed the rest.

Only the Spaniards remained. Arrogant, high-nosed young men, scions of ancient families, swift to take offense at any slight to their honor, real or imagined. They were lately come to the court of the Pope, who still considered Valencia to be home, and had been drawn inevitably to the company of his son.

"Who is this?" one of them demanded, resolutely ignorant.

Cesare Borgia rose unsteadily, adjusted his breeches, and made a token effort to straighten himself. He smiled grudgingly.

"My conscience, alas."

Outside in the street, surrounded by the condottieri, he held his face up to the cool night air. A fine mist carried the tang of the sea miles off at Ostia. He breathed it in deeply, as did I. For a moment, the lure of far-off places and different lives filled us.

"Say you couldn't find me."

"It wouldn't make any difference if I did. Your father would just send someone else. Be glad he sent your own guards and not his."

He sighed. "Have you no pity? My life is ending."

I fought a smile and lost. He was so young still, this boy-man with whom my own life was so unexpectedly entwined.

"You are scarcely eighteen years old and you are about to acquire more power and wealth than most can ever dream of. Do not expect anyone to weep for you."

"All well and good, but this isn't how I wanted to get either. You know that."

"Who among us gets what we want?"

"My father has."

I conceded the point with a slight nod. "True enough. Now let us see if he can keep it."

Torches burned in brackets set into the walls of the palazzo near the Campo, illuminating the marble statues in the entrance and the loggia beyond. Despite the hour, the servants were all awake and scurrying about. I went with Cesare up the curving stairs to his private quarters and waited as he threw off his clothes and sank into a steaming-hot bath. As he sweated out the effects of his indulgence, I mixed a restorative from powders I carried in a small bag that hung at my waist. I never went anywhere without that bag or without the knife nestled in a leather sheath next to my heart.

He swallowed the potion I handed him without delay, testament to his trust in me. Watching him, I wondered how many people I knew would do the same. A dozen, at most, if I really stretched? And half of those would at least hesitate.

"That's vile," he said.

The tub was carved from a single piece of marble and

decorated with ample-breasted mermaids. I sat on a stool next to it. "You'll be glad of it all the same."

He was leaning back, his head against the rim, his eyes closed, but he opened one to look at me. "You could get in."

"I could. . . ." I appeared to consider it. "But you know what would happen. Tired as we both are, we'd fall asleep afterward and then we'd drown. *Che scandalo*."

He laughed, accepting my refusal with better grace than I had expected. I took that as evidence of how truly low his spirits were.

When the water had cooled, he rose and stood naked, legs braced and arms held away from his sides. Droplets sluiced down his skin kissed by the sun. He was leaving the lankiness of youth behind, coming into his own as a man and a warrior. His shoulders had broadened first, followed by his torso, but lately the bands of muscle across his abdomen and thighs had become even more evident. So far at least, his body was without imperfection, a condition he lamented as he longed to prove himself on the field of honor. Scars, he insisted, were the true mark of a man; all else was pretense. His father, Christ's Vicar on Earth, thought otherwise, and his will ruled, at least for now.

"This really doesn't bother you?" Cesare asked as his long-suffering valet finished patting him dry.

I shrugged. "Why should it?"

He looked so uncertain suddenly that I went to him, wrapped my arms around his broad chest, and pressed a light kiss against his lips, the softness of which surprised me, as always. He stirred against me, making me laugh and causing my gaze to drift just for a moment in the direction of the bed. Only the light stealing through the high windows gave me pause. That and the great bells of Saint Peter's that just began to ring on the far side of the river, heralding the dawn.

"Of course it makes no difference. How could it possibly?"

The valet cleared his throat. "Pardon me, signore. It is time to dress."

I sat in a comfortable chair with my feet up and sipped a light cider from the first apple pressing while I waited. The procedure took longer than usual, no doubt because Cesare was donning clothes he had never worn before. When he emerged finally from the dressing room, my breath caught. I rose, smiling.

"You look exceedingly handsome."

"This is not what I want," he said and kicked at the long red skirts of his cassock in disgust.

I would have replied, but just then the bells of Saint Peter's grew louder, their voices joined by the bells of churches all over Rome. Together they hailed the day of consecration for Holy Mother Church's newest and most unwilling prince.

The bells were still ringing as I made my way across Rome. Despite its being Sunday, most of the shops were open and the streets were busy. His Holiness—a man of commerce himself—had designated virtually every enterprise in the city as "necessary," and therefore exempt from closing on holy days. For that, and for reining in the crime that had been rampant in the streets during the tenure of his predecessor, Romans loved him. But theirs was no longer the giddy love of first infatuation that brings a blush to the cheek and a glow to the eyes. Rather it was the brittle love of experience that teeters on the edge of disillusionment, when the faithlessness of the beloved is becoming all too evident.

In Borgia's case, his boundless lust for women, power, privilege, and wealth was a mere beginning. What he really wanted—what he was determined to have—was nothing short of immortality. He intended to so remake the world in his own image that his name would ring down through the ages, never diminished, never forgotten, forever glorious. I imagine that he envisioned himself sitting Jove-like in the heavens, gazing down benignly at what he had wrought. Unfortunately, his enemies were coming to the same conclusion, and they were determined to stop him.

Despite the shadow they cast, the sun was out, a benediction after the constant rain of late. For a moment, a fragment of my interrupted dream flitted through my mind. I could just as easily turn toward the Campo and visit Rocco. The recent announcement of his betrothal to Carlotta d'Agnelli had made no difference to our friendship, and why would it? True, there had been a time when Rocco fancied that he and I should wed, but given what he now knew of my dark nature, he should surely be glad of his escape. Even so, we liked and trusted each other in the way of colleagues bound by mutual interests. If I still longed on occasion for what could not be, that was my secret to bear and keep. I owed him a visit, just not quite yet.

After more than a year in His Holiness's service, living constantly within the darkest aspects of my nature, I could no longer ignore the anxious melancholia that hung over me on even the brightest day. In front of Cesare or His Holiness himself, I managed to maintain the appearance of confidence, but it was no more than a thin façade over my deepest fears. Constantly on guard, seeing danger in every shadow, I was haunted by the conviction that my soul, insofar as it still existed, would never see the light for which I yearned so desperately. Out of sheer bravado, I told myself that to be damned was a kind of liberation. Not for me the endless cycle of sin, confession, and bought absolution. But having gone beyond all that, I found myself in a purgatory all my own.

A cloud moved across the sun. I shivered in the sudden chill and pressed on. The Tiber having overflowed its banks, I was forced to hold up my skirts as I made my way through filthy water to the small apothecary shop secluded down a narrow lane. Several customers were inside. I waited, loitering just out of sight, as they were seen to one by one. When the last had gone, I stepped through the door.

Within, all was clean and ordered: every bottle and packet properly stowed, the worktable scrubbed down with sand, the air bearing the scent of drying herbs. No hint lingered of the suffering and death that had played out within those walls the previous year when desperate refugees—expelled from Spain at the order of Their Most Catholic Majesties Ferdinand and Isabella—had streamed into Rome, their condition stark testament to man's inhumanity to man. Any normal person would welcome the relative tranquility as evidence of the mercy of God, who, it is said, never sends us more than we can bear. To me, it had more the quality of stillness that precedes a great storm.

Sofia Montefiore finished rinsing her hands in the vinegar she used as a protection against spreading disease and reached for a towel. Seeing me, she frowned.

"You look a wreck."

Friends can always be counted on to soothe one's vanity; only good friends tell the truth. Sofia, a middle-aged woman with a sturdy build and a cloud of silver hair pinned up haphazardly around her plain but pleasant face, cared too much for my well-being to be less than honest. I could not do otherwise, especially as my best efforts to deceive her invariably failed.

"I haven't been sleeping well."

"That's nothing new. What have you been doing about it?"

"Drinking," I admitted. "Likely too much."

"Nothing else?" When I hesitated, she came around the table to look at me more closely. I resisted the urge to squirm under her scrutiny.

"No opium?" she asked.

As much as I would have liked to feign shock, I could not manage it. Sofia knew what all of Rome knew: the Turkish sultan, who paid well to assure that his younger brother and rival remained a captive in the Vatican, supplied said brother with all manner of indulgences intended to keep him weak and complacent. Chief among these was opium, which the generous Prince Djem shared with his friends in the Church and among the nobility.

"I've tried it," I admitted. Shortly before Cesare's investiture, when he was in the throes of realizing that his father would not relent and let him become the war leader he yearned to be, he had procured some for us to sample together. The euphoria it evoked was seductive in the extreme, but the drawbacks were obvious. "It dulls the senses too much. I have to be able to work."

Sofia looked relieved. "It is as well you realize that. There is much you can do to help yourself without relying on—"

I did not let her finish but interjected, "There was opium in the sleeping powder you gave me a few months ago, wasn't there? That's why you refused to continue providing it."

She did not deny it but said, "That was a mistake. I thought that if your sleep could be adjusted to a more normal pattern, it would remain that way after the powder was withdrawn. Now it seems that I may have only sparked a craving that lingers still."

"My only craving is for sleep. I am desperate for it. Surely, under your care, following your instructions, I could take some form of the powder safely?"

I was prepared for her to reject the idea out of hand, in which case I had rehearsed my argument. Borgia was the Jews' pope as much as he was anyone's, insofar as they had provided the sums needed to elect him. In return, he had pledged them his protection. I, in turn, protected him. Sofia must see the benefits of keeping me functioning.

But before I could begin to convince her, she gestured for me to sit. Leaving me for a moment, she returned with hot water from the stove in the rear of the shop. As she prepared an infusion of chamomile and rose hip, she said, "David is back."

I swallowed my impatience; no great task, as her news interested me. David ben Eliezer was the leader of a band of renegade Jews prepared to fight for the survival of their people. He and I had joined forces before to that end. The last I had heard, he was in Florence keeping an eye on the fanatical monk Savonarola, who, when he wasn't railing against the corruption of Holy Mother Church, kept busy calling for the extermination of the Jews. Savonarola had an ally, a priest named Bernando Morozzi, who I believed was the man ultimately behind my father's death. David had been watching him as well. Whatever had made him break off and return to the Holy City must be important indeed.

"What brings him to Rome?" I asked.

"The same concerns that keep you wakeful, I imagine. Borgia seems intent on collecting enemies, including some with the capacity to be deadly."

I could not deny it. "He is determined to advance the interest of *la famiglia* at all cost. Witness his insistence on making Cesare a cardinal despite how it has outraged so many of the prelates."

"Such hubris will be his downfall," Sofia said with a sigh. She filled two stoneware cups with the infusion and handed one to me. As I sipped, she added, "I fear that we will have a new pope or we will have war. Most likely both."

I could not dismiss either possibility, but had I been willing to accept them as inevitable, I would not have been sitting in her shop.

"If there is one thing I have learned," I said, "it is never to bet against Borgia. Everyone who has done that is the poorer for it, assuming they're still with us at all."

Sofia did not hide her skepticism. "You really believe that he can survive?"

"Most definitely. The longer he does, the more frustrated and divided his enemies become. Eventually, at least some of them will seek an accord with him." Or so I most profoundly hoped, for every other possibility loomed grim and lethal.

Before she could comment, I went on quickly. "But I need help, Sofia." I gestured with my cup. "I am far beyond such remedies as this. Will you give me what I need or not?"

She took a breath and let it out slowly. "What will you do if I refuse?"

"I hadn't thought of that." It was a lie, but I hoped a small one. I had considered various alternatives; I just hadn't been able to come up with any that were remotely good.

Her eyebrows rose. "We both know that when it comes to such matters, your expertise surpasses my own."

"You give me too much credit. I wish to sleep only for a few hours, not eternally."

What I needed was beyond the limits of my dark calling. While I knew a hundred ways and more to kill, I knew next to nothing of how to heal. What little I had managed to learn I owed entirely to Sofia's efforts to reform me.

A smile tugged at the corners of her mouth, but her gaze remained serious. "In that case, I will see what I can do. But you must promise that you will follow my instructions without exception."

Having assured her that I would not dream of doing less, I thought to linger longer in her company, but just then a customer arrived. I took my leave, greatly relieved now that I knew help was at hand. With the improvement in my mood, I was tempted once again to seek out Rocco. But when I reached his shop in the Via dei Vertrarari, the street of the glassmakers, I found it shuttered. Likely he and his young son, Nando, were visiting with Carlotta and her family.

Determined to ignore the sudden hollowness where my heart was, I returned to my own apartments. There I spent the remainder of the day pursuing an investigation that had sparked my interest. Recently, there had been a spate of deaths among older gentlemen who had in common both wealth and young wives. All had died after complaining of sharp stomach pains and passing blood in their urine. Naturally, this had prompted rumors of foul deeds. Ever on the lookout for signs that a poisoner might be at work in the city, and therefore a possible threat to Borgia, I made my own inquiries.

As it turned out, all of the gentlemen had been taking a commonly available compound made from the dried husks of the Spanish fly, which is in fact a rather pretty emerald-green beetle, renowned for stimulating the flagging vigor of the male member. I had become curious about how this effect was accomplished and had gone so far as to inquire of Cesare what he knew of it. After he got over being both offended and amused by my assumption that he would have any such knowledge, he relented enough to tell me that the compound appeared to greatly increase the flow of humors through the body, most especially that of the blood. While the result could be an impressive erection, it also could overstrain the heart, cause severe pain in the stomach, and interfere with urination. Despite so mixed a reputation, it remained much in demand among men desperate to hold on to their virility.

All that made me wonder: If a little of the cantharidin, as it was known, could accomplish so much, what might a more concentrated dosage do? Without dwelling on the details, I quickly discovered that the problem lay in the purity and strength of the substance. The gentlemen in question had had the misfortune to encounter an unusually potent supply. The source, a back alley seller unworthy of the title of apothecary, had agreed to sell me all of his remaining stock shortly before he departed Rome in considerable haste. I had set myself to study the effects—and how they might be made even more potent and deadly.

So occupied was I that I failed to notice the storm blowing in from the west. Wind-driven rain was splattering the floor of my workroom before I realized what was happening and hurried to close the shutters over the tall windows. As I did so, I happened to glance down into the courtyard. A figure was standing there, wrapped in an enveloping cloak and sheltered from the rain by an overhang. I could not make out any features, but the angle of the head made it appear that the watcher was looking up at me.

Having shut the windows and pulled the shutters closed, I told myself that my imagination was overwrought. With so little sleep and so much worry, likely I had conjured the watcher from shadows. Yet before I finally retired for the night, I glanced outside again. Nothing stirred in the courtyard, not even a bedraggled rat.

Perversely, I slept well, at least for me, waking shortly after dawn to the lingering scent of rain and the sound of trumpets blaring the news of a papal proclamation.

2

The old man with a bulbous red nose and bushy gray hair growing out of his ears spat as the Pope rode past. The great wad of phlegm he hocked up landed on the sodden ground just beyond the rump of His Holiness's fine white horse. Borgia appeared not to notice. He continued making the sign of the cross above the heads of the sullen peasants driven from nearby fields to honor his passage.

Without breaking stride, a man-at-arms cuffed the miscreant, sending him sprawling into the mud. The grizzled *paesano* lay where he fell, staring up at the leaden sky. He appeared to have suffered no great injury and, for all the contentment of his expression, may have been contemplating the accolades he would receive from his neighbors as soon as the procession was out of sight.

So it had been every plodding step along the old Via

Cassia north from Rome toward the allegedly charming town of Viterbo, our way proceeded by heralds and men-at-arms proclaiming the intent of His Holiness to make his first papal progression outside of Rome. A convoy of priests carried on their shoulders the glorious gold and jeweled Tabernacle of the Eucharist brought from Saint Peter's Basilica. Borgia had announced that he was taking the Tabernacle along as a sign of his piety and personal devotion to the Savior. Romans like a good joke, and they appreciated that one. The truth, as everyone knew, was that he wanted a ready source of convertible wealth close at hand in case worse came to worst.

Not that anyone could tell that he was less than entirely secure. His Holiness rode immediately behind the Tabernacle, arrayed in scarlet and gold with the tripartite papal crown seemingly rock steady on his head. Despite his years and the burden of his office, he sat erect in the saddle. For a man about whom it was said that he was better suited to rule in Hell than reign in Christendom, he made a very convincing pope. Given the low state of Holy Mother Church, riddled by corruption and venality to rival a poxy whore, perhaps that was no great challenge.

Behind him dozens of prelates followed—among them several cardinals who still claimed to support him—as well as his personal household, including his young daughter, Lucrezia, and her husband of four months, the increasingly dour Giovanni Sforza. Il Papa had forbidden consummation of their marriage on the grounds that thirteen-year-old Lucrezia was too young for carnal intercourse. All the world, including Lucrezia, knew that His Holiness's true intent was to preserve an easy path to annulment should the political winds, which were blowing particularly fiercely of late, suddenly shift.

I rode with the rest of the papal household, close enough to observe His Holiness but far enough back to avoid being spat upon. Renaldo d'Marco rode beside me. Borgia's steward caught my eye and frowned.

"Did you see that?" he asked.

Renaldo had the misfortune to bear an uncanny resemblance to the common ferret in both manner and appearance. A small, perpetually nervous man, he fussed over the minutest detail and lived in dread of ever making a mistake. Accuracy was his shield against a world he too often found overwhelming, yet he had proven a true enough friend to me, whom others walked in fear of and shunned. Bound together by our mutual obligation to serve and protect *la famiglia,* we had long since fallen into the habit of talking over matters of shared interest.

"The old man?" I replied. "What of him?"

"He wasn't the first. There was a fellow about an hour ago who waited until just as His Holiness was passing to pull out his cock and take a piss."

I shrugged. "Who can explain the curious customs of country folk?"

Under his breath, Renaldo said, "You can't dismiss such behavior, Francesca. The peasants are emboldened to show their contempt for our master because they do not believe he will be pope much longer."

Equally quietly, I replied, "They do not know him as we do. If they did, they would be far more circumspect in their behavior."

The steward looked unconvinced. "Perhaps, but this cursed progress was ill-advised. It makes it look as though he is running away."

It was true that Borgia's departure from Rome could be seen in that light, and his enemies would not hesitate to present it as such. But his real purpose in going was no secret.

"By personally inspecting the fortifications at Viterbo and elsewhere to the north," I said, "he is declaring that he will not shy away from war, should it come to that."

"Heaven and all the saints forbid," Renaldo muttered.

I shared his sentiment even though I nurtured little hope of divine intervention. We were all of us gamblers to one extent or another, but no one gambled so furiously or for such high stakes as did Christ's Vicar. His boundless ambitions for *la famiglia* had put him on a collision course with some of the most powerful rulers in Europe and made war, as Sofia had said, inevitable. Any such conflict would threaten Borgia's papacy and give his enemies within the Church the opportunity they sought to unseat him. How, precisely, he intended to work his way out of this particular problem remained a mystery. I was confident only that, being Borgia, he had a plan—or, more likely, several.

"What if it really does come to war?" Renaldo asked. "What then?"

"Then I can think of one person at least who will be very happy."

The steward did not have to ask whom I meant. My relationship with Cesare was hardly a secret, but I had not seen my sometime lover since shortly after his consecration as a prince of Holy Mother Church the previous week. Rather than deal with the ongoing recriminations spewing from his son, Borgia had put him to use by sending him ahead to Viterbo, ostensibly to keep him safe from the plague rumored to be stirring in Rome but really to rally the local nobility and strengthen the garrison. In his absence, my bed had grown cold.

"Cesare's attitude toward becoming a cardinal hasn't improved at all, has it?" Renaldo prompted. "He remains unreconciled to his father's will."

"Did you imagine it would be otherwise? He has dreamed his whole life of winning great victories on the field of battle. To be bound in a red cassock and chained to a desk in the Vatican is unbearable."

"Even so," Renaldo said, "the touts are giving five to two against there being a falling-out between them anytime in the next year."

I was not surprised. Romans will bet on anything—the number of bodies pulled from the Tiber on a given day, the sex of a cardinal's next bastard, the longevity of a pope, all are fodder for the spinning wheel of fortune upon which our lives are balanced and where, on occasion, there is money to be made.

"And if there is war?" I asked. "How go the odds then?"

"Three to two that Il Papa will prevail."

"Interesting . . . considering that he has virtually no army in comparison to the French and that the support of the Spaniards is more vital than it is certain."

Renaldo did not disagree, though he did point out what I knew to be true. "But he has such brio, such a sense of his own inevitability. He's like a force of nature. Who really wants to bet against him, especially when the alternative is that old stick, della Rovere?"

I laughed despite myself and won a smile in turn from the steward. We were passing along an aisle framed by beech trees, approaching the inn at Ronciglione where we were to spend the night. An army of carpenters, glaziers, and painters had worked ceaselessly for the better part of a week to assure that His Holiness would be properly housed for the single night he intended to stay at the inn. Wagonloads of servants, furniture, wall hangings, artwork, and other necessities had been brought from Rome. The entire upper floor had been set aside for His Holiness's use, leaving the ground floor to accommodate all the prelates and their staffs. Dismounting, I heard grumblings about the arrangements, but there was nothing to be done for it; Borgia loved his privileges and loved even more to make lesser men accept them as his due.

He also had a fondness for generating chaos, or so it seemed by the level of activity ever swirling about him. I stepped aside quickly as a troop of men-at-arms went by at a run, only just missing trampling me. A wagon driver bellowed in anger as another blocked his way. Pages and kitchen boys scurried about, helping to unload a steady stream of boxes and barrels when they weren't tripping over their own feet. Anyone would have been pardoned for thinking that the papal court was settling in for a month or more rather than for a few scant hours.

Next to the inn a large, unadorned building of raw wood planks had been thrown up to house the traveling kitchens.

Fires had been lit, spits were turning, and delectable smells filled the air. I sniffed appreciatively. The mundane truth of my profession is that most of it involves food; and with good reason, for nothing is easier to poison. Grains of arsenic can be slipped between folds of beef, cheese can be wrapped in poisoned cloth that will transmit its deadly properties, and so on. With the proper tools, it is even possible to introduce poison into a fresh egg still in its shell. As a result, I not only inspected every item that Borgia might ingest with the greatest care, I also made sure that my presence was felt where it could do the most good.

Having bid Renaldo farewell for the moment, I had walked only a short distance through the well-churned mud toward the kitchens when my way was blocked by a dour-faced condottiere wearing the sash of a captain of the papal guard. Vittoro Romano was in his fifties, still straight-backed and strong-shouldered despite a rough-and-tumble life, whose saturnine nature lulled the unwary into believing that he took little notice of anything around him. I knew better, having observed him through all my years growing up in Borgia's household. Since I had assumed my father's duties and sworn to take vengeance on his killer, Vittoro and I had become friends. I counted on him to tell me anything I might need to know, and he did the same with me. Only rarely did we disappoint each other, and never without good reason.

"Francesca," he said, speaking quietly so that we could not be overheard. His manner was such that we might have been discussing the weather, mercifully drier than of late, the rain holding off until just then, when the first dank drops began to fall.

"There has been an incident." Vittoro took my arm as he spoke, guiding me around the back of the inn. When we were alone, he said, "A kitchen boy was found dead an hour ago."

Any sudden mortality within the Pope's household was always brought to my attention on the chance, however remote, that it might signal a danger to His Holiness. Thus far, every death I had investigated had proved to be from natural causes, but I did not presume that that would always be so.

Vittoro had arranged for the body to be placed in a wagon drawn up along the far edge of a field, where it was not likely to attract notice. As we approached, two men-at-arms emerged from behind nearby trees. Seeing their captain, they stood aside for us to pass.

"I have cautioned those who are aware of the boy's death not to speak of it to anyone," Vittoro said.

That would buy us a little time, but not much. Climbing into the back of the wagon, I paused for a few moments to let my eyes adjust to the dimmer light. The rain had begun to fall more heavily. It splattered on the canvas covering strung over the wagon bed. The boy was laid out on a plank of wood supported at either end by a crate of supplies. He was naked.

"Who removed his clothes?" I asked.

"I did," Vittoro said. "I wore gloves." After a moment, he added, "There is plague in Rome, or so it is said."

He spoke calmly, but I understood his dread. If it was plague, we could all be dead within days, if not hours. Quickly, I lifted the boy's arm and looked under it. The telltale buboes from which the scourge took its name were absent both there and in the groin. That did not absolutely rule out the possibility of plague, but it did make it unlikely.

Nor was there any sign that a contact poison had killed the boy. Had there been, I would have found signs of a pinprick rash and overall bluing of the skin where the poison had touched him.

"Did he vomit or soil himself?" I asked.

"I found no evidence of either."

That ruled out many poisons, though not by any means all. Steeling myself, I began at the top of his head and moved my gaze slowly down over every inch of his body. When I had finished with the front, Vittoro and I turned him carefully so that I could examine the back. There were no obvious signs of wounds, punctures, or other injuries. The boy's skin where it had been exposed to the sun was tanned, the rest of him being pale enough for me to make out the blue etching of his veins just below the surface. His hair was brown, as were his eyes beneath the film of death when I lifted the lids to examine them. I judged him to be about thirteen, which made him a little tall for his age and gracefully built.

We turned him again. Fortunately, the rigor that follows death had not yet set in so it was not necessary to break the jaw. I found no foam in the mouth or around the lips. Inhaling, I observed that the boy had eaten garlic not long before his death; hardly unusual, as it is greatly favored not only for its flavor but as a protection against illness. Slipping a hand beneath the bodice of my gown, I withdrew the knife I habitually carried and made a small slit along the side of the boy's neck. At once, his blood began to flow. The color was dark red.

"Not cyanide," I said. Had it been, the nicked vein would have produced bright cherry-red blood, the only certain indication that the poison is present. One of the reasons cyanide is so popular among those of my profession is because the public, in its infinite wisdom, believes that it can be readily detected by the scent of almonds it gives off. But the scent is easily masked by any number of substances, including garlic, thereby instilling a false sense of security that can be very useful.

"What else might it be, then?" Vittoro asked.

"I don't know. Was there anything unusual about his posture when he was found? Anything that might indicate that he'd had convulsions?"

"There didn't seem to be. He just looked as though he collapsed."

"Where are his clothes?"

Vittoro handed them to me. They were in good condition for the boy's station and ample enough to have kept him warm. Inhaling, I smelled damp wool, wood smoke, and a faint but not very intense odor of sweat. Nothing to indicate that he had been ill.

"If you want to open him up . . . ," Vittoro began. Holy Mother Church forbid such treatment of the dead, even when it was the only means of establishing what had killed them. The prohibition had not stopped me in the past and would not have done so then, but there was no time. As I could not rule out the possibility that the boy had been poisoned, I had no choice but to act. His Holiness was about to dine.

I jumped from the wagon, caught up my skirts, and ran. My presence was noted the moment I stepped into the kitchen. Work sputtered to a halt before the *maestro di maestri* barked a command and everyone snapped back into action.

I forced a smile. "Is that pork I smell? For His Holiness?"

The maestro assured me that it was, to be accompanied by Il Papa's favorite apricot sauce as well as the savory peas he enjoyed and golden rounds of lightly fried chestnut meal, the achievement of such a meal under such lamentably primitive conditions being mentioned only once or twice—or thrice—as though in passing.

"You have whetted my appetite," I declared. "I must have a taste of everything." This was not an unheard-of demand from me. During the frequent state dinners at the Vatican, Borgia liked for me to be present as a reminder of the care he took with his own safety and of the weapon he could unleash should he choose to do so. On such occasions, I preferred to eat first in the kitchens, where I customarily enjoyed a portion of the food prepared for His Holiness.

I was not, contrary as it may seem, being entirely reckless; only somewhat. Most poisons in food can be detected by sight and smell, provided one knows what to look for. Of course, cooking and the addition of sauces make that task more difficult, but it was for just that reason that Borgia—like any sensible prince—employed someone of my dark calling.

His Holiness's dinner was already plated on gold serving pieces to be carried forth by pages wearing the mulberry and gold colors of the House of Borgia. They froze as I approached, their outstretched arms suddenly trembling under the weight of what they bore. I told myself that I had inspected the pork with the greatest care. The same was true of the apricots, peas, chestnut meal, and every other ingredient, as well as the wine. Every *maestro di cucina* knew better than to use anything that had not been sealed by me to indicate that it was safe. Forgeries were possible, but my father had caused the seal ring that he had used before it became mine to be wrought so intricately as to make copying it unusually difficult. Moreover, I changed the color of the wax I used daily, selecting randomly from among dozens of hues. The plain truth was that I had taken every possible precaution to assure that Borgia would dine in perfect safety. If I had any real confidence in my own skills, the death from as-yet-unknown causes of one kitchen boy would not deter me from testing them.

The pork was succulent, crisp-skinned and moist. The apricot sauce was a perfect accompaniment. I took only a small piece so as not to disturb the arrangement on the platter overly much and swallowed it quickly. So, too, did I taste everything else intended for His Holiness, including his wine. Truly the man ate well. A hush had fallen over the kitchen. Every eye was on me. No one moved, and few seemed even to breathe.

When I was done, I cleaned my fingers on a cloth while I did a quick assessment: no burning in the mouth or throat; no tingling in the extremities; no cramping in the stomach or lower down; no blurred vision. Granted, certain poisons could be slow-acting, but they required multiple doses administered over time. Whatever had killed the kitchen boy, it was not in Borgia's dinner.

"Superb, as always," I said. "My compliments, maestro. You have outdone yourself."

The poor man almost sagged in relief but caught himself in time and inclined his head to me instead. We both knew that had poison been found in Borgia's food, things would have gone very badly for the maestro and everyone else who worked in the kitchens. But had it not been found—had it slipped through somehow and actually reached Borgia—that would have been even worse, for therein lay the difference between the hope of a swift death and the certainty of prolonged agony that makes death a blessing.

Not exactly the most cheerful atmosphere in which to work, but every job has its drawbacks, and Borgia paid very well.

The pages hurried off, and activity in the kitchen returned to normal. I stepped outside, followed by Vittoro, who was tight-lipped and glaring out of concern for me but said nothing because, as we both knew full well, I had done nothing not in keeping with the responsibilities of my position.

"I'll see that the boy is buried," he said. Under the circumstances, it was the wisest course. To do otherwise would invite speculation. Still, I regretted not having the opportunity to determine what had killed him.

Suddenly weary, I nodded. With the immediate crisis passed, all I wanted was to wash off the dirt of the road and go to bed. I managed only the first. Having patted the last drop of apricot sauce from his lips, the Pope wasted no time summoning his poisoner.

3

In that October of Anno Domino 1493, Christ's Vicar was sixty-two years old, still a bull of a man with a barrel chest, strong limbs, heavy-lidded eyes, and a full, sensual mouth. Of late, the demands of the office he had sought with such unrelenting ambition had taken a toll, but he remained, as Renaldo had described him, a force of nature possessed of so indefatigable a will as to send his opponents scrambling for shelter as though from the burning sun.

"My queen is in danger," he said as I entered his private chamber. He did not bother to look up from the chessboard, certain as he was that only the person he had summoned would be allowed to enter past the cordon of condottieri keeping watch. Lush tapestries hung on the walls, golden candelabras provided light, the air bore the scent of newly laid rushes, and a cheerful fire burned nearby. Borgia's papers were spread out over the inlaid chestnut desk he traveled with, but his secretaries were nowhere in evidence.

"I have no skill at this game," I said as I approached. In fact, my father had taught me to play chess passably well, but I had persevered only to please him. Since his death, I found the exercise pointless.

"Take a look all the same," Borgia said as he straightened.

I obeyed reluctantly. He was right, of course; his queen was under attack. But the remedy seemed obvious.

"Take the bishop," I said.

"You mean the cardinal, don't you? Della Rovere is a thorn I would pluck from my side."

I suppressed a sigh. Cardinal Giuliano della Rovere was Borgia's great rival for the papacy. The two had vied for the ultimate jewel in Christendom's crown at the conclave the previous year. Della Rovere had skulked off to lick his wounds, but he made no pretense of accepting his loss. Borgia suspected him of being responsible for at least some of the failed attempts on his life, and there was nothing to say that he was wrong. I lived in dread of the moment when Christ's Vicar decided that the time had come to remove his rival from the board once and for all.

"You have the means," I reminded him despite the sudden hollowness in my stomach, "provided you are willing to sacrifice a faithful pawn."

He laughed and snared two goblets, into which he poured a deep red claret. It was his custom to drink with me when we were alone. I suspect he was one of those who believed that so long as he drank in company, he was not a drunkard. Handing me one of the goblets, he said, "That being you, I suppose?"

I hesitated before taking a sip. I had promised Sofia that I would not drink. When she brought me a supply of the sleeping powder just before the papal procession left Rome, she had stressed the need to abstain from all spirits.

But if I did not drink with him, Borgia would wonder why. Lest any suspicion of me be planted in his mind, I raised my goblet, drank, and said, "You will forgive me if I do not wish to be thrown away lightly. You have worse enemies than the cardinal."

Several months before, I had devised a means of killing della Rovere that even I will admit was ingenious, albeit extraordinarily expensive, involving as it did crushed diamonds that would lacerate the cardinal's intestines and condemn him to a cruel death by infection. Of necessity, I would have to get very close to him in order to introduce the poison. Entering his stronghold at Savona would be difficult, although I believed it could be done. Leaving again, especially if my presence aroused any suspicion, was another matter entirely. My hope was that my future usefulness to His Holiness outweighed the benefit to him of my killing della Rovere at this juncture.

Borgia sat down in a high-backed chair also brought from his quarters at the Vatican and gestured me to a stool nearby.

"Worse . . . perhaps not," he said, giving no sign that the abundance of his foes troubled him. "But it is true, I do not lack for challenges. Speaking of which, I perceive that Cesare is not yet reconciled to the great honor I have bestowed upon him by making him a cardinal. I am concerned that he may be led astray."

I nodded, not because I agreed with him but in acknowledgment that we had come to the true purpose for his summoning me. "By whom?"

Il Papa spread his hands, as though appealing to the air. "Who knows? The French, the Neapolitans, the Turks, a pretty dancing girl, his own vanity? Anything is possible."

I thought that unfair to Cesare, who was made of considerably sterner stuff than his father recognized, but I resisted saying so. Instead, I took a breath and said, "May I ask why you tell me this?"

"I want your help. Make him mindful of his good fortune. Keep him from doing anything foolish. The Spaniards flock to him because they think he is the future. Let him do nothing to disabuse them of that notion."

"You overestimate my influence."

"Women fall at his feet, but it is you he returns to again and again."

That was true, although I had to hope that Borgia had not thought too deeply about why his son should be drawn to me. Between Cesare and me simmered an attraction born of the deficits in our natures that set us apart from other people and nurtured by the discovery, however fragile, that alone in all the world, we might be able to trust each other. We had both grown up in his father's palazzo on the Corso, he the cardinal's bastard son and I the poisoner's daughter. What began as wary glances progressed over the years until the night he came upon me in the library. I was reading Dante, ever my favorite; he was drunk and in pain after yet another argument with his father. I could claim that his passion took me by surprise, but the truth is that I had my way with Cesare as much as he had his with me; perhaps more. The darkness within me was drawn to him, constructed as he was of raw appetites that left no room for morality or conscience. He was without sin in the sense that he recognized none. With him, I came as close as I could ever hope in those years to being myself.

"I am not asking you to betray him," Borgia continued. "On the contrary. Help him to be the man he is meant to be. Not merely a great prince of the Church but a future pope, leading the world into a bright new age. That is what you want, isn't it?"

Borgia knew full well that it was. My late father had belonged to a secret organization of scholars and alchemists, pursuers of truth who called themselves Lux for the light they hoped to bring into the world. After his death, I was accepted as a member. Borgia had reason to know the lengths I would go to to protect Lux. Even so . . .

"I cannot stand guarantor for your son's behavior."

"A pity since I expect you to do exactly that."

The very powerful have an advantage over the rest of us; they can engage in the most blatant unfairness without recourse. Like it or not, I was Borgia's servant. I disobeyed his edicts at my own peril.

"I will do my best," I promised him and drained the wine to its dregs.

The next day we came to Viterbo.

4

Cesare was not among the notables on hand to welcome his father to the fortified hilltop town that for centuries had been a favorite of popes in times of trouble. Accepting the greetings of the mayor and the commander of the garrison, Borgia did not comment on his son's glaring lapse in propriety, but the thin white line around his mouth hinted at his anger.

Mindful of it, I set out to find the wayward son without delay. Out of respect for Sofia, I had resisted using the sleeping powder the night before, but my restraint had left me with dragging steps and a bad headache. Not to mention that I had spent yet another day on a horse. All in all, I doubt that I was a sight to gladden any man's heart.

It was late afternoon. Sunlight slanted from the west across the scrubbed paving stones of the small courtyard behind the roofless loggia, its seven arched bays looking southward over the town while in the opposite direction it provided an unobstructed view of the steep Faul valley. The air was cool and scented with the aromas of wood smoke, newly cut grass, and the late-blooming roses in the nearby palace garden. A fountain bedecked with lions gurgled softly. Other faint sounds filtered up from the surrounding streets, but little disturbed the silence that, as always, set my nerves on edge. The backdrop of noise ever present in Rome provides reassurance when all is as it should be and prompt warning when it is not. Silence, on the other hand, gives away nothing while having the added disadvantage of amplifying one's own thoughts.

A page directed me to the sandy field of the old amphitheater adjacent to the palace. I went anxious to discover what so commanded Cesare's attention that he would fail to greet his father. The crumbling stone tiers where once Romans sat to cheer their favorite gladiators had drawn a motley crowd of retainers, servants, hangers-on, and the same Spanish lords who had been present with Cesare in the taverna. Quickly enough, I discovered why they were all there.

Two men stood at the center of the field, posed in an oval of golden light. Both were stripped down to their shirts and breeches, both armed with rapiers. The clash of their swords rang out against the stillness and the swiftly inhaled breath of their audience. They were similar in height and build, although the one I perceived to be Spanish—judging by the encouragement and advice shouted by his countrymen—moved with greater urgency, as though eager for a swift conclusion.

Not so his opponent, who appeared to be enjoying the contest for its own sake.

Cesare was smiling as he balanced lightly on feet set shoulder-width apart in the classic stance of the swordsman. He appeared almost as still as a statue until, in a sudden explosion of movement, he whirled to parry a thrust and meet it with his own. He had the coordination of a natural athlete and a fondness for making everything he did appear effortless. Young as he was—he was then just eighteen—he understood already how that could madden an opponent.

At first, he and the Spaniard appeared well matched, for all that their fighting styles were clearly different. The Spaniard, of a swarthy visage dominated by a thin, sharp nose that resembled the beak of a hawk, struck me as impatient. I wondered if, being of an arrogant race, he had made the mistake of assuming that the Pope's son would offer him little challenge. Cesare, by contrast, was far more controlled and deliberate, unusually so for his age, when hot blood and hot temper tend to march together. The cheers of the Spaniards faded away as they began to perceive that their man might not have as easy a time of it as they had expected. A hush settled over the crowd.

I took a seat on one of the stone tiers a little apart from the others and watched with unfeigned interest heightened by concern for the larger implications of the contest. The Spanish being vitally important to Borgia's strategy for survival against both della Rovere and the French, Cesare could not put the fellow in the dust as he no doubt wished to. He had to preserve some measure of the man's dignity even as pride would drive him to leave no doubt as to which of them was the more skilled. And he had to do it even as the Spaniard's attack turned increasingly fierce, the cut and thrust of his sword coming ever closer to wounding. Faced with the prospect of defeat, he appeared to forget that this was merely a sparring session and not actual combat.

My heart leaped when the point of the Spaniard's rapier slashed the air perilously close to Cesare's chest. An instant later, I breathed again when the son of Jove, having apparently had enough of the exercise, agilely sidestepped the blow, thrust through the Spaniard's defenses, and deliberately brought the point of his blade up against the other man's eye. It was a move intended to intimidate, and it worked. The Spaniard flinched and fell back a pace. Cesare drove forward and this time brought his blade up against the other's man's throat. His smile never faltered even as his lips shaped a single word: "Yield."

A dark flare of anger moved across the Spaniard's face, but he clearly had no choice. Scowling, he lowered his blade, but he failed to incline his head, as the rules of honorable combat required.

Grudgingly, he said, "The bout is yours, signore."

At once, Cesare lowered his own weapon and slapped the Spaniard heartily on the back. "Well played, Don Miguel!" he said, loudly enough for all to hear. "I swear I thought you had me beat a time or two."

Whether anyone believed that was questionable, but the Spaniard at least appeared mollified. "Next time," he boasted as they walked together from the field, "I will leave you in no such doubt."

From the corner of his eye, Cesare met my gaze. I raised a brow. He grinned, dropped back behind the Spaniards, and came over to me.

"Have you been sent to retrieve me yet again?" He took a seat beside me, pulled his shirt away from his skin, and sighed. "Don Miguel wanted to fight. Had I begged off, he would have taken it as an insult no matter what the reason."

I stared out across the rapidly emptying amphitheater. Venus winked in the eastern sky. With the setting sun, a chill wind was springing up. I shivered slightly and wrapped my arms around myself.

"You don't owe me any explanation. Save it for your father."

"There's no point. He's made up his mind that I'm an ungrateful son. Nothing I say will make any difference."

He spoke casually, as though accepting of the reality and untroubled by it, but I was not fooled. Cesare yearned for his father's approval as a man will lust after water in the desert. The problem was that they were too alike, being possessed of fiery temperaments and indomitable wills, yet also different in crucial ways. Whereas his father was genuinely outgoing, boisterous and high-spirited, Cesare's nature took a much more secretive and inward-looking turn. He was inclined to suspicion and the nurturing of grudges, although he did his best to conceal both tendencies. Between us, there was no room for any such pretense. I would not allow it.

"But you are ungrateful, aren't you?" I asked. Or was I supposed to believe that he had reconciled himself to becoming a cardinal? He who had dreamed all his life of the armies he would lead and the glory he would win with his sword.

"It is not . . . entirely as bad as I thought it would be. I don't actually have to do anything priestly, thank God. I've been working to strengthen the fortifications and improve training for the garrison. And I've been looking after the Spaniards, of course. They take a great deal of tending."

I smiled despite myself. Cesare had held various church offices since childhood, none requiring anything of him but all filling his coffers through the payments of benefices and the like. However, by the time a man—even one so young—advanced to the point of becoming a cardinal, he was expected to also be a priest. The holy orders of chastity, poverty, obedience meant nothing, being routinely ignored even by the lower clergy. Cesare had every reason to know that he would remain entirely free to acquire mistresses, sire children and see to their advancement, and so on, just as his father had done. Perhaps even more important given his warlike temperament, he had the example of no less than Borgia's great rival, Giuliano della Rovere, who when already a cardinal had personally led an army to subdue Umbria.

Yet Cesare had, at least so far, avoided committing himself entirely to the church that Il Papa expected him to lead one day. Preoccupied as he was by the prospect of war, His Holiness had let the matter slide for the moment, but I doubted that could continue indefinitely. Especially not if it fed the rumors that the Pope's eldest son would not vow himself to the Christian god because he was a secret follower of Mithra, worshipped by Roman soldiers in hidden caves and grottos, many of which still existed.

Such rumors titillate the average Roman dinner party, but in the mouths of enemies, they can be deadly. Ultimately, Cesare would have to decide where his loyalties lay. I could only hope that when the time came, he would make an entirely rational decision unimpeded by loyalty to any god, pagan or otherwise. For truly, I think the Greeks had it right when they claimed the gods only amuse themselves with humans, wagering with our lives as children will with tokens of clay.

"That one just now, the one you were dueling with," I said. "Who is he?"

"Don Miguel de Lopez y Herrera, Ferdinand and Isabella's beloved nephew. They have sent him to encourage friendship between us and, of course, to spy on me."

"What does he tell them, do you suppose?"

"As he finds my household considerably more congenial than that of Their Most Catholic Majesties, he tells them what I encourage him to say. We are Spain's most faithful ally, but we are beset by enemies who are also theirs. It is in their interest to support us unstintingly."

"Do you think they believe him?"

Cesare shrugged. "I can only hope that they do. Given my father's talent for making enemies, we need all the friends we can get. This insane notion he has of making Juan king of Naples . . ."

Long rivals for their father's approval, Cesare and his brother despised each other. Having no siblings of my own, I could not claim to understand the depth of the enmity between them. But I did know that Juan was a dangerous fool who should not be trusted with the simplest task. To leap him over all the other pieces on the board and crown him in glory was such breathtaking folly that even I could only marvel at it. Yet such was Borgia's intent. As a first step, he had married Juan off to a cousin of King Ferdinand's. The happy bridegroom was in Spain, where he was expected to be making himself pleasant to Their Most Catholic Majesties.

"Be assured," I said quickly, "that I will take every precaution to keep Il Papa safe. But His Holiness is unlikely to agree to any measure that could give the impression that he is afraid. He will continue to go wherever he wishes and meet with whomever he pleases."

"We will have to find other ways to protect him," Cesare said. Bending a little closer, he lifted my hand and brushed a kiss across my palm. His breath warm on my skin, he asked, "Come to my bed tonight. I will slip away from the Spaniards as early as I can."

Anticipation shimmered through me. I thought of what Borgia had said, of the women who threw themselves at the feet of his son. I would never be one of them.

"Come to mine," I said and took my leave.

After a quick visit to my rooms to wash away the mud of the road and don fresh clothes, I made my way to the grand hall of the palazzo, where His Holiness was to dine in state with the dignitaries of his own court as well as the town notables. Later, he would take most of his meals in private; but on these first few nights in Viterbo, he intended to show himself grandly.

Cesare was seated to his father's right, with the young Spanish lords arrayed nearby. Despite the courtesy with which he had been treated on the dueling field, Don Miguel de Lopez y Herrera appeared to be in a foul temper. As I watched, he shoved a serving man offering a basin for hand washing so harshly that the fellow stumbled back and would have fallen had he not been caught and steadied by another. The water splashed over the floor and had to be mopped up hastily by a page. Cesare frowned but said nothing, his silence a reminder of how vital the friendship of the Spaniards had become.

Drifting around the edges of the assembly, I kept an eye out for anything unusual, any break in routine that might signal trouble. Finding nothing, I let my attention stray back to the guests. Lucrezia sat at her father's other side, a slim figure garbed in gold with her blond hair arranged in ringlets around her face. She was laughing at something Borgia had said and appeared to be ignoring her Sforza husband entirely. I sighed, thinking of how excited she had been at the prospect of marriage and how she had romanticized her husband-to-be before ever meeting him.

The plain fact was that Borgia had sold her to the peacock-proud Sforzas in return for their support in getting him elected pope. With that goal obtained, the alliance with them had lost much of its appeal. Betting was five-to-three in the streets of Rome that the thrice-betrothed Lucrezia would be twice-married before too long. Predictably enough, her present husband was not amused, but he seemed genuinely smitten with her and disinclined to take any action that might further sour his formidable father-in-law. There were times when the darkness of my nature that precluded any such tender longings did not seem so great a disadvantage after all.

As the evening wore down, I sought my quarters, there to await Cesare. Wrapped in a black lace robe that I knew he particularly liked, I sat propped up in bed with a favorite book, Boccaccio's *On Famous Women*. I was in the midst of the life of Medea when a loud knocking interrupted me. Puzzled as to why Cesare would make such a clamor, I slipped my knife into my hand and eased open the door, finding myself face-to-face with a harried Spanish servant who made no pretense of addressing me politely but said only, *"Venga."*

5

The servant led me down corridors and around corners, past guardsmen who scrupulously averted their eyes as we went by and scurrying servants who did the same, until we arrived at the wing of the palazzo that housed Cesare and his father. Beyond the cordon of guards put in place by Vittoro, we approached the wide bronze doors of Cesare's apartment, passed through the antechamber where the new young cardinal met with petitioners and counselors, and came at last to his private quarters tucked away in a corner overlooking the gardens.

Lamps had been lit, casting long shadows over the century-old murals depicting the martyrdom of Saint John the Baptist. Treacherous Salome came off particularly well in the artist's rendering. His Eminence, as Cesare was now known, lay on a vast bed shrouded in curtains and roofed by a tapestry canopy.

Herrera hovered over him. The Spanish grandee had the look of a man queasy with the shock of sudden sobriety.

Cesare, by contrast, appeared pale but otherwise entirely himself, except for the long red gash down his left arm. He was bare-chested and absent his boots.

"It's not that bad," he assured me in response to my scowl. To the Spaniard, he said, *"Gracias, Don Miguel. Déjame con la señora, si se quiere."*

I was unsure exactly what Cesare had said, as he had spoken in the Castilian of the Spanish court. Among themselves, the Borgias spoke the Catalan of their forbearers. Those of us who served them found it useful to learn something of that language, similar to yet sufficiently distinct from Castilian to make understanding what he had just said difficult. Even so, I realized that he had thanked Don Miguel and asked to be left alone with me.

The Spaniard rattled off a rapid-fire response of which I caught precisely nothing and took his leave, but not without a contemptuous glance in my direction. The servant who had fetched me departed with him. Cesare and I were left alone. I made haste to examine his injury. The gash extended from below his left shoulder down the length of his arm to the elbow. A little deeper and it would have done serious damage to the muscles and tendons.

"Just clean this up for me, if you would," he said. "I'd rather no one else knows about it."

A basin of bloody water, evidence of his own efforts to deal with the wound, was on a table beside his bed, along with a needle and thread. There was no sign of his valet, who I gathered had been banished.

All too aware of my own limitations, I hesitated. "You do understand that my . . . expertise lies in a different direction?"

"I don't care about that. How's your sewing?"

"Appalling. I can barely thread a needle."

I was not exaggerating; the needlework expected of every properly reared young woman had ever been my bane. But given the circumstances, I would have to gird myself to do better.

"How did it happen?" I asked as I refilled the basin with clean water from an ewer near the bed. I tried to sound at ease although inwardly I was trembling. I cope well enough with the monthly results of being female, but otherwise I have a particular horror of blood and avoid it whenever possible. Except, of course, for those times when the darkness comes upon me. Then I have killed bloodily and wallowed in the results.

I am a contrary creature, to be sure.

"Herrera mistook an officer's wife for a woman of the town," Cesare said. He sounded weary and more than a little exasperated. "The officer took offense, there was a fight, I intervened."

"You took the blow meant for a drunken lout because he happens to be a nephew of the Spanish monarchs?"

The notion angered me more than I would have expected. Cesare was no child and had not been one for many years. Yet just then I felt an odd sort of protectiveness toward him, which I told myself came solely from my responsibilities for the welfare of *la famiglia*.

Cesare shrugged. "Something like that. It doesn't matter. What is important is that this go no further. Herrera is already screaming that he was insulted and wants the officer's head. Can you imagine the reaction of the garrison to that?"

The garrison of the town Il Papa was counting on to protect the route an enemy army would have to take into Rome.

Stabbing thread through a needle, I said, "Has there been trouble before this?"

Cesare glanced at what I had in my hand and looked away. "The charms of Viterbo have paled quickly. The Spaniards are bored. For that matter, so am I."

"Not to worry. The usual hangers-on came in your father's wake. There's a fresh supply of whores, touts, entertainers, and thieves to keep everyone occupied."

Likely an assortment of spies, intriguers, and troublemakers as well, but I said nothing of that.

Cesare started to laugh, caught his breath as I took the first stitch, and remained resolutely silent as I finished the job. The hours I had spent in Sofia's company had taught me more than I had realized.

"You underrate yourself," Cesare said when I was done. He examined my work closely before I bandaged the wound and appeared satisfied. "I'm going to tell Lucrezia how good you are with needlework. She can put you to work on that altar cloth she's making."

"I know at least a hundred ways to poison you, each more agonizing than the last."

He did laugh then and, wrapping an arm around my waist,

drew me down to him. "Stay with me," he said. "I've missed you."

I was tempted, but I hesitated all the same. "You should not exert yourself."

Blue shadows were deepening beneath his eyes. He tried to stifle a yawn and failed. "I honestly don't think I could."

A frank admission for one of his age and temperament. I laid my hand against his brow and was relieved to find no sign of fever. Even so, his condition could worsen during the night. It was best that he not be alone.

So did I justify my natural yearnings. Intimacy—not of the sexual kind but borne of the true communion of minds—was exceedingly rare in my life. I told myself that was just as well, yet there were still times when I longed for it.

"As you wish," I said and settled into the bed beside him, drawing a light cover over us both.

He turned on his side, fitting me into the curve of his body. Scant moments passed before his breathing grew deep and regular. I lay snug against him as my mind drifted back to the problems posed by the cantharidin and how they might be solved. I had gotten to the point of considering whether the time had come to test what I had accomplished so far when I became aware that Cesare was no longer asleep.

Ah, the resiliency of youth! Still on my side, gazing away from him into the darkness of the bed hangings, I made no demure when he raised the hem of my gown to bare my thighs, nor when his hand slipped between them. I needed only to shift a little to accommodate him. We moved as one, urgency coupled with familiarity. I knew his rhythms; he knew mine. Yet still I was surprised by how quickly pleasure mounted. Whether from unmet need or the strange eroticism of the largely silent encounter, release overtook us both between one breath and the next.

A normal woman, so well sated, would have slipped unfettered into sleep and dreamed only of her lover. Not I. Scarcely had slumber overtaken me than the nightmare came.

The same dream had tormented me for as long as I can remember. I am in a very small space behind a wall. There is a tiny hole through which I can see into a room filled with shadows, some of them moving. The darkness is broken by shards of light that flashes again and again. Blood pours from it—a giant wave of blood lapping against the walls of the room and threatening to drown me. I can hear a woman screaming. A few months before, waking suddenly, I heard myself call out her name: "Mamma." But that was absurd. My mother died when I was born. She could not possibly be the woman in the blood-soaked room.

I woke as usual in the clammy grip of terror, but from long practice lay unmoving, forcing myself to breathe slowly and deeply. I was determined not to disturb Cesare, who surely needed his rest at least as much as I did. Besides, I did not want to have to explain to him yet again about the nightmare. We shared a bed often enough that he needed no reminding of it.

For the rest of the night, I dozed lightly, waking while Cesare still slept soundly, one arm thrown across my hip. Carefully, I slipped out of the bed and made my way back to my quarters on the other side of the palazzo. The guards were changing posts as I went, giving me some hope that I would not be seen. Not that it mattered. Borgia's agents were everywhere, their reports flowing to him as a river fed by many streams before being swallowed by the ocean itself. For certain, he would know of the altercation in the town, but I suspected he would also approve of what his son had done, though he would not tell him so. At all costs, the Spaniards had to be kept sweet, until the pendulum swung as it always does. Then who knew what price Borgia would exact for having to endure them?

In my own rooms, I bathed quickly, not bothering to wait for a servant to bring hot water. Simply dressed with my hair secured in a braid around my head, I hastened down to the kitchens; but did not linger there. Before long, I was on my way again with a roll stuffed with hazelnut cream in one hand and a sturdy market basket in the other.

My father, in his days as poisoner to the House of Borgia, understood the risk of being so focused on what is nearby as to overlook what is on the periphery. He was a great believer in getting out and about, instructing me in the finer points of how to look, listen, even smell a scene so as to understand it and, even more important, how to know early on when something is wrong. He also understood that the right prop could explain one's presence without calling attention to it. Hence the basket.

I went down the wide stone steps of the palazzo and set off to the southeast in the direction that a stammering serving boy told me led to Viterbo's central square. The day was pleasantly cool with only thin traces of cloud to mar the otherwise pristine sky. Bright autumnal flowers trailed from window pots, their perfumes mingling with the bite of the lye soap used to scrub the paving stones. Having long been a favorite haunt of popes, the town overflowed with churches, many of them centuries old, constructed mainly of stone that had yellowed softly over the years. In that respect—and only that—it bore the faintest possible resemblance to my beloved Rome. Otherwise, everything appeared small, shrunken, and still far too quiet for my taste.

The old *porta romana* giving entrance to the town through the high stone walls punctuated by watchtowers would have been opened at dawn; already travelers were making their way toward the palazzo in hope of doing business with the papal household. Members of Viterbo's garrison were in evidence, patrolling in breastplates and plumed helmets with spiked halberds in hand. But I also saw men of the Pope's own household guard on patrol in the town. I could not help but wonder how much the show of their presence had to do with protecting the Pope and how much was intended to quell the spreading resentment of the Spaniards.

In the central market adjacent to the main piazza decorated with carvings of lions and palm trees, the town's twin symbols—stalls overflowed with heaps of newly harvested grapes and olives. Vats of virgin olive oil and raw wine were stacked near wicker cages of chickens, ducks, and rabbits. I smelled rounds of tart pecorino and the sweet aroma of pearly ricotta. Salted pink hams hung from rafters beside the stalls. Heaps of thorny artichokes vied with a surprisingly good selection of mushrooms. I bought some of each, filling my basket.

All the while, I listened. The good wives of Viterbo, many

in high conical bonnets and rich lace bodices, were serious about their marketing. Like sensible hagglers everywhere, they scoffed at the prices being asked before settling on what all parties could consider fair.

I was eavesdropping on an exchange regarding red borlotti beans when several cooks I recognized as being from Borgia's household entered the market. These *maestri di cucina,* garbed in their customary white tunics emblazoned with the papal seal and trailed by kitchen boys brought along to carry their purchases, began to pick through the displays. They seemed unaware that the mood among the townspeople had changed abruptly. It was as though a dark cloud had moved across the otherwise sunny sky.

"Damn Romans," the matron near me muttered. Forgetting her interest in the borlotti beans, she stomped away. Nor was she alone. One by one, the good wives of Viterbo shot scowls at the new arrivals and took their leave.

A loud argument broke out not far from where I stood. A stout butcher draped in a blood-splattered leather apron was refusing to haggle over the price of a haunch of beef, declaring that the red-faced cook could pay him what he demanded or do without.

"Don't be an idiot," the maestro protested. "No one will pay what you're asking."

"An idiot, am I?" The butcher's expression darkened as he picked up a cleaver and smacked it down hard into a wooden chopping board. "If you don't like how we do things here, why don't you go back to Rome?"

A rumbling of agreement rose from the surrounding stalls.

In the midst of it, someone else said, "And take the goddamn Spaniards with you."

"Better yet," another shouted, "send them back to Spain. We don't want their kind here."

"Or yours!"

"Put that on His Holiness's plate, why don't you?"

At the mention of Borgia, I froze. Discontent over the behavior of the Spaniards was reasonable enough, given what Cesare had told me. But when it spilled over to include the Pope himself . . . A handful of peasants on the route north could make asses of themselves without my worrying unduly. But if the people of the very town Borgia was counting on to block a French advance were emboldened to behave in such a matter, the situation was considerably worse than I had realized.

Catcalls and hoots followed the cooks as they retreated amid hurled threats and shaken fists back up the street toward the palazzo. With their hasty departure, the good wives reappeared. Save for a rippling undercurrent of satisfaction, the market returned swiftly to normal. I made my way back to the palazzo slowly, thinking over what I had witnessed. Had the Spanish truly been so boorish in their behavior as to deserve such hostility, or was it possible that the mood of the town was being stirred by an unseen hand? Della Rovere's, perhaps, acting in concert with the French? Rumor had it that the cardinal who hungered to replace Borgia on Saint Peter's Throne had struck an agreement with the young French king whereby Charles would receive Naples in return for della Rovere's ascent to the papacy.

A sudden blaring of horns up ahead interrupted my thoughts. A troop of horsemen was approaching at high speed down the winding street leading from the palazzo. They came at a gallop, banners flying, spurs gleaming in the sun. I saw at a glance Cesare riding with Herrera, the other Spaniards ranged out behind them. Baying dogs ran alongside, signaling their intent to hunt.

Parties of young aristocrats make a show of themselves galloping through the streets of Rome all the time. But they stay to the broad avenues and for the most part cause little trouble. Not so here. There was a moment when everyone in the byway seemed to stand stock-still with surprise at what was happening. Then pandemonium broke out.

I dove into the nearest doorway as people all around me did the same. Peddlers rushed to push their carts into alleys, while those unfortunate enough to be driving wagons whipped their animals frantically as they struggled to get out of the way. I saw a man fling himself into the road to scoop up a small girl as chickens beat their wings in panic and a white cat who reminded me of mine arched her back and hissed in fury.

So, must I admit, did anger surge in me. That men should show such contempt for the peace of the town was infuriating. That Cesare should be among them passed all bearing. Had I the means, I would gladly have thrown him from the saddle to crack his thick head on the paving stones, consequences be damned.

Turned away as I was to avoid flying dust and small bits of stone struck loose by the horses' pounding hooves, I was certain that Cesare took no more notice of me than he did of anyone else in the road. He and the other riders went by in a blur of silver spurs, foam-flecked dogs, and panting handlers racing to keep up.

When they were gone, I stood for a moment, listening to the fading sounds of their passing. My basket had tilted, and several of the artichokes had rolled out into the road. I bent to retrieve them, becoming aware as I did so of the muttering all around me.

Straightening slowly, I dared a glance at those standing nearby. Uniformly, the face of every man and woman I could see was bright with anger. What good would the strongest walls be to Borgia if a disgruntled populace welcomed his enemies in their hearts?

Such was my preoccupation with that thorny question that I must have grasped one of the artichokes too tightly. The sharp end of a fleshy leaf pierced the palm of my hand. I stared down at the bright drops of blood as dark apprehension rippled through me.

6

Venison, served still bloody as Borgia liked it, graced the Pope's plate that evening. The sight of it made me queasy as well as reminded me that I was angry at Cesare. His feckless accommodation of the Spaniards still rankled. Herrera was seated next to him at dinner and seemed able to make him laugh at will.

I did not linger in the hall as was my custom but instead threw a cloak over my shoulders and stepped outside. Wood smoke curled from the chimney pots that dotted the tiled rooftops of the town. To the west, the sun's last rays filtered through mist and the promise of rain. Although it would be vespers soon, the square directly in front of the palazzo remained busy. Merchants of every stripe jostled with priests, peddlers, prostitutes, and the occasional penitent, all avid for a bit of papal business. The guards kept the crowd orderly enough, but as the hour aged and the prospect of a day's trade dimmed, the press of bodies clamoring to be heard grew more urgent.

Failing to find the peace I sought, I was about to go back inside the palazzo when a sudden splash of color on the edge of my vision stopped me. From one of the *corsi* leading into the square came a figure out of fantasy, dressed in a patchwork tunic and leggings and wearing on his head a pointed felt hat on which spangles glinted in the fading sun. He was banging a drum at the same time as he blew a horn and shook his head to make the spangles clang. He looked as much a jester as any to ply his trade from court to court, but there was also something oddly familiar about him.

Advancing across the piazza in leaps and bounds, he came at last very near to where I stood. Seeing me, he paused and with a smile swept the hat from his head and executed a more than passable bow.

Having secured my attention, he lingered only a moment before he straightened and gamboled off back toward the town. I took a breath, let it out slowly, and followed him.

David ben Eliezer and I found a quiet place to sit in the back of a taverna catering to a motley crew of jugglers, jongleurs, jesters, and pantomime players. They were a rowdy bunch, their raucous laughter making it unlikely that we could be overheard. A buxom young woman took our orders, not so preoccupied that she didn't manage an appreciative glance at David. Having removed his hat again and set aside the other accoutrements of his borrowed occupation, he looked like a figure out of a

Botticelli painting, all dark liquid eyes and fierce grace. Yet the jester costume remained a brilliant disguise. No one would think to look behind it for a renegade Jew determined to protect his people with guile if he could but with the sword if he must.

"I'm sorry I had to leave Rome before we could meet," I said when the barmaid had gone again. In the rush of activity leading up to Il Papa's departure from the Holy City, there had been no time to seek out David. As glad as I was to see him, his sudden appearance in Viterbo could not be good.

He inclined his head in understanding. "I, too, was occupied. There is much to speak of. But first, I've brought letters." Sliding them across the table, he added, "One from Sofia, another from Rocco, and a message from a woman named Portia, who won't tell me how she found me but who wants you to know that your cat is fine. She hopes you are the same." He looked at me all too perceptively. "You aren't, are you?"

I slipped the letters into my pouch. Sofia's I welcomed. As for Rocco's . . . I would not think of that just then.

"I am well enough." David and I had braved death together, and only just escaped it, but I was reluctant all the same to burden him with my troubles. We spoke of lighter matters until both of us were satisfied that we were not attracting any undue attention. Only then did I ask why he had come to Viterbo.

"I wouldn't have," he said in answer to my query, "had not His Holiness decided to hie himself here. Not that Rome has much to recommend it these days. The weather is foul, the plague is stirring, and the populace is more than usually disgruntled."

"Save for the plague, Viterbo isn't much better." I leaned a little closer across the table. "His Holiness's servants are insulted openly in the marketplace. As for the garrison . . . let's just say that at the moment, I would not put money on their loyalty."

"That is unfortunate." David fell silent as our cups of wine arrived, along with a plate of bread and a saucer of pale green oil. We dipped and sipped before he said, "I bring news that I could not entrust to a letter."

Sourness stirred in my stomach. I set down the wine. "Tell me."

"An assassin is en route to Viterbo, may indeed already be here."

I was not about to disregard any threat to Borgia, yet the thought that one more would-be killer was stirring in the weeds hardly shocked me.

"Yet another?" I said, picking up my cup again. "More seem to sprout with every rain."

"Unfortunately, this one may be different. The amount of money involved suggests that whoever has been hired is more dangerous than anyone else you've confronted in the past."

Just as poisoners vary in their degree of skill and, consequently, their price, assassins do the same. Yet I remained cautious.

"How do you know this?"

"You are aware that we still have contacts in Spain?"

"I had assumed as much." Tens of thousands of Jews had fled from there the previous year, expelled at the order of Their Most Catholic Majesties. But others, having seen what was coming, had chosen to remain as conversos, converts to Christianity. They lived under constant suspicion, although at least a few were nestled securely within the ranks of Holy Mother Church and the royal court itself.

"Funds are moving between banks here and in Spain," David said. "The objective seems to be to obscure their origins as much as to conceal the recipient. Someone is going to great effort to strike at Borgia. With all respect, I fear that this time they could succeed."

Far from resenting his assessment, I welcomed it. Only a true fool would reject the counsel of one who had proven himself as good and trustworthy a friend as David.

"Do you know anything more?" I asked.

"Not yet, but I thought it best to come here as soon as I got word of what was happening. We paid to the heavens and beyond for Borgia's promise that as pope he would extend the hand of tolerance to us. So far, he has made good on his word. But if he falls . . ."

I nodded grimly. "All the current crop of candidates to replace him see their power as rooted in Holy Mother Church. They will use any scapegoat to keep it from being blamed for the mounting ills of the world."

"You really think Borgia is different?"

"I do. He sees his power as coming from within himself. The Church is only a means to an end. He would cheerfully tear it apart and rebuild it in some entirely new form if that meant he would achieve his own goals more readily."

"You are saying that in the vastness of his ambition, there is room for other men to breathe?"

I could not have put it so eloquently, but it was true all the same. "Yes, I suppose I am. So, my friend, how are we to keep him alive?"

David flashed a wolf's smile. However high the stakes might be, he could still find pleasure in the contest. "You would be amazed at what people will say in the presence of a fool. If anyone in Viterbo has seen or heard anything that points to the identity of the assassin, I will find it out."

I did not doubt him, but I did have a suggestion. "As this information comes from Spain, you would do well to keep an eye on the Spaniards in particular."

David raised a brow. "Are you saying that Borgia's own countrymen, his supposed allies, could be behind the threat to him?"

In truth, I would not have thought so except that the known perfidy of Their Most Catholic Majesties was enough to give any sensible person pause. Fairly or not, I had to consider that despite the lengths Borgia had gone to woo them—giving them the lion's share of Novus Orbis, the New World, for example—they still might not be steadfast in their loyalty.

Even so, I answered mildly. "I am saying nothing, but neither do I want to overlook any possibility."

He thought for a moment, then nodded. "Fair enough. Can you get me close to them?"

It was my turn to smile. "Nothing adorns a great prince so well as a great fool. I will speak to Borgia."

We lingered a little longer, talking of Rome and mutual friends, before I took my leave and returned to the palazzo. There beneath the wooden-hammer-beam roof from which the banners of the popes dating back centuries were displayed,

Borgia was still holding court. Herrera appeared to be attending courteously to whatever it was that Il Papa was saying, but I caught the mocking roll of his eyes when His Holiness turned away for a moment.

When the meal concluded, I withdrew to my rooms, where, after some hesitation, I opened the letter from Sofia. She wrote to say that she hoped I was taking every care for my health, by which I assumed she meant that I was not abusing the sleeping powder she had provided. Plague was in the city but as yet seemed contained by the usual measure of boarding up the houses of the afflicted, leaving all within to live or die as God willed. I should write to let her know how I fared, and if I needed anything, I should tell her that as well.

I set the letter aside and reached for the one from Rocco. Did my hand shake slightly as I opened it? I do not wish to think so, but the possibility remains.

He was well and hoped I was the same. Nando had produced a drawing of their street that his father enclosed. He thanked me again for encouraging the boy's artistic leanings. They had acquired a dog, some mix of greyhound and who-knew-what. Nando had insisted on naming her Bella. Rocco thought the sentiment far off the mark but admitted that with decent feeding, a warm place to sleep, and a bath, Bella was proving worth her mettle. He was keeping busy with commissions and had devised a new method of adding color to molten glass that he thought I would find interesting. He wondered when I would be returning to the city.

Of Carlotta d'Agnelli, his wife-to-be, he said nothing at all.

No doubt that was mere oversight. He had filled the page

with his writing and did not think to turn to the other side. Or he had simply run out of time. Otherwise, he surely would have gone on and on about her.

Smiling, I folded the letter carefully and put it away, but I kept out the drawing. Nando truly had captured the sense of life and motion in the street of the glassmakers. I could almost smell the coal smoke of the kilns mingling with the distinctive dry scent that sand emits in the moment before it turns to liquid.

With renewed vigor, I unpacked one of the chests I had brought from Rome. Within it, secured in fitted cases, were the apparatus that I used in my investigations. Bringing them along was difficult and somewhat risky, but I refused to allow my enforced stay in *la campagna* to inconvenience me any more than was absolutely necessary. Having arranged the retorts, lenses, burners, and scales on a table, I set to work and presently was well occupied testing concentrations of cantharidin against various reagents in an effort to determine its potency.

My late father had stressed the need to keep meticulous records regarding all such investigations, and I maintained that habit. Already, I had filled the better part of a notebook with my observations regarding cantharidin. While it was far from the most potent poison familiar to me, if it lived up to its promise it would have one overwhelming advantage: namely, that men would take it willingly. The administration of a poison, slipping it past someone's guard, is often the greater part of the challenge facing one of my calling. But to actually have a poison that men asked for . . . I could not help but smile at the possibilities.

Several hours sped by. My anger at Cesare having dulled, I wondered in passing if he might visit me, but I failed to muster enthusiasm at the thought. The truth was that as time crept on, the arms of Morpheus appeared more seductive. Still I resisted sleep, fearing that the nightmare would overtake me again.

Finally, I bargained with myself. I had drunk only a single cup of wine with David, and that long enough ago that surely its effect had worn off. Persuaded by my own logic, I packed everything away again—a tedious process but better than raising curiosity about my activities. By the time I had finished, I was so weary that my hand shook as I prepared the powder. I downed the result with a grimace and made haste to bed. That was just as well, for the effects took me swiftly enough to make me wonder if perhaps I had overdone the dosage just a little.

Not that it mattered. I slipped into sleep with a smile, and if I dreamed at all, I had no awareness of it.

7

"Have you heard?"

I turned my head to find Renaldo standing beside me. It was the next morning. We were in the corridor that led to Borgia's apartments. The steward had approached so stealthily as to escape my notice. Either that or I was far too preoccupied for my own good.

"Heard what?"

His sharp nose twitched with excitement. "The dispatch riders from Rome report that there was a violent thunderstorm in the city last night. The papal apartments in the Vatican were struck by lightning. Two of His Holiness's secretaries were knocked to the ground and rendered unconscious."

This was indeed startling news. Thunderstorms in Rome in early autumn are not common, and for the Vatican itself to have been struck . . .

"Clearly," I said, "the fact that this happened *after* His Holiness's departure from the city is a sign of God's favor."

Renaldo snorted. "It could be taken as such. But the betting is running five to two that the Almighty simply missed."

"Surely that is sacrilege." I meant no criticism, matters of religion being impenetrable to me. I was merely concerned that Renaldo might be placing himself at some risk by repeating such a thing. However, the possibility did not seem to worry him overly much.

"That is humor or what passes for it these days," he said. Leaning a little closer, he imparted the rest of what he had heard. "Satan protects our master, so the street whispers. Hence, Borgia's departure from the city in advance of divine retribution."

The charge that Borgia was a servant of the Devil had been around for as long as I could remember. Such can be said of all men who achieve great worldly ambitions. Even so, if it was now being rumbled about in the streets, something was afoot.

"How big a spoon do you think it takes to stir such a pot?" I asked.

Renaldo shrugged. "More to the point, who wields the spoon?"

Who indeed? In Rome, I had my own sources of information. While they could not begin to rival Borgia's, they were effective all the same, reaching as they did from the Jewish Quarter deep into the network of smugglers who populated the city's underground. By contrast, in Viterbo I was fumbling in the dark, trying to find my way in a place too alien for me to be sure of anything.

"You will tell me if you hear more?" I asked Renaldo.

He nodded gravely. "You and I are of the same mind, Donna Francesca. We both want only what is best for our master."

On that I was in full accord. The problem was that our master did not always seem to understand what was best for him. Nor did his son. No matter. My first duty was to tell Borgia what I had learned from David. But as so often happens with good intentions, there were problems.

"His Holiness is occupied with matters of state," the high-nosed secretary informed me. All of Borgia's secretaries viewed me with suspicion and dislike, for which I could hardly blame them. I was, after all, a woman who had the confidence of the Pope, in their eyes an aberration of nature even without the added complication of my dark profession.

"Serious matters," the secretary emphasized. "I doubt that I can fit you in unless—"

He broke off as an angry voice penetrated the wall between the antechamber and the inner office. The words were indistinct, but there was no mistaking the tone, or the fact that the speaker was Borgia himself. Clearly, something had displeased Il Papa.

"Unless," the secretary resumed, "the matter is urgent . . ." He looked at me almost hopefully.

Borgia and I had an understanding, Under certain circumstances, he would see me immediately. I had only to declare that it was urgent for him to do so and all barriers would melt away. He had made it so because he understood full well that there were times when such access could be vital to his survival.

"*¡Aquesta lloba!*" His Holiness exclaimed, his voice rising loudly enough as to leave no further doubt of his meaning. "That she-wolf! How dare she do this? *¿Qui cony es creu que és?*"

I could not say who the Queen of Spain thought she was, apart from the obvious, but Borgia's pungency in his native Catalan made his sentiments about her more than clear. His Holiness rarely showed anger in public, and then usually only for effect, but in this case he seemed genuinely enraged. Whatever Isabella had done, she appeared to have earned his enmity and more.

"Do you know what has provoked him?" I asked the secretary.

He hesitated, reluctant to share anything he knew with me, but anxiety—always high among those who served Il Papa—got the better of him. "The Spanish have arrested Juan, charging him with immoral behavior." He sniffed faintly. "As though they should have expected any other kind."

I could not conceal my shock. To arrest the Pope's son hard on the heels of his marriage into the Spanish royal family seemed an act of feckless hostility. But perhaps I should not have been so surprised. I had never trusted Their Most Catholic Majesties. Their decision the previous year to expel the Jews from Spain had smacked of the worst sort of fanaticism combined with a shortsighted ruthlessness that did not bode well for anyone allied with them. I blamed them for much of what had happened since, not the least encouraging the atmosphere of hatred that led to my father's murder.

Without delay, I announced, "It is urgent that I see His Holiness."

The magic word having been uttered, the secretary stood aside. I entered as Borgia was in the midst of a graphic—and, I believe, anatomically impossible—description of the Spanish queen's begetting. Seeing me, he broke off. With one hand, he dabbed with a cloth at the sweat pouring off his forehead. With the other, he accepted the goblet of wine that a timorous servant held out to him.

Having taken a long swallow, he eyed me. "What do *you* want, poisoner?"

By all means, take that moment to remind the world of who and what I was, a weapon only waiting to be unleashed at his whim.

"A few moments of your time, if you please, Your Holiness." I spoke so meekly that even Borgia in his black mood could not restrain the flicker of a smile.

"Out!" he bellowed to the others.

The breeze cast up by the haste with which his secretaries and hangers-on fled his office ruffled the skirts of his cassock. Borgia and I were alone.

"Get on with it," he ordered with a wave of his hand. "What new trouble do you bring?"

Experience had taught me that when dealing with a man as seeped in intrigue and duplicity as Borgia, nothing was more effective than the blunt, unvarnished truth.

"An assassin is en route to Viterbo, or possibly even already here."

His Holiness shrugged. "Another? All to the good. I wouldn't want your skills to grow dull."

What in another man would have been a show of bravado

was, in Borgia's case, evidence of genuine personal courage. He wasted no time fearing what his enemies might do to him, preferring to make them fear him instead. That was admirable, but I could not allow my own success in keeping him alive to lead to overconfidence.

"This one may not be like the others we have seen," I said. "A great deal of money is moving between banks, both here and in Spain. More than the usual effort is being made to conceal where it is coming from and where it is going."

His gaze narrowed. Borgia prided himself on his army of spies, and rightly so; very rarely was he taken by surprise. Yet even many-eyed Argus had his blind spots.

"How do you know this?"

"David ben Eliezer brought word. Do you remember him?"

"The renegade Jew, the one who wants to fight?"

"I don't think he wants to, necessarily. He just doesn't believe that the meek really will inherit the Earth. Or even be around to see who does."

Borgia grunted. He walked around the expanse of his desk and sat down in the thronelike chair. Lacing his hands over his stomach, he said, "I can't say I disagree with him. Do you trust his sources?"

"He hasn't told me what they are, but I wouldn't expect him to. What is more important is that I trust the man. David believes the threat is real. We should take that seriously."

"And do what?" Before I could reply, Borgia added, "Don't suggest that I limit where I go or whom I see; I'll have none of that. If you had your way, I'd be living as an anchoress immured in convent walls."

The thought of Borgia as a virgin nun sealed off from the world caused me to press my lips together in an effort not to burst out laughing. When I was sure that the impulse had safely passed, I said, "As a first step, I suggest that you put your own men on the town gate to scrutinize everyone coming and going." It might already have been too late to stop the assassin from entering Viterbo, but I thought that the effort would be worthwhile all the same. If nothing else, it would remind the garrison that Borgia's personal guard was a force to be reckoned within its own right.

Borgia grunted. "Not a bad idea. What else?"

"I'd like to bring David into the palazzo. Disguised, of course. Another pair of eyes and ears could be very helpful, and he's good in a tough situation."

"Done; but I want it clear to both of you that this has to be handled delicately."

I understood his concerns, or at least I thought that I did, but even so I said, "With all respect, Your Holiness, we have an assassin, possibly a very good one. There is nothing delicate about that."

"Is there not? Then tell me this, who is the target?"

Perhaps I had already been too long in Borgia's employ, or all those years living under his roof as a child had warped my thinking. Had I breathed in conspiracy with the air, imbibed it with the water? Whatever the case, I understood the question all too readily. I also realized that his asking it meant that he had deciphered in an instant what it had taken me all night to figure out.

It was the Spanish banks that had troubled me. Not that Spain doesn't have fine assassins, but Italy and France are known to breed better. Why send the money through Spain, then? I could think of only one reason.

"Obviously," I said, "you may be the target."

His eyebrows arched. "Only 'may'? Who else would be worthy of so costly an assassin?" He spoke as a tutor to a promising pupil. I did not mind, understanding as I did how much I had to learn from him.

"Your enemies have been trying to kill you almost since the day you were elected pope, but you're still here. I fear that they may have finally realized that they don't actually need to attack you directly. They only need to weaken you enough so that you will fall on your own."

A lesser man would have rejected the notion that his success did not depend entirely on himself but was owed at least in part to other forces. Borgia, who understood better than any other the rickety scaffolding upon which power rests, gazed at the marble and gold chessboard set up on his desk as though he had no greater concern than his next move. Almost absently, he asked, "How might they accomplish that?"

The game had changed, I saw. The queen was no longer in danger. A bishop of her own had come forward to protect her, supported by a knight.

"By destroying the one thing you must have in order to survive: your alliance with Spain."

"Ah, yes, Spain again. Funny how often it comes up lately."

His gaze shifted to me. "What do you think of this business with Juan? Do you think it's related?"

"I wouldn't discount the possibility, but to be perfectly frank, Juan is too far away for me to concern myself with him. I have to concentrate on the situation at hand."

Borgia grunted his approval. "Fair enough. If you were this highly paid assassin, what would you do?"

I could only hope that the promptness with which I answered would be taken as an indication of my devotion to safeguarding Il Papa and not as evidence that I entertained disloyal thoughts.

"One possibility would be to harm someone close to you in such a way that you would be made to believe that Herrera and the other Spaniards were responsible. In that event, you would be driven to kill them and thereby end the alliance yourself."

His Holiness nodded slowly. "Quite right; it is well known that I would destroy anyone who strikes at my children."

That was the one thing he truly feared, more even than falling at the hands of an assassin. Borgia's children were his promise of immortality. I suppose that was why any resistance to his will in matters regarding them prompted him to fury.

"Obviously, we can take every precaution to protect Cesare and Lucrezia, but we're already doing that. Which means that they are likely not the target. Someone else is."

I waited, letting him work through it for himself as he was always wont to do. No one liked a puzzle better than Borgia, and no one was better at unraveling them. After a moment, the corners of his mouth twitched. He took another swallow of the wine and set the goblet down.

"Herrera himself?"

I nodded. "To die in such way that you would be blamed. The Spanish would be infuriated, or at least they would claim to be, and the alliance would be shattered beyond all hope of repair."

"You realize that this may be all Ferdinand and Isabella's doing? They may simply want an excuse to betray me. If that is the case, you think they would go so far as to arrange the murder of their own nephew?"

"I do not rule it out." Not that there weren't plenty of other candidates. The French king, for one, but also the rival families within Italy itself—the Orsinis, Sforzas, Medicis, della Roveres, Farneses . . . the list went on and on. In the end, it didn't matter. Regardless of who had sent the assassin, my only real concern was to stop him.

Without resentment, for he was ever a man who appreciated a clever stratagem, Borgia said, "It's ingenious, don't you think?"

"It *may* be. But we would be well advised to keep all the possibilities in mind and protect against them. However, we may also wish to consider an . . . unorthodox solution."

I stopped there. As with most men of power, much of the art of managing Borgia had to do with planting a seed, then stepping back to let it take root. Fortunately, his mind was quick and agile. I did not have to wait long.

His smile was genuine, if a little chiding. "Francesca, you

aren't seriously proposing . . . ?" His smile broadened. "Good Lord, you are."

And I would make no apology for it. We both knew that I was in his employ not merely for my skill with poisons but because I was willing to consider what others, in their moral nicety, termed "unthinkable." As though the mind of man—and woman—has not conceived of every cruelty and horror under the sun.

"I am merely saying that we might wish to act preemptively."

"Ha!" Borgia slapped his big hand down on the desk so hard that the porcelain nymph on the corner shook so hard she almost fell off. "You mean it. You want to kill Herrera."

It was true, I did. To my mind, that was the simplest and most effective response to the threat. There was everything to gain and virtually nothing to lose, provided that it was done right.

"Whether he is to be blamed for harming you or yours," I said, "or you are to be blamed for harming him, either way he is a liability. Of course, it would have to be done properly, so as to give the appearance of a tragic accident."

"And how would you manage that?"

He was indulging me, but I still hoped I could appeal to a mind that I knew to be at least as ruthless as my own.

"There are any number of ways. He could tumble off the side of a hill into the valley below us, which, it should be noted, is conveniently steep. Or he could drown in one of the many nearby lakes. Or take a bad spill from his horse.

Any or all of those misfortunes can befall a man under the influence of certain substances that cause dizziness and disorientation while leaving no trace of themselves. In addition, there are numerous other ways to kill that are as undetectable. For example—"

Borgia held up a hand, stopping me. "Enough. I don't know whether to applaud your ingenuity or be terrified of it. So kill Herrera. An accident . . . tragic . . . all of us overcome with grief . . . the promise of a brilliant life snuffed out, and so forth. It has a certain appeal, but—" Reluctantly, he concluded, "Unfortunately, this business with Juan changes things. We need the Spaniard."

"With all respect, alive he will continue to be a target for anyone who seeks to undo you."

His Holiness's eyes narrowed on me. "It's been a while since you killed anyone, hasn't it? The last time was that fellow a few months ago at the Basilica di Santa Maria in Rome, am I right?"

"That was self-defense," I reminded him, which it had been, if only strictly speaking. Besides, that particular miscreant had died after a mere nick from a knife dipped in a contact poison that killed within minutes. When it came to releasing the darkness inside me, I preferred the knife alone. In such situations, the dread I had of blood was transformed into a kind of rapture that both terrified and exalted me.

"Of course it was, but our present situation can benefit from a show of restraint."

"You could take him hostage," I suggested. It was a poor

alternative in my view but one that might serve Borgia all the same. "Demand Juan's release in return for him."

Borgia brushed that aside as unworthy of consideration. "Too crude by far, and even worse, a wasted opportunity. No, this is the perfect time to take the high road. Show that she-wolf and her gutless mate for the backstabbing ingrates they are and myself the better man."

This was the side of Borgia that his adversaries missed, to their own peril. He could be in the grip of the most powerful emotions and yet remain relentlessly rational. It was as though he had the capacity to step apart even from himself, viewing the world with ruthless objectivity. Granted, everything he did was based on the assumption that only what he wanted mattered, but even so the conclusions he came to were more often right than wrong.

I sighed, sensing the inevitable but still driven to make one more attempt, however futile. "Surely, honor demands—"

"Honor is never a substitute for results, Francesca. Remember that. The beloved nephew lives, at least for now." Borgia shot me a warning glance, as though to make sure that I understood him. Any lethal urges I felt would have to be restrained. Worse yet, it would not be enough for me to safeguard *la famiglia.* I would also have to extend my protection to Herrera, a man I already heartily disliked.

I had several hours to ponder the misfortune of that before the clatter of hoofs in the courtyard heralded Cesare and the Spaniards' return. Their visit to the baths appeared to have restored them to good humor. They were all backslapping camaraderie and boisterous cheer as they disappeared up the wide stairs and into the palazzo.

I waited long enough for Cesare to reach his own quarters before seeking him out. He was in his bedchamber, having thrown off his cloak but still wearing his mud-splattered boots and breeches. When I entered, he was in close conversation with one of his secretaries, who, I supposed, was telling him the news from Spain. I could not help but admire how well the newly fledged cardinal controlled himself. Not until the man departed and we were alone did Cesare burst out laughing.

"Juan arrested!" He sketched a deep bow. "My heartfelt apologies to Their Most Catholic Majesties. I freely admit that I have not had the best opinion of them, but clearly I was wrong."

"No doubt your brother deserves what has happened to him," I said. "But it still presents a problem."

He nodded, his quick mind leaping ahead. Of all *la famiglia,* Cesare was consistently the most intelligent, only one of the reasons why he would also prove to be the most dangerous.

"As you have already discussed with Il Papa," he said.

I suppressed a sigh. The Borgias would vie over anything—a pretty jewel, a swift horse, the loyalty of a privileged servant; for that was what I was when all was said and done, and I would be a fool to ever forget it. Yet I was fool enough to be Cesare's lover, a complication a wiser woman would have avoided.

"Had you been here when the news arrived," I said as diplomatically as I could manage, "I am certain that His Holiness would have sought your counsel before all others."

Cesare sat on a curved wooden stool and began pulling off his boots. In public, the son of Jove played the prince to perfection. But in private, he eschewed ceremony, performing tasks for himself that others of lesser standing than his own would never have dreamed of doing. He had told me with relish of nights spent sleeping on the ground on the extended hunting trips he took with the men of his personal guard, who were as close to him as a band of brothers. For a fortnight and more, they would range over rough terrain in exercises that bore an uncanny resemblance to training for war, even though Cesare insisted that they were mere amusement.

Borgia knew of the deception and disliked it, but so far at least he had not insisted that his eldest son pursue more sedentary activities both better suited to his new position as cardinal and less alarming to his fellow prelates. The Spaniards, however, had managed to accomplish what Il Papa had not. Since their arrival, Cesare had been forced to rein in his natural impulses and give their amusements preference over his own.

The effort had left him more impatient than he would otherwise have been, and chafing for action. He tossed the second boot aside and stood.

"You should know that there is something else in addition to the problem of your brother," I said. "David ben Eliezer has brought word that an assassin is on the way to Viterbo." I hesitated before adding, "Obviously, you, your father, and Lucrezia are all at risk, but it also occurred to me that the target could be Herrera."

Cesare showed no particular concern that he or either of the others might be marked for death. He had grown up understanding the danger inherent in seeking to scale the heights of power. Fortuna was a capricious goddess who might at any moment withdraw her favor and send the most ambitious plunging into the deepest abyss.

Still, the mention of Herrera surprised him, if only for a moment. "An interesting notion. Should I be concerned for the Spaniard?" At my raised brow, he laughed. "Really, Francesca, you didn't make a bid for removing him in some seemingly innocent way before the assassin can strike?"

A little stiffly, I said, "His Holiness does not think that useful, at the moment." Surely I could not be so obvious to everyone as I apparently was to Borgia *padre e figlio* or I would not have survived even a year in my present occupation.

Cesare laughed. He slipped an arm around my waist and drew me to him. " I am profoundly relieved that Il Papa is acting with his usual wisdom. And yet, so much tension remains." He bent closer, nuzzling the curve of my neck. "I missed you yesterday morning. You slipped away before I was awake."

"You could have sought me out last night."

He drew back enough to look at me. "The Spaniards—"

"Require constant tending. Yes, I know." If Cesare was to be believed, everything he did was for the sake of his father's ambitions, having set aside his own as a good and faithful son. Indulging the Spaniards had nothing whatsoever to do with his own intensely sensual nature or his need to vent the frustration that had been growing in him daily since his ascension to the cardinalate.

"How was your visit to the baths?" I inquired pleasantly.

"Purifying. After a sweat and a good soak in the mud, they scrub you down. I don't know what they use exactly, but—"

I bent a little closer, the better to inhale his scent. "Eucalyptus, sea salt, and a bit of citron. Did you enjoy yourself?"

He laughed, understanding my meaning full well, and pressed me closer. "Do you think I did?"

"I am always impressed by your stamina." That was as close as I would come to admitting that I was pleased by his unmistakable arousal, and aroused in turn by it. "How is it that you are not more . . . relaxed?"

The principal attraction of the baths being the pretty girls and boys who attended the patrons, I had assumed that Cesare would have partaken of such pleasures as were to his taste. But perhaps I was mistaken.

"You can thank the Spaniards for that," he said. "The sight of them at the trough is enough to steal any man's appetite."

"Their company palls?"

He laughed and slipped his hand down my back to cup me. "It palled before we ever got to Viterbo." His lips moved to the exact spot behind my ear where I was most exquisitely sensitive. "I have even," he whispered, "wondered if there might not be some good in the celibate state after all."

"I can tell you that there is not," I said and reached for him.

"Why is it," he asked as he eased my skirts up, "that we prefer each other as we do?"

My fingers were at work on the laces of his breeches as

I answered, "Because our natures are so well attuned? We were friends before we were lovers."

His hands stroked my thighs, slipping between them. "Are you still my friend, Francesca? Can I truly trust you?"

I gasped softly. "Why do you ask?"

"Because," he said as he grasped my leg and bent it up over his hip, "there are times when the weight of this mask I must wear becomes unbearable. I have to believe that there is one person in this world with whom I can be myself."

I bit my lip to keep from crying out when he stroked me, my fingers digging into his broad shoulders. With difficulty, I managed to answer.

"You must know that I feel the same." And yet there was much I had never told Cesare, most particularly not about my feelings for Rocco, the man who stirred me to dreams of a better self and a better life. Of that, Cesare knew nothing at all, nor should he, for I had no wish to either hurt or anger him. And besides, what point would there be? Rocco lived in the light that I did not believe I could ever reach. He was as unattainable by one of my dark nature as was Heaven itself.

How fortunate then that there were still the pleasures of this earth to be savored.

Cesare slipped into me with a groan, his mouth hot against my own. At another time, I would have preferred the comfort of a bed, but just then nothing mattered except the quick release of the passion swiftly building to intolerable heights within us both. I felt the coolness of the stucco wall against my back as he lifted me higher, plunging deeper. The world with all its trials and woes spiraled away into nothingness. I sank my teeth into the tender flesh at the base of his throat, tasted the salt tang of his blood on my tongue, and let the fire he lit scorch away all fear and dread.

8

Cesare was still asleep when I left his bed. In my own rooms, I bathed and changed, then set out to find David and tell him that I had arranged his entry into the palazzo. A light drizzle had begun to fall as I made my way along the winding streets toward the town gate. Once there, I saw that Borgia had wasted no time deploying his personal guard. Vittoro himself was on hand, directing his men as they moved to take command of the area surrounding the gate. Men from the garrison were standing aside, clearly uncertain of how or even whether to respond. By the time their officers decided what to do, it would be too late. Effectively, Borgia had taken control of the single, vital point in and out of Viterbo.

Instead of a steady stream of traffic passing through the gates, every man and woman seeking to enter the town was being stopped and scrutinized with care. The crowd waiting to be admitted was growing by the moment. The murmur of angry voices could be heard coming from outside the walls.

By dint of pushing and shoving, I managed to get closer to the gate. A party of pilgrims, their travel cloaks marked by the crossed-arm patches signifying their intent to pray at the tomb of blessed Saint Francis of Assisi, was being held up by the guards. Their leader, a portly, red-faced merchant, protested vehemently, but to no effect. As I watched, each of the dozen or so men and women in the group was subjected to the same scrutiny as the most common peddler. To be fair, with the exception of their leader, they appeared to take it with good grace, although I did hear one woman mutter that it was not enough to be delayed by problems on the road north, they had to put up at a town that clearly had no idea how to treat respectable people.

I was about to move on when my attention was caught by a member of the pilgrim party. A nun in the undyed wool habit of a Poor Clare was staring at me. The pale oval of her face, framed by her wimple and veil, had the unlined beauty of those whose holy lives seem to protect them from the depredations of time that mark the rest of us. I could not tell her age, but by the gravity of her manner I guessed that she was in her middle years. The heavy wooden cross at her waist also indicated that she had a position of authority in her order. As our eyes met, she hesitated and then, quite unmistakably, smiled.

A moment later, the press of the crowd took her from my view. As she vanished, I was left to wonder if I had imagined her.

The thought was fleeting. Quickly enough, I returned to

my study of those newly arrived in Viterbo. If David was right, somewhere amid the motley throng of merchants, lawyers, emissaries, soldiers, mercenaries, peddlers, gypsies, entertainers, and the like, all having business in the town now that the Pope was in residence, could be the secret enemy bent on destroying Borgia. I had only to find him before he could strike.

I had called myself Borgia's pawn and had no illusions otherwise. But a pawn who advances deep enough into the fray and survives is promoted under the arcane rules of the game into a queen, wielding the lethal power of that high estate. To that end, I would dare all.

But first, I sought out David, finding him in the same taverna we had frequented the day before. He was finishing a bowl of potato soup as I slipped onto the bench across from him.

"Borgia has agreed that you should come to the palazzo," I said after making sure we would not be overheard. "He is taking your warning seriously."

"I am glad to hear it. You still want me to keep a particular eye on the Spaniards?"

I nodded and briefly explained to him why I thought Herrera might be the target. Of course, I didn't trouble David with my idea of dealing with the beloved nephew before the assassin could do so. Borgia had ruled that out . . . at least for the moment.

After David had collected his belongings, I accompanied him back to the palazzo. Together, we sought out Renaldo in the small office he had commandeered off the main hall. The steward looked even more harried and preoccupied than usual.

"Who is this, Francesca?" Implicit in the question was why I would bother him with so lowly a creature as a jester.

"A friend," I said. Quickly, I explained about the assassin.

"Another one," Renaldo moaned when I was done. "And this one more skilled than those who have come before. Is there to be no end?"

"Borgia is being tested," David replied before I could. "He's managed to plant his posterior in Saint Peter's Chair, but now he has to prove that he can keep it there."

Renaldo looked at him more closely, beyond the spangled hat and parti-colored costume. "Do I know you?"

"David has been helpful in the past," I said. "That's why he's here."

The steward nodded in comprehension. "All right, then. We'll slip you in among the entertainers. But if there is going to be any sort of general mayhem, I would appreciate a little advance warning."

I left as David was assuring him that his intentions were entirely peaceful and Renaldo had nothing whatsoever to worry about. He lied almost as well as I did.

Speaking of lies . . .

Given both the weather and the hour, I looked for Lucrezia in the solar on the uppermost floor of the palazzo. I needed to alert her to the possibility of danger, but at the same time, I was curious to see how she was coping with her sham marriage.

Several of her ladies were there, working on the altar cloth that Cesare had mentioned, but there was no sign of Lucrezia herself. At sight of me, they startled like so many pretty birds discovering a hungry and rather mangy cat among them. I withdrew quickly, murmuring my apologies for having disturbed them, and sought Lucrezia elsewhere.

The bedchamber she occupied alone was near Borgia's and Cesare's apartments. Her husband, the hapless Sforza, had been assigned quarters in a separate wing of the palazzo, as far removed from her as it was possible to be while still remaining under the same expansive roof. Yet it was his voice I heard as I approached Lucrezia's door. Giovanni Sforza, Lord of Pesaro and a scion of the powerful House of Sforza, did not sound pleased.

"I am telling you," he said, loudly enough for me to hear him through the solid oak door, "we should be gone from this place! You are my wife, and you belong at my side, in Pesaro!"

Lucrezia replied more softly but with such firmness that I had no difficulty making out her words. That and the fact that by then my ear was pressed up against the door.

"My father says otherwise. You may be willing to defy him, but I am not. If you wish to return to Pesaro, by all means do so, but do not expect me to go with you."

For a thirteen-year-old confronted by an angry man twice her age who had at least nominal authority over her as her husband, Lucrezia sounded remarkably calm and self-possessed. But then she had grown up under the tutelage of a father who believed that any show of uncertainty was a confession of weakness deserving of the crushing response that it inevitably received in a harsh world.

"Of course," Sforza replied. "Why would you? We are only married, after all, in the sight of God and man. That counts for nothing when compared to the will of your exalted father!"

"You are speaking of His Holiness the Pope. He decides what is pleasing to God, not you." On a more conciliatory note, Lucrezia added, "Is it so hard to remain here in Viterbo? The town is charming, and we have a chance to get to know each other away from the intrigues of Rome."

"But not away from your father, who is curiously possessive of you. He does not accept our marriage. Indeed, I have begun to wonder if he would accept your being truly married to anyone."

"What do you mean?" Young as she was, Lucrezia was far from ignorant. She knew the depths to which Borgia's enemies went in their efforts to defame him, even dragging his relationship with his young daughter through the vilest muck. I sucked in my breath as I realized what a mistake it was for Sforza to remind her of that, and an even worse one for him to entertain any such suspicions himself.

But the Lord of Pesaro seemed to have no sense of that. To the contrary, he seemed to have no sense at all. "I merely wonder whether if we were allowed to live together as husband and wife, I would find that you—"

Find what? That she was not a virgin because of the disgusting slander against her and her father? I slammed a hand over my mouth to contain my gasp. How could Sforza be so foolish? And so cruel?

"Get out!" Lucrezia screamed, her self-control finally shattering, if only for a moment. Or perhaps, like her father, she understood the selective use of rage. "Get out and do not come back!"

"You cannot order me about! I am your husband—"

"If you do not leave now, I will tell my father what you just said. Papa believes me too sheltered to know about the filth his enemies spread. I will let him think that was so until *you* put them in my mind. Do you have any idea how enraged he will be or what he will do to you in turn?"

Weakly, Sforza said, "He needs my family's support—"

"He did need it in order to gain the papacy, but he is pope now and unless you are very careful, he will come to see all you Sforzas as a liability. Instead of making him regret that he ever agreed to our marriage, you should be seeking ways to win his favor."

"I don't know how." A hard confession on the part of a member of one of the wiliest and most guileful families in all of Italy, but then no one had ever claimed that Giovanni Sforza was overly endowed with either intelligence or daring. Lucrezia possessed far more of both, as she did not hesitate to demonstrate.

"You may start by doing as I said—leave."

A long moment of silence followed. I imagined the two of them staring at each other—golden-haired Lucrezia with her angelic face and dark, brooding Sforza, who was, to be fair, a handsome man. Under other circumstances, they might actually have been happy with each other. But the world was as it was, and it left very little room for matters of the heart.

Caught up in the drama happening just out of sight, I barely had the presence of mind to dart behind a nearby column before the door to Lucrezia's apartment banged open and Sforza stomped out in a fury. I waited until he had vanished down the far end of the corridor before approaching tentatively.

Half expecting to find Borgia's daughter in tears, I was surprised to discover her in a window seat, reading calmly.

As I entered, she looked up and smiled. "Francesca, how good to see you. Come, sit down." She patted the stool beside her. "I hope you have gossip to share. I am most dreadfully bored."

The strain around her eyes suggested she was in the grip of far more turbulent feelings, but I understood her determination to conceal them. From a tender age, Lucrezia and I had both recognized the perils of revealing too much to the world.

"Let me see . . . ," I began as I settled onto the stool. A servant brought goblets of warmed wine. I sipped mine gladly, remembering only then that I had not yet eaten. Intent on diverting her, I embarked on a fanciful rendition of recent events in Viterbo.

"If rumor is to be believed, two housewives almost came to blows in the market over a particularly nice round of cheese. A pig got loose as a result, creating havoc. Someone took advantage of the uproar to steal several apples. While the thief was being pursued, a vat of wine was upended, its contents spilling all over the road. To the dismay of those who tried to sop it up, the wine was found to be sour. Now the winemaker is blaming the cooper who made the vat; the cooper says it was the fault of the fellow who hauled it to market, who says in turn that the problem lies in the winemaker using dregs fit only for vinegar. Several lawyers newly arrived from Rome have inserted themselves into the matter, so Heaven only knows when or how it will end."

Lucrezia laughed, her altercation with Sforza seemingly forgotten. "Never, provided there are enough lawyers involved.

Centuries from now no one will remember where the town of Viterbo stood, but they will know that the matter of its sour wine remains unresolved."

I smiled at her whimsy, but I was not fooled by it. What Sforza had suggested truly was unforgivable. She would bide her time, but I was certain that in the end, she would exact a price for the insult he had done her and her father both. She was, after all, a Borgia.

"I need to speak with you about a matter of some seriousness," I said. As young as she was, Lucrezia had a right to know why her security was being increased, if only so that she could be more vigilant about her own safety. I still did not believe that she or Cesare was a likely target, but precautions had to be taken in any case.

When I told her of the assassin, she showed no surprise but merely sighed. "Sometimes I wonder what it is like to live an entirely normal life, far from any such turmoil."

As I wondered the same on occasion, I sympathized with her. However, I also pointed out, "Such a life may seem enviable, but it offers little opportunity to influence one's own destiny. Ordinary people are always being surprised by events, usually unpleasantly."

"Perhaps," Lucrezia allowed. "But as I have no control over my own destiny under any circumstances, I still think that I would prefer such a life."

It was on the tip of my tongue to tell her that she might have more control than she knew, provided that she acted with care and circumspection, but I suspected that she would find that out for herself in time.

We nibbled almonds and sipped more wine, talking of Rome, fashion, and her vapid ladies, whose company she was happy to do without. At length, she fell silent. I perceived that something weighed on her mind and thought it must be Sforza, but she surprised me.

"Do you think Cesare will ever accept the life our father has chosen for him?" she asked.

I hesitated. Any suggestion of a conflict between father and son was inherently dangerous. Surrounded by enemies as they were, it was essential that *la famiglia* stand as one.

"He will do what he must," I said.

"But how does he feel about it?"

"He . . . accepts what cannot be changed, at least for now."

She nodded, seemingly satisfied, but she was not done. "What of you, Francesca? What life do you envision for yourself?"

I finished the last of the wine and rose to go. "I find it best not to dwell on such matters. Are you coming down to dinner?"

She took my refusal to answer with good grace and said, "Would I miss an opportunity to enjoy the wit of surly Spaniards and pompous prelates?"

I smiled despite myself. "There is a new jester."

She brightened at that. "Really? Well, then I will come. Perhaps he will show us for the fools we are."

"Or perhaps he will merely make you laugh." I hoped that David could. Indeed, I hoped that he would make her laugh enough to forget, for some little time, Sforza, his vile accusations, and the price she was paying—indeed, we were all paying—for Borgia's ambitions.

For myself, I had no interest in totaling up the cost, nor could I have done so even if I had been inclined to try. I could only hope that there would be room, as David had said, for other men to breathe.

All the same, Lucrezia's question lingered in my mind. I could not tell her that it was not the future that weighed on me but the past. Until I found some way to put that to rest, I was trapped in a nightmare that had no end.

9

Renaldo found me in the great hall early the next morning. Despite the threat hanging over us, he looked better than he had the night before. A merchant venture he had invested in had paid off nicely, and he was beginning to dream of his retirement.

"A villa in Capri, perhaps," he said as we both drew our cloaks closer against the dank weather. Rain dripped from the palazzo eaves, splattering in puddles across the piazza. Rain, rain, endless rain. I was beginning to long for winter and at least the chance of snow. "A place to sit in the sun, doves cooing, a nice, plump wife . . ."

"Sounds lovely," I allowed. "But what would we do without you?"

"Nothing lasts forever," he said with a shrug. "Change is the only constant. Heraclitus said that, didn't he? That Greek fellow who dreamed up the idea of Logos, the source and order of the cosmos. Scripture says the same: 'In the beginning was the Word.' But the 'word' is Logos. What are we to make of that?"

There had been a time when I assumed that Renaldo kept his nose securely in his ledgers. I had since learned otherwise, and therefore was unsurprised by such erudition.

"Heraclitus also said that the cosmos was not created by God or man but simply is," I replied. "Which, I suppose, helps to explain why Holy Mother Church does not fully embrace the rebirth of ancient learning."

Renaldo nodded gravely. "That is so. By the way, there is a nun looking for you."

"A nun? Did she say what she wanted?"

"Not that I know of. I have to admit that I was surprised when the doorkeeper told me. Not that a nun looking for you is odd. We all know nuns, but—"

"I don't."

Renaldo's eyes were watery and bulged a little, the result of too many hours bent over his accounts. He blinked slowly. "What's that?"

"I don't know any nuns and I have no idea why one would be looking for me. When was she here?"

Renaldo looked uncertain. "A few minutes ago, perhaps a little more."

I looked around the hall, hoping to catch sight of her. When I did not, I took my leave of the steward and moved toward the wide double doors giving out onto the piazza. Despite the spitting rain, priests, merchants, petitioners, and hangers-on jostled for space as they tried to make their way toward the palazzo or simply stood about watching the gloriously attired prelates and their entourages coming and going.

No, not quite everyone. A nun was crossing the square in the opposite direction toward the nearby church of Santa Maria della Salute. As I watched, she glanced back over her shoulder toward the palazzo. In that moment, I recognized the pale face of the woman who had smiled at me near the town gates.

Without pausing to think, I hurried down the wide stone steps to the piazza. The nun was disappearing into the church. I followed quickly, sloshing through puddles that had collected between the cobblestones. Stepping inside, I looked in all directions, but saw no sign of her. By the time I had walked halfway down the nave, I was beginning to wonder if my imagination had been playing tricks on me. But a moment later, I caught sight of the nun kneeling at prayer before an altar dedicated to blessed Saint Clare.

Unsure of what I hoped to gain by following her, I hesitated. Irreligious as I was, even I knew that it wasn't right to interrupt a nun at her prayers. Besides, what would I say to her? As it happened, I need not have been concerned. Even as I debated what to do, she crossed herself and rose. Turning, with her hands clasped together at her waist, she caught sight of me. Her lovely, serene face lit up with a smile.

"How astounding is the way of our Lord," she said. "You were just now in my thoughts, and here you are before me."

At a loss as to how to respond, I could only ask, "You came to the palazzo?"

She nodded. "To inquire about you, but alas, the doorkeeper was not very forthcoming."

That did not surprise me. Few members of Borgia's household would want to speak of me at all, much less involve themselves in any matter having to do with me.

"What was your purpose?" I asked. "Why do you seek me?"

She hesitated. We were both speaking softly in deference to our surroundings, but the nun glanced around as though to be sure that we could not be overheard.

"You are Francesca Giordano, are you not?"

When I nodded, she clasped her hands more tightly, as though to contain her excitement.

"I thought as much yesterday when I saw you by the town gate," she said. "Forgive me, but the shock was so unsettling that I really didn't know what to do. I prayed for guidance and woke this morning certain that I had to speak with you."

"I don't understand . . ." My profession was shocking, to be sure, but there was nothing particularly remarkable about my appearance. Certainly nothing that required praying over.

Without warning, the nun reached out and took my hands in hers. I stiffened in surprise but did not attempt to pull away. Looking into my eyes, she said, "Has no one ever told you? You are the very image of your mother. The moment I saw you, I knew that you had to be dear Adriana's daughter."

We sat on a stone bench near the altar to Saint Clare. The nun was silent, her fingers working the plain wooden beads of her rosary. When the tightness in my chest eased, I was able to speak.

"Other than my father, I have never met anyone who knew my mother."

She lowered her beads and looked at me. Once again, I was struck by the smooth serenity of her features; testament, I assumed, to her sanctity, which protected her from the trials of ordinary life.

"I am sorry to hear that," she said softly. "Please forgive me for taking you by surprise. My name is Mother Benedette. I am abbess of a religious house in Anzio. Adriana and I were friends when we were both girls in Milan. Our lives took very different paths, but I have never forgotten her."

"You have nothing to apologize for. I am . . . glad to have a chance to speak of her." In fact, I was overwhelmed. My long-dead mother was an imagined ideal for whom I yearned with all the desperation of a child's wounded heart. On occasion, I even fancied that I could remember her singing to me. Given that she had died at my birth, I could only conclude that my grip on sanity was even more precarious than I wanted to admit.

Hesitantly, because this was all so new and fraught, I asked, "Do I really look like her?" My father had spoken of my mother very little, I supposed because of the lingering pain of her loss. And I, a deeply troubled child with a disturbing talent for the art of death, had never wanted to burden him with questions.

"For a moment when I saw you near the gate," the abbess

said, "I thought that time had rolled back and I was seeing Adriana. The resemblance is that uncanny." She paused for a moment, then added, "Your mother and I were so close; like sisters, really. It is the blessing of God that has guided me to you."

She would not think so when she knew the truth about me. It could not be very long before some well-intentioned soul whispered in her ear that I was the pope's poisoner and a witch in the bargain. Oh, yes, and a *puttana* who took a prince of Holy Mother Church to my bed. Before that happened, I was determined to seize the opportunity to learn everything from her that I could.

"What was my mother like?" I asked.

As though she understood my hunger, the abbess said, "Adriana was the kindest, most caring person I have ever known. She was also very high-spirited. She always preferred to run anywhere rather than walk. She loved music and played the lute very well. As for her needlework—"

"She wasn't good at it?" My heart leaped at the thought that my mother and I might be alike in some way, however small. Such a possibility had never occurred to me.

Mother Benedette chuckled. "It was her bane. Her threads were always tangled, her stitches uneven. Once, I remember, we were both set samplers to do. I sped through mine while Adriana labored, pricking her fingers over and over until the linen was stained with her blood. I could not bear that and offered to do the work for her, but she knew that such duplicity was wrong and would not allow me to fall into sin. Fortunately, the embroidery mistress was a sensible woman who, seeing what Adriana had produced despite so great an effort, suggested that she pursue drawing instead."

"And did she?" I had never so much as picked up a piece of charcoal, although I enjoyed watching others, especially Rocco's young son, Nando, draw. The process fascinated me.

"Oh, yes, quite successfully. Her best drawings were of animals. She truly loved them and was forever bringing home strays."

My father and I had used stray animals to test new poisons on, a practice he accepted only reluctantly as a regrettable necessity. Seeing how it troubled him, I suggested using humans instead. When he recovered from his shock that I would think of such a thing, I was able to persuade him that it was an act of mercy to grant a quicker, less painful death to those otherwise condemned to torturous execution. Such had been my practice ever since. That the results are more accurate, and therefore more useful, surely does not make the act of compassion any less.

"Do you know how she met my father?"

Mother Benedette nodded. "Adriana's mother was stung by a wasp. The injury became infected and the poor woman was suffering horribly. The physicians were useless, as usual, but Giovanni, who was earning a reputation for himself as an apothecary, devised a poultice that drew the poison out and allowed her to heal."

"I suppose the family was grateful?"

"They certainly should have been, but like so many others, they preferred not to deal with Jews. They had turned to Giovanni only as a last resort. Adriana thought their behavior was unkind. She sought your father out privately to tell him that."

I had only recently come to terms with the fact that my father had been born a Jew, a fact he had concealed from me all my life. Granted, he had converted to Christianity and, so far as I knew, had been sincere in his faith. But my mother had known him before that happened. I wondered how she had possessed the courage to seek him out.

"I would like to tell you more," Mother Benedette said as she stood. "But it is almost time for vespers. Perhaps we can meet again?"

I rose reluctantly. "Yes, of course. I would like that very much. You know I am at the palazzo?"

That was as close as I could come to asking what she knew of me. Her smile did not falter.

"I am aware that you serve His Holiness."

"I should perhaps tell you—"

The abbess held up a hand. "Francesca, I did not seek you out in order to judge you. From what I understand, you protect the life of Christ's Vicar on Earth and do so very ably. That is enough for me to know."

I looked away quickly before she could see how nearly her words undid me. Such generosity of spirit was almost unknown in my experience. I was accustomed to being viewed with a mixture of fear and revulsion, if not outright hatred, by all but the very small number of people I could call friends.

The abbess and I parted a short time later, having made plans to meet again the following morning. As I crossed the square to the palazzo, my thoughts were of my mother and what I had learned of her. For the first time, I allowed myself to wonder what my life would have been like if she had lived. What I would have been like.

Most probably, I would be married, with children of my own. My experience with normal women was very limited, but I did know a few. Would that other self be like Vittoro's daughters, all good girls well married and busy presenting him with grandchildren? Would she spend her days keeping house, tending her growing brood, and pleasing her husband, as every proper woman surely lived to do? Without the nightmare to plague her, what would she dream of? What would she think, feel, desire? My imagination faltered. Sadly, I recognized that she was as great a stranger to me as anyone I might pass in the street.

The rain had lessened, but even so I felt its chill through my wet cloak. As I entered the palazzo, I was thinking of nothing other than a warm fire in my rooms and dry clothes. I almost missed Herrera, who was lounging just inside the entrance, where he had a clear view of the piazza. Had he not spoken, I likely would not have noticed him at all.

"I am astounded that you dare to enter a church," he said. "Has it occurred to you that you offend God by doing so?"

Good sense dictated that I ignore the insult and keep going. But under the circumstances, I had scant patience for the man I remained convinced would better serve us dead.

"Indeed," I said. "I live in expectation that the ground will open under me and I will fall through a fiery chasm into Hades. And yet, curiously enough, that has yet to happen."

Clearly, the beloved nephew was not accustomed to being

addressed in such a manner by one he regarded as an inferior. His face darkened as he straightened away from the wall and glared at me. "You blaspheme."

"Do I? No doubt your depravity makes you an expert on the subject."

The words were out before I could think better of them, as well I should have. It was not in my nature to provoke anyone. I much preferred the single, deadly blow delivered without warning. Even so, I was surprised by the violence of Herrera's reaction.

"How dare you!" His hand shot out, grasping my arm. Abruptly, it occurred to me that I had pushed the vainglorious scion of the Spanish royal family too far. Worse yet, I could not manage to care.

"Puta maligna!" he exclaimed. "You pollute the bed of a prince of the Church who may well be pope one day. Your malevolence threatens the Throne of Saint Peter itself. The sooner His Holiness realizes the threat you represent and disposes of you, the better!"

Pain shot through me. My arm was in danger of being wrenched from its socket, but all I really knew was that he was very close; I could feel the heat of his breath and smell his sweat. He had made a serious mistake. Unfortunately, most anyone who could have told him that was already dead.

A red mist moved before my eyes. The knife I wore in a leather sheath over my heart slipped into my hand with ease. In an instant, the point of it was lodged under the Spaniard's chin. The darkness within me stirred, a hungry beast rousing itself to feed.

While I still retained a shred of control, I said, "Consider, if this knife is coated with a contact poison that need only enter through the smallest prick in your skin in order to kill you, shouldn't you be making yourself more pleasant to me?"

Herrera began to speak, but the pressure of my knife against his flesh stopped him. Though he did not release me, his grip on my arm loosened. I was distantly aware that all those in the hall were staring at us, some in shock but most with avid curiosity. The Spaniard had not made himself loved. More than a few of our audience looked as though they would not mind seeing him die. Another few moments and they would be taking bets.

Of course, I knew that I could not kill him. Borgia had forbidden it, and besides, there were witnesses. All the same, my hand tightened on the knife. I let the Spaniard feel the tip of it just a little more.

There was no contact poison on the blade, not then. True, I had killed the man in the Basilica di Santa Maria a few months before in such a manner. Perhaps Herrera had heard of it. That could explain his pasty complexion and the nerve that leaped to life in his clenched jaw.

God forgive me, but I was enjoying myself.

Too soon reality intruded. Our audience faded away in every direction. I sensed a presence behind me and heard the clearing of a throat.

"Francesca?"

Without moving the knife, I glanced over my shoulder. Cesare stood with his hands on his hips, regarding me quizzically.

Herrera mewed. The son of Jove ignored him.

"Is there a problem?" Cesare asked me courteously.

I shrugged. "Your friend here called me a malignant whore." Never mind that he had also tried to break my arm.

Cesare frowned. "Did he? What an infelicitous choice of words."

"I want him to apologize." Such was my disgust at the Spaniard that I was at least partly serious. Cesare was trying to look stern, but it was a losing battle. He knew as well as I the utter impossibility of what I was insisting on.

"I want him to apologize, too," Cesare said. "But there is a problem. Don Miguel is a Spaniard. He is as proud as I am. The odds of him begging your pardon, as I am sure he would really like to do under the present circumstances, are about equal to him flapping his wings and flying to the moon."

I made a show of looking behind Herrera's back. When I failed to find any evidence of wings, I sighed. Considering my point to have been made—and Cesare's patience to have been strained about as far as it would go—I sheathed my knife.

Herrera released me, but in the same instant, he raised his arm to strike a blow that at the very least would have thrown me against the nearby stone wall and probably shattered a bone in the bargain. Cesare did not hesitate. He stepped between us, in the process elbowing the Spaniard with enough force to drive the breath out of him. Taking both my hands in his, he looked deeply into my eyes.

"Allow me to entreat your pardon on my friend's behalf."

A smile tugged at the corners of my mouth. We were, both of us, behaving shamelessly, to my delight.

"Well, if you insist."

"I do, absolutely." He stepped closer and pressed a kiss into each of my palms, first one, then the other, his mouth lingering on my suddenly heated skin.

Herrera made a sound of disgust and whirled away. When he was gone, Cesare dropped my hands and took a step back. He stared at me with what looked like real concern.

"What were you thinking, Francesca? This will be all over Viterbo before sunset and in Rome in time for breakfast. Like it or not, we need Herrera. You provoke him at your own peril . . . and ours."

"I know, and I am sorry. It's just that—" How to explain what I had done, even to myself? Above all else, I counted on being able to control myself, at least in public. To conceal the darkness that drove me beneath a veneer of professionalism and to go about my daily tasks as though I wasn't really all that different from ordinary people, merely equipped by chance with a peculiar set of skills. But in that instant when my knife flew from its sheath, I could cheerfully have slit Herrera's throat and waded in his blood. The realization of how tempted I still was to do that was startling. Was Borgia right? Had it been too long since I had killed?

"Something happened," I said. The admission cost me. As a rule, I never admitted to any weakness, even with those I counted as friends.

Cesare drew me a little aside, down a passage where we would be less observed. His hand on my elbow, he said, "Tell me."

"I met a nun . . . an abbess. She knew my mother."

Cesare drew a breath and let it out slowly. Young as he was, he knew me well enough to understand the import of that.

"I thought your mother died when you were born." I had told him that and, inevitably given our intimacy, he knew of the nightmare that visited me so often.

"Mother Benedette and she were friends when they were girls together in Milan. I am meeting her again tomorrow. She has much to tell me."

Cesare regarded me closely. He had a complex relationship with his own mother, the redoubtable Vannozza dei Cattanei. Though she had not shared Borgia's bed in years, His Holiness continued to visit her regularly to enjoy her famed lemon cakes and discuss mutual interests, chief among them the future of their children. Rumor had it that Vannozza had been the first to suggest Juan's Spanish marriage and that she had raised no opposition when Borgia revealed his intent to make Cesare a cardinal. Despite his mother's showing no more interest in helping her son achieve his own dreams than did Borgia himself, Cesare remained devoted to her.

"It is only natural that you want to know about your mother," he began, "but . . ."

I understood his hesitation. Clearly, I could not return from every encounter with the abbess in the mood to pull a knife on Herrera or anyone else. As delicately as he could, Cesare was reminding me of the need to control my darker impulses lest they interfere with my ability to serve his father.

"What are you thinking?" he asked.

I lied, fluently and well. And yet, there was a particle of truth in what I said. "Of Capri. I may retire there, assuming that I live long enough."

He laughed and drew me closer. "You wish to live among the Sirens, luring the unwary to their deaths?"

"I wish to have done with death." Done and done a thousand times over. That, at least, was the truth.

"Unfortunately," Cesare said, "we are not free to follow our hearts."

Truth again, sour though it was. I leaned my head against his chest; he stroked my hair. We took such comfort from each other as we could and pretended that it was enough.

10

Herrera was absent from the hall that night. Rumor had it that he was off sulking with his fellow Spaniards. Cesare had gone with them. Borgia bestowed a chiding glance on me when I appeared, but he said nothing. He was deep in conversation with his prelates, who, tame though they might be, were beginning to show signs of restlessness. I heard della Rovere mentioned, and the French. Of Juan, there was not a word.

David was gone as well, no doubt keeping an eye on the Spaniards. They are great ones for fools, although I hear that they prefer them to be dwarves. Perhaps I should have sent for Portia. I was wondering if she could still execute a backflip as in her days as one of Rome's most popular acrobats when Vittoro joined me.

"What were you thinking?" the captain murmured. Such

was the understanding between us that he did not need to say more.

I flushed and hoped he did not see. "Clearly, not much. I realize it should not have happened." That was as close as I could come to admitting that my response to Herrera had been ill-advised. Even so, I could not completely regret what I had done. Never would I be anyone's helpless victim. Far better to die fighting.

Wryly, Vittoro said, "Perhaps you meant to impress the Spaniard with your skill so that he would trust you to protect him?"

I laughed despite myself. "We both know that I am not that clever. I do understand that he is unlikely to let me anywhere near him."

Satisfied that I grasped the seriousness of what I had done, Vittoro moved to reassure me. "We'll find a way around that. Meanwhile, we're keeping a close eye on everyone arriving in Viterbo. But with the roads flooded to the north, there are many stranded travelers, which is complicating the task. Do you have any more thoughts on who this assassin is or what his plan may be?"

"Cesare told you about the money?"

Vittoro nodded. "Ben Eliezer says it comes from Spain, which, of course, makes one think that the assassin does as well." He hesitated a moment, then added, "I have the greatest respect for David, you know. He is not a man I would ever underestimate."

"Nor would I."

"I am glad to hear that. He's lately come to Viterbo, hasn't he? Indeed, he's right here in the palazzo."

I shot Vittoro a quick glance. "He is. And your point . . . ?"

"Herrera is the beloved nephew of Their Most Catholic Majesties, who expelled the Jews from Spain."

My breath caught even as my mind raced. The Jews had suffered terribly because of the expulsion. They had lost wealth, true enough, but many had also lost their lives, whether through deliberate violence or through the spread of disease engendered by chaos. In my mind, Ferdinand and Isabella had committed a great crime, for which all of Christendom could justly be called to answer. But that had nothing to do with one particular Jew.

"Vittoro, you can't think that—"

He shrugged almost imperceptibly. "A champion of his people could be pardoned for wanting to avenge an act that cost thousands of lives and inflicted terrible suffering on countless more."

"But it was David who brought news of the assassin," I reminded him. "Why would he have done that if—?"

"To deflect suspicion from himself, perhaps? We both know that His Holiness has a formidable network of spies throughout Europe and beyond. Isn't it likely that he would have learned of the assassin quickly enough from his own sources?"

"That is true, but the Jews need Borgia to protect them. Why would they do anything to threaten his papacy?"

"They wouldn't, but they *would* act in such a manner that they believed would strengthen it."

I shook my head, unable to comprehend what he was saying. "By destroying his alliance with Spain? The alliance that he must have if he is going to survive?"

"Survive on his present course," Vittoro corrected. "But what if instead he was left with no choice but to seek reconciliation with the other great families in Italy and beyond? Wouldn't that ultimately protect his papacy even more?"

Actually, it might, but the likelihood of Borgia doing any such thing was remote. For decades he had nurtured the vision of *la famiglia* supreme above all others in the Church and in the world. By such means, he intended to secure his own immortality. Like the greatest of the Caesars, his name would live forever. Yet he was also a consummate realist who, more than any man I had ever known, looked at the unvarnished truth and did not blink.

"Compelled to do so by the loss of the Spanish alliance?" I asked.

Vittoro nodded. "Exactly. Forcing Borgia's hand in such a way would be risky, perhaps too risky to even consider. I'm not saying that is what is happening. All I'm asking is that you not blind yourself to any possibility."

The very idea struck me hard, for David was my friend. But so, too, did the realization that I should have thought of it myself.

"Does this come from you or from Borgia?" I asked. His Holiness consulted with the captain of his guard as least as often as he did with me. I was not privy to what was said between them, but I knew that as much as Borgia trusted any man, he trusted Vittoro.

"Neither. It comes from Cesare."

I could not conceal my surprise, not that the son of Jove would see the possibility of such treachery, but that he had not told me of it himself. "Why did he leave this to you?"

Vittoro shrugged. "He knows that you count ben Eliezer a friend. Perhaps he thought you would take it better coming from me. Besides, wherever it comes from, it is worth considering. All right?"

Having assured him that I would keep uppermost in my mind the possibility that the man I had introduced into Borgia's household was an assassin who threatened all I was sworn to protect, I excused myself. His Holiness could linger as long as he liked at table. I was for a bath and a much-needed dose of Sofia's powder. If God was merciful, I would sleep without dreams.

Despite the drug, I woke early. For a moment, I lay on my back staring up at the canopy above, wondering what seemed odd. Only gradually did I realize that it was not raining. Indeed, I could just make out a watery ray of sunshine filtering through the shutters. Quickly, I rose and dressed. There being some little time before Mother Benedette and I were to meet again, I thought to find Cesare and ask him directly about his suspicion. But I had scarcely left my rooms when Renaldo intercepted me. The steward was pale and sweating. For a moment, I feared that he was ill, but quickly enough I discovered the cause of his distress.

Dabbing his brow with a cloth, he whispered, "A laundress

has been found dead. Vittoro is with the body now. He thinks you should take a look."

We hurried down a narrow stone staircase into the lower level of the palazzo, where the laundries were located close to the interior wells sunk deep into the earth beneath. As we approached, wet, steamy air rose up to envelop us.

"What happened?" I asked.

"Heaven if I know. All I was told was that she was found facedown in one of the rinsing tubs."

I had visited the laundries shortly after arriving in Viterbo, finding them a smaller version of those in the papal palace in Rome. Under vast, arched ceilings, women and a few men labored amid boilers kept constantly stoked to provide hot water, bubbling vats of lye, tall wooden wringers, and enormous tubs that held alternately hot soapy water or cool water for rinsing. Nearby, ropes were strung to receive linens and garments belonging to the household staff and the guard. The laundries had not concerned me very much because everything worn or otherwise used by *la famiglia* was cared for elsewhere by skilled servants devoted solely to that task. Now I had to wonder if I should not have been more watchful.

"She drowned?" I asked.

"I suppose," Renaldo replied. "But why would she have fallen into a tub? And if she did, what stopped her from climbing back out?"

I had no answer. Vittoro had directed that the body be laid out on the slate floor of a small antechamber nearby. The laundress was plump with well muscled arms and appeared to have been a woman of middle years. I bent down and looked at her closely. Her face was smooth, without any sign of pain or struggle in the final moments of her life.

"According to the women working on either side of her," Vittoro said, "she seemed perfectly normal right up to the moment when she gasped, caught at her chest, and toppled over into the tub. They wrestled her out as quickly as they could, but it was too late. She was gone."

I nodded and bent closer, easing up first one eyelid and then the other. If the woman had drowned, I would find small pinpricks of blood in the whites of her eyes. Instead, there were none.

"She was dead when she went into the water," I said.

"What would kill a seemingly healthy woman so suddenly?" Renaldo asked. He had remained off to the side and looked ready to bolt at any moment, but to his credit he stood his ground.

"We will have to find out," I said. "Does she have family here?" If she did, they would insist on taking possession of the body in order to prepare it for burial. It would be impossible to hide what I needed to do.

"I will ask," the steward offered. He hurried off, seemingly glad of a reason to be gone, but returned in only a few minutes.

"She is from Palermo. No one here really knows her. The assumption is that the authorities will take charge of the body."

Vittoro and I exchanged a look. Turning to Renaldo, I said, "No doubt there are pressing matters that require your attention elsewhere."

He nodded gratefully and removed himself in all haste. Guards carried the body to a small room on the opposite side of the palazzo, as far removed from the laundries as it was possible to get. High slit windows admitted some light, but I called for braziers as well. Excusing myself briefly, I fetched the case containing various implements that I kept in the false bottom of the puzzle chest I had inherited from my father. In addition, I rolled up and brought with me a large canvas apron.

As Vittoro stood watch, I undressed the woman and performed a rough but adequate autopsy. There was no time for anything more. If we were discovered, the outcry would be extreme. As the desecrator of a Christian body and a rumored witch in the bargain, I might not survive it.

My aversion to blood, except when I have killed with the knife, made the procedure difficult. That and the fact that I had little experience with such things. Generally, a poisoner would not concern herself with the workings of the body except insofar as they can be brought to a halt. But my father was interested in anatomy, even to the extent of possessing several learned treatises, and Sofia had furthered my education in the subject. Even so, I hesitated before making the initial cut and opening the chest. As blood began to ooze from the body, the darkness in me stirred like a great beast restive in its slumber. With the greatest effort of will, I turned my mind from that abyss and focused all my attention on the task at hand.

"No one has been allowed to leave the laundries," Vittoro said as I worked. "My men are on guard. But I have to tell you, people are close to panic. Some are afraid that it is the plague."

"It isn't." Cold beads of sweat had formed on my forehead,

but I was still there, still in control of myself, and for that I was deeply grateful.

"You're certain? Because if there is any chance of that, we must get His Holiness away from here with all speed."

"There would be little point in doing so. No one can outrun plague that kills this quickly. But we need not concern ourselves with that."

"I'm glad to hear it," Vittoro said. "There are also whispers that this is proof of Satan's presence here."

I straightened and looked at him. "The Devil killed her?"

"Essentially, yes, that is what people are saying. And once word spreads of this death, someone is going to remember the kitchen boy. They'll be talking about him as well."

Shaking my head, I returned to my work. It did not take long to find what I sought. When I was finished, I stitched the woman's chest back up and clothed her once more. At the last, I touched my hand lightly to her brow and murmured the hope that she would forgive me for what I had been compelled to do.

"Well?" Vittoro asked as I washed my hands in a basin of water. Blood swirled away in pale eddies. I took a breath against the tightness of my chest.

"There is a clot in her heart, large enough to stop it from beating."

He had the look of a man who wanted to believe me but wasn't quite there yet. "Then this is a natural death?"

I shrugged. "It could be. But there are poisons that can have the same effect."

Vittoro's eyes widened slightly. "There are?"

Nodding, I reached for a towel. Unable to hide my frustration, I said, "So once again, it's impossible to tell whether or not this was murder. But two sudden deaths within a handful of days, both of seemingly healthy people in service to His Holiness . . . I don't like it."

"Nor do I. What are we to do?"

"What can we do except redouble our vigilance yet again? That and take every precaution to quell panic. If this were to get out into the town . . ."

"It will not," Vittoro assured me. "For once, the poor state of relations between the townspeople and His Holiness's servants works to our advantage."

I hoped that he was right and also that the mysterious deaths would stop. But as I left Vittoro to see to the interment, I had to wonder what could be gained by killing a kitchen boy and a laundress. And if they really had been murdered, who would be next?

11

Pausing at the top of the broad steps leading down from the palazzo, I sought a measure of calm, without great success. The ray of sunshine I had so briefly glimpsed had vanished. Rain threatened once again. Resigned to a day that seemed bleak in every respect, I hastened across the piazza. Santa Maria della Salute was empty when I entered. The air inside the old stone walls felt dank. I drew my cloak more tightly around myself and looked down the shadowed length of the apse.

Not seeing the abbess, I sat down on the stone bench near the altar to Saint Clare. I waited long enough to begin to wonder if, after an opportunity for reflection, Mother Benedette might have thought better of befriending me. Just as I was debating whether I should try to find where she was staying in the town, she appeared, a little out of breath and walking hastily.

When she reached my side, she said, “My apologies. I was delayed by the dear sisters at the convent where I am staying. They mean well, but even so . . .” She broke off and looked at me. Something of my impatience must have communicated itself to her because she said, “I hope you haven’t been waiting long?”

“Not at all,” I assured her as I moved over to make room for her on the bench. My relief at her presence erased all else, and was exceeded only by my eagerness to hear more of what she had to say.

I am sure that she sensed my need, for she smiled slightly as she took her seat and said, “We have much to speak of. But first, I have something for you.” She drew a small basket from beside her and offered it to me with a smile.

I lifted the wicker lid and peered inside. Nestled within a white linen cloth were half a dozen small loaves shaped like little cylinders. The aroma rising from them was enticing.

“The bakers of Milan vie to produce the finest bread of this sort, which they call *panetto,*” Mother Benedette said. “Your mother had a particular fondness for it.”

I had never heard of the little breads, but the gesture touched me. “Did you bake these?”

The abbess nodded. “To be frank, there is very little to do in the convent where I am staying until the road north clears and we can continue on our pilgrimage to Assisi. The sisters there are very kind, of course, but I am accustomed to being busy.” She gestured at the basket. “Adriana and I used to make these together. It has been so long that I wondered if I would remember the recipe, but it seems that I did.”

Sitting beside her, I lifted the lid again and breathed in the aroma of the little loaves. The thought of my mother baking filled me with an odd feeling, at once yearning yet oddly nostalgic. For a moment, I saw a woman behind a fire, singing softly to herself as a smell, such as lingered in the air now, filled a snug room. In the next breath, the impression was gone as though it had never been.

"This was very kind of you," I said. Courtesy has many uses, but among them is that it gives us certain responses we can make without thought to conceal what is truly in our minds.

"Oh, I confess to loving them myself. I cannot remember when I last had one."

"Let us remedy that," I said and held the basket out to her.

With a smile, she took one of the little loaves; I helped myself to another. As Borgia had no fondness for sweets, few were prepared in his kitchens. I had not felt the lack, but when the first bite of the still-warm bread flavored with honey and raisins touched my tongue, a sigh of pleasure escaped me.

"This is delicious," I said. "What did you call it?"

Mother Benedette wiped a crumb delicately from the corner of her mouth. "*Panetto.* Some bakers add other fruits or even nuts, but Adriana liked them just this way. I thought you might, too."

"I do; they're marvelous. You are a wonderful cook."

The abbess laughed softly. "Best my dear sisters in Anzio not hear you say that or they would be wickedly amused. I swear that I was made abbess in order to keep me out of the kitchens."

When I laughed and insisted that could not possibly be

the case, she said, "I exaggerate, but not entirely. There are a few dishes I do well enough, mostly because I learned them from Adriana. She loved to cook, and she was forever finding interesting ingredients to combine in novel ways. I won't say that all her efforts were equally successful, but quite a few of them were very good."

I thought of myself, forever experimenting with ingredients for new poisons, and grimaced.

"Is something wrong, child?" the abbess asked.

"Not at all; I'm just regretting my own lack of domestic skills. I can cook a little, though I usually only inflict the results on myself." I had cooked for Borgia when he smuggled me, disguised as a boy, into the conclave that elected him pope. But that was only because he trusted no one else to keep him safe while he was locked away with his fellow cardinals.

"My father did his best, but he raised me alone and there are some things that I never learned." Also a great deal that I had, but I saw no reason to dwell on that.

"I was very sorry to learn of your father's death. He was a good man."

My throat tightened. As always, it was difficult for me to hear anyone speak of my father, although the more time that passed since his death, the fewer there were who seemed to remember him. Even I sometimes had difficulty remembering his face, except in my dreams, in which he figured often. My father was a great walker, and from time to time I dreamed of him walking with me through a particular neighborhood of Rome that we had both enjoyed. On such occasions, I longed to talk to him of the troubles that beset me and receive his wise counsel, but he never spoke, and inevitably when I tried to press him, I awoke. I had been left to figure out matters for myself despite feeling ill equipped to do so.

"He gave his life trying to protect others," I said. "His murderer remains at large."

"Surely, with all his power His Holiness could . . ."

I did not want to speak of Borgia's response—or lack thereof—to my father's murder. Had my father succeeded in killing the loathsome Pope Innocent VIII, who sought to prolong his dissipated life by taking mother's milk and drinking the blood of young boys who suffered horribly for his sake, he would have cleared the way for Borgia to assume the papacy. Instead, he had died for his efforts, leaving me to complete his work. I still had no idea whether Innocent had perished by my hand or from natural causes, and I cannot say that I cared. That could wait until I was held to account for my sins in the world beyond, assuming there was any such place.

"His Holiness has much to concern him," I said noncommittally.

"Yes, of course. Forgive me for speaking as I did. It is just that I remember the great love your father and mother shared. It was clear to anyone with eyes that they were meant for each other."

I thought of Rocco and of what it meant to care for someone even in the face of seemingly insurmountable barriers. Did I have more of my mother in me than I had ever imagined?

"It must have been so difficult for them," I said. "A Jew and a young Christian girl of good family. How did they even dare to think that they could be together?"

"At first, your father did his best to deny Adriana, but she refused to be discouraged. She pointed out, reasonably enough, that had he been born Christian, her family would have welcomed him as their son-in-law. Adriana's father was a middling successful spice importer. He did well enough, but he had nothing like the wealth needed to marry her into one of the great merchant families or acquire her a titled husband. Giovanni was clearly more skilled than the average apothecary and could make a good future for himself. The only problem was that he was a Jew."

"But he converted," I pointed out. Whether for love of my mother or from real conviction, I had no idea. Nor did I think it mattered.

"You know conversos have always been viewed with suspicion," the abbess said. "They are the first to be accused of being heretics."

"Is that why her family didn't want her to marry him? Because they feared she would be endangered?"

As hard as that would be, I could understand it. Rocco protected his young son, Nando, fiercely, and even I, surely the most unlikely mother, had risked my life to save the boy. Love of the young and the preservation of their safety had to be among the most fundamental human instincts.

Or so I thought.

Mother Benedette was silent for several moments. Finally, she said, "Your mother's family did not want her to marry your father because their hatred of the Jews blinded them to every other consideration. I am sorry to say that in the end, nothing else mattered to them. When they realized that Giovanni had converted, and that he and Adriana had contrived to marry without their permission, they declared themselves shamed by her and refused to have any further contact."

I knew a little of what it meant to be consumed by hatred, but never could I imagine being so ruled by it as to cast out a child.

"At least she and my father were able to make a life together."

"It is a testament to both of them that they did so." With a gentle smile, Mother Benedette indicated the basket of *panetti.* "Come, eat a little more and let us speak of happier things. Adriana would not wish either of us to be so cast down. She had an irrepressible sense of optimism that, I will admit, sometimes led us into situations we did not quite expect. For instance, there was the time she enlisted my help in a project to find homes for what she claimed was a litter of kittens but which turned out to be wild lynxes. . . ."

As she described the antics of the two young girls, the abbess coaxed smiles from me, and finally laughter. By the time I left her, having agreed to meet her again soon, I was filled as much with stories about my mother as with the good *panetto.* As I crossed the square back toward the palazzo, my buoyant mood matched the lightness of my step. Thanks to the abbess, my mother was emerging from the shadow of death to come alive in my mind. Already, it seemed as though I could see her, a young woman filled with love and happiness, hurrying about the business of being a wife as she looked forward to the birth of her child.

There she was, brown-haired like me, wearing a simple

white gown beneath a green surcoat, with the handle of her basket tucked in the crook of her arm. She turned her head and smiled in my direction. So vivid was the impression of her that I stretched out a hand and called her name.

"Mamma!"

She did not answer, nor could she, for in the next instant I stared in horror as blood spurted from a dozen wounds that appeared suddenly all over her body. A crimson tide flowed across the cobblestone street, flowing faster and thicker, racing toward me. My mother bent over, clutching herself. She cast me a long last look before she crumpled to the ground.

"Mamma!"

My voice carried on the same wind that blew away the ashes that were all that was left of her.

I staggered back against a nearby wall, clamping a hand over my mouth to hold back my screams. A part of me knew that what I saw was not real. I had experienced such visions in the past—glimpses of a macabre world filled with death and despair. Whether such horrors were phantasms of my disordered mind or warnings of damnation, I could not be sure. But I had become, if not accustomed to them, at least able to fend off their worse effects. This was different.

The sight of my mother's life flowing from her consumed me with pain and terror unlike any I had ever known. For a horrible moment, I feared that I would lose all control of myself, becoming a spectacle for the avid crowd, who would conclude I must be a witch possessed by demons. Not even Borgia would be able to save me then.

Spurred by nothing more than raw horror and the instinct

for survival, I turned and ran across the piazza and up the steps of the palazzo. Bile burned in my throat, and my limbs felt weighted down with irons. My heart pounded so frantically that I thought it must surely burst. At the top of the steps, I paused and forced myself to look back. The usual motley collection of townspeople and visitors was passing through the square. No one appeared to have noticed what I had seen. My mother was gone; no sign of her remained.

I drew as deep a breath as I could manage as I fought for a semblance of calm. Despite the coolness of the day, my palms were wet and slick. The handle of the basket containing the remaining *panetti* slipped in my hand. Hysterical laughter rose in me as I realized that, despite everything, I had managed to hold on to it.

In my rooms, I paced back and forth, consumed with raging energy that could scarcely be contained. Jagged bits of color appeared and disappeared before my eyes. My chest ached from the raggedness of my breathing, but I scarcely noticed. I moved unceasingly for an unknown time, stopping only when I became aware that my legs were throbbing and that the bells were ringing for sext. As soon as prayers were over, the midday meal would begin. If I did not appear in the hall as expected, questions would be raised.

With difficulty, I managed to wash, refashion my hair, and don fresh clothes. Before I was done, my hands were shaking violently. I could not possibly go before Borgia and the others in such a state. In desperation, I took out the vial containing Sofia's powder. She would be horrified if she knew that I was taking it for any reason other than to sleep. But she had no way of understanding how dire my circumstances had become. Nor was it right that she should judge me from the distance of Rome and its relative safety.

Having that easily convinced myself of the rightness of my urges, I mixed a small quantity of powder with an ounce or so of wine and swallowed it quickly. Thus armored, I ventured forth. Uppermost in my mind was the fear that my weakness would be seen and seized upon. I felt myself surrounded by enemies only waiting to pounce. Cesare, David, Vittoro, and all the rest—any of them could conceal enmity behind false smiles and soft words. My hand flew to the knife beneath my bodice. Touching it gave me some faint comfort.

In the hall, everything appeared as normal. No one seemed to take more than passing notice of me. The bloody vision I had seen continued to dart through my mind again and again, but such was the effect of the powder that shortly I was able to observe it as though from a distance, almost as something that had happened to a stranger. By the time the dragée of spicy hypocrase accompanied by figs and oranges—intended to end the meal and promote digestion—was brought forth, I felt almost myself again.

Relief and elation filled me in equal measure. I struggled not to smile. Cesare, glancing in my direction, raised a brow. Beside him, seemingly attentive to whatever His Holiness was saying, Herrera smirked.

My thoughts raced. If the Spanish alliance were to shatter . . .

Borgia would need an army quickly. An army strong enough to convince his enemies to negotiate an accord that left him in possession of Peter's Throne. Juan was a prisoner of the Spanish and an idiot in the bargain; he could be of no use to his father. But there was Cesare, the eldest son, who had dreamed all his life of leading men in battle.

Cui bono? Who benefits? That is always the question in any great matter.

The handsome jester leaned close to whisper a joke in the ear of the beloved nephew, who had no sense of how close he trod to eternity. Beside him, the red prince laughed and raised his cup. I watched them all as the false comfort of the powder dissolved, leaving me marooned on the inhospitable shores of reality.

12

In the two days that followed, I had no further visions of my mother, but—despite my increased use of Sofia's powder—the nightmare came again and again, plunging me into blood-soaked darkness, from which I woke in terror, sobbing and gasping for breath.

The second night, Cesare was with me and roused when I did. Experienced as he was with my often fractured sleep, he did not bother with questions but simply offered me the comfort of his arms. Shorn of pride, I clung to him until dawn finally crept up over the horizon.

Waking, I did not speak but turned to him in mindless frenzy, driven by the desperate need to escape my demons. He was young and virile, and he responded as he always did, but plunging into release, I had no thought of him. At that moment, he was merely a means to an end.

As we rose to dress, he asked, "Are you angry with me?"

A fragment of memory: a summer afternoon. We were in the courtyard at the center of Il Cardinale's palazzo. Borgia and his eldest son were arguing, something about Cesare's being sent off to the university at Firenze when what he really wanted was to go into the army. Ugly words were said. Afterward, I followed Cesare around a corner of the loggia and waited while he vomited.

I dropped a shift over my head and said, "Of course not. Why would I be?"

"Ben Eliezer is your friend." Neither of us had mentioned his suspicions about David before now, but they had remained uppermost in my mind, along with what they led me to wonder about Cesare himself.

"True," I said, "but do you really think that he could be the assassin?"

"I think you don't want him to be."

He sat down on the bed to pull on his boots. I went to help him. Straddling his leg, I said, "Suppose for a moment that it isn't David. Who else could benefit from the loss of the Spanish alliance?"

"Any of my father's enemies."

"I mean someone here, close enough to do harm."

"Why do you ask?"

Over my shoulder, I said, "There have been two unexplained deaths. A kitchen boy while we were on the way here and a laundress a few days ago."

"Were they poisoned?"

"I don't know. Their deaths could have been natural. But if

they weren't, the poison used would have had to be very sophisticated."

I finished pulling up one boot and turned to the other.

"Why would anyone bother to do that?" Cesare asked. "They were just ordinary people, weren't they?"

"So far as I can tell."

"Then it makes no sense that anyone would take the trouble to kill them in such a way." More gently, he added, "People do just die, Francesca. You know that."

"Of course I do, but—"

He patted my bottom and stood. Tucking in his shirt, he said, "Better you concentrate on real dangers rather than conjure them where they don't exist."

I knew that he meant that kindly, but it still stung. If the kitchen boy and the laundress had been poisoned, it was because I had failed to protect them. Not that I was expected to. Examining every item meant for *la famiglia* was time-consuming enough; to do so for the entire papal household was impossible. The assumption had always been, as Cesare said, that no one would trouble to kill ordinary people by such means. I could not imagine why that would suddenly have changed, but neither could I shake the sense that the deaths were not natural.

In an effort to rein in my anxious thoughts, I took a little time after breakfast to catch up on correspondence. To Sofia, I sent assurances that I was sleeping better than ever and thanked her again for the powder. I did not mention that I was taking more than she had intended, nor that I had not entirely stopped drinking wine.

"You may be interested to hear," I wrote, "that I have met a friend of my mother's, an abbess who knew her when they were both girls growing up in Milan. She has told me how my parents came to fall in love and that my mother was a wonderful cook who also showed great skill at drawing. I hope to learn much more from her."

I said nothing of the bloody vision of my mother that still haunted me. It would only worry Sofia to no good purpose.

When I had finished the letter, sealing it and setting it aside to give to the dispatch riders later in the day, I took a fresh sheet of paper and spread it out before me with the intention of writing to Rocco. Several times, I raised my pen to begin, but the words would not come. I wanted to thank him for Nando's sketch, congratulate him on acquiring an undoubtedly fine dog, and ask how he was, but instead all I could think of was that he had said nothing of Carlotta. Was she still in the city or had her family left to avoid the plague? Were she and Rocco making plans for their wedding? Had a date been set? Did he love her?

The quill snapped between my fingers. Cursing, I tossed the pieces aside and stood. This was not the time to be mooning over Rocco and what could never be. Impatient with myself, I sought distraction in work. As I entered the kitchens, the usual chatter of conversation stopped abruptly. Being resigned to such behavior, I thought nothing of it at first. But when, after a few minutes, the mood did not return to normal, I realized that I was the target of sullen, fearful stares. Apparently, the personal risk I had taken only a few days before to assure Borgia's safety—and thereby their own—no longer mattered. Perhaps they were upset by the laundress's death coming so quickly after that of the kitchen boy, whom many of them must have known. Yet they had no reason to blame me for either.

Unless they thought, as Vittoro had warned, that the deaths were evidence of Satan's handiwork. Who better to do his bidding than a witch with a talent for killing?

Resolved to see to my duties regardless of the circumstances, I worked steadily through newly arrived crates of cheeses, apples, mushrooms, and asparagus meant for *la famiglia* and their noble guests, as well as several barrels of cider, a half-dozen sacks of flour, the split carcasses of a cow, and a hundred oysters packed in seaweed. No one attempted to hinder me, but I was aware of being constantly watched. Several of the cooks went so far as to make the horned sign against the evil eye when they thought I wasn't looking.

Though I kept my composure, my mood was grim by the time I finished and left the kitchens. At the top of the short flight of steps leading up toward the palazzo's main floor, I stopped and slumped against the wall. Whether because I had been thinking about my parents and what they had shared or because Rocco had crept into my mind as though he had never left it, the strain of being so isolated from normal human life seemed unbearable. I squeezed my eyes shut and drew a ragged breath. I could not risk being seen in such a state. Above all, I had to hide my weakness from any who might take advantage of it.

A little of the powder would calm me. But if I kept taking it as I had been doing, I risked exhausting my supply before

I could return to Rome and cajole Sofia into giving me more. Or find a different source. I would have to deal with that problem when I came to it. For the moment, I seized on the fact that I could resist the urge for the powder, if only temporarily, as evidence that Sofia's concerns were overblown. Clearly, I had nothing to fear from it.

Reluctant still to encounter anyone, I slipped into a narrow-walled *passetto* that wrapped around the outer wall of the palazzo. Such discrete passageways are common in noble residences. As a child, I had made good use of them within Borgia's palace on the Corso. I hoped to do the same right then, but I had not gotten very far when a sudden flicker of movement up ahead stopped me. Instinctively, I pulled back into the shadows.

A door opened, revealing a young man. He was about my age, well built, with reddish-brown hair and strong features. As I watched, he bounced a handful of coins in his palm, grinned, and hurried off in the opposite direction. Relieved not to have been seen, I was about to continue on when the door opened again. Herrera stepped into the corridor.

The Spaniard looked in both directions and then, having failed to notice me, came toward where I stood. There was no opportunity to conceal myself and no possibility of retreat. With no alternative, I stepped forward quickly, as though I were hurrying on my way with no thought other than for my destination.

Abruptly, the beloved nephew stopped. He looked first shocked, then enraged.

"*You!* What are you doing here?"

"I'm going to . . . it doesn't matter where." I tried to move around him, but he blocked the way forward.

"You are following me! Spying on me!"

I could understand his concern. He was taking a chance trysting with the young man. Borgia wouldn't care, nor would many others at the court. But if word got back to Their Most Catholic Majesties . . .

"I am doing no such thing." Again I tried to go around. Again he stopped me.

Herrera's fists clenched at his sides. He took a step forward. I resisted the urge to reach for the leather sheath under my bodice.

As calmly as I could manage, I said, "There is no reason for trouble between us, senor."

He looked at me as though I truly were a madwoman. "Have you forgotten that you put a knife to my throat?"

"Yes . . . well, you were trying to break my arm at the time." Reluctantly, I reminded myself that however I felt about him, nothing could be gained from another confrontation between us. "But I went too far. I apologize for doing so."

It wasn't enough. Still glaring, Herrera said, "You humiliated me in front of him."

Silently, I railed against Cesare for trampling on the Spaniard's vanity even as I sought to soothe it.

"I assure you, His Eminence reprimanded me in the sternest possible terms."

Herrera brushed that off. Furiously, he said, "He doesn't love you, not really, no matter how he acts."

Ah, so that was it, was it? Why hadn't I seen it sooner?

Resistant as I was to Cupid's dart, I should at least be able to recognize the pain it caused.

"Of course he doesn't," I said.

"Then let him go! Stop imperiling his soul!"

"You mistake my purpose. I wish only to protect—"

"Enough! You lie with every foul breath. And now you will tell lies about me! But I will not allow it. By God and all the saints, I will not!"

He came at me. I had an instant to decide: go for the knife and hope Borgia believed I spoke the truth when I swore that I had killed the Spaniard in self-defense or . . .

Deep within, the darkness stirred. Before it could awaken, I turned and ran. Behind me, I heard Herrera follow, cursing. Spurred by fear of myself far more than by fear of him, I raced ahead. Plunging through a door in the *passetto,* I came out into a busy part of the palazzo. Surrounded by servants and hangers-on, I stopped abruptly. So, too, did Herrera, who stumbled out a moment later.

As unwilling to draw attention as I was, he could only watch as I walked away. I don't know where I intended to go—anywhere so long as I put distance between myself and the furious Spaniard. I could have told Herrera that I understood all too well the cost of having to conceal one's true self from the world, but he would not have heard me. It was a pity, really; we actually had something in common in addition to our concern for Cesare.

Before I got very far, a page sidled up and thrust a note into my hand, fleeing immediately as though he feared that any contact with me would contaminate him. I opened the paper and scanned it quickly. At once, my spirits rose. Mother Benedette had managed to slip away from the convent where she was staying and hoped that I could meet her at Santa Maria della Salute.

The abbess was seated in her usual place when I arrived. This time, she had brought a small basket of *torrone,* a confection of honey, sugar, egg whites, and almonds that I accepted gladly but declined to try just then, promising her that I would when my stomach was more settled. The encounter with Herrera coming after so much else made me disinclined to eat anything just then.

"Are you feeling all right?" she asked, her brow furrowed with concern.

"I'm perfectly fine. It's just that I've been inspecting food all day and that has robbed me of my appetite."

She seemed content with that, and quickly we fell to talking of my mother. "Adriana loved to sing. I do myself, but my voice was never the equal of hers."

A memory stirred in me. A woman's voice singing softly . . .

Firefly, firefly, yellow and bright,
Bridle the filly under your light,
The child of my heart is ready to ride,
Firefly, firefly, fly by her side.

"Again, Mamma. Sing it again."

But that was impossible. My mother had died when I was born. How often had I been told that? I might have heard her groan or even scream, but most assuredly I could never have heard her sing. Not that it mattered, for I could not possibly remember anything to do with her.

"Did she . . . ever sing about a firefly?"

Mother Benedette frowned. "A firefly? I don't recall." Suddenly she said, "Wait, there is an old folk song. How does it go . . . 'Firefly, firefly, yellow and bright'? Yes, that's it! 'Bridle the filly under your light.' I haven't thought of that song in years, but your mother loved it. She sang it when she was pregnant with you."

What was I to make of that? That somehow, against all belief, I had heard and remembered a song my mother sang while I was still in her womb? The practical side of my nature, that part of me that seeks the light of reason, knew that could not be true. Yet how I longed for it to be so. Because the alternative . . .

"Were you with my mother when she died?"

The day was overcast; the church dimly lit. I could not be sure, but I thought the abbess paled. She rose hastily. "I was in Anzio. Forgive me, I cannot tarry. I'm expected back at the convent. Please, enjoy the *torrone*."

Gazing down at me, she asked, "Can we meet tomorrow? I should be able to get away for longer then."

I hesitated, surprised by the abruptness of her departure. "Yes, of course." With a nod to the basket, I added, "Thank you for this. I'm sure it is delicious."

"Enjoy it." With a hasty smile, Mother Benedette departed.

Shortly, I did the same. After a day of unsettling encounters, I was glad to retire to my chambers, where I resumed my investigations into the cantharidin. Soon it would need to be tested. As I said, my father had procured stray animals for such a purpose, but I had convinced him that it was better to try new poisons on humans. The thought horrified him at first, especially coming from a child, but quickly enough he saw the sense of it. Better a swift death by poison than a far longer, more drawn out execution according to the hideous methods so favored by courts and bloodthirsty crowds alike. I take it as a sad commentary on our age that when my father, and then I in turn, appeared in the dank, subterranean cells that housed the condemned, we were greeted as saviors rather than as the monsters the more fortunate of this world would call us.

I showed myself at dinner that evening in the great hall, but did not linger. As soon as I decently could, I returned to my rooms and made use of the powder. In the last moments before sleep claimed me, I thought of my other self, the woman I imagined I would have been if fate had not made me what I was. That woman, hurrying about her blessedly normal life, turned to glance at me over her shoulder and smiled.

I braced myself, expecting the image to turn, as it had in my waking vision of my mother, into a nightmare of blood and terror. But instead I found myself looking up through soft shadows at the face of a woman who was singing quietly:

Firefly, firefly, yellow and bright,
Bridle the filly under your light,
The child of my heart is ready to ride,
Firefly, firefly, fly by her side.

The child of her heart. A child who was safe, secure, loved. How could I know what that felt like when I had never been that child? Had never known my mother's touch, her voice, the comfort of her presence?

Yet I remembered her all the same.

In the still hours of the night, I left the bed, threw on a robe, and went to sit by the window. Cracking the shutter open, I gazed out at the sere autumn garden wreathed in darkness. Dawn was hours off. In the distance, I could see the torches that burned all night, providing illumination for the guards who patrolled constantly. There were more of them than usual and soon their numbers would grow further, but their presence gave me no comfort. When the real enemy came—as I was certain that it would—it would be from the shadows, in some way I could not yet see. I could not afford to be distracted, especially not by old pain and old yearnings that had no place in the present dangerous day.

And yet, despite my best intentions, one question loomed uppermost in my mind: How—and when—had my mother died?

13

In the morning, I sipped warm cider and nibbled on the *torrone* I had remembered belatedly. Sweet and melting on my tongue, it was as delicious as the *panetto,* but my appetite was still lacking. I put it down after a few bites and dressed hurriedly. Though the rain had eased, there were reports of flooding to the north, making me hope that the road to Assisi would not reopen before I had a chance to learn all I could from Mother Benedette.

Renaldo caught up with me as I crossed the hall. "Have you heard?"

A sharp pain stirred behind my eyes. Determined to ignore it, I said, "Apparently not. Tell me."

"Sforza is being packed off to Pesaro. Supposedly it's because his presence can no longer be spared there, but in fact it's because he and Cesare came to blows last night. The Spaniard, Herrera, had to separate them."

"What were they fighting about?"

"I probably shouldn't say, but"—he leaned closer—"it had to do with Donna Lucrezia and . . ." A look of disgust flitted across the steward's face.

I sighed. "That again. Sforza is a fool."

"No one has ever accused him of being anything else. But where does this leave His Holiness? The Sforzas helped to put Borgia in power and would help to keep him there, but now . . ."

"He grows more isolated," I agreed. "And more dependent than ever on the Spanish."

"Even as the assassin is out there somewhere waiting to work his mischief." He paused for a moment, then asked, "Has your friend learned anything?"

"Not that he has said. I will have to speak with him." The headache was growing worse. I shut my eyes for a moment, opening them again to discover that the light in the hall seemed overly bright, even glaring.

"Has it stopped raining?" I asked.

"What? No, it's never going to stop. We should all be building arks."

I tried to laugh, but the effort hurt too much.

"Vittoro is calling up more men, I hear," Renaldo said.

"You hear everything." I only partly meant to flatter him. He had an uncanny talent for ferreting out useful information amid the daily chatter.

The steward preened a little but quickly turned serious

again. "I suspect that he is concerned about the loyalty of the garrison. If they were to throw their support to one of Borgia's rivals—say della Rovere—we could be murdered in our beds."

Though he spoke matter-of-factly, the threat was real. Any hint of weakness on Borgia's part invited catastrophe.

I nodded, but his words seemed to come from a distance. Shadows were moving along the inside walls of the palazzo. Peering more closely, I saw the dark shapes resolve into the forms of armed men coming with speed and stealth.

I turned, I believe with the intention of alerting Renaldo to what was happening, but before I could do so, the scene exploded. Without warning, the palazzo was under attack. Screams rent the air, fire burst forth, death and devastation were everywhere.

Nor did the horror stop there. A thick, red mist rose before my eyes. Through it, I saw a world soaked in blood, bodies writhing across a landscape of utter bleakness, and above it all, immense carrion crows, their beaks gleaming, swooping down from a black, lightning-torn sky.

I gasped, or perhaps I screamed; I really can't say. The gruesome vision spun wildly, taking me with it. I fell a great distance in the instant before consciousness left me.

When I was again myself, I was seated on a bench a little distance away from where I had been standing. Renaldo hovered over me, shielding me from view. I could smell the damp wool of his cloak and the hint of sausage from his breakfast. My senses remained uncomfortably heightened, but at least the pain behind my eyes had lessened.

"Francesca, are you all right?" His voice was low, yet I

heard the dread in it all the same. He was my friend; I had to remind myself of that. He had seen me in extremis before and yet he did not shun me.

"I . . ." Belatedly, I realized that I was clutching his hand as though it could somehow anchor me to the world. "I am getting worse."

My greatest fear was coming to pass, and I could not even keep myself from voicing it. Since I had left Rome, and been separated from all that was familiar, the darkness within me had grown, taking on even more of its own life, to the peril of my soul. Despite Sofia's powder, the nightmare was more intense and more frequent. I had begun to sense danger everywhere, even going so far as to not dismiss the notion that David might be an enemy. David! With whom I had shared danger and death, and whom I had every reason to trust absolutely. As though that were not enough, my encounter with Mother Benedette and the thoughts she prompted regarding my mother's death further fed my demons.

Renaldo's attempt at a smile, no doubt meant to be reassuring, fell far short of the mark. He tried a different approach. "Your . . . infirmity does not seem to worry our master. His confidence in you is undiminished."

"He sees what he wants to see." That had not always been the case. Much of Borgia's success as a prince of the Church had come from his ability to rise above his own desires and view circumstances with ruthless objectivity. But since achieving the papacy, his vision of *la famiglia* spawning a dynasty of popes and kings absorbed him to the exclusion of all else. Juan on the throne of Naples was only the beginning. If Il Papa had his way, Cesare would follow him onto the Throne of Saint Peter, to be followed in turn by his own heirs. They would be Borgia's legacy . . . and his immortality.

Perhaps emboldened by the intimacy of the moment, Renaldo asked, "Is it true that he believes you are a seer?"

I grimaced. Of all the aspects of my relationship with Borgia, I found that the most troubling. Through the pain that was finally ebbing behind my eyes, I said, "His Holiness has alluded to the possibility." However, he retained for himself the right to determine which of my visions were a true glimpse of the future and which were merely the disordered workings of my troubled mind. I had no such luxury.

"You do not want what I see to be the future." The very thought made me shudder.

No doubt Renaldo was tempted to ask what it was that I saw, but he thought better of it. Instead, he said, "Whatever you see does not have to come to pass. After all, we possess free will, among the greatest of the Almighty's gifts, second only to life itself."

To look at him, you would have thought the steward cared for nothing other than the healthiness of his accounts, both those he kept for Borgia and the plump ledgers in which he recorded his own growing wealth. But he had interests beyond the pecuniary, even extending into the realm of theology and natural philosophy.

"What are you suggesting?" I asked.

"If Il Papa is right about you, is it not possible for us to alter our behavior in order to avoid at least the worst of what you see?"

Since my father's death and my assumption of his position in Borgia's household, I had been forced to confront what seemed the likelihood that I was damned or possessed or both. In that case, I could expect to spend all of eternity suffering the grotesque torments described so vividly by Dante in his masterful *Divina Commedia,* a work to which I was drawn again and again with unhealthy fascination. Inevitably, I had wondered if I did not deserve all that and worse, because not even the fear of it could persuade me to give up my dark ways. But never had I thought that my "infirmity," as Renaldo so delicately put it, might actually be useful.

Hesitantly, I said, "What I . . . see is not very specific."

The steward was not to be dissuaded. Helping me to my feet, he said, "The pronouncements of the Oracle of Delphi were open to broad interpretation, yet they were taken very seriously. And what about more recently? Saint Catherine of Sienna's visions brought the papacy back to Rome. Not to forget that poor French girl, Joan. Such a shame what happened to her."

The same Church that had allowed the Maid of Orleans to be burned had recognized her, once she was safely dead, as a martyr. There was even talk that she might be canonized someday.

"Surely you don't mean to compare me to such holy women?" Despite everything, I could not help but be amused. Perhaps that was Renaldo's intent.

"I am only saying that you might consider that there could be some benefit from whatever it is that you are experiencing."

I was still mulling that over when we parted a short time

later. It seemed unlikely that Renaldo could be right, yet the temptation to believe otherwise was too great for me to resist entirely.

Even so, I did not dwell on it very long. The hour was fast approaching when I intended to seek Mother Benedette again. I crossed the piazza against a damp wind, my cloak drawn tightly around me. Finding the church nearly empty, I took my seat across from the altar to Saint Clare and waited what was probably no more than a few minutes but what seemed an interminable time. I had almost decided that the abbess was not coming, and that I would have to seek her out at the convent where she had told me she was staying, when the heavy wooden door to the church creaked open and she appeared. For a moment, illuminated by the dreary day behind her and the pale gray light filtering through the clerestory windows, she looked grim and anxious. The skirt of her undyed wool habit flapped around her legs as she hastened down the central nave. When she saw me, a smile of relief flitted across her face.

"I am sorry to have kept you waiting. I hope you haven't been here long?"

"Just a few minutes." I slid aside to make room for her on the stone bench. "You needn't have hurried."

She sat, took a breath to steady herself, and folded her hands in her lap. They were slender, white and well-formed, the nails neatly clipped and lightly buffed. More the hands of a gentlewoman than were my own, which bore the stains and scars of my profession.

"I am so used to being occupied day and night with the

business of the abbey," she said. "Here I have scant idea what to do with myself. My mind wonders in all directions. Were it not for the bells summoning us to prayer, I would lose track of time entirely."

Before I could suggest that it was no bad thing for her to have a rest, she went on quickly, "The last time we met, I left you with unseemly haste. If you will allow, I would like to make amends."

"There is no need—"

"Please. Otherwise, I cannot help but think that I have forfeited all right to your friendship." From a pouch secured to her belt, the abbess withdrew a small book about the size of her palm and held it out to me. "This was your mother's. I would like you to have it."

I hesitated, unsure how to respond. For my mother to have owned a book at all was a surprise. For it to suddenly appear before me was almost more than I could comprehend.

At Mother Benedette's urging, I took the volume bound in dark brown leather and turned it over carefully. Pale gold writing was inscribed on the spine, but a sudden blur of moisture in my eyes made it impossible for me to read the words.

"What is this?"

"A psalter, containing the Book of Psalms and various canticles from the Old and New Testaments. Your mother received it on her thirteenth birthday. It was her most cherished possession."

"She was devout?" I had not considered that possibility.

"Not particularly, but she loved to read, and the very idea of books fascinated her."

I, too, had a fascination with the written word, but my taste tended more toward treatises on alchemy, poisons, and the like. I had a small number of items that had belonged to my mother—her bridal chest with its carved scene of the Sabine women; her locket. But a book that she had held and treasured, that had occupied her mind and stirred her imagination . . . Holding the smooth, well-worn volume, my hands trembled.

Gathering my courage, I asked, "How did you come to have this?"

In the back of my mind was the half-formed hope that she would tell me some pleasant story, that my mother had given her the psalter as a reminder of their friendship when the abbess entered the convent. Instead, she looked at me sadly. "Your father brought it to me afterward."

Afterward. Such a wealth of meaning in that word. After the world shatters, all the pieces flying apart, never to be put right again. After the shroud of grief descends, trapping the hapless survivors in a cruel mimicry of life shorn of light or hope.

"After my mother died?"

Mother Benedette's brow furrowed. "Perhaps I should not have brought it. Believe me when I say that the last thing I want is to cause you any more pain."

My grip on the book tightened, as though I feared irrationally that she might try to take it back. Lights danced in the corners of my eyes. Fireflies.

"I want to know the truth about what happened to her."

The abbess stiffened. I heard the sharp inhalation of her breath. "Francesca . . ."

"I must know!" The harshness of my voice was grating. For a moment I was a child again, lying in a bed in a house I could not remember, unable to speak, scarcely able to move, adrift in a sea of echoing silence from which I never wanted to emerge.

"Knowledge, once given, can never be withdrawn," the abbess said quietly. "Eve learned that to her sorrow."

The anger, already building in me in anticipation of what I might learn, turned in her direction. "Does that make you the serpent?" I asked.

She started as a dark flush bloomed across her cheeks. I regretted my outburst at once, but before I could attempt to repair it, she said, "Your father loved you. He thought that if you didn't know what really happened, you would be protected from the memory of it."

The fireflies were brighter and swarmed even more thickly. I blinked, trying to banish them, but without success. A sudden, unanticipated rush of loathing for what my father had done swelled up in me. It was so at odds with my normal feelings for him that it shook me to the core. I had lived all my life trying to please him, because he was good and kind to me but also because in the darkest corners of my mind I wondered if he didn't blame me for my mother's dying at my birth, as he had told me was her fate. I wanted to make amends for that, as I yearned to avenge his death not only as my final gift to my father but also as the ultimate proof that I had deserved to live.

But if he had lied, if all that I thought I knew was

false . . . Where was the truth, then? In what obscure corner of the darkness did it crouch?

I clutched the psalter tightly, as though it might otherwise dissolve into dust and I with it. Blinded by the brilliance of the fireflies, I said, "As you loved my mother, tell me how she died."

14

Three days at most," Giovanni said. "Four at the outside. You understand why I must go?"

Adriana laughed, her face turned to the sun, her eyes shining. Her skin bore the tint of apricots; a smattering of freckles marched across her nose. She looked young, filled with life and, incredible as he always found it, love for him.

"It is the best opportunity you have ever been offered," she said. "Apothecary in the household of the Duke himself. You deserve no less."

"Assistant apothecary, one of many. Still, it would mean a great deal more money and a better life for us all."

"We have a good life right now. Even so, I understand. This town is charming but too small for your aspirations. Go, then, and awe the majordomo or whomever it is that you must impress. I will start packing."

He laughed and seized her around the waist, swinging her in a wide arc so that her skirt billowed out like a sail about to carry them all away on some marvelous adventure. Nearby, the child watched, solemn-eyed but with a smile tugging at the corners of her mouth. Rather than the usual infant fare, her father told her tales of great voyages when he tucked her into bed at night. The Portuguese were plunging down the coast of Africa, even claiming that they would find the southern tip of it and discover a new route to the spice wealth of the Indies. He wanted her to share his wonder in the new age into which she had been born. She was too young to understand completely, but such was her trust in him that she believed all the same. He felt the responsibility of that, knew he should never break faith so innocently given.

At the moment of parting, he hesitated, a sudden sense of apprehension moving through him. He was a Jew by birth and, as such, accustomed to always looking over his shoulder in an unfriendly land. But he had embraced the Christian faith with sincerity, if also with some regret that he kept entirely private within himself. Mounted on the borrowed horse, he shook off his dread and turned to look at the woman and child. Though the rising dust of summer clouded his vision, he saw his wife smile once again and raise her hand in farewell.

When he was gone, the child sat outside and drew with a stick in the dirt. The shapes she traced were simple: a lopsided circle, an almost square, lines that wandered off to nowhere. The lack of rain in the days that followed preserved the markings.

Evening came; the candles were lit, and her mother spooned soup into a bowl and helped her to eat. They were finishing when a dog barked in the road just beyond the shop. Or some other sound drew their attention. The child dipped a small piece of bread in the bottom of the bowl and sucked on it. Her mother went to the window. She opened a shutter and peered down.

Or so Giovanni imagined when he sat in the room afterward, trying to grasp what had happened. There were tiny signs: the bread left on the table beside the bowl, the shutters drawn a little apart, the overturned stool where the child would have been sitting just before her mother grabbed her up.

He tried to see it all in his mind's eye even as the ghost of his butchered wife stood at his shoulder, gazing at him with great sorrow.

The next tenants would have to sand the wood floor to get the bloodstains out, and even that might not work. So much blood—incredible to think that the body of one small woman could have contained all that.

As for the child . . .

She had not spoken, might never again. Her mind was broken in some way that, for all his skill as an apothecary, he could not heal.

How much had she seen? Understood? There had been three men, he thought, working backward from the number of stab wounds in his wife's body and the footprints in her blood. She must have recognized them in that moment when she looked from the window. They had worried her enough for her to hide the child, but not herself.

Perhaps she had feared that failing to find her, they would tear the place apart and discover the child as well.

Or perhaps she simply had not been able to believe that men she knew would do what they had.

It was his fault. In his vanity, he had believed that the letter summoning him to the ducal palace was real. Believed that he—a converted Jew of humble origins—would be offered a position for which the ablest and best-connected men vied. Arriving to the discovery that no one had any knowledge of him had been merely annoying at first. He had wasted precious hours trying to rectify what turned out to be no one's mistake but his own. By the time he started for home, it was too late.

So much blood . . . Slipping and falling in it, he cried her name, gathering her into his arms, refusing to believe what all his senses told him. The woman who had filled his world with light and love was gone, leaving nothing but a torn, empty shell.

And the child. Scrambling frantically to his feet, he looked in all directions, terrified that he would find the tiny body.

"Francesca!"

Nothing, no sound. Was she dead? Had she fled? Was she out there somewhere wandering, alone and afraid?

Or—

He tore desperately at the wall that he had built despite Adriana's laughing protestations, knowing in his soul that hatred never slept.

"Francesca!"

Was there a sound? Not a voice, only a soft rustling. He ripped the last plank away and fell to his knees, grasping the small, still body. Still but alive. Alive but . . . away.

"That was the word he used when he spoke of you," Mother Benedette said as she finished her recitation of the events as told to her by my grief-stricken father. "You were there . . . but not. It was as though your mind were somewhere else and he had no idea how to reach you."

Floating in a sea of silence for how long? A year? Two? My memory was such that I had difficulty remembering much of anything until the day we came to the grand palazzo on the Corso, the home of the renowned prince of Holy Mother Church, Cardinal Rodrigo Borgia, who had hired my father in some capacity I did not then understand. At that moment, walking through the doors into Borgia's domain, my life seemed to begin again.

Yet, contrary to my father's hopes, the past had never given up its grip on me. Its talons were wedged deeper than ever into my soul.

"Who killed her?" I heard my voice as though from a great distance. The wall loomed before me, pressing me down into a narrow, confined space from which there had never been any real escape.

"All the signs pointed to her family being responsible. They never forgave her for marrying a Jew."

"Are they still alive?" Why did I ask? Because I had a sudden, fierce need to seek them out and kill them one by one as they had killed my mother?

"Two years later, a plague swept through Milan. They did not survive it."

The thought of my anonymous, faceless relations writhing in Hell failed to satisfy me. Plainly, I lacked sufficient trust in divine retribution.

"Your father blamed himself for not being there, for putting your mother in such jeopardy by marrying her, for everything. You were all he had left, the sole reason for his continuing to live. He could think of nothing except protecting you."

Perhaps that was true, but it was equally true that my father's lie had left me exposed to the hideous nightmare that haunted me. Robbed of the right to acknowledge it as memory, and deal with it as such, I could only conclude that I was mad or damned, or both. My fear, as I sat on the stone bench clutching my mother's psalter, was that the truth had come too late to save me. Could I be anything other than what I had so long believed myself to be? Did I even want to try? My infirmity, as Renaldo had so delicately called it, was the price I paid for my armor against the world. Without it, how could I live?

"I must go." The world tilted as I stood. I reached out a hand to steady myself. My legs turned to water and my head spun. Only with an effort was I able to right myself.

"You are not well," Mother Benedette said as she, too, rose. "Let me help you."

I had difficulty hearing her, so thick had the fireflies become. But I managed to shake my head. "I'm fine, really, and I have much to do. This business with Herrera—"

I broke off, abruptly aware that I had begun to speak of matters entirely private to His Holiness. Even so, the look that flitted across the abbess's smooth face suggested that she had heard about the incident with the officer's wife.

"The Spaniard," she said. "He is not liked."

Apparently, the gossip of the town breached even convent walls. "The affection of the mob is always capricious," I replied absently. Borgia had said that one night when we were drinking together, shortly after his election to pope. Cesare had come in and found us most of the way through a goodly amount of Lombardy red. He had thought it all very amusing.

"I must go," I said again. The echo of my words rang hollowly within the church walls.

The abbess touched my arm to keep me a moment. "Read your mother's psalter. It will give you comfort."

I nodded and slipped the book into the pouch I wore beneath my gown so that the sight of it would not spark anxious speculation as to its contents.

"One more thing," she said. "The road to Assisi is still closed, but I am of a mind to remain here awhile in any case. If you have need of me—"

I murmured something to the effect that I would be in touch with her as soon as circumstances allowed. I think I also thanked her for the psalter, but I am not certain. The world was splintering into a thousand pieces, like the shards of a mosaic suddenly free of the mortar that had held it in place. I feared that I would do the same if I did not get away quickly. Having bade the abbess farewell, I left the church and hurried across the piazza. My heart beat rapidly, and each breath I took was painful. I could scarcely feel the ground beneath me.

The guards on watch in front of the palazzo stiffened as I approached. No doubt I did not look my best, fleeing a church as though pursued by unseen demons. They made way for me with haste, all but falling over each other. Once in my quarters, I attempted to secure my mother's psalter in the puzzle chest, only to discover that my fingers had turned to clumsy lumps unable to perform the complex series of movements needed to unlock the chest. Worse yet, I could not remember the sequence for more than a second or two before it flitted from my mind.

Hardly aware that I did so, I sat down on the floor in front of the chest. My heart beat frantically and my breath was ragged. I was in desperate need of a calmative, but when I looked, I discovered that less of Sofia's powder remained than I had thought. Panic flared. Clearly, I had to restrain my use of it or I would be left without. Yet my need was great. I stumbled to my feet and set off for the cellars, thinking only of finding an alternative. I had in mind to help myself to a small cask of brandy, not that I would drink very much of it; not at all. Just enough to soothe my jangled nerves. Surely I deserved that much, given what had just been revealed to me?

At the bottom of the stone steps, I paused. I had visited the cellars once shortly after arriving in Viterbo, but with every bottle, barrel, vat, and cask intended for *la famiglia* secure under my seal, there had been no reason to return. For a moment, I could not remember where in the maze of redbrick chambers the brandy was stored. As my eyes adjusted to the dim light filtering through window slits at ground level, I began to get my bearings. Setting off in what I thought was the right direction, I soon came to an arched chamber lined with wooden stands holding supplies for the papal household.

A flicker off to the side distracted me. Out of the corner of my eye, I thought I glimpsed a figure moving along the aisle that ran the length of the cellars. At once, I stiffened, fearful that the terrifying vision I had experienced earlier was about to return. When it did not, I looked again, but the figure had disappeared. With a sigh of relief, I stepped into the chamber.

Only to trip and almost fall over an obstruction in my path. Thrusting out an arm, I caught hold of a barrel to steady myself. Slowly, I straightened. In the dim light, it looked as though a large sack had been dropped carelessly just inside the chamber. I knelt, reached out a hand, and felt the unmistakable shape of a body.

Looking more closely, I saw that the eyes were open and as yet unclouded by death. The skin, when I touched two fingers to the side of the neck, was warm. The young man staring up at me wore the mulberry and gold colors reserved for His Holiness's personal household staff.

I leaped up, ran out of the chamber, and looked in all directions. In the shadows, I could just make out the figure, too far away for me to catch. It was moving swiftly.

I took the stairs I had come down two at a time. For a change, Fortune favored me. Vittoro was in the hall, preparing to go out on patrol. As soon as he saw me, he stepped away from his men so that we could speak privately.

Quickly, I said, "A page is dead. In the cellars. The killer may also still be down there."

Without hesitation, he called an officer over. "Fifty men. *Now.* Half block all stairs to the cellars, the rest come with me."

There followed shouted orders, a rush of motion, the pounding of booted feet, and—off to the sides—the startled faces of high and low alike, suddenly awakening to the presence of danger within the walls they had counted on to keep them safe.

Following with all speed, I told myself that I was certain

of what I had seen, but was I really? That day alone my mind had conjured up a vision of a blood-soaked world, the pretty spectacle of fireflies dancing beneath the roof of a church, and reality turned into a shattered mosaic. How could I even consider trusting my senses?

Yet they were reliable at least as regarded the dead man. The page remained where I had found him. His face, revealed more clearly by torches swiftly lit by the guards, appeared serene. Like the others, he gave every evidence of having died suddenly and with very little awareness of what was happening to him. As Vittoro's men spread out, searching for anyone hiding in the cellars, I knelt beside the body. A quick examination confirmed the absence of any wound or other sign of violence. I was considering whether to look deeper when Vittoro returned.

"Whomever you may have seen down here is gone," he said. Looking down at the body, he asked, "The same as the others?"

"I think so." Rising, I added, "These deaths coming right now cannot be a coincidence. The assassin is here in Viterbo."

"If you could give a description . . ."

I shook my head. "The light was too dim. I saw a figure moving. Nothing more."

Vittoro nodded slowly. He put a hand on my shoulder. "What brought you down here at this time of day?"

Briefly, I considered telling him the truth, but I could not bear for him to see me as weak or pitiable.

"You know what has been happening. I wanted to check everything again."

"No other reason?"

"What other reason could there be?"

He hesitated a moment. "You have become very regular in your devotions."

"What do you mean?"

"You were seen not long ago returning again from Santa Maria della Salute."

"What are you saying? Am I being watched?"

Vittoro stepped back a little. In the light from the torches, he looked brooding and worried. "When the Pope's poisoner suddenly feels the need to make regular church visits, tongues are going to wag."

I had not thought of that. In my blind absorption with my own concerns, it had not occurred to me how my actions might be interpreted. Cesare knew a little about Mother Benedette, and Renaldo was aware that a nun had come looking for me, but I had to hope that no one else had any notion of who she was or why I would be speaking with her.

In a bid for time to think, I asked, "Do these wagging tongues offer an explanation for my behavior?"

Vittoro smiled faintly. "The consensus is that His Holiness has charged you to do something so terrible that you feel compelled to beseech Almighty God's forgiveness in advance. The difficulty lies in imagining what you would consider that bad, but everyone is much diverted trying to figure it out."

"Oh, well, as long as they're diverted. . . ."

"Seriously, Francesca, if there is something I should know, I would like to hear it now."

"It is a private matter, not touching on my responsibility to

His Holiness." I spoke too quickly; Vittoro would know that I was unnerved. But he was my friend and I was counting on him to understand that I did not want to discuss the matter. Of course, he would also make his own inquiries in the meantime, but that was only to be expected.

"As you wish," he said. "If you remember anything more about what you saw down here—"

"I will tell you at once. I trust your men to keep a good lookout."

"Of course. Someone is going to a great deal of trouble and risk. There has to be a reason."

I was no closer to determining what that might be when together we left the cellars and returned to the palazzo above. Throughout the remainder of the day, my thoughts were jumbled and unclear. I was missing something, but worse yet, in my present state I had scant hope of unraveling the skeins of danger and intrigue that were drawing us all deeper and deeper into a deadly web.

15

Water sloshed from the wooden bucket and splattered across the floor. The maids gasped and fell to their knees, mopping frantically with their aprons. I thought to reassure them that a little spill was not such a calamity, but instead I pretended not to notice. In the hours since the page's death, the usual fear and dread that my dark calling inspired had intensified beyond all my previous experience. Everywhere I went, I encountered sullen, angry looks and worse. Now, when my sole wish was an end to the torturous day, I could not bear to see such condemnation in the eyes of the two young girls sent to fill my bath.

When they were gone, running in their haste, I stripped off my clothes and sank into the water. Leaning my head back against the rim of the tub, I closed my eyes and tried to relax. Thoughts of the dead page intruded, but I pushed them away.

My only hope of preventing further deaths was to find the assassin before he could strike again. I would not do that by dwelling on what it was too late to change. For a time, my efforts seemed to work. The pain behind my eyes lessened, as did the aching stiffness in my back and shoulders. But with the easing of bodily discomfort, other thoughts intruded.

My father had told a great lie. By denying the truth of what had happened to my mother, he had denied the horror I had witnessed. No matter how good and loving his purpose, he had left me alone to deal with memories no child should ever have to endure. For a time, I had retreated into a place where nothing could touch me. But when I emerged, the memories were there waiting for me. They had become the nightmare that haunted me.

Nothing would ever lessen the love I had for my father or my determination to avenge his death. Even so, anger at what he had done threatened to overwhelm me. Unbidden, I suddenly found myself wondering what Rocco would make of it all. He and my father had been good friends; under other circumstances they might also have been father- and son-in-law. What would he think of such a deception? As he was a father himself, I suspected he would be better able to understand it than I could. And as a former monk, he would certainly be more inclined to forgive.

I missed Rocco. Whatever else there might have been between us, he was my dear friend, to whom I had turned in times of great trouble and whose wise counsel I had the good sense to value. Or at least he had been. Surely I deluded myself if I thought that could continue after he and Carlotta wed. She could hardly be expected to welcome my coming by the shop, taking him from his work, and involving him in dangerous matters. She would see to it that he was far too busy for any of that.

What would I do without him? There was Cesare, of course, but my relationship with him was entirely different, and besides, he would be occupied with his father's business. I had other friends—Sofia, Vittoro, a handful more—but none was as close as Rocco. If he were here right now, I would—

I would what? I was not a foolish girl who mooned over what could not be. The pain was back behind my eyes. I sat up in the tub and stared down into the water, struggling to find a measure of calm.

And found instead my mother, her face looking back at me. The sight stirred such yearning that I had to believe I truly did remember her. Remembered, too, the knife as it flashed, cutting through flesh, destroying hope, dreams, all that was good. Bringing only blood.

The water in the tub was gone. I was bathing in blood, drowning in it, and I could not even scream. I was paralyzed, unable to move. My mind was shattering, threatening to fly away in a thousand jagged pieces like the mosaic I had seen. When next I was aware, I was standing beside the tub, naked and shivering. Choking on sobs, hardly able to breathe, I staggered to the bed. Slumped there, hugging my knees, I managed finally to pull a blanket over myself, but I could not stop the convulsions that wracked me. I reached out for the small box in which I kept Sofia's powder, only to knock it onto the floor. The lid flew off and the powder spilled. Frantically, I scrambled to retrieve as much of it as I could. In my haste, I sent more drifting up into the air, dispersing beyond my grasp. Much of the rest was lost in the threads of the carpet. I was left with only a faint tracing, which I licked in desperation from my fingers, the bitter taste mingling with the salt of the tears that coursed down my face.

Exhausted and aching, I finally accepted that the powder was gone. Only the clawing hunger for it remained. Sleep was out of the question, but I forced myself to rise and with trembling hands dropped a nightgown over my head and straightened the bed. Achieving that small degree of order soothed me a little, but I needed much more. Looking around for some source of comfort, I remembered my mother's psalter.

When I had retrieved it from the puzzle chest, I crawled back into bed holding the small book. Cupping it in the palm of my hand, I spread my fingers and let it fall open as it would. My eyes alit on the delicately inscribed words:

The Lord is the keeper of little ones: I was little and He delivered me.
Turn, O my soul, into thy rest: for the Lord hath been bountiful to thee.
For He hath delivered my soul from death: my eyes from tears, my feet from falling.
I will please the Lord in the land of the living.

Abruptly, I slammed the psalter shut; heedless of what damage I might do to it. Hot tears trickled down my face. How cruel the promise of those words. I was little and he did not deliver me. I was still falling, far from the land of the living. There was nothing and nowhere for me to catch onto.

Except the memory of the mother who had hidden me and turned to face the darkness by herself.

My throat was thick and my eyes burned as I slowly opened the psalter again. Though I could barely see at first, I turned each page with care, my fingers lingering where she had touched as though I might feel what she had felt—her courage, her joy . . . her love.

I don't remember falling asleep, but I must have done so because the nightmare came. I was behind the wall, peering out through the small hole in it. It was a game, my mother had said. There was no reason to be afraid. Her words echoed in my ears.

"Don't move, sweetheart, and don't make a sound until I get you out."

Three men came into the room. They all seemed very large, much taller and broader than my mother. One wore a brown felt hat pulled low over his brow. She called him brother.

"Why are you here?" she asked.

"You know why." He punched his right hand in his left and cracked the knuckles. "Where is the child?"

"With friends. Aldo, listen to me. We only want to be left in peace."

He snarled and spit a great wad of phlegm that landed almost on her feet. "You should have thought of that before you married one of them."

"My husband is a Christian!"

"Your husband is a filthy Jew! You have brought shame on

us all! Father drinks all day. Mother . . . she just weeps and weeps. We cannot endure this any longer."

"Then they should accept him! We can be a family again!" She held out her hands, pleading. The other two men circled to either side around her. They looked bored.

"A family? You stupid bitch!"

That was a *bad* word! Young as I was, I knew that. Frightened, I forgot what she had told me and opened my mouth.

"Mamma!"

My cry was lost beneath her scream as a knife flashed. My mother fell to her knees, clutching her chest. The knife rose and fell again. The other men were joining in, their own blades drawn. Her brother was shouting, but I could no longer hear. The rush of blood in my ears drowned out all else. Disbelief and horror overwhelmed me.

I had to get away! *Had to.* Away from the wall, away from the terror, and most especially, away from the knowledge that what I was seeing was not the product of a disordered mind but was actually real. I had witnessed my mother's brutal murder and lived for three days trapped with her butchered body. Because of my father's deception—however well meant—I had never been able to speak of it. It had been left to fester inside me, an oozing wound poisoning me from within. The stark truth of that was as terrifying in its own way as the memory itself. Of course, there could be no escape from it, but even so, every instinct I possessed spurred me to flee.

A well of darkness beckoned. I leaped into it, racing away from the hideous scene, running with all my strength. My breath came in gasps, my heart beat frantically, but I ran on and on, heedless of the sharp stones tearing at my feet, of the cold and damp, of the endless night that threatened to swallow me forever. On and on I ran until at last I could run no more. I collapsed and lay still, my arms wrapped around my upturned knees, trying to make myself as small as possible so that I might, at long last, disappear.

"Francesca?"

A man's voice—deep, familiar.

"Francesca, can you hear me?"

Odd question. Why wouldn't I be able to?

Slowly, I opened my eyes to find myself staring at blades of grass directly in front of me, illuminated by the glow of a torch. So close were they that I could make out each separate, glistening drop of dew clinging to them. I stared at them in fascination. If I had the capacity to move, I had no desire to do so.

Strong arms lifted me. I was wrapped in a cloak, held against a broad chest, carried.

"Cesare?" My voice came out as no more than a croak. A flicker of fear stirred in me. What had happened?

"Hush," he said and walked on, up a flight of steps, down a hallway, past stone-faced guards, into rooms I recognized as his own.

I winced as he sat me down on the side of the bed. My feet throbbed, and the rest of me was stiff and aching. I looked up to find him standing over me. His Eminence, thankfully not in his crimson clerical regalia but casually dressed in a loose shirt and trousers, stared back. He looked at once displeased and worried.

Honest confusion drove me to ask, "What has happened?"

"You will have to tell me, for I have no idea." Without waiting for a reply, he gestured to his valet. That hapless fellow, who I only just then realized was hovering in the background, was holding out a silver tray. Cesare put a goblet in my hand and closed my fingers around it.

"Drink," he ordered.

Vaguely, I remembered wanting a drink. Or several. Perhaps I had gotten drunk. My head hurt, but not with the deep, resonate throb of a serious hangover.

I started to sip the brandy, than thought better of it and took a long swallow. Though the liquid burned going down, it also revived me. Belatedly, I became aware that I was wearing only Cesare's cloak and a nightgown. My feet were bare. They were also cut, bloody, and dirty.

Slowly, I said, "I don't understand. What happened?"

"I came to your rooms an hour ago. I assumed you would be asleep, but there was no sign of you. Fortunately, you had been seen by several of the guards. They were able to point me in the right direction."

"Where?"

"Running, as one said, 'as though pursued by demons.'" Before I could respond, he added, "Don't worry, they won't say anything."

I hadn't thought of that, caught as I was by the sudden return of memory. The nightmare . . . my struggle to escape . . .

"They should have stopped you," Cesare went on. "For their failure, they are being posted elsewhere."

I didn't inquire as to where the men were going, there being so many unpleasant possibilities. Instead, I concentrated on the problem at hand: namely, reassuring Cesare that I was not entirely mad. That was complicated by the fact that I was not at all certain of that.

"This must look very odd to you," I began.

"Let me see your feet."

"I can take care of—"

"Damn it, Francesca, do as I say!"

Reluctant to anger him further, I obeyed. At once, Cesare seized my feet in his hands and looked at them carefully.

"You couldn't possibly have done this much damage going only so far as the garden."

"Is that where you found me?"

He nodded. "Do you remember where else you went?"

I shook my head. "I only know that I had the nightmare and I had to run. This has never happened before." The tremor in my hand made it difficult for me to raise the goblet again but I managed and downed the rest of the brandy.

"I have heard of people walking in their sleep," Cesare said.

"I wasn't walking; I was running."

"To where?"

"I have no idea."

He made a sound of dismay—or was it disgust?—and let go of me. Turning to the valet, he said, "Bring water, soap, and bandages. Then go to Donna Francesca's quarters and find her some clean clothes." The man was about to obey when Cesare held up a hand, stopping him. To me, he said, "Where is your knife?"

"My knife?" I truly was bewildered. The circumstances were worrisome to be sure, but Cesare seemed more upset than was justified, and his mind appeared to be darting about in odd directions.

"The knife I gave you," he said. "The one you have used on more than one occasion. Where is it?"

I didn't know, but I could guess. "Under my pillow." Where I always kept it at night, as he had reason to know.

"Bring that as well," Cesare ordered the valet, who hastened off with an understandable look of apprehension.

"Why this interest in my knife?" I asked when he was gone. As I spoke, I swung my legs onto the bed in the vain search for a more comfortable position. The brandy helped, but the more aware I became, the more I hurt from head to toe.

Cesare sighed and slumped into a nearby chair. Looking at me, he said, "One of the Spaniards has been murdered."

My breath left me in a rush. "Not Herrera?"

"No, thank God. It was a servant sent into town to fetch some whores. When he didn't return, a guard went to find him. He'd been stabbed to death."

Shock roared through me. I fumbled for words. "Why? Who?"

"That's what everyone is going to want to know." With another sigh, he added, "Unfortunately, you picked a bad time for whatever it is that happened to you."

Darkness swirled at the edge of my mind. Cesare and I shared a bed on occasion, but—far more important from my perspective—we also shared a bond of common experience and outlook. Alone among almost everyone in the world, he knew me. Or so I had believed.

"You think that I—?"

He waved a hand dismissively. "Given the hatred toward the Spaniards here and the growing animosity to Il Papa, any number of people could have killed the man. But you can be sure they can all account for their whereabouts, truthfully or not. All except you. If this escapade of yours—running about in the middle of the night like a madwoman—becomes known, you will be suspected. Only too many people will jump at the chance to blame you, starting with Herrera himself."

I sighed and held out my empty goblet. Cesare was right, of course. The Spanish servant's death put me at serious risk and would do so unless I could discover who really had killed him. "Is there any indication at all of who did do it?"

Pouring brandy for us both, Cesare shook his head. "You won't be surprised that no witnesses have come forward. That being the case and given the mood in the town, we may never know."

He sat down beside me on the bed, swirled his drink and said, "Francesca, we need you—my father, Lucrezia, and I. *La famiglia* needs you. If something is wrong—"

Perhaps the brandy was to blame, but before I could stop myself, I laughed. Did he truly not see me as I was? Dirty, disheveled, with bloody feet, having been driven into a frenzy by a nightmare? Did he imagine that there was anything remotely *right* with me? Or did he simply not want to admit what seemed increasingly evident, that I was descending further and further into madness, from which I might never be able to emerge?

"You mean more than usual?" I asked. "Be honest, Cesare; neither of us has ever pretended that I'm like other people."

With a sublime lack of concern that appeared to be completely genuine, he shrugged. "If you were, you wouldn't be of any use to the family, and you certainly wouldn't be as interesting to me as you are."

Like all the Borgias, Cesare saw the world in the mirror of his own desires. If something suited him, it was good, regardless of how it might discomfort anyone else.

"Oh, well, that makes it all worthwhile."

He cast me a chiding glance. "Francesca . . . It's not that I don't care about what's happening with you, whatever that is. It's just that we have to be realistic. If you are not up to the task of protecting my father—"

"You'll what? Find another poisoner who is more capable? It's too late. The assassin is already here, in Viterbo. Besides, threatening me with losing my position to some imaginary poisoner who will do my job better than I can is pointless. All it does is make me think about what I could be doing if you Borgias had no part in my life."

It was not the first time I had thought of that. Several months before, after sacrificing an opportunity to kill my father's murderer in order to protect *la famiglia,* I had threatened to leave Borgia's employ. In the end, I stayed because I had no other access to the power I needed in order to avenge my father's murder.

Apparently, Cesare had also been considering an alternative life for me and had come to his own conclusions about what it would involve.

"You'd be married to Pocco," he said.

I sputtered, all but choking on the brandy. "What?"

"You know, that glassmaker, Pocco."

"Rocco." That Cesare would think of him was a shock, but perhaps it should not have been. For all his worldly nature, His Eminence had a gift for seeing into men's souls—and women's.

Cesare shrugged. "You'd be married to him."

"I am not suited to marriage." I hoped to put a quick end to that particular topic, but Cesare had other ideas.

"But you would be, if you were different. That's what you're saying, isn't it? You could have had an entirely different life."

"That I do not is not because of you or your father." To the contrary, thanks to Mother Benedette, I knew better than ever what forces had shaped me. I was the product of murderous evil made even more powerful by a well-meant but flawed effort to deny its existence. Only by facing it starkly could I have any hope of ever defeating it.

He set down his glass and ran both his hands from my knees to my poor battered feet. "You would do better to accept yourself as you are. Forget everything else."

Forget. Is any possibility more enticing . . . or more terrifying? No consequences for anything we do or for what is done to us. No festering pain. But also no promise of a future, no pretense that anything extends beyond the next breath.

"It's not that simple."

"Isn't it?" He stroked a warm hand upward along my thigh. "You've seen someone tortured, haven't you?"

A sudden flash of memory: the cell beneath the palazzo on the Corso. Borgia was in his final months as a mere cardinal, before his apotheosis to pope. One of the men responsible for my father's death was in his custody. A drone, no more; not the man who had ordered the crime. A flash of the knife . . . not the one I had now but the one pressed into my hands by Borgia himself.

"Kill him," he said.

I acted out of the urge to be merciful as much as I did from hate. The twin sides of human nature, so at odds with each other, so intertwined.

"Why torture yourself?" Cesare asked. "What is the point?"

"I . . ." What could I say? How could I explain what drove me? "All this has to have some purpose."

He laughed. The prince of the Church, the future pope, was amused by my stab at faith.

"What do you think, that somehow you can balance the scales? Your father's death for the death of the one who killed him? The cosmos can be evened out, maintained in order?"

The valet returned just then with a basin of water, sparing me the need to reply. That was fortunate as I had no idea how to answer. Cesare had given voice to an inchoate yearning I had not even known I possessed but which when presented with it, I could not deny. The cosmos in balance, predictable. Safe.

For all the disorder of my mind, even I knew the unattainable when I encountered it.

Cesare cupped my feet in his warm, roughened palms. Despite my feeble effort at protest, he insisted on washing away the blood and dirt inflicted by my mad flight.

As he did so, he said, "I do care about you. I know you think that I don't, that I'm not capable of caring about anyone other than myself. Everything would be much easier if you were right, but you aren't."

"Cesare . . ."

His gaze held mine. "Trust me."

God help me, I wanted to. My very soul yearned to yield to him, to put my fate in his hands and surrender all responsibility for what was to come. But I could not. The memory of my butchered mother—she who had followed her heart—stopped me.

"Trust me," I said instead and reached for him.

The valet came back. Finding us preoccupied, he withdrew quickly, but he left what Cesare had charged him to recover from my quarters. Later, in the gray light of early dawn, the prince of Holy Mother Church stood naked beside the bed and turned my knife over in his hands, examining it.

"Clean," he said.

I smiled to hide my own relief, but questions remained: Where had I gone in my frenzy? What had I done?

"Did you doubt it?" I asked.

He bent a knee on the bed and stroked my cheek. "Of course not."

I knew he lied, but it didn't matter. Cesare had urged me

to accept myself, and I knew that I had no other choice. I was as I was, God help me. My only hope lay in confronting what had made me—and destroying it.

The knife, unstained for now, could not long remain so.

16

It's a sad day," David said, "when a jester with a hat full of Jew jokes can't get a laugh out of a drunken Spaniard."

"Sad indeed," I agreed.

We were in the kitchens, where I had gone out of a sense of duty and because I knew that if I did not eat something, I would be sick. The realization of how fragile my mind had become terrified me. I feared even to breathe lest I shatter into pieces. For the first time, I understood how powerful the instinct to hide could be and why, as a child, I had not been able to resist it.

David was ladling porridge into bowls for both of us. Although preparations for the midday meal were already under way, everyone from the most exalted *maestro di cucina* to the humblest spit boy had discovered a sudden need to be elsewhere the moment I appeared. Unpleasant as that was, it gave David and me a chance to talk alone.

"Herrera is baying for your blood," David said as we took our seats at one of the long wooden tables. "He is convinced that you killed his servant."

I winced. Although the evidence suggested that I was not responsible, the fact that I had no memory of the hours I had lost troubled me deeply.

"Does he say why I would do such a thing?"

He hesitated but finally said, "There's a rumor going around that you were seen last night in a state that some take as proof that you are possessed by demons."

So much for Cesare's belief that he had banished the witnesses before they could talk.

"I see."

"Are you all right?"

"I'm fine." Lying to friends was becoming a habit, but even if I had been willing to tell him the truth, I saw no benefit to distressing him. "Who do you think did kill the servant?"

"I have no idea. Given the mood in the town, it could have been anyone."

I swallowed a little of the porridge and looked at him. "Was it you?"

There was a time for discretion, but this was not it. Matters were coming to a head. I had to know where I stood.

David lowered his spoon and stared at me. "You're not serious?"

"Cesare has a theory. He thinks you may believe that

Borgia's papacy is more likely to survive if he makes peace with his enemies. But Il Papa won't do that as long as he has the support of Spain. As Herrera is Their Most Catholic Majesties' beloved nephew, killing him would not only destroy the alliance, it would also be some measure of revenge for the suffering they have caused your people."

"Cesare thought of that? Does he always seek such convoluted explanations for events?"

"He has a fondness for intrigue," I admitted. "That doesn't mean he's wrong."

David sat back a little and looked at me. A faint smile played at the corners of his mouth. "Well, then . . . let's say I am the assassin. Why would I kill the servant?"

"Perhaps he found out something about you that he shouldn't have?"

"Perhaps, but why haven't I struck at Herrera already?"

"There hasn't been an opportunity? You yourself said that his men are well trained and capable."

"When they aren't listening to their master rant about you, they find me quite amusing. I could slit Herrera's throat and probably several others before they realized what was happening."

"Then you're waiting for something."

His smile broadened. "I'm starting to enjoy this. What am I waiting for?"

I knew David too well to be deterred by his seeming unwillingness to take me seriously. He had not survived so long as a fighter for his people without the ability to conceal his true thoughts and motives, even from those most determined to discover them.

"You said yourself that if the alliance were shattered, Borgia's enemies would move at once to destroy him. There wouldn't be any time for him to reconcile with them . . . unless that process was already under way."

"Is it?"

"Not that I know of, but I wouldn't put anything past Il Papa. He could pretend to be interested in a reconciliation in order to force the Spanish to release Juan. But if circumstances changed . . ."

"If someone happened to kill Herrera?"

I nodded. "His hand would be forced. He would have to make the reconciliation real."

"Go on. You've almost convinced me that I am the assassin."

I admit to being a little hurt. We were friends, yet he seemed oblivious to the danger confronting me.

"It's not a joking matter, David. Under the present circumstances, if Herrera is killed, I'm likely to be the one who's blamed."

Abruptly, his smile vanished. "You're referring to the fact that several dozen people saw you put a knife to his throat?"

"Among other reasons. In that event, His Holiness would no longer have the benefit of my services." That was as close as I would come to acknowledging that Herrera's fate and my own were now inextricably linked. If he died, in all likelihood so would I.

David nodded slowly. "Destroy the alliance *and* strip Borgia of the protection you afford him. You're right; there's nothing to laugh about."

"I'm glad you understand that. If you are the assassin, I hope you realize this means that your plan is fatally flawed. The moment I'm taken off the board, there is a very real risk that Borgia's enemies will strike. There will be no chance for any reconciliation."

I rose to go. "On the other hand, if you aren't the assassin, I hope you'll help me find out who is."

David sighed. "I'll dust off the Jew jokes and try again." More seriously, he said, "But Francesca, you have to realize what could really be happening here. Cesare has every reason to loathe Juan. He'd like nothing better than for him to rot in a Spanish prison. And if the alliance crumbles, His Holiness will need an army fast. Whom do you suppose he will trust to lead it?"

My stomach tightened. He was right, of course, but I should have thought of that myself. And I would have had my mind not been so disordered.

Cesare or David? David or Cesare? Two men I both liked and cared for, one of whom might be set on a course of action that I could not survive.

"You be careful as well," I said. "Whatever your true purpose in being here, the next few days could prove deadly for any of us."

I left him to consider that and went out through the empty kitchens and across the courtyard. Uppermost in my mind was the thought that I had to find out who had killed the servant. But how to accomplish that when almost no one in the palazzo would look me in the eye, much less tell me anything of use?

A shout rang out in the direction of the field behind the palazzo. Through the archways, I glimpsed Vittoro drilling his men. Seeing me, he called for a lieutenant to take over and came to where I stood.

"Are you all right?" he asked at once.

I restrained a sigh. "It was a nightmare, nothing more."

"An inopportune time for that to happen."

"Indeed." Before he could pursue the matter further, I went on. "I have a favor to ask. People in the town will be gossiping about the servant's death, but they will be reluctant to speak to me. If I had a means of encouraging them . . ."

"What do you have in mind?"

"Perhaps Donna Felicia would like some company while she is shopping?"

Vittoro's wife was a plump and cheerful matron, mother to three daughters, grandmother to a growing horde, who had insisted on accompanying her husband to Viterbo. Something about their having been separated quite enough during his career and her unwillingness to tolerate any more such partings.

Nor had she come alone. The entire brood, sons-in-law included, was also in residence, jammed into a little house just beyond the palazzo. I took their presence as evidence of Vittoro's concern about conditions in Rome and the safety of the Holy City should everything go catastrophically amiss.

"You think the good citizens of Viterbo will be more likely to talk to her than to you?" he asked.

I shrugged, acknowledging the obvious. "We both know that people can be uncomfortable around me, even when they don't know who I am." As though they had an instinct for what was outside the norm, and therefore dangerous.

He did not dispute that but said, "You understand that I couldn't agree to her being involved in anything dangerous?"

"A simple shopping trip," I promised. "Nothing more. And remember, a good outcome to all of this is to her benefit as well."

"Very well, then. Just one thing." I waited, knowing that I would have to agree to whatever he was about to say. Vittoro had expressed concern about my visits to Santa Maria della Salute. If he insisted that I tell him what I had been doing there—

"See if you can find some nice mutton shanks, would you? Felicia hasn't made them in weeks, and I've got a craving."

With a quick smile to conceal my relief, I promised that he would not long go shankless. As I had hoped given the hour, Felicia was about to set out for the market when I reached the house. But not before cleaning the dirt from one grandchild's face, helping another into his shoes, and admiring the doll thrust into her hands by yet a third. Her daughters were lining up to go with her, but, seeing me, Felicia waved them back inside.

"There is laundry to be done and mending, and the flagstones in the kitchen need scrubbing," she said.

With varying degrees of disappointment, they obeyed and left us to ourselves. I marveled at Felicia's authority even as I had the sense to respect it.

"I don't mind helping you," she said when I had explained why I wanted to go with her. "But my girls aren't to be involved in anything that is going on, whatever that might be, understood?"

"Of course, absolutely. There's really nothing to be concerned about. This is just a little trip to the market; a bit of gossip, that's all."

She cast me a frankly skeptical glance and thrust a basket into my hands. As we started down the street, she said, "Terrible business, that murder. Who do you think did it?"

"That's the problem: I have no idea. I'm hoping to pick up a whiff or two to point me in the right direction."

"Oh, you'll get more than that. Everyone will have an opinion, most of them useless."

"Then where do we begin?"

Felicia furrowed her brow beneath her neat kerchief, from which wisps of gray-brown hair trailed. She had been pretty in her youth and now she was . . . something more. Wise, vibrant, very much alive. I could understand why Vittoro was so devoted to her.

"The poor soul was killed in the alley behind a butcher shop," she said. "We should start there."

We did, only to discover the place so crowded with the curious—and the butcher himself so intent on basking in his newfound celebrity—that we got nothing of use, neither information nor mutton shanks. Fortunately, Viterbo was large and prosperous enough to support more than one butcher. The rival establishment, just on the other side of the road, was nearly empty. A ruddy-faced, morose fellow in a blood-splattered leather apron manned the chopping block.

Wielding his cleaver with quick jabs, he produced a quantity of shanks to Donna Felicia's specifications as she complimented him on the freshness of the carcasses dangling on hooks above our heads.

"My husband will thank you," she said. I noticed that in speaking to him, her Roman accent—which some claim to find harsh—had faded, replaced by the softer tones associated with country folk. "There's nothing he likes better than a nice braise of mutton." With a sigh, she added, "I do, too, normally, but I must admit, my appetite isn't what it should be." She leaned a little closer, as though to impart a confidence. "I fear I'm quite undone by the terrible events across the way there. How anyone can still buy their meat where that man was butchered—"

"Oh, they aren't buying," I interjected. "They're just standing around gawking. I daresay the poor fellow who owns that shop is desperate watching his goods spoil."

Cheered by the notion, the rival butcher said, "Shame, isn't it?" *Whack.* "But it was a Spaniard, after all. Can't expect anyone to be too upset about that." *Whack.*

"I suppose not, what with the way they've behaved," Felicia said. "Still, I have to wonder who would take a knife to one of them."

"I can't say." *Whack.*

"You don't think it could be someone from here, do you?" I asked.

"Could be." *Whack.* "Maybe someone from the garrison. But likelier it was one of their own out to stir up trouble." *Whack.*

I didn't dismiss that possibility out of hand, but neither could I conceive of any reason why Herrera and the rest of the Spaniards would want more trouble than they already had. As we left the shop with the shanks tucked into Felicia's basket, I asked her, "What do you make of that?"

She shrugged. "Good mutton at a fair price, but he doesn't know anything about what happened. Don't worry, there are plenty of other shops. Someone's bound to know something."

Buoyed by her confidence, we set out through the market, stopping in succession at a vintner, who claimed the French were to blame because they produced inferior wine and were known to cheat people; at a cheesemonger, who opined as to how the killer was likely a Turk since, as everyone knew, they excelled at close knife work; and finally at a fruit stand, where an anxious young woman hoped the Spaniards would leave and take their demons with them before Viterbo suffered even more serious calamity.

Munching on late pears, we stopped for a brief rest, leaning our rumps against a handy stone wall. "It's almost as though no one wants to know what happened," Felicia said as she wiped juice from her chin.

The same thought had occurred to me, but I thought I knew the reason. "They are afraid." Of Borgia and what he could bring down on them, and of the shifting sands of power beneath their feet that threatened the very foundation of their lives. Where there was fear, there was also often anger . . . and violence.

Felicia tossed the core of a spent pear into the bushes and turned to look at me. "They aren't alone. Vittoro insisted that we come here because he doesn't think Rome is safe right now, and not just because of the floods and the plague. But Viterbo strikes me as a very uncertain refuge. If there is war—"

"We have to hope there won't be."

She raised a brow at once questioning and mocking. "Hope? Is that what I tell my daughters when they worry for their children? They should hope that His Holiness prevails against his enemies, numerous and powerful as they are? What if he does not?"

Then we would all go down to disaster, as Donna Felicia no doubt knew quite well. Not even the smallest and most innocent among us was likely to be spared. I thought of the little granddaughter with her doll and sighed.

"It would help," I said, "if I could discover who killed the Spanish servant."

"Why? How does he figure into all of this?"

"I don't know," I admitted. "But if I can find that out, I may be able to protect Borgia better, which is to say, protect all of us."

She plucked a handful of sunflower seeds from her pouch and offered them to me. I took several, separating the shells between my teeth. Together, we spit.

"Back to business, then," she said.

We returned to the market. The day wore on as we visited

a seemingly endless array of shops and stalls—how did Viterbo possess so many?—and still we learned nothing of use. My basket grew heavy with figs, dates, pomegranates, olive oil, bunches of dried herbs, bags of pearl barley and peppercorns, heads of kale and cabbage, and all manner of other items that Felicia considered necessary to the comfort and well-being of her family. My injured feet hurt, my back ached, and as for my patience . . . it had just about expired when my companion remembered that we had yet to purchase fish.

"A nice bit of cod," she said, giving every appearance of being as fresh and energetic as when we had started out. I admired her stamina even as I despaired of sharing it. "And perhaps some anchovies," she added.

I nodded wearily. We waited beside a stall as a pair of Viterbo's housewives rattled on about the murder in between haggling over herring. When they completed their business and were gone, Felicia said, "Silly creatures. Not a notion in their head about what really happened, wouldn't you say?"

The fishwife—an old woman with a nose full of broken veins and one cloudy eye—shrugged. Even so, she looked pleased to be asked her opinion.

"Brutal, it was," she said, smacking her lips. "Absolutely brutal. He was stabbed through and through, with gore running everywhere. That's what I hear."

Felicia shook her head in appreciative dismay. "Who could have done such a terrible thing?"

"A whore from the Priory, so the wind says."

As all the world knows, brothels are commonly found on Church property—where they provide a tidy source of revenue for our Holy Mother's faithful servants. That being the case, the name did not surprise me. Moreover, the possibility made sense. Cesare had said that the servant was sent to fetch whores for the Spaniards. Perhaps that was actually true.

"Do you have any idea why a whore would have killed him?" I asked.

The old woman hesitated until Felicia added, "Come, now. My friend and I aren't innocent girls to take offense at anything you say."

"Well, then . . . might be she didn't like how the Spaniards treated her. Odd creatures, aren't they? Who knows what they get up to?"

"Indeed," I murmured.

The fishwife leaned a little closer, filling the air with the aroma of cod, brine, and rotting entrails. "They shouldn't even be here," she hissed. "Wouldn't be if it weren't for a certain Spanish someone."

A moment passed before I realized that she meant Borgia, whose family hailed from Valencia, in Spain. The reminder of how much His Holiness was disliked in Viterbo, and what the consequences of that could be, sent a shiver through me.

"A whore," Felicia said thoughtfully as we left with enough cod for a month of Fridays, not to mention what had to be far too many anchovies. "I suppose that's possible."

I set aside my concerns about the mood in the town for the moment, and said, "It's not that easy for a woman to kill a man, except with poison, of course. To be successful with a knife would require training." Such as Cesare had so thoughtfully provided for me. But then I also had a certain natural talent for the weapon, unfortunately.

"Maybe she took him by surprise," Felicia suggested, "or just got lucky."

"Perhaps. . . ."

"We can keep looking," she offered.

I intended to do just that, but I didn't think I should involve her any further. She had already extended herself more than I had any right to ask.

"I'm sure your daughters are wondering what has become of you. Besides, can we really carry anything more?"

With a laugh, she admitted that we probably could not. Together, we trundled up the hill lugging our overladen baskets. Outside the small house, Felicia bid me farewell, but not before inviting me to dinner.

"Come for the mutton shanks; they really are good. We eat earlier than His Holiness, so you can be back before he dines."

For a moment, I was unsure what to do. I spent so little time in normal company that I wasn't entirely certain of how to comport myself. But Felicia's kindness and my friendship with Vittoro made refusing impossible.

"I'll bring wine," I said. "His Holiness favors a hearty Tuscan Sangiovese that is excellent with mutton."

"We'll drink to his health with it," Felicia said.

She would, I knew, also pour a splash of the wine on the floor in an offering . . . not to the gods of old, for only the very powerful can flirt with heresy. To some saint or other, whomever Felicia favored, who might favor us in turn. If nothing else, it would give her some comfort to do so.

There was little enough of that to be had in Viterbo, where with each passing moment the mood seemed to darken further. Or perhaps it was my own spleen that I was sensing. I pushed the thought aside. Before I could sit down to Felicia's good mutton, much remained to be done.

17

I returned to my rooms long enough to apply a salve to my feet. The damage to them was not extensive, but it did make me wonder again where I had gone in my mad flight. The floors throughout the palazzo were far too smooth to have inflicted any such injury. Besides, if I had remained inside, far more than a mere handful of guards would have seen me.

Clearly, I had gone outside, but where? Back in the corridor, I looked in either direction. The wing of the palazzo where I was housed contained numerous other guest apartments, but mine was set a little apart on a corner. Just beyond it, a door led to a curving stone staircase that gave out onto a lane running off the piazza.

If I had gone down those stairs the night before, they held no sense of familiarity. Nor did the scene that greeted me when I stepped out onto the lane. A cat, drowsing in the afternoon sunlight, raised her head, blinked at me, and flicked her tail. Pigeons cooing in the eaves above fell silent. Small, smoothly rounded cobblestones covered the ground. I could not possibly have hurt myself on them.

At the far end of the lane the ground was rougher, with some of the paving stones broken in places, leaving sharp edges. In my distress, had I crossed the square to the church where I had been meeting with Mother Benedette? Again, no memory stirred.

I turned completely around, looking in every possible direction, but no solution presented itself. I had left the palazzo, that much seemed certain, and I had returned at least as far as the garden. It was on the opposite side of the palace from the square, near the courtyard behind the roofless loggia that looked out over the steep Faul valley.

Had I gone to the crumbling arena where I had watched Cesare duel with Herrera? The sandy ground there could not account for the condition of my feet. But looking out across the fallen tiers of seats where ancient Romans had gathered to watch gladiatorial contests, I noticed the thick covering of *pino* growing just beyond, along the steep slope leading down into the valley. The low, thorny bushes were a perfect hiding place for animals small enough to find shelter within their prickly defenses. But for anyone unfortunate enough to step on them barefoot . . .

The memory of needles driving into my feet made me gasp. Was it pain that had stopped me from plunging into the abyss, driving me back instead to the safety of the garden? If so, I had to be grateful for it.

A flattening of the ground nearby caught my eye. When I peered closer, I realized that a narrow path led down through the bushes along the slope and around the side of the palazzo. That must be how I had reached it, but what drove me to do so? Where had I imagined I was going?

Nowhere. I had been running not to but from. A shadowy figure had pursued me. A robed being no less terrifying than Death itself. Even in bright sunlight, my breath caught at the memory. I had fled along the path leading up the slope, straying from it often enough to catch my feet in the thorn bushes. And I had hidden. There, in the shadowed cleft that I had glimpsed for the first time when I sought out Cesare the day I arrived in Viterbo and forgotten until the moment when I desperately sought refuge. Like so many of the surrounding hills, the slope leading to the valley was riddled with small caves, most only large enough to hold a single person. In one I had sought to conceal myself. The ground, when I examined it, was still tamped down by the body, my own, that had lain there. When the moment availed itself, I had fled into the garden, where Cesare had found me. But something was left behind.

I bent closer, following the glint of sunlight reaching into the obscurity of the cave and reflecting off . . . steel. A knife. Not unlike my own but slightly smaller. There were dark stains on it.

I raised the knife in my hand and inhaled deeply.

The copper tang of blood rose above the deeper note of steel. So close that I could taste them, I stared at the scattered splotches along the blade. *Absolutely brutal. He was stabbed through and through, with gore running everywhere.*

The condition of the knife supported what the fishwife had heard. It had stabbed deeply and repeatedly as it drained the life from the Spaniard and left him an empty husk lying under a cold night sky.

I staggered back, still grasping the knife, and with a quick glance toward the palazzo, shoved the blade into the pouch beneath my skirts. If the knife was found . . . if I was associated with it . . .

I walked, as calmly as I could manage, back toward the palazzo, across the loggia, through the great hall, and out the main entrance. In the piazza, I thought quickly. I had to find the whore. Please God, she existed, in which case I was perfectly willing to agree that she had ample good reason for whatever she had done and should be given the liberty of Viterbo as reward, just so long as I could be sure that I was not responsible.

Delay being out of the question, I slipped away from the palazzo again and returned to the town. Following the main course down toward the gates, I shortly found the Priory, a solid timber and wattle building a stone's throw from them. Three-storied, with iron grilles over the windows, it announced its purpose with the image of a mermaid on the sign above the door.

A very large, red-faced man with a single brow and a stoic manner occupied the entrance. He glanced up as I appeared, looked me up and down, and said, "It's Thursday."

"So it is. How clever of you to know."

"No hiring on Thursday. Come back on Saturday. In the morning."

Being taken for an out-of-work whore was not remotely as offensive as being called a demon-possessed spawn of Satan. Keeping that in mind, I said, "Thank you, but I'm not here for employment."

The fellow scrutinized me again, reassessing my economic standing and, apparently, my proclivities. "Your pardon, I'm sure. You want the Brindle Mare, around the corner. They're more . . . versatile in their clientele." I must have looked puzzled, for he felt called upon to explain. "We just run to the usual. Man-woman, you know."

I had some idea, but I wanted to be sure. "There aren't actually any horses at the Brindle Mare, are there?"

"Lord, no. If that's what you're after, you've got to go to the Cote. It's on the road west out of town. Big place; you can't miss it."

And here I had been thinking of Viterbo as a provincial backwater when in fact it had entertainment options to rival Rome's.

"I'm actually just here to talk to the proprietor."

The single brow furrowed. "What about?"

"I work for His Holiness."

At once, the fellow brightened. Borgia might not be popular in the town as a whole, but in certain quarters he could still prompt a smile.

"We've been wondering when we'd hear from him. Come in, then."

Just beyond the door of the brothel, I stepped into a large room hung with middling-good tapestries and furnished with an assortment of Roman-style couches upon which I assumed customers reclined to assess the goods. At that hour, the area was deserted. I watched dust motes dance in sunbeams filtering through the slanting shutters until a motion on the stairs diverted me.

The person who descended from above appeared to be neither male nor female, but was possibly both. About the size of a ten-year-old child but with the face of an ancient, he—or she—wore a red velvet robe draped over a plump form and carried a small, entirely hairless dog with large ears and protruding eyes. I stared at the animal in fascination. It surely had to be one of the ugliest things I had ever seen, yet at the same time, it was oddly engaging.

A polite cough recalled my attention. "I am Erato. And you are . . . ?"

"My name is Francesca Giordano." I waited, but not long. Not long at all.

Erato stiffened. He . . . she . . . descended the remaining steps, stopped in front of me, and forced a smile. "I have heard of you."

"Good; that makes things simpler. You are the proprietor here?"

"I am. We would, of course, be delighted to serve His Holiness."

"And so you will. At the moment, he requires information; nothing more, and not to your harm. Whatever I learn, I will gladly keep to myself."

The dog curled back its lips to expose pointed teeth. It emitted a long, low snarl.

"Even so," Erato said, "I doubt—"

"A Spaniard died in the town last night. Rumor has it one of your girls killed him."

"A lie! Put out by my competitors."

The dog barked. Flecks of foam dotted its chin.

"How vile of them," I replied. "No doubt you are anxious to clear your name."

Erato sighed. She—I decided to think of her as female, if merely for convenience—patted the dog and gestured toward a small room off the reception area. "I don't really have any choice, do I? This is a dreadful business."

Unsure whether she meant prostitution in general or the murder in particular, I followed her into the cozily furnished chamber. She gestured me into a chair on the opposite side of a small desk. After placing the dog on a tasseled cushion nearby, she said, "None of my girls was involved. I am absolutely certain of that."

"Yes," I agreed, "I know you are. I saw the bars on the windows."

"Grilles," Erato corrected. "They are ornamental."

"My mistake. I assumed they were there to assure that no one could leave without your knowledge."

Erato sat back in her chair and observed me closely. After a moment, she said, "May I offer you a liqueur? I have a very nice lemon infusion newly arrived from Sorrento."

Generally, I tried not to mix business and drinking, but under the circumstances I thought it would be impolitic to refuse.

"That sounds delightful, thank you."

A servant appeared at the ringing of a bell, coming so quickly as to suggest that he had been hovering just on the other side of the door. Instructions were given and the drinks were swiftly produced, presented in small glass goblets.

I took an appreciative sip. The presence of lemons was very strong, but underneath I caught hints of pepper and . . . bay leaf?

"That's excellent," Erato said when I hazarded a guess. "You have a sensitive palate."

"Useful in my line of work. So . . . your girls were all here last night? None of them was called away elsewhere?"

"With the roads flooded to the north, the town is quite full. We've been unusually busy. I couldn't have let anyone go even if there had been a reason to do so."

"The Spaniards didn't want anyone from here sent up to the palazzo?"

"Not last night, which was just as well."

I took another sip and thought of the orchards of lemon trees south of Rome. When the wind blows from the right direction, their fragrance overwhelms the city. Romans claim to enjoy these sudden invasions from the countryside, but that isn't true. There is always great relief when the smell abates, replaced by the familiar, well-loved stench of the Tiber.

"You don't want the Spaniards' business?" I asked.

"Their coin is as good as anyone else's."

"But—"

Erato shrugged. She selected a wafer from a small silver plate and fed it to the dog, who crunched it noisily. "They drink too much. Half the time, my girls end up sitting around doing nothing."

"And?"

"Then they complain when other clients expect more of them."

I sipped a little more of the liqueur and nodded. "That must make it difficult for you."

The dog licked Erato's fingers assiduously. She allowed it for a moment or two, then withdrew her hand.

"Every business has its challenges," she said. "Our clients expect a certain standard of service. Not every girl is up to that."

"What happens to a girl who can't take the pace or just isn't up to your standards? Where does she go when she leaves here?"

A deep, rich chuckle emerged from within the folds of red velvet. "Why, she marries her favorite client, of course, the fellow who has been coming to see her for months, often paying her for no more than conversation and bringing her lovely gifts. She goes off with him to a new town where no one knows her and begins a new life as a respectable housewife."

Such were the dreams of whores. Not all of them unfulfilled, if rumor is to be believed. Supposedly the lineages of most of the great families include—But I digress.

"No, seriously, where does she go?"

"Oh, well, if we must be serious . . . I usually recommend Ostia. The port is thriving, and a whore who would be considered used up here can still earn a living there. Otherwise, she ends up on the street, plying her trade in back alleys."

"Such as the one where the Spaniard was killed?"

"What are you suggesting?"

"You know how rumors are. They start from a little seed. A girl who used to work here and is now on the streets saw something last night. She told someone. That person told someone else, and so on. Somewhere along the line, someone remembered that the girl used to be here at the Priory. The story sounds better if she is still here. Better still if what she saw becomes what she did. And now you have a problem."

"Which I can solve by—"

"Give me her name and tell me where I can find her."

Erato shook her head. "There have been many girls—"

"One who didn't take your advice but instead stayed here in Viterbo. Maybe she had a reason to do so. A child, perhaps?"

It was a stab in the dark, but it found its mark. Erato shook her head in exasperation. "She would have been better off if she had left. The child died. So many of them do."

"But she still stayed?"

"I suppose she didn't see much point in leaving after that."

"She—?"

"Magdalene. A professional name, of course. I thought she had great promise, but she proved to be a disappointment. The last I heard, she works the alleys, when she isn't too drunk to stand up."

"Where can I find her?"

Erato wrinkled her nose in distaste. "There is a crib off Tanners Lane. The last refuge of the down-and-out. You could look there."

Ideally, the tanning of animal hides should be done well

away from any place of general habitation. Unfortunately, the process requires urine, which is most easily collected from humans. Viterbo was large enough to supply that in sufficient quantity to attract a small but apparently thriving tanning industry. It was perched just beyond the town walls, next to a noxious little stream clogged with the sludge of cast-off waste.

The sensible thing would have been to go back to the palazzo, find Vittoro, and request an escort to accompany me. But good sense had never been high among my attributes. Added to that was the fact that I had a keen and ever-growing conviction that time was running out.

I had no difficulty finding Tanners Lane just on the other side of the town walls; the smell led me to it unerringly. Breathing as shallowly as possible, I approached the ramshackle wooden building that appeared to have been added on to in fits and starts with no thought to structural integrity. A good wind could have knocked it over. A cluster of women—all looking well past their prime but likely little older than I was—were seated outside. They wore a motley collection of rags over their thin bodies. Most stared off into space, seemingly aware of nothing. But one thrust out a scrawny arm in supplication. "Alms, donna? Spare a penny for a poor girl down on her luck? The saints will bless you."

I knew she was asking for no more than one of the debased coins—more copper than silver—that could be found everywhere. But the penny I drew from my pouch was pure silver, as she quickly determined by rubbing it between her fingers. When her skin failed to turn black, she stared at me suspiciously.

"What do you want, donna?"

"I'm looking for Magdalene."

She stretched her mouth wide in a parody of a grin. There were sores on the inside of her lips that appeared to be cracked and bleeding. "We're all Magdalene here, donna; or didn't you know that?"

"I'm looking for a girl who used to work at the Priory. She had a child who died. Help me find her and you'll have another of those."

The temptation was clearly irresistible, meaning as it did access to food, shelter, drink, and whatever else she needed to make life bearable, but still she hesitated. "What sort of lady comes to a place like this?"

"The kind you don't want to anger."

It was cruel, not unlike kicking a sick dog. But it had the desired effect. The girl stumbled to her feet and, gripping the silver penny, led me into the building. At once, I nearly gagged. As vile as the stench was outside, it was even worse within. Beneath a ceiling so low that I almost had to stoop, dozens of stalls ran off in every direction. Some were equipped with tattered curtains to provide a semblance of privacy, but most were open to all eyes. Instead of bedding, filthy straw covered the floor. All the windows were sealed over, plunging the place into unrelenting gloom and concentrating the stench of unwashed bodies, waste, and despair. Thin, pale-faced men and women alike peered dazedly at us or merely stared off into space as though they had fled all connection with the world. Some were racked by coughs, but others appeared too weak to do anything but moan. Others sat hunched over, rocking back and forth and crooning to themselves, oblivious to everything going on around them.

If it was possible for human beings to dwell in greater degradation, I could not imagine how. The Church was supposed to care for such pitiable creatures, but here in Viterbo, seat of popes, no provision had been made for them. They were left to live—and die—without regard for their most basic dignity or the condition of their souls.

I told myself that I could not afford to care, the matters concerning me being too grave to allow for any distraction. Yet I could not deny the dismay that filled me as I plunged deeper into what might as well have been one of the circles of Hell. Surely, if Dante had ever visited such a place, he would have had no trouble recognizing what it was.

Deep within the building, my guide stopped and pointed. Peering through the gloom, I could just make out a huddled form crouched against a wall.

"Wait for me," I said, doubting that I could find my way out. She nodded and withdrew, sliding down onto her haunches.

Bending low, I stepped into the stall. "Magdalene?"

When no response came, I inched a little closer. Her hair was so dirty and matted that I could not make out its color. Her cheeks were sunken, and I could see the telltale sores near her mouth. Not six months before, the great Cristoforo Colombo had returned from his voyage to what he still claimed were the Indies but which cooler heads realized was Novus Orbis, the New World. He brought back several natives of strikingly handsome appearance, a very small quantity of gold, a strange plant called tobacco, and a disease. One of his subcaptains, Pinzón of *La Pinta,* came ashore covered in strange pustules and consumed by fever. Nor was he alone; several other men who had sailed with the great discoverer were similarly stricken. Very shortly, the same symptoms appeared among the whores of Barcelona, the city to which many returning crew members had gone. Since then, the illness had spread with frightening speed, carried from town to town by sailors, merchants, and pilgrims. Some of its victims were able to survive the sickness, but among the poor and hungry, it cut like Death's own scythe. Apparently, it had reached Viterbo.

"I want to help you," I said, bending closer. That was true, even though my help came at a price. I needed for her to tell me what had happened in the alley behind the butcher's shop. But as I moved nearer, I began to doubt that she would be able to do so.

Her eyes were open but glassy and unblinking. She stank of rotgut, the refuge of those too poor to afford even grain alcohol, and often poisonous. It was known to induce periods of frozen absence during which the imbiber seemed completely removed from the world. That, of course, was the whole point of drinking it. However, just as I debated what to do, the pitiful creature stirred. Becoming aware of my presence, she flinched and tried to draw away.

"Easy," I said quickly. "I won't hurt you. I just want to talk." Behind my words was relief that, so far at least, she gave no sign of recognizing me. If she really had been in the alley when the Spaniard was killed, I had to hope that meant I had not been there as well.

A gurgling noise rose from her throat. Her lips moved, but stiffly. I leaned closer in an effort to hear what she was mumbling. ". . . pray for us sinners." She swallowed with difficulty and continued. "Hail Mary, full of grace, the Lord . . ." Her voice trailed away. She looked confused.

Pity stirred in me. On impulse, I took both her hands in mine. Looking into her eyes, I recited, "Hail Mary, full of grace, the Lord is with thee; blessed art thou among women, and blessed is the fruit of thy womb, Jesus. Holy Mary, Mother of God, pray for us sinners, now and at the hour of our death. Amen."

One of my many secrets is that although I have no gift for prayer, I do on occasion try to pray to Mary. While God the Almighty Father is incomprehensible to me, she seems entirely real and vastly more approachable. I had felt particularly drawn to her ever since I killed the man in the Basilica di Santa Maria several months before. The nave of the basilica is lined with richly carved capitals that, it is said, bear the face of an older Queen of Heaven, the one called Isis, the capitals having been taken from her temple on the nearby Janiculum. Somehow, I conceived the notion that the goddess understood what I had done and perhaps even approved of it.

A deep sigh escaped Magdalene. "Yes," she murmured. "Oh, yes." She was silent for a moment before she said, "I had the sweetest baby boy." A tear trickled down her ashen cheek.

My throat was thick, no doubt because of the foul air. I sat back a little but kept hold of her hands. "I can help you, but you have to tell me what you saw in the alley."

She looked at me as though not entirely sure that I was real. "The alley?"

"Behind the butcher's shop. Were you there last night?"

Slowly, she nodded. Almost at once, a look of terror crossed her face, forcing her into frenzied coherence. "I didn't do it! I swear by all the saints!"

"I don't believe that you did," I said quickly. "But I need to know what you saw."

"Nothing . . . just a man. He had a girl . . . I couldn't see her . . . the shadows . . ."

"What did you see?"

"She . . . thrust something into his side. He fell. By the time I realized he was dead, she was gone."

"Did you see her face?"

"No. . . . I scarcely saw her at all, I swear."

"Did you see a knife?"

"No, no knife, just blood, slow like, seeping into the ground."

A single wound, then; perhaps delivered between the ribs? Done right, there would have been no spurting of blood, only the steady flow the girl was describing. And the knife gone, which lent credence to my fear that it was the same blade I had found where I lay near the thornbushes.

"You're certain that it was a woman?"

"I thought so because they were . . . you know. But there's plenty that like it different. Still, there was something about the way she moved . . ."

A woman or someone pretending to be one? That brought

me no closer to the truth; neither did it exonerate me. I hesitated, debating what to do. As the rumor spread that a girl from the Priory had killed the Spaniard, I would not be the only one looking for Magdalene. Once found by someone else—Herrera, for example—she might be induced to say anything. She might even be encouraged to believe that the woman she saw in the alley was none other than me.

It would have been a simple matter to solve that problem right then and there. Certain substances I always carried with me would have done the job quickly and more or less painlessly. Yet I could not bring myself to kill so blameless a creature, despite the danger she presented.

Slowly, I loosened her hands and rose. Though Rome was hardly the best place to be just then, if I could get her into Sofia's care, she might have a chance. I would have to act quickly, but with luck I could have her out of Viterbo before nightfall.

My guide reappeared as I emerged from the stall. Swiftly, I handed her another penny, then added two more. While she was gaping at them, I asked, "Is there somewhere near here she can be moved to, just temporarily?"

"I don't know—"

"Anywhere she won't be found . . . a shed, perhaps?"

Slowly, the woman nodded. "Perhaps, but—"

"Come, then; help me."

Together, we managed to get Magdalene on her feet and out of the stall. The going was slow and difficult—we had to stop several times to let both women rest—but finally we stepped out into the sunlight beyond the wretched building. The shed was only a short distance away.

"Can you get food for her and bring it here without being noticed?" I asked when we had gotten Magdalene inside.

The woman nodded without great conviction. "I can try. How long—"

"A few hours, no more. If she's found by anyone else, she will be in danger and so will anyone around her. Do you understand?"

"Yes. I will do as you say, donna."

I had to be content with that, but for good measure, I added, "When this is over, you will be well rewarded."

Though she managed a wan smile, I wondered how much she really understood. Not that it mattered; I had no better options. I took my leave, but not before taking off my cloak. It was a small gesture, all I could do at the time; as I draped it around Magdalene, I hoped it would bring her some small comfort. As swiftly as my throbbing feet could manage, I climbed the road to the palazzo once again.

18

It was then midafternoon. I had promised to dine that evening with Vittoro, Felicia, and their brood. If I sent an excuse, I would arouse the good captain's curiosity. The last thing I needed was Vittoro looking too closely at my activities. Accordingly, I went in search of Cesare, finding him, rather to my surprise, in the otherwise deserted chapel.

His Eminence was stretched out on the marble steps leading up to the gilded altar set beneath an elaborately carved stone canopy. He had a bottle of wine in one hand and a volume of Boethius—his *Consolation of Philosophy*—in the other. When I entered, he glanced up.

"Don't tell me you've been shopping all this time?"

Taking a seat beside him, I replied, "Why did I bother to seek the gossip in town when there is so much of it right here?"

"Boredom elicits an unhealthy interest in the lives of

others. Speaking of which . . ." He indicated the volume. "Do you think it's really possible to detach ourselves from misfortune and simply accept hardship while remaining apart from it?"

"Only if you're writing in prison while awaiting execution. What attitude would you expect Boethius to have taken?"

"I suppose. Herrera is insisting that you be put to questioning regarding the death of his servant. He's driving me mad."

"Which is why you are here, hiding from him?"

Cesare did not deny it. To the contrary, he said, "This is the one place I'm sure the beloved nephew of Their Most Catholic Majesties won't set foot. At any rate, was your foray successful?"

"I found a witness who may or may not be reliable. Tell me, how many times was the Spaniard stabbed?"

"Once, between the ribs, a quick in and out."

So Magdalene really had been there. That could be a problem.

"I want to get her out of Viterbo."

"The witness is a woman?"

I nodded. "She believes that the killer is a fellow prostitute. But I am concerned that with a little persuading by the wrong people, she might say something else."

"Pointing to you?"

"It is possible. She is ill, starving, and in the grip of melancholia. All that makes her vulnerable."

He passed me the wine. I took a swallow as he asked, "Where do you wish to take her?"

Handing the bottle back, I replied, "Rome. Do you remember Sofia Montefiore?" It was not the most politic question, given that Sofia had been involved in a plan of mine that led Cesare to believe I was dead and caused him more upset than I had anticipated. He had not yet completely forgiven me for that.

"The Jewish apothecary?" he asked. "Of course I remember her. You think she would take this girl in?"

"Sofia has a kind heart." I did not add that she would also have a sensible appreciation for the need to learn as much as possible about the scourge that I feared afflicted Magdalene.

"What exactly did the girl see?"

"Enough for her to believe that the killer is a woman."

"And you believe her?"

"I do, yes."

"Francesca . . ." He hesitated, and I knew what was coming. I could not even blame him for it. "You still have no idea where you were during the time you were missing?"

Lying on the steep slope beyond the arena where I later found the knife I believed killed the Spaniard. And before then—

"Very little," I replied. "But Magdalene—that is her name—gives no hint of recognizing me."

"You just said she saw very little."

Having my own words thrown back at me was irksome. If he was reconsidering my guilt, I would not trouble him further. But neither would I give up so easily. It was bad enough that I feared for my own sanity. I could not have Cesare do the same.

"What reason would I have to kill the Spaniard?" I countered. "Or, for that matter, why would I have gone down into the town while in the grip of a nightmare? I cut my feet on the thornbushes behind the arena, of that I am certain. But there is no evidence that I went beyond the piazza."

"It's not that I don't believe you," Cesare said too promptly. "The servant's killing really may be nothing more than the work of an angry whore. When do you want to get the girl out of here?"

"Before nightfall. The sooner she is on the road to Rome, the better. Unfortunately, I promised to dine with Vittoro and Felicia."

He shot me a surprised look. We both knew that socializing was not my strong point. "You wish me to act in your stead?" The notion seemed to amuse him, and why not? Poisoners, no matter how skilled, do not delegate tasks to princes of the Church. To the contrary. I was prepared to wheedle if need be, but I tried diplomacy first.

"If you could be persuaded to do so. There is no one else to whom I can turn."

He dismissed my flattery for what it was—simple truth—and agreed graciously. "So it shall be. Where is she?"

When I told him, he nodded. "I have heard of the place, but I have not seen it for myself."

"Dante would take up his pen again if he saw it. It is a condemnation of Christian charity that such horrors are allowed to exist."

That was as close as I had ever come to criticizing Christ's Vicar on Earth. Given all that Borgia had to concern him—the threats posed by rival princes of the Church, rapacious nobles, and foreign rulers, as well as his own determination to make *la famiglia* supreme in all of Christendom—it was hardly surprising that he had no interest in the actual teachings of Christ.

Cesare took that in stride, which is to say he ignored it. "Go. Give my regards to Vittoro, his charming wife, his lovely daughters, his fortunate sons-in-law, and his ever-growing collection of grandchildren. I'll see to your Magdalene."

I thanked him most sincerely, but as I stood, I also said, "Be gentle with her, please. She is . . . very fragile."

If the request surprised him, he gave no sign. I had to hope that he would not interpret my actions as a sign of weakness. Concerned that the stench of where I had been still clung to me, I went to bathe and change my clothes. My wardrobe had grown considerably since I had assumed the duties of Borgia's poisoner, in large part due to Lucrezia's insistence, but I had gladly left most of it behind in Rome. What I had brought with me was simple and serviceable, and, most important from my perspective, did not require the assistance of a maid. My underskirt of forest green wool looked good enough paired with a bodice of russet velvet.

I refused to wear my skirts as long as was the current style, thinking it ridiculous that I should have to tuck them into a belt in order to move about without tripping over them. However, I had bowed to Lucrezia's insistence that my bodices be both snugly fitted and tapering to points that emphasized the narrowness and length of my waist. Personally, I thought it was all a great deal of foolishness, but it had not escaped me that when I made at least some effort to conform to fashion, people seemed a shade more comfortable with me. My hair I wore as I almost always did, in braids wound around my head, but in honor of the occasion, I added a black velvet cap hemmed with silk braid and decorated with small amber beads.

As always, I secured my knife in its leather sheath beneath my bodice, but I hesitated as to what to do with my pouch. I would take it, of course; I could not imagine being without it. But the bloody knife I had recovered weighed the pouch down; it jostled against my leg as I moved. After hesitating a moment, I withdrew the knife and secured it in my puzzle chest.

When I was properly arrayed, I paid another visit to the kitchens, appropriating several bottles of the Sangiovese in the process, then made my way across the piazza to the cheerful little house that Vittoro was renting. The delectable aromas wafting from it made my stomach growl and reminded me that I had not eaten a proper meal all day.

Vittoro greeted me at the door. Instead of the solemn and always proper condottiere I was accustomed to, he looked rumpled and a little distracted as he attempted to soothe a fractious child he held in his arms.

"He has a tooth coming in," he said as he passed the little boy to a pretty blond woman who gave me a quick smile before she hastened off. Meanwhile, men whom I took to be the sons-in-law were busy assembling a large table from trestles and planks of wood otherwise kept stacked against the wall of the main room. Vittoro poured the wine I had brought; we drank to Borgia's health, and, as I had expected, Felicia spilled a little into the rushes for, she said, Saint Vesta, patroness of home and hearth.

Vesta is a goddess, not a saint, as I am quite sure Felicia knew, but no matter.

The mutton shanks were every bit as good as their aroma promised. After a day of dark turmoil and uncertainty, my mood slowly brightened. Good wine, good food, and, above all, good company will drive most demons away for at least a little while. We finished with a pear tart made by one of the daughters. I, who clung to solitude as a protection from the world, found myself basking in the moment. When a small child crawled up into my lap, I froze, but only briefly. She smiled around the thumb stuck in her mouth and seemed to require that I do no more than breathe. After a time, she fell asleep. When Felicia lifted her gently to take her off to bed, I was startled by a sense of loss.

Too soon duty beckoned. After many thanks and promises to sup with them again, I returned to the palazzo in time to be present at the more fashionable hour when Borgia dined. I was also anxious to see if Cesare had returned. In this I was not disappointed. He was there, looking princely in black velvet and crimson silk, but when I caught his gaze, he turned away.

I was forced to wait through the seemingly interminable meal as the Spaniards made asses of themselves as usual, Herrera braying above all the rest about the general vileness of the town, as evinced by his servant's murder. I would have sworn that he did not even know the fellow's name, for he never used it, but he went on and on as though they had been inseparable.

From time to time, I caught him glancing in my direction. Sadly, I was no Medusa; the sight of me failed utterly to turn him to stone. I was reflecting on what a handy talent that would be to have when Borgia finally rose, signaling the meal's end.

On the way out of the hall, I tried again to catch Cesare's eye. Clearly he was avoiding me, but why? Had he been unable to arrange Magdalene's departure? Or had he reconsidered doing so? In either case, he should have told me. I would not have idled away the hours, first eating mutton shanks and then enduring Herrera's cold stare, if I had known that she still languished in the shed where I had left her.

I had worked myself up to the point of being angry at Cesare's failure when he finally managed to disentangle himself from the Spaniards. Slipping into an alcove, he tipped his head to indicate that I should follow.

Face-to-face with him, I did not wait. "What happened? Did you find her? Is she—"

I meant to ask if she was on her way to Rome, but I didn't get the chance. Without warning, Cesare said, "Your Magdalene is dead. I found her where you said she would be. There were no wounds or any other sign of violence. She appears to have simply . . . died."

Shock roared through me. Of course, I understood that she was ill and malnourished. But to expire so suddenly just when she was on the verge of being rescued—

"Did anyone know what happened . . . when she died?"

"They all made themselves scarce the moment we got there.

She'll have a proper burial, but you would be wise not to tell anyone else that you found her."

It took me a moment to understand what he was saying. When I did, bile rose in my throat.

"You think I killed her?"

His dark, almond-shaped eyes glinted. "The possibility crossed my mind."

Instinctively, I knew that there was no point in trying to appeal to any feelings Cesare might have for me. Everything about his manner at that moment proclaimed that I faced not a friend and lover but a stern and unyielding prince for whom there was neither morality nor immorality, only expediency.

Either that or David was right and Cesare really was behind the plot to force his father to a reconciliation with his enemies. If that was the case, there was every likelihood that I had sent Magdalene's killer to her.

As calmly as I could, I said, "I did not kill her." True enough, I had considered doing so, but only fleetingly.

"She may have died of natural causes," Cesare allowed. "But the Spanish servant most certainly did not, and she witnessed his death."

"She didn't see the killer's face."

"So you say."

We had come to the crux of it. Could my word be trusted? In the grip of madness brought on by the realization of what had happened to my mother and how my father had deceived me, had I killed the Spaniard? Then hunted down and slain the witness whose testimony could send me to the stake?

I had killed before, more than a few times. Usually, I acted out of necessity and with strict professionalism. But there had been incidences when the darkness overwhelmed me and I killed with relish, savoring every moment.

Yet never had I killed an innocent, nor had I ever considered that I could do so.

Could Cesare?

"Find the assassin David claims has come to Viterbo," he said over his shoulder as he walked away, adding, "Do that and nothing else will matter."

And if I could not, whether because David was wrong or simply because I had finally met my match? What then?

It is said that there are places in the Indies where the mad are held to be sacred and are revered as second only to the gods. Here where the god of Abraham holds sway, it is different. The mad are left to waste away their days in babble and frenzy, if they are fortunate. Otherwise, they are condemned as harborers of demons that can only be driven out in the purifying fire.

Standing alone in the alcove, feeling the darkness of night closing in around me, I was certain of only one thing: I would swallow a dose of my own poison before I let either of those fates become my own.

19

I did not sleep that night. As though Cesare's suspicions of me and my own fears regarding him were not enough to keep me awake, upon returning to my rooms, I discovered that they had been searched. The signs were faint but unmistakable. I had not brought so many belongings to Viterbo that I would be unaware when they were disturbed. My suspicion was aroused first when I noticed that the drawer in the table beside the bed had not been closed entirely. My hairbrush and combs were where I had left them, but they were pushed to one side of the drawer instead of being in the middle. As I investigated further, I discovered that the clothes I had folded neatly and placed in a wardrobe were all slightly askew, as though hasty hands had searched beneath and behind them. My precious books, kept in a small wooden chest on a table, were still in there, but they were no longer in the order in which I had left them.

Worse yet, my puzzle chest had been completely turned around so that the front left now faced the wall, something I would never do. Quickly, I searched for any sign that it had been broken into, but to my relief, I found none. The chest, which my father had said was made by a sailor from the Indies, was of heavy, tough ebony. The weight of it alone would be daunting to anyone thinking of getting inside it quickly.

From all this I gleaned that whoever had searched my quarters had done so in haste, no doubt taking advantage of my absence from the palazzo. As desperately as I did not want to believe that Cesare could be responsible, the shadow of suspicion between us made me fear exactly that.

Hunger for Sofia's powder stirred within me. In a bid to distance myself from it, I picked up *The City of Ladies* by the extraordinary Venetian Christine de Pizan, who dared to argue that women were the equal of men and deserving of regard. For such heretical notions, she had been libeled in her own time; but she had persevered, never yielding in her defense of the worthiness of our sex. I read her words that night as a consolation to my wounded spirit and for strength against the deep tidal pull of fear that threatened to drag me under and drown me.

Toward dawn, I finally dozed off sitting up in a chair. A knock at the door snapped me back to awareness. I rose stiff and sore to answer it. Did I hope, even in passing, that Cesare had come to make peace and allay my concerns about him? I could confide in him about the search of my rooms. He would have some ready explanation for it or, even better, know nothing but join me in determination to find the culprit.

Renaldo dropped his hand when I opened the door and peered at him. He looked as he always did—harassed, worried, anxious—yet he mustered a smile that appeared genuine. I had no idea how much he knew (to this day I do not), but I was certain it was more than he would ever tell.

"You're awake," he said. "Good. The rain has stopped; the sun is out. It's actually a nice day. Our master has announced his intention to inspect the fortifications between here and Orvieto. We are to accompany him."

Belatedly, I recalled that the inspection of fortifications was Borgia's stated reason for making the trip to Viterbo. The fact that his current mistress, the exquisite and very young Giulia Farnese, called La Bella and reputed to be the most beautiful woman in all of Italy, was staying at her family's estate near Orvieto doubtless played no part in His Holiness's travel plans.

"When are we leaving?" I asked.

"Hark and you will hear our master bellowing," Renaldo replied. "Apparently, we should all have been on the road before dawn and would have been but for the fact that he only just thought to mention it a short time ago."

"I need to pack and—"

Renaldo was shaking his head before I could finish. "We travel light or we do not. Grab what you can and be ready with all speed." He tossed a pair of saddlebags on the bed. "These and no more," he said as he hurried off.

Cursing Borgia and his everlasting love of frantic activity

bordering on chaos, I made haste. Stuffing clothes into one of the bags, I ignored everything Lucrezia had tried to teach me about how to put together an appropriate ensemble and only hoped that I would be suitably attired for however long we were to be away. Into the other bag I put what I regarded as the bare necessities of my trade—including the very few substances that, provided they are administered in time, can offer some remedy for poisoning.

At the last moment, I hesitated over the puzzle chest. This time I would be away not for a few hours but at least overnight and well into the following day. A determined searcher would have time to pry his way into the chest no matter how difficult that task. Of course, it would be impossible to conceal such an effort, but that might not be as great a concern as was finding proof of my alleged guilt. With that possibility in my mind, I went through the sequence of movements needed to unlock the chest and withdrew the knife that had killed the Spaniard, returning the weapon to my pouch. I hesitated over the various poisons contained within the chest, as well as the ground diamonds intended to kill della Rovere, but there was a limit to how much I could carry; and besides, I doubted that I was dealing with a mere thief.

Having secured the chest once again, I flung a bag over each shoulder and hurried as best I could along the corridor, down the steps, and through the great hall. Outside in the piazza, I could hear Borgia booming.

"I am away! Cesare, to me! The rest of you sluggards, lie abed as you will, being good for nothing else."

Glancing back over my shoulder, I saw the upper windows

of the palazzo crowded with an assortment of befuddled prelates and their entourages, all caught unawares by Borgia's intentions. No doubt exactly as he had planned.

Which is not to say that His Holiness was alone. Vittoro was there, along with at least a hundred men-at-arms. Cesare was already mounted beside his father, accompanied by Herrera and a bevy of the Spaniards. Frantically, I looked around for Renaldo, spying him finally on a sturdy gray, his traveling desk strapped to his chest. With one hand he controlled his own horse, and with the other he held on to mine. Apparently, in snatching a mount for me, the steward had not considered my dislike of riding, far less my general ineptitude. The chestnut mare pawed the ground and snorted even as she rolled her eyes in my direction.

"Away!" Borgia shouted and set his spurs. With no choice whatsoever, I threw the saddlebags over the mare and launched myself onto her. She bucked; I held on with fierce desperation, and too quickly found myself rattling down the same road where I had almost been trampled by Cesare and the Spaniards. Down we went, dogs barking, trumpets blaring, townspeople scattering. In the blink of an eye—or so it seemed—we were through the market and out past the gate. The mulberry and gold banners of Il Papa streamed out in the wind as we turned north onto the continuation of the old Via Cassia, in the direction of Orvieto.

At some point, I finally managed to breathe. So, too, I was able to adjust myself in the saddle at least so much that I no longer felt as though I was about to be thrown from it. The mare ran full out, apparently determined to keep to the front.

All my efforts to persuade her otherwise were ignored. I could only hold on and hope that before too long Borgia would moderate his pace.

By the time he finally did so, we were well away from the town, trotting along the tree-lined road. Renaldo came up beside me. The steward was flushed and bright-eyed, apparently exhilarated by the sudden adventure.

"Our master never does anything halfway, does he?" he asked, grinning.

Given that my posterior felt like it was being pounded against an anvil, the jarring motion traveling all the way up my spine to make my teeth rattle, I think I responded with admirable calm.

"A little moderation would not necessarily be a bad thing. What hornet stung him that he should take off like this, do you know?"

"Something in the dispatch bag, I think. It arrived just before he announced that we were going."

"But you have no idea what it was?"

"I didn't say that, did I? As it happens, there is a possibility that His Holiness has a scheme up his sleeve that surpasses even his usual cleverness."

We were riding close enough together that Renaldo could keep his voice very low. I did the same. "What scheme? What is he plotting?"

"I dare not say, it is that audacious. But if it comes to pass, we will have a better understanding of why he left Rome in the first place and why he has just abandoned all those prelates who came with him to Viterbo."

"Renaldo—" I was torn between remonstrating with him for his coyness and pleading with him to satisfy my curiosity. But the steward would not be swayed.

"Just keep an eye on the Spaniards," he advised. "If what I suspect is true, they are in for a nasty surprise."

That cheered me just enough for me to hold my tongue. The miles passed in a blur as the morning wore on and the air warmed. Up ahead, I could see Borgia, who looked to be in high good humor. Not so Cesare, who appeared watchful and subdued. I had to wonder if he was aware of what his father was planning or if, like the rest of us, he had been kept in the dark.

We had come to the foothills surrounding Lake Bolsena, which I had heard of but never seen before, at least not so far as I knew. It was possible that my father and I had traveled along its shores on our way to Rome when I was a child, but as that time is lost to me in darkness, I had no recollection of the area. I did, however, have the sense to appreciate the beauty of the landscape that unfolded before me. Rolling hills flowed down to the shores of the immense oval-shaped lake in which two small islands nestled comfortably. At the southern end of the lake lay a small, pretty town set beside a broad river that flowed out of the lake and away toward the sea. A villa lay a short distance beyond the town. We appeared to be heading for it.

"Are we stopping here?" I wondered out loud, on the off chance that Renaldo would relent and reveal why he was looking so puffed up and pleased with himself. As for me, I welcomed a chance to put distance between my posterior and the mare, if only temporarily. However, I saw no sign of the fortifications that Borgia had supposedly come to inspect.

The steward gestured toward the river. "That's the Marta. Pretty name, don't you think? A very useful river. It runs all the way from this lake to the port at Corneto. An enterprising traveler, wishing to avoid Rome for whatever reason, could put in there and avail himself of one of the wherries that ply the Marta in both directions. Oh, look, there's one of those now docked just beside that villa."

I observed the low flat boat equipped with oars at the same time as I said, "Enough, for pity's sake! What traveler?" A sudden suspicion surfaced in my mind. Surely it wasn't possible that—

"Has Borgia come here to meet someone?" I demanded.

To my utter astonishment, Renaldo smiled and in a singsongy voice that mocked my ignorance said, *"Il vaut mieux être marteau qu'enclume."*

I speak very little French and that badly, so I had no real idea what he had said, although it was something about a hammer. However, that scarcely mattered. It was the French itself that counted.

The French.

The Spaniards' great rival, their sometime enemy, whose bellicose young king had his eye on Naples and whom Borgia's most dangerous rival for the papacy, Cardinal della Rovere, was counting on as his ally.

And, quite possibly, the signal that we had entered the end game. Whatever was to happen was hard upon us, and I still had no idea from which direction the danger would come.

I dug my spurs into the sides of the mare and clattered after Borgia as he made for the villa with all speed. Behind me, I was aware of the Spaniards, still in Cesare's care and, from what I could see as I went by, with no notion of what was happening.

I dismounted in front of the villa moments after Borgia did the same. A woman stood on the stone terrace overlooking the lake. She was young, exquisitely beautiful, and visibly pregnant. I recognized her in an instant, as, I am sure, did the rest of the company. Giulia Farnese, justifiably known as La Bella, was considered to be the greatest beauty of our age. At nineteen—with long, golden hair, a complexion as pure as cream, and a slender but curvaceous form—she possessed the ability to turn the most stalwart man into a besotted fool.

Borgia was no exception; he adored her and cosseted her in every way. His decision a month or so before to send her from Rome to the comfort of her family's estate outside Orvieto had been taken as a sign that His Holiness did not regard the city as entirely secure for his mistress and their unborn child. Now here she was in the villa beside the Marta, seemingly overwhelmed with joy to see her lover.

For his part, Borgia bounded up the steps to her with all the eagerness of a much younger man. Taking both her hands in his, he kissed them passionately before embracing her. They were cooing to each other when a man I had never seen before walked out of the villa onto the terrace.

As though caught by surprise, Borgia startled. Looking down into La Bella's lovely face, he asked loudly enough for all to hear, "Who is this?"

She gave a charming little laugh and replied, "A visitor from the French court, my lord. Only just learning that you were about to arrive, he asked if he might stay to greet you. I hope I did not do wrong to tell him that he could?"

For just a moment, Borgia looked at her sternly, but then, as any man could be expected to do, he yielded. Releasing his beloved, he turned to greet the Frenchman. Together, they went into the villa. La Bella, whose smile had begun to waver, took a breath and sagged a little.

At once, I went to her. There were no other women present, but in addition, I had a particular reason for being concerned about her. Despite my best efforts, La Bella had lost a baby the previous year after being poisoned. Now she had been brought from the comfort of Orvieto to provide cover for Borgia's meeting with the Frenchman. I could understand if she felt ill-used and in need of rest.

"Are you in any difficulty?" I asked quietly when I reached her side.

Recognizing me, she mustered a smile and shook her head. "Just tired and a bit concerned . . . you know."

In fact, I did. Serving a man as powerful and willful as Borgia is never easy in any capacity.

I took her arm and we started into the villa. Behind me, I heard an angry exclamation from Herrera and glanced back over my shoulder in time to see Cesare shrug. Apparently, he had just told the Spaniard whom His Holiness was meeting with.

The fiction that an emissary of the French king had just happened to turn up in the neighborhood of Lake Bolsena at the same time that Borgia arrived there to visit his mistress would not fool anyone, nor was it meant to. Il Papa had brought the beloved nephew of Their Most Catholic Majesties along precisely so that Herrera could witness the meeting with the Frenchman and send word of it to King Ferdinand and Queen Isabella.

"Who is the emissary?" I asked as Giulia and I made our way to the pretty white-and-gold rooms she was occupying overlooking the lake. With a sigh, she settled into a chair. I took the stool beside her.

"Comte François de Rochanaud, the French king's minister of state," she replied. "He seems a charming man."

No doubt he was to La Bella, but I rather thought Herrera would view him differently. The sheer audacity of what Borgia was doing stunned me. With all attention focused on the Spanish alliance and the threats to it, including from the still unknown assassin, His Holiness had pivoted in an entirely unexpected direction. By arranging to meet with a representative of the French king—an extremely high-ranking one at that—he signaled to the Spaniards that he was far less reliant on their support than they had presumed. He was Borgia the Bull and he had no equal. His enemies were lesser men who could never defeat him. When the dust settled, he would still be on Saint Peter's Throne and they would be nothing.

It was a bluff, of course. Borgia was Spanish himself; he would never favor the French over his own kinsmen, no matter how difficult or tiresome Their Most Catholic Majesties might be. Unless, of course, he was forced to do so by circumstances beyond his control.

"I didn't know he was bringing the Spaniards," Giulia said wearily. "Does that strike you as wise?"

"It seems he wants to make sure that they—and Ferdinand and Isabella—understand that he has options apart from them," I said.

"I suppose," La Bella agreed. She slipped off her shoes and wiggled her small, plump toes. "I think I will dine here tonight. You are welcome to join me."

I thanked her for her thoughtfulness but declined. Petty though it was of me, I wanted to see Herrera's reaction for myself, all the better to savor it.

Leaving La Bella to rest, I was looking for a room to claim for the night when I encountered Renaldo. He appeared flustered and in a great rush.

"They are threatening to leave!" the steward exclaimed. "Herrera is in such a state, he claims he won't remain here a moment longer. He says he has been insulted beyond bearing and he's going back to Spain."

As appealing as the notion was, I thought it highly unlikely. "And tell Their Most Catholic Majesties what, exactly? That the alliance is finished because the beloved nephew has been outmaneuvered?"

Renaldo grinned. "I heard Cesare tell him to go if he wished but he would be ceding the field to the French."

Anxious to see what Herrera would do, I followed Renaldo out toward the terrace. On the way, I asked, "How did you know this was happening?"

He glanced around to be sure no one else could hear, then said, "His Holiness personally instructed me to send supplies here to the villa. I couldn't imagine why. Supplies to Orvieto would have made sense if he were going there to visit La Bella, but to here? So I asked myself, what does this place have that would recommend it to Il Papa?"

"And the answer?"

"The river, of course. A visitor who wished to be discreet could hardly come to Rome, or to Viterbo for that matter, without being seen and recognized before he got anywhere near Borgia. The prelates would have been up in arms, each wanting to have his say. Nothing of any significance could be accomplished. But the port at Corneto and a quick trip up the Marta, that would do quite well. By the time the emissary's presence was known, it would be too late to do anything about it."

I stared at him in admiration. "You are wasted as Borgia's steward. You should be his co-conspirator."

Renaldo chuckled. "Five to three the Spaniards stay, what do you think?"

I shook my head. "No bet, but let's go see all the same."

We reached the terrace in time to find Cesare, his arm thrown around Herrera's shoulders, smiling in apparent good humor as all around them hounds yelped and bayed, and handlers hurried to ready the horses. Herrera did not appear at all mollified, but apparently he had been convinced to go hunting rather than go back to Spain.

I should have been relieved, and perhaps I would have been had I not been all too vividly aware that by remaining, Herrera continued to make himself a target. Perhaps of the very man who was making every effort just then to appear to be his dearest friend.

20

His Holiness and the French emissary remained closeted together into the afternoon and beyond. What they had to say to each other was anyone's guess, as no servants, attendants, or secretaries were permitted in the room. Both men being fluent in Latin, there was no impediment to their entirely private conversation. Even so, the intimacy of their meeting was bound to distress the Spaniards even more.

With Borgia occupied and Cesare absent, I found a small but pleasant chamber for myself. Keeping in mind that my rooms in Viterbo had been searched, I left my clothes strewn about to give a false appearance of disorder that would in fact reveal any tampering. I also took care to secure the small box of supplies I had brought with me. Generally, I have found that most places have a loose floorboard or two with space beneath to conceal small items. The villa was no exception.

As weary as I was, having slept little and poorly the night before in addition to enduring the mad ride from Viterbo, I had to fight the impulse to lie down. Instead, I made my way to the kitchens. The staff, sent from La Bella's family estate near Orvieto, knew me by name and reputation. I was welcomed with whispers and anxious looks, which I ignored.

His Holiness would dine that evening on shad stuffed with minced oysters in a light basil sauce, seared lake duck with dried cherries soaked in liqueur, and a succulent custard of eggs, cream, lemons, and ginger. I made a point of sampling some of each, but only in very small portions. My stomach was unsettled, and I could not shake a sense of nausea creeping over me. That and the unsettled state of my nerves I reluctantly ascribed to having gone as long as I had without Sofia's powder. Her warning to me of its dangers no longer seemed overblown.

By the time the company gathered in the small but gracious hall of the villa, Borgia appeared to be in a considerably better mood than he had earlier in the day. He emerged from his consultations in the company of Comte François de Rochanaud, the two of them rattling away like the oldest and best of friends.

By contrast, Herrera looked positively sullen.

"The hunting didn't go well," Renaldo said as he joined me where I stood against one of the walls, a position from which we could observe the proceedings without getting caught up in them. "Either the deer hereabouts are too swift or Herrera was too slow, but they came back empty-handed."

"No matter," I said. "The cooks have outdone themselves."

Borgia seemed to think so, as did the Comte, for they fell to with good appetites. Herrera, on the other hand, ignored what was set before him in favor of drinking steadily. Several times I caught him watching me. While I pretended not to notice, the truth is that I would have had to be a fool to ignore his animosity, or to fail to wonder how far he would go to bring about my destruction.

The French emissary, proving himself a consummate diplomat, made an effort to be pleasant to Herrera, but he was rebuffed crudely. He shrugged that off with a worldly smile and gave his attention to Cesare, whose measure he seemed intent on taking.

As the evening wore on, it became more and more difficult for me to fight off the fatigue weighing me down. I did not dare lean against the wall for fear that I might slip into sleep. Seeing my difficulty, Renaldo urged me to withdraw.

"Aside from Herrera getting drunk and sulking," he said, "nothing is going to happen. Tomorrow we return to Viterbo. You should get some rest while you can."

The reminder that I would be back on a horse in a few short hours was enough to decide me. With a quick nod of thanks to the steward, I slipped away.

Although the villa was small, I was so tired that I took a wrong turn and had to make my way back down one corridor and along another before I finally found the room I had chosen. With no thought other than sleep, I opened the door.

And walked into chaos.

Everything in the room had been turned upside down. The mattress had been pulled off the bed and thrown to one side. The bed hangings had been yanked down and were crumpled on the floor. My clothing lay in heaps. The saddlebags I had used had been slit open. Tables, a chair, and two stools had been hurled into the corners so carelessly that several were smashed.

Nor was the violence finished. The two men in the room were in the act of pulling up the loose floorboard where I had hidden my box of supplies. As I entered, they turned and saw me. One of the men leaped to his feet and came at me in a rush.

Shocked as I was, instinct took over. I drew my knife, flicked it in his direction, and said, "Come any closer and you die."

He did hesitate, but only long enough to bellow for the second man, who, seeing his fellow's difficulty, joined him in coming at me. What did they think? That for all my fearsome reputation, I was only a woman and therefore helpless? Or that the punishment their master would exact if they failed was worse than anything I might do? There is even the possibility that they believed they would win great favor with him if they did away with me right then and there. Or perhaps they did not think at all. In my experience, it is often a mistake to assume that people do so.

I had fought before with a knife, but never against two men at the same time. Moreover, there was no poison on the blade. Killing—or even defending myself—would require far more than a mere nick.

My skirt hindered me. I pulled it back with one hand while with the other I brandished my knife. I have a very clear memory of saying, "I have no wish to hurt you."

And then I remember nothing more. Or almost nothing.

It is easiest to claim that I have no memory of what followed, and that is mostly true, but fragments still replay in my mind. The snarling face of one of the men as he launched himself at me with his own knife drawn, aimed for my heart. The ribbon of blood that appeared across his throat where I slashed him. The strength I drew from the darkness that welled up within me. The second man, drawing his own blade, coming at me, his mouth wide in a scream of mingled terror and rage. I pivoted on one foot, locked my arm at the elbow, and drove my knife into his belly up to my wrist. We hung together, he and I, in a macabre embrace, until at last I pulled the blade out. He sank down at my feet as his life ran out of him.

I think I staggered back against the door, but again, I cannot be sure. I do know that I was covered with blood. It was in my hair, on my face, saturating my clothes. It caked my nostrils, and when I tried to breathe through my mouth, I gagged on the stench of copper. Horror filled me, and in that instant, something inside me snapped. Frantically, I tore at my garments, my hair, my face, all in a futile effort to escape the effects of what I had done. But there was no escape; I was saturated in blood, drowning in it. I reeled on the edge of an abyss as my mind threatened to shatter completely.

In that writhing darkness, a single cord of light appeared. I seized hold of it, clinging desperately, knowing that it was all that kept me from plummeting into endless darkness.

I would like to believe that it was my longing for Rocco and the dream of a better life that gave me the strength to hold on. Or my love for my friends—David, Sofia, Portia, and others. Or that it was of Cesare and the intimacy that we shared that I thought as I crawled my way back up into the world of reason. But none of that would be true.

I thought instead of myself, of the child I had been, so helpless and terrified, hiding first behind a wall that could not protect me and then behind the wall of my own mind. Against all odds, that child had survived. She was still there, somewhere inside me. If I perished, so would all that was left of the innocence and goodness of my soul.

And those who had done all the dark and terrible things, who had inflicted so much pain and suffering, would win.

Never again would I flee from the agony of the world. I would confront it with all the strength I possessed, beginning with the carnage I had just wrought. Two men were dead—butchered. And I . . . I had to look like a figure from the Hell to which so many were eager to consign me.

But, I reminded myself, I had acted in self-defense. Most women would not have been able to do so, as the men had clearly expected that I would not. They had died for their ignorance, but surely no one could blame me for reacting as I had?

Even as I tried to convince myself that I had acted well within the right of any person to defend his or her own life, I heard the pounding of approaching feet. Belatedly, I remembered that one of the men had screamed as he came at me. And perhaps also as he died. The sounds of our struggle had reached well beyond the room, alerting others to what was happening.

I looked around quickly with some thought of trying to straighten myself as best I could, but it was too late. A pair of

Vittoro's men-at-arms came on the double, only to halt suddenly when they saw me.

"Donna?" one managed to say as his face drained of all color.

"Go to His Eminence, Cardinal Cesare Borgia," I directed. Even to my own ears, my voice sounded unnaturally flat. A strange calm had settled over me, as though I were part of the world yet somehow standing apart from it. In such unexpected ways do we sometimes find evidence of a merciful god. "Tell him I have need of him."

I had only the smallest hope that the men would be discreet, therefore I was not overly surprised when Cesare did not come alone. A bevy of others trailed after him—his own attendants, Vittoro and more men-at-arms, Renaldo, and, I saw with sinking heart, Herrera and the other Spaniards, with David close behind. Of His Holiness there was no sign, or of the French emissary. Both men were far too wily and experienced to involve themselves in such a matter.

"I was attacked," I said before anyone else spoke. "These men were searching my room. When I discovered them, they came at me armed. I warned them, but they would not listen."

"Devil!" Herrera screamed. Lapsing into his native Castilian, he went on, *"¡Puta! ¡Engendro de Satanás! ¡Destructor de todo lo que es bueno y puro!"*

I caught "whore" and something about Satan before I stopped listening. Herrera was coming toward me. David was moving to stop him. I braced myself, gripping the hilt of my knife tightly.

Cesare stepped between us. Grabbing the Spaniard by the shoulders, he demanded, "Are these your men?"

At first I thought that Herrera would not answer him. His eyes were wild with rage, and flecks of foam shone on the corners of his mouth. He appeared to have no thought other than to get at me.

"Are they?" Cesare demanded and shook him hard.

Abruptly, Herrera became aware that the man he believed to be his friend was speaking to him. He took a breath, then another, and said, "Of course they are. Someone has to protect you from her."

Revulsion overcame me. I turned away, staggering, and would have fallen had not Renaldo—bless him—somehow found the courage to reach out and steady me. Though he held me at arm's length to minimize the damage to his fine garments, he kept me on my feet.

Cesare glanced around the room, then down at the dead men. Loudly enough for all to hear, he said, "The condition of this chamber and the fact that both men were armed makes it clear that Donna Francesca is speaking the truth. She acted to defend herself."

"You cannot believe that!" Herrera exclaimed. He looked stricken with horror at the thought. "No normal woman would be able to do what she has done. She is the spawn of the Devil! You put your very soul at risk by having anything to do with her. You must reject her and everything she represents!"

"Miguel—" Cesare began, as though about to make a sincere effort to explain to the other man why he had it all backwards, why sending men to search a room and then attack a woman was wrong even if one did believe her to be a servant of the Devil. But if that was what he meant to say, he reconsidered.

Falling silent, he stared at the Spaniard for a long moment before he looked to Vittoro.

"Escort Don Miguel and his retinue to their quarters and make sure that they stay there. Not one of them goes anywhere until morning, is that understood?"

Herrera protested loudly, but Cesare ignored him. The Spaniards were quickly surrounded by men-at-arms, who marched them out of the room and out of sight.

I breathed a sigh of relief when they were gone, only to realize that the problem was far from solved. The room remained in chaos, and there were the two dead bodies, as well as so much blood . . .

"Renaldo," Cesare said, "find a priest, then muster the servants. See to it that these men are buried with all speed and that the room is cleaned. I don't care if it takes all night, I don't want any hint left of what happened here."

"Of course, Your Eminence," Renaldo said, as though he had been carrying out such orders all his life.

Cesare turned to me. He gripped my arm, shook me hard, and said, "Look at me, Francesca."

I looked, seeing in his face the question I dreaded he would ask. Had I been in my right mind when I killed the men?

"They attacked me," I said again, but the words sounded weak to my own ears. I had been attacked; I had acted to defend myself. But I had killed in the grip of the darkness that I could neither control nor deny. If I was not what I was, the men would still be alive.

"Lucky for you," he said and strode down the corridor with me in tow.

I had to run to keep up with him even as I struggled to understand what he was saying. Did he really believe that I would have killed the men without provocation, simply because I came upon them searching my room? Or worse, merely because I needed to kill? Was there any chance that he was right?

Cesare had left his valet behind in Viterbo; we were alone. In the middle of the room, he released me.

"Take off your clothes." When I hesitated, still grappling with the notion that he thought I could have killed so wantonly, he said, "They're covered with blood. Take them off."

Reminded of my condition, I moved as quickly as I could to comply, but my hands were shaking too much to be of any use. Cesare made a sound of impatience and took charge. He used the blade he wore at his side to cut through the laces and ties holding my garments in place. As he worked, they fell away. I was left in nothing other than the short chemise I wore against my skin.

"That, too," he said.

I glanced down to see that the blood had soaked through all the layers of my clothing even to the chemise. Quickly, fearing that I was about to retch, I pulled it off over my head.

Cesare gathered the clothes and dropped them in a far corner of the room. I stood naked and shivering, watching him as he did so. He returned to me holding out a blanket.

"You need to wash."

Neither of us was of a mind to endure servants trooping in and out to fill the bathtub in the adjacent room. Instead, I made do with the contents of the ewer provided when Cesare returned from hunting and long since cooled to the temperature of the room. That didn't matter; nothing did except that there was water and soap. With Cesare's help, I was able to wash the blood from my hair, my face, my body, and most especially from my hands, which were caked with it. He even produced a small brush to help me remove the last traces from around and under my nails. I scrubbed and scrubbed until finally he stopped me.

"Enough. You will injure yourself."

By then, I was shaking so hard that I could scarcely stand. Cesare led me over to the bed and sat me down. Gripping the blanket around myself, I said, "You taught me to use a knife."

My intention may have been to remind him that there was an entirely plausible explanation for how I had managed to kill the men. However, he was not persuaded.

"You are too modest. I have trained men who would not have been able to do what you did."

"What do you think, then? That Herrera is right and I am possessed by the Devil?" Without giving him a chance to answer, I added, "The Spaniard would burn me, you know, if he could. And he is far from alone."

Cesare sat down on the bed beside me. Quietly, he said, "He cannot. Besides, none of this is really because of you. You just have the bad luck to be involved with me."

Accustomed as I was to the Borgias' believing that Creation itself revolved around them, I was surprised all the same. Until I remembered what I had discovered about the Spaniard in the *passetto*.

"You have to understand about Don Miguel," Cesare continued. "He's actually an intelligent, well-educated man, not to mention a gifted architect. He's shown me a design of his for a dome that, assuming his calculations regarding the weight-bearing stones are correct, would be revolutionary."

I stared at him in bewilderment. Here I had thought that all Cesare and Herrera did together was hunt, whore, and drink. But they had actually been poring over architectural plans and discussing the finer points of dome construction?

"I'm not excusing anything he has done," Cesare continued. "I'm just saying that Miguel fights a constant battle with his own nature. Not surprisingly, that puts a great strain on him, as it would on anyone. You, above all, should understand that."

I should understand Herrera? I should . . . what? Accept that he wanted to consign me to the flames because he was in love with Cesare?

"Oh, yes," I said. "By all means, let's make allowances for his wounded heart."

Cesare shrugged. "Of course, even if my proclivities did run in that direction, I could not allow myself to return his affections."

"Why not?"

"Because while I remain the object of his unfulfilled desire, he will do everything he possibly can to please me. Such is the nature of all men, regardless of whom they like to climb into bed with."

He was right, of course. Ruthless and heartless, but definitely right. However, that raised a question. "Why are you telling me this?"

"Because I need you to help save him from the assassin, no matter how much reason you have to hate and fear him."

In a way, I was relieved. Cesare's concern seemed to suggest that he was not playing a deep game against his own father's wishes. Or perhaps he simply wanted me to believe that.

"Surely," I said, "neither Herrera nor the alliance is so important now that Il Papa and the Comte have become such great friends."

"Do not be misled by the false bonhomie of schemers as clever as that pair. The French king's hunger for land and power is equaled only by my father's. Inevitably, they will clash, and when they do, *la famiglia* will need the Spanish more than ever."

Which meant that Cesare would need Herrera, albeit for entirely cold-blooded reasons.

Grudgingly, I said, "So long as he refrains from trying to consign me to the pits of Hell, I have no particular reason to want him dead."

"Or his servants?"

"Are we not in agreement that I was provoked and acted in self-defense?"

Cesare stood up. He went over to the heap of bloodied clothes that he had dropped in a corner. When he returned, he was holding my pouch. Opening it, he withdrew the knife I had found near the thornbushes.

"I thought this felt unusually heavy," he said as he tossed the pouch aside. Turning the knife over in his hands, he said,

"The shape, even when concealed, is quite distinctive. This is the type of knife carried by Herrera's servants."

"I didn't know that," I said, despising the weakness of my voice. I had meant to tell him about the knife, I really had. But the opportunity had never presented itself, and besides, with him entertaining the notion that I had killed the servant in the alley, how could I be expected to tell him anyway?

"I only thought it had been used to kill the man," I added.

"You thought that, did you? When?"

"When I discovered it on the slope of the hill near where you found me the other night."

"The night when you can't remember where you went or what you did?"

I nodded, fully realizing how damning that sounded. "That night. But surely I don't have to point out the obvious? When you found me, there was blood on my feet but nowhere else." I gestured toward the pile of clothes that I could only think would have to be burned. "If I had killed that man, everything I was wearing would have been covered with blood just as it is now."

I could think of few benefits to killing two men as I had done, apart from the obvious one of preserving my own life. But being forcefully reminded of just how messy a business killing is, especially when done with a knife, removed from me all fear that I could have killed the Spanish servant while in the frenzy of terror caused by the nightmare. Among all my many sins, that was not one of them.

"Yes," Cesare said, "I know."

"You do?" I had feared that my possession of the knife

would convince him that I was responsible for the man's death, but apparently it had done exactly the opposite.

"Where did you say you found this?"

"On the slope beyond the arena. The ground there is covered with thornbushes, which I think are the reason why my feet were cut. A narrow path leads through them and around the side of the palazzo toward the piazza. I believe I came that way."

"I know the place. How did you happen to see the knife?"

"I didn't, not at first. But I noticed a depression where it looked as though someone might have lain for a time. The knife was there."

"And you didn't tell me because you feared that I would think you dropped the knife, having taken it from the man and used it to kill him?"

Reluctantly, I nodded. "We both know that I haven't been . . . entirely myself lately."

He sighed and put an arm around me, drawing me close. More exhausted than I could ever remember being and aching in every bone, I accepted the comfort he offered without hesitation. Stroking my hair, he said mildly, "You don't do well away from Rome."

The notion that my distress was caused by a sojourn in the countryside was so absurd that I could not help but laugh. As, of course, Cesare intended.

"Perhaps you found the knife somewhere and carried it to the slope," he suggested after a moment.

"If I did, I have no memory of doing so."

"Then perhaps someone else left it there."

Dimly, I recalled the shadowy figure I had glimpsed. A robed being no less terrifying than Death itself. But surely only a product of my disordered mind?

"In the place where I happened to be? What is the chance of that?"

"I don't know," Cesare admitted. Or at least I think he did. No matter how any of us tries to hold off Morpheus, the capricious god always wins in the end.

"I am missing something," I murmured, but my voice was slurred and I could barely understand my own words. Likely Cesare did not hear me, for I don't think that he replied. I knew when he laid me down on the bed and covered me, and then I knew nothing at all.

21

Herrera and the other Spaniards left the villa at first light. David went with them, which I hoped meant that he was still in their good graces despite his instinctive move to help me. Comte de Rochanaud departed shortly thereafter, setting off with many expressions of mutual amicability between himself and Borgia. Scarcely had the boat carrying the French emissary disappeared around a bend of the river than His Holiness was off to spend a few hours with La Bella.

The sun was high when we finally departed. During the ride back to Viterbo, I had no opportunity to speak with Il Papa, nor did he address me. While I was certain that he knew full well what I had done, apparently there was no reason for us to discuss it.

I did, however, have ample time to reflect on what had

occurred. Borgia's suggestion that I needed to kill was not without merit. Yet whatever relief I gained from doing so was transitory. Although I did not have any doubts about the moral rightness of defending one's own life, I was gripped by a hollow sadness that not even Cesare's understanding could ease. Moreover, I was all too vividly aware that I was, yet again, the target of fearful and condemning stares from even the hard-bitten men-at-arms in His Holiness's escort. I have observed that there are advantages to having a dark reputation, but riding along the Via Cassia that afternoon, I could not remember any of them.

Coming into Viterbo, it was clear to me that word of events at the villa had already spread, as no doubt Borgia had intended when he sent the Spaniards back so early. With thoughts of peace with the French uppermost in every mind, Il Papa was greeted far more enthusiastically than usual as he entered the town and made his way through the winding streets up to the palazzo. He seemed to enjoy the novel reception, for he waved and offered blessings enthusiastically. As for me, I kept my eyes straight ahead and did my best to ignore the whispers that followed in my wake.

The prelates, having been denied any role in the discussions with France, were out in force when we arrived. To a man, they demanded His Holiness's attention. He gave it, if grudgingly. Cesare went along, most likely to mediate, although he had scant patience for his fellow prelates and was far more likely to shout them down than to listen to them. Sorry though I was to miss that, I was free to see to my own needs. Or so I thought.

Before I reached my rooms, Renaldo caught up with me. He had gone ahead in the company of the Spaniards, and I assumed he had something to tell me regarding them. But instead he surprised me. "That nun is back. She is asking to see you."

I swallowed a groan. Of all the people I wanted to deal with just then, Mother Benedette was not among them. I dreaded the thought of facing her, given what she must surely think of me now that she knew what I was capable of doing.

"She's quite a charming woman," Renaldo added. "We had a nice chat."

"Did you?" I could only imagine about what.

He nodded gently. "She knew your mother."

My head was throbbing. I had slept, but not enough. I needed a proper bath and a chance to collect my thoughts, but apparently I would not get either.

"They were friends together growing up in Milan," I said.

"So she told me. I put her in my office. I thought she would be more comfortable there."

Renaldo's office, whether in Borgia's old palazzo on the Corso or at the Vatican or in Viterbo, was at once his inner sanctum and the command post from which he maintained his oversight of all aspects of the papal household. I had been allowed to call upon him there from time to time, but visitors were generally not welcome. For him to have made an exception for Mother Benedette suggested that he was impressed with her indeed. Or perhaps he was simply trying to do me a kindness.

"I'll just have a quick word with her," I said. "We won't be long."

To my surprise, he replied, "Take as much time as you like. I'm having a new counting table built and I want to see how it's coming along. If the beads aren't perfectly smooth or properly balanced . . ." He shuddered at the havoc that could wreak.

I thanked him and withdrew long enough to freshen myself before following in his wake. Renaldo's office was down a short corridor from the great hall. When the door to it was open, he had a view from his desk of all comings and goings. Although we had been in Viterbo only a few days, the office was heaped with piles of ledgers, rolled parchments, and stacks of paper. I suspected that Renaldo used them as a kind of fortification against the chaotic world.

In their midst, perched on the edge of a chair facing the desk, I found Mother Benedette. The abbess's eyes were closed and she was fingering the wooden rosary beads she wore at her waist. She appeared lost in prayer.

I hesitated, reluctant to interrupt her; but she seemed to sense my presence, for she opened her eyes, peered at me, and smiled wanly.

"My dear child. I hope you can forgive me for coming like this?"

Considering that I had brutally killed two men scant hours before, I rather thought that I was the one who should be asking for forgiveness, but so be it. Quickly, I took the seat beside her. "Of course. I am glad to see you."

"It is kind of you to say so. You could hardly be blamed if you never wished to be in my company again."

Whatever I had expected, it was not that. Surely any

offense she imagined that she had committed paled in comparison to mine. "I don't understand. Why would you think that?"

"Because I was far too hasty and clumsy in telling you of your mother as I did. I am so sorry for the distress I must have caused. I fear it may have led you to—" She broke off, but her expression made it clear what she thought I had done in response to learning how my mother died.

Distress was too mild a word by far for what I was still experiencing as I struggled to come to terms with my mother's fate and my father's deception, but I would not for the world tell her that. Instead, I replied, "I acted in self-defense. But beyond that, a truth withheld for so many years can never be revealed with too great haste. You only did what was right."

For a moment, I feared that she might give in to the tears glistening in her eyes, but she blinked them away hastily and nodded.

"Then I thank God for guiding me as He has done, and I tell you truly, your friendship means as much to me as your mother's ever did."

In the aftermath of the events at the villa, her kindness all but overwhelmed me. I needed a moment before I could respond. "Be assured that I feel the same way. When you have completed your pilgrimage to Assisi, perhaps we can—"

I was about to voice my hope that she might stop in Viterbo again on the way back to her abbey, or visit me in Rome if we had, please God, returned to the city before then, but Mother Benedette forestalled me. "In that spirit of that friendship, I must speak with you honestly," she said.

Bracing myself for what I was sure must be her concerns about the state of my soul, I said, "By all means."

"I fear that you are in great danger, Francesca."

"I would be the last person to claim that I am without sin, but—"

She looked at me in surprise. "Oh, I don't mean that. I'm concerned because people are saying that you must also have been responsible for the death of the Spanish servant. And that is not all they are blaming you for."

"There is more?"

"People want to believe that His Holiness will not take us into war, but they still have grave doubts about him and his intentions. They fear that he cares for nothing but the well-being of his own family and that he will do anything to increase his own power—even if that means that ordinary people are put in great peril."

She was right, of course. But that did not mean that Borgia was a poor choice for pope. Without doubt, there were far worse.

"There is some truth to that," I admitted. "But Borgia is a man of vision and daring. He supports the rebirth of classical learning, natural philosophy, the arts, and much more. He decries superstition and hypocrisy. He believes that the Church has become mired in ways that no longer work in the world and he wants to change that."

"All well and good," Mother Benedette said. "But people are caught between wanting to put their trust in him and being unable to do so. In that situation, it is very easy for them to convince themselves that his failure to be what they want him to be is proof of a malign influence at work on him. More and more, they suspect you of being that influence."

"Me?" It was absurd, utterly ridiculous, past all reason. To begin with, I had no particular influence over Borgia, but that he should be absolved of his failings and I held responsible for them . . . I took a breath, forcing myself to remain calm. After all, there was nothing I could do about what was being said in the streets.

"Words cannot hurt me," I said with rather more confidence than I felt.

"Dismiss it if you will," Mother Benedette said, "but I would feel terrible if I went on to Assisi, leaving you in danger."

Though her concern touched me deeply, it also surprised me. "What happens to me is not your responsibility."

"In a way, it is. After all, I put myself in your life, taking it upon myself to stir up memories that you might have dealt with better in a calmer time. If you are confused or distracted as a result, and therefore less able to deal with the problems that confront you, I do have some responsibility for that."

I could not help but think that she was taking too much upon herself, but rather than say so, I replied, "Even so, I don't see how you could help."

Mother Benedette sighed. She folded her hands in her lap and looked at me beseechingly.

"Your mother was as stubborn, always believing that she had to handle problems for herself. She had to meet your father and fall in love with him before she realized that we are not meant to face the trials and tribulations of this life alone. If there is anyone else you can trust to stand with you . . ."

David had stepped forward when Herrera came at me, yet I was still not entirely certain of his motives. Cesare had done the same, but I was no more sure of his intent. Vittoro could be counted on, and Renaldo, too, but they both had their own burdens.

"I cannot ask you—" I began.

"You do not have to. I am offering—nay, I am pleading. Let me be your friend as I was your mother's. I could not help her, but, God willing, I can help you."

What could I say? On the one hand, I was not accustomed to trusting anyone outside the very small circle of people in Rome on whom I could rely. However, they were not with me now; I was alone. Mother Benedette seemed to be a woman of sincerity and strength. I could do far worse in an ally.

Besides, being seen in the company of a holy woman would do me no harm. To the contrary, it would make it more difficult for Herrera and others to label me a witch in need of burning. The thought of thwarting the Spaniard settled the matter for me.

"I accept," I said with a smile, "on the condition that you agree to stay here in the palazzo. If I am to impose on you in such a way, I want to be certain that you have every comfort."

Mother Benedette laughed and squeezed my hands. "Only remember that I am a simple bride of Christ unaccustomed to the ways of the great and powerful."

"I am sure you will hold your own." I had to hope that would prove to be true, but the more I considered it, the better the plan seemed. As soon as Renaldo returned from inspecting his new counting table—he reported that it was coming along nicely—I asked his help in finding suitable accommodations for the abbess.

"She has gone to fetch her things and bid farewell to the other nuns, who are traveling on to Assisi now that the roads are reopening," I told him.

"Excellent. The apartment opposite yours is free."

Most likely, I thought, because no one was eager to sleep across the hall from a poisoner.

"She can have that," Renaldo continued. "I'll make sure the majordomo knows that she is to be made very comfortable." He reflected for a moment, then added, "I hope you won't mind my being so frank, but I am very glad that she is staying. The Spaniards in particular are . . . getting a bit out of hand."

"I daresay we can manage them," I replied.

He went off happily as I hastened to make my usual rounds. By the time I was finished, the abbess had returned. She carried a small bundle bound in a length of homespun cloth, no more elaborate than would be expected of a nun, and was slightly flushed.

"The good sisters tried to persuade me to go on to Assisi with them," she said. "But I think in the end I convinced them that this is where I am called to be."

I had to hope she would not have cause to regret that. After I showed her to her quarters—which she described as breathtaking and beyond anything she could have expected—I offered her a tour of the palazzo.

"Finding your way around isn't as difficult as it may seem at first," I said. "But I want to make sure that you don't get lost."

"If I do, I'm afraid that I will wander for days."

She did appear a bit overwhelmed, which worried me until we came to the lion fountain at the center of the arched loggia overlooking the town. Just as Mother Benedette was admiring the vista, there was a flurry of movement at a door leading to the opposite wing of the palazzo. Borgia appeared, surrounded by a retinue of his secretaries and various of the prelates.

Seeing me, he paused. I kept my head high and met his scrutiny without flinching. I had no doubt that he was looking for any sign of weakness in the aftermath of what had happened. If I showed the smallest glimmer of self-doubt, his confidence in me would be weakened and my own fate made all the more uncertain for that. Truly, it helped to have a friend at my side.

At last, his gaze shifted to Mother Benedette. "Who would this be?" he inquired.

"Your Holiness, may I have the honor to present to you Mother Benedette, abbess of the Convent of Saint Clare in Anzio."

Borgia extended his hand. With a look of reverence, Mother Benedette took it and pressed her lips to the papal ring. "Your Holiness," she murmured.

Staring over her bent head at me, the Vicar of Christ raised a brow in inquiry.

"Mother Benedette and my mother were dear friends."

I watched him as I spoke, curious to see how he would react. It defied credulity that he would have hired my father in the ultrasensitive post of poisoner without investigating him thoroughly first. I wondered how long he had known the truth about my mother's fate and whether he had ever intended to tell me.

"I remember Francesca so well from when she was very small," the abbess said. "It is the blessing of God that I have found her again."

Before Borgia could reply, I added, "I hope you will not mind, Your Holiness, but I have asked Mother Benedette to stay with me here in the palazzo for a time so that she and I may become better acquainted."

His look of surprise was gratifying, so rarely did it occur, but I knew it would not last. Quickly enough, he assessed the situation and came to his own conclusions regarding the abbess.

"You are more than welcome, Mother Benedette," Il Papa said with a warmth rarely seen in him. "I am certain that Francesca will benefit from your presence here." Belatedly, he added, "So shall we all."

As the abbess murmured something about His Holiness's great kindness and generosity, Borgia bent closer. Softly, so that only I could hear him, he said, "Nicely played. It appears that you have Herrera in check."

By which I concluded that I was still in His Holiness's good graces.

When he had passed on, Mother Benedette smiled, apparently not at all overwhelmed by her sudden encounter with Christ's Vicar. "Quite an impressive man. I can see that you have your hands full protecting him."

"It can be challenging," I allowed. "Perhaps you would like to see the kitchens next?" The more people who saw us out and about together, the more quickly news of my warm relationship with the abbess would spread. And the more quickly Herrera's campaign to slander me would be undone.

"I would like nothing better," Mother Benedette said, and took my arm.

22

Renaldo leaned back in his chair, folded his arms behind his head, and gazed up at the ceiling. Deep in thought, he asked, "Mother Benedette has been here how long? Two days?"

Seated across from him in his office, sipping a very decent burgundy he had offered with no apology for its being French, I replied, "About that."

He nodded. "Thus far all of the following is being said with great authority: She received a visitation from Saint Clare, who told her to come to you. Alternatively, His Holiness sent for her because he fears for the state of your soul. Or you sent for her because you fear for the state of His Holiness's soul. Or you received a visitation from Saint Clare or Saint Mary Magdalene or the Devil—there is some disagreement about which—and you sent for her for the sake of your own soul."

I swallowed half the burgundy and said, "The rumormongers have been even busier than usual." I strongly suspected that I was speaking to one of them, but I didn't fault Renaldo's intentions.

"They have," he agreed. "The best part is that Herrera and the other Spaniards are enraged but stymied. They're convinced this is a trick of some sort, but they can't decide how you've managed it."

"I'm surprised they aren't suggesting that, as a servant of the Devil, I didn't just conjure Mother Benedette."

"They would if they could, but she is just so . . . genuine. That homespun habit of hers, the wooden rosary, the aura of sanctity that shines all around her . . ."

"Really? Aura of sanctity?" I liked Mother Benedette well enough, but I saw no halo on her.

"Oh, yes, definitely. I think we should make frequent references to that whenever we speak of her."

"You're seriously suggesting that we—?"

"Look at the facts, Donna Francesca. She arrives in Viterbo, seemingly from nowhere, in the midst of great danger and upheaval. She appeals to you directly, and really, who has more power to preserve the life of His Holiness than you?"

"Vittoro . . . the pope's personal army . . . all the mercenaries he has hired . . . his own incessant but usually brilliant scheming . . ."

Renaldo brushed all that aside as though it was of no consequence. "I am speaking in a more spiritual sense, touching on the eternal battle between good and evil, which surely you personify. She arrives, but she doesn't seek out the Spaniards or His Holiness or anyone except you, a woman like Mary Magdalene herself, tainted by all sorts of aspersions on her character. And what do you do? Like Lot in Sodom, you take her in. You give her refuge and you listen to her wise counsel."

"Lot's wife ended up a pillar of salt, didn't she? And isn't there something about him lying with his own daughters?"

"Details, nothing more. My point is—*the* point is—our Lord has reached out to succor and protect His Holiness despite Borgia's personal weaknesses and in the face of all his enemies. Moreover, He has chosen you as the instrument of His divine will."

"You're drunk." And rather adorably so. Renaldo and I had retired to his office after dinner in the great hall, which we had both observed from the sidelines in our respective roles as steward and poisoner. Mother Benedette, on the other hand, had dined in good company, having been invited to sit next to Lucrezia, who showed her much kind attention. She had since retired, leaving the court agog over her presence.

"I am inspired," Renaldo corrected. "And I am also drunk, but that is only because I don't normally drink enough to not be drunk now."

"I see. Did you really say that I personify the struggle between good and evil?"

"I did, and you do. Whatever the Spaniards are putting about, we both know that you are a fundamentally good person. Yet you have chosen an occupation that assures you will be called upon to kill."

"I did not choose it. It chose me. My father's death left me no alternative." So did I justify my actions to myself and anyone else who cared to listen, including God.

"Yes, I know. As a lone woman, you had no means of avenging his murder, but as Borgia's poisoner—" He shrugged, leaving unsaid what we both knew: that I had so far failed to bring his murderer to justice precisely because of the responsibilities that came with the power that I had gone to such pains to acquire.

"Was not Joan of Arc sent by Almighty God to make Charles the Seventh king of all France?" Renaldo asked.

With no idea why we were suddenly discussing the Maid of Orleans, I countered, "Was she not burned at the stake for her pains?"

"Only because she fell into the hands of Charles's enemies. I am not suggesting for a moment that we let the same happen to Mother Benedette; although, frankly, having a martyr on our side wouldn't be a bad thing."

I didn't take him seriously . . . at least not entirely. "Just so long as it isn't me. Can you imagine centuries from now, good Christians praying to Saint Francesca of the Poisoned Chalice or some such? Truly, I fear for the fate of our Holy Mother were that ever to come to pass."

Renaldo choked on his wine, spewed a quantity out his nose, and fell back in his chair. "You don't worry about Hell at all, do you?"

I thought of what I had seen in Tanners Lane. "Has it ever occurred to you that we are already there?"

He considered the possibility. "That would explain quite a

lot. So what do you think? We put it about that Mother Benedette—maybe we should hint that she's actually an angel disguised as a humble abbess—that her presence is proof that God loves Borgia. Give him a cloak of sanctity, as it were, over his nakedness. Heaven knows he could use it."

"And people say I'm evil." I meant it as a compliment, as I was sure he would know.

"People have only ever said that I'm a little man obsessed with his ledgers. I wouldn't mind being thought of as rather more than that."

"All right, then; but no martyring. When this is all said and done, Mother Benedette goes back to her abbey in Anzio without ever being the wiser as to how we have used her."

"Fair enough. I'll put a word in the right ears. Oh, and it wouldn't hurt if you showed yourself at Mass with her. The weather is bidding fair, so we shouldn't have to worry about any lightning strikes."

I thought of what had happened to Borgia's office in the Vatican and grinned. "If I must be damned, Renaldo, I am grateful to be in such good company."

He was fairly beaming when I departed a short time later. It was by then the deep part of the night, when all the world seems hushed and expectant. Holy Mother Church is said to spend such hours in vigil, awaiting the return of her bridegroom, Christ. Accordingly, the monks were at prayer in the chapel as I walked by. The flowing cadence of their voices as they chanted the office of matins was a balm to the jagged edges of my spirit. I paused for a few moments to listen before going on to my rooms.

Having had almost no sleep now for a second night, I forced myself to lie down on the bed. Sofia's powder beckoned, and—after wrestling briefly with my better sense—I took most of what remained of it. When next I opened my eyes, it was morning.

Having dressed hurriedly, I went in search of Mother Benedette, finding her about to depart for morning services.

"There you are, dear," she said. "I hope you slept well?"

"I did, yes." Remembering Renaldo's suggestion, I added, "Would you mind if I accompany you?"

"On the contrary; I would be delighted."

We proceeded to the chapel, where, to my surprise, there was a far larger crowd than was usual. Seeing the steward, who appeared no worse for his excesses of the night before, I asked, "Isn't it early for so many to be up and about, much less in the mood for prayer?"

Renaldo inclined his head to Mother Benedette, bestowed a smile on me, and said, "His Holiness has sent word that he will conduct Mass this morning."

The rarity of that event and the curiosity it naturally provoked explained the crowd. But it gave no hint of what Borgia was thinking. Although technically he had taken holy orders decades before—a dozen years after becoming a cardinal—and was therefore required to say Mass daily, he had not done so in several months. Indeed, I wasn't entirely sure when he had last attended Mass. In Rome, he enjoyed visiting the Sistine Chapel, adorned with magnificent frescoes by Ghirlandaio, Botticelli, Perugino, and Cosimo Rosselli depicting the lives of Moses and of Christ, but he went there at odd hours, when no services were under way. Rumor had it that he had his eye on the vast ceiling with the thought of commissioning a great work for it. However, the funding to do so continued to elude him. As for the adjacent Saint Peter's Basilica with its overall air of dilapidation, to the best of my knowledge His Holiness had not set foot there since the roof had almost quite literally come down on his head a few months before.

"Someone will be on hand in case his memory is rusty?" I asked.

Renaldo rolled his eyes. "We can only hope. Come, let's get a good seat."

In honor of His Holiness's presence and to accommodate all the dignitaries, benches were set up in the chapel. Renaldo had secured us places not far from the altar. We had an excellent view of Borgia as he processed to it, resplendent in his red and gold vestments, with the magnificent three-tiered jeweled crown that symbolized the papacy on his head. It was well understood that Il Papa had brought an immense amount of portable wealth from the papal treasury with him to Viterbo, but the sight of the triple crown sent a ripple through the crowd. Everyone loves a show, and Borgia seemed intent on providing one.

He got down to business forthwith and proceeded fluidly, never once pausing or tripping. So expert was his performance that an uninformed observer could have been forgiven for believing that he said Mass daily. The Latin rolled smoothly from his tongue, but, it must be said, it lacked grace. I had heard Renaldo read lines of figures with more feeling than

Borgia brought to the mystical transformation of bread and wine into the body and blood of our Savior.

Never mind; he got through it well enough. Steeling myself, I joined the others in the line wending toward the altar. Despite my occasional tendency to shed blood with wanton abandon, I have a strong aversion to it, no doubt the result of what I had experienced as a child. Until recently, the taking of Communion had been a trial for me, but I had decided in the privacy of my own mind that wine was wine and no amount of prayer would ever make it blood. That is heresy, of course, but it was also a comfort to me. Naturally, I can understand why the Church punishes such thinking. The moment people begin to decide for themselves what they believe, it will not be merely Saint Peter's roof that crumbles.

With the Mass over, we exited the chapel. I was about to ask Mother Benedette if she would like to accompany me on my rounds when I became aware of nervous glances being thrown in our direction. A quick look over my shoulder told me why. Herrera, somber in the black velvet and silver that the Spaniards seemed to favor, was cutting a path toward us. Mindful of my last encounter with him, I resolved to restrain myself.

Coming to a halt in front of me, he ignored the abbess and said, "Do not think for a moment that you are fooling anyone, *bruja.* I know what you did, God knows, and soon everyone will know."

At once, I flinched. "Witch" was "witch," regardless of what language it was uttered in, Italian or Castilian. It required no great leap of imagination to understand that he was accusing me of killing his servant, as was rumored in the town. If I failed to respond, I would be acceding to my own guilt. A movement to the side momentarily distracted me. Cesare stood a little apart, watching us. I had not noticed him in the chapel, but that was no surprise. He had even less love for the trappings of faith than did his father, and less tolerance for them.

Because I had no other choice, I said, "Be so good as to enlighten me, signore. What exactly is it that you think I have done?"

"You have surrendered your soul to the Devil himself! You do his bidding in a frenzy, like the ancient Bacchae who tore men apart in their madness. And like them you will descend into Hell and be condemned through all eternity."

Herrera's tirade did not surprise me; I understood full well that fear of what I could reveal about him was added to his genuine dislike for me, creating a vitriolic mixture. But he had managed to shock Mother Benedette.

Before I could even think to stop her, she blurted out, "Signore, you abuse a young woman who desires only to preserve the safety and well-being of Our Holy Father. Surely you wish the same?"

Her audacity took me aback, but no one was more astonished than Herrera himself. He stared at her down the long blade of his nose. "If you are a woman of faith, as you claim, you should separate yourself from this . . . this *thing* with all speed."

I waited, thinking that she would be cowed by him. He was, after all, a powerful man, well accustomed to intimidating lesser mortals. But Mother Benedette did not so much as flinch.

With perfect calm, she said, "God does not send us into the fire to warm our bones. He sends us there to test us. I will not abandon a soul in need."

The Spaniard stared at her in bewilderment. Clearly, he had no notion of how to deal with a woman of genuine sanctity. Cesare took advantage of his confusion and stepped up smoothly. A word in Herrera's ear, a hand on his arm, and he was drawing him away.

Mother Benedette and I continued on. Very shortly, I became aware that she was muttering under her breath. At first I thought she was praying, but it quickly became obvious that she was not.

"Dreadful man," she said. "Absolutely dreadful."

Her anger in the aftermath of her calm reproach of Herrera left me at a loss for words. "Indeed." A bit lamely, I added, "There is more to him than may appear. For instance, I have it on good report that he is a gifted architect."

The abbess looked at me as though I were daft. "How could that possibly matter? He wants to do you harm, and I, for one, am not inclined to let him. All the same, I will fast in repentance for my wicked thoughts. But you must eat; you will need all your strength to deal with him."

I realized just then that I was hungry, but I had no wish to eat alone. After a bit of cajoling, Mother Benedette agreed to postpone her fast and join me. We breakfasted in my rooms, sharing a loaf of still-warm semolina, a soft Ligurian cheese, and a handful of hard-cooked eggs sliced and seasoned with thyme. I also enjoyed a few slices of *culatello,* the ham that is soaked in wine until it emerges rosy red, but the abbess refrained from eating meat. With the servants come and gone, we were free to speak.

Nibbling on a slice of egg, Mother Benedette said, "I had no real understanding of what you are facing here until this morning. How do you bear it?"

The question took me unawares. I had not thought in terms of having a choice.

"His Holiness must be protected. I do what I can."

"But that man, Herrera, is doing everything he can to undermine you. To think that he is the nephew of Their Most Catholic Majesties. Are they blind to the vileness of his character?"

"They must think well enough of him, since he is their emissary. The unfortunate fact is that without his support, the Spanish alliance might well collapse."

"Surely that does not matter now with the French—"

"I would not put too much store in that."

Mother Benedette's gaze sharpened. "Would you not? Well, then, what if the alliance with the Spaniards did come to an end? What would happen?"

I hesitated. The temptation to unburden myself to my mother's friend—now mine—was very great, but so, too, was the habit of silence.

When I did not answer at once, she took a bit more cheese and said, "You do not have to discuss such matters with me, of course. I understand completely. The problem is that you don't know whom to trust, and whom can blame you for that, given the world that you live in? Only know that you can speak to me in perfect confidence. I will never share what you say with anyone, and even though I am only a simple abbess, it is possible that fresh ears and eyes might help you see more clearly."

She was right, of course. And I was in desperate need of sage counsel. Slowly, I said, "Herrera may be the target of an assassin who has been sent to Viterbo."

Mother Benedette laid down her knife. She looked at me closely. "And you are charged with protecting him? What a conundrum for you. You must preserve the life of a man who would be happy to take yours."

I nodded. "It doesn't help that I killed two of his men, no matter how provoked I was. Or that when I tried to investigate the death of his servant, the only witness to that killing also died."

The abbess shook her head slowly. "Truly, you are beset with difficulties. But this is not the time to lose faith. On the contrary, you must cling to it as never before."

"In all honesty, my faith has never been that strong."

"I am sorry to hear that, but I do understand it. You were forced to confront evil at a very young age. It is no wonder that you are filled with doubt regarding spiritual matters."

"It is true that I have struggled to understand why a loving God who is all powerful permits such cruelties to afflict us," I admitted. Indeed, I had studied the matter at some length, seeking wisdom in learned texts. Unfortunately, I had yet to find it. "Saint Augustine claimed that evil is nothing more than the absence of good, but to be very frank, that seems too convenient an explanation."

The abbess did not appear to be offended by my candor,

but neither did she seem impressed by the saint's conclusions. "Augustine was a clever man," she said. "There is no doubt of that. But there is another explanation. This world of physical existence and material obsession is inherently evil. Goodness is to be found solely in the spiritual realm. From there comes the divine light that exists in all of us and gives us our only hope of redemption."

The notion was provocative, but it also seemed somehow familiar. I had encountered a similar idea—no, exactly that idea—elsewhere. Yet within Holy Mother Church, Augustine was regarded as the absolute authority on the nature of evil. His teachings left no room for different interpretations, much less one that suggested that God's Creation was evil in and of itself. Where then had I . . . ?

Abruptly, I remembered. The Mysterium Mundi beneath the Vatican, that secret repository of forbidden knowledge to which Borgia had reluctantly given me access when I had threatened to leave his employ a few months before. I had barely begun to explore the richness of what it contained, but though my interests lay primarily in the realm of natural philosophy and alchemy, documents touching on entirely different matters had compelled my attention. Although I was well aware of the great schism that had torn the Church apart for decades, and from which our Holy Mother was still healing, I had known nothing of earlier challenges to the rule of Rome. Most particularly, I had never heard of the Cathars until I encountered their sacred texts preserved in the hidden chamber beneath the papal palace.

It was the Cathars who believed that this world was evil

by its very nature. According to them, we dwelled not in the creation of a loving God, as the Church taught, but in the kingdom of Satan. God existed, but He was entirely separate in a realm of purity and light vastly beyond the physical world. No priesthood was needed in order to reach Him; to the contrary, His truth was available to every man and woman with the grace to seek it. As for the Church, its material wealth and opulence was all the proof needed that it served not God, as it claimed, but Satan.

Not surprisingly, Holy Mother Church had repressed the Cathars with fire and sword. But their writings had been preserved against the day when the threat they represented might reappear. So far as I knew, all mention of them had been purged from the ordinary discourse of the faithful. Mother Benedette could not possibly know that she was repeating heresy.

"An interesting view," I said carefully.

"Of no real consequence," the abbess said. "My point is that evil is a potent force. We can sit around debating its nature or we can come to grips with preventing its worse effects."

"And how," I ventured, "might we do that?"

She was silent for a moment before she said, "Herrera will not let you protect him. To the contrary; he will do everything to hold you at bay. I, on the other hand, can win his confidence."

"But you despise him. You said so yourself."

"That is not important. I will put aside my personal feelings in the interest of helping you."

As much as I hated to impose on her any more than I was already, the fact remained that I was stymied when it came to the Spaniard. His opinion of me—from whatever source it sprang—made it impossible for me to protect him adequately. Moreover, I was concerned that David might be unable, or unwilling, to do so.

"You actually think that you can get close enough to him to see a threat if it comes?"

"Do you have a better alternative?"

Honesty forced me to admit that I did not. But I did say, "If you intend to befriend him, he will expect you to repudiate me."

"I will never do that," the abbess said emphatically. "But he must have some chink, some weakness, that will help me to reach him."

"He . . . admires Cesare. But he knows that His Eminence and I are—" I broke off, reluctant to shock her.

But apparently Mother Benedette understood me—and the ways of the world—better than I knew. "Then I will tell him that I am working to persuade you that your relationship with a prince of Holy Mother Church is wrong and that, for the sake of both your souls, you should withdraw to a convent."

The notion of my poor self taking holy vows was ludicrous . . . and yet as a ploy it had much to recommend it. "Do you really think you can convince him of that?"

She shrugged as though the answer were self-evident. With certainty that I could only envy, she said, "People will always believe what they want to believe."

23

Two days passed. In all my public encounters with the abbess, I endeavored to appear solemn and thoughtful as befitted someone coming to terms with her own sinfulness. Privately, I vacillated between concern and relief. On the one hand, Herrera seemed willing to grant her access to him. But on the other, I feared that she was putting herself in danger on my behalf.

"Nonsense," she said on the second night, when we were alone in my rooms. By all evidence, the abbess was enjoying her new role. Her customary composure had given way to a sense of excitement that made her seem even more youthful and energetic.

"He has no notion that I am there to keep an eye on anything other than the welfare of his soul," she said with confidence. "Which, by the way, needs much attending to."

"He confides in you?"

"Not in the least, except to rant about you and Cesare. But his household priests have let drop that rumors of his behavior here have reached Spain. Word has come back that Their Most Catholic Majesties are not pleased. They may recall him. I suspect that is why he has allowed me to befriend him."

David had not mentioned that to me in the one brief encounter we had managed since returning to Viterbo. He claimed to still be in the good graces of the Spaniards despite his instinctive move at the villa to help me, but I had my doubts. He had also expressed his concern about the wisdom of using Mother Benedette, but I put that down to his understandable suspicion of Christians and did not worry overly much about it.

Listening to her, I was reconfirmed in that decision. The news about the Spanish monarchs was important. I wondered if Borgia was aware of it. "Much good that would do the alliance," I said.

"I don't think it will come to that. Once your assassin makes his move and is caught, surely Queen Isabella and King Ferdinand will realize that they have no choice but to continue to support His Holiness, or risk the triumph of someone who is both his enemy and theirs?"

"That is to be hoped. Of course, it all hinges on catching the assassin before he can kill Herrera. I take it that you have encountered no one suspicious?"

"Regrettably not, but be assured that I will persevere."

I nodded, grateful for her help even as I still regretted involving her in the matter.

Several hours after she had crossed the hall to her own quarters, I was awake and mulling over those regrets when my door suddenly opened. As a matter of routine, I kept it secured; but locks are made to be picked, and it seemed that someone had done just that. At once, I reached for the knife under my pillow, only to quickly slip it out of sight again when Cesare entered, pocketing a key I had not known he had.

He must have caught a glimpse of the knife, for he smiled and said, "However did you restrain yourself from throwing that at me?"

I did my best to appear unruffled by his sudden appearance, but the truth is that my heart beat more rapidly than I would have liked. In the light from the glowing embers in the braziers, he looked disheveled, weary, and all too desirable.

"Alas, I've only ever used it close in," I said. Perhaps it was not wise to remind him of what I had done with a knife such a short time before, but I felt an overwhelming need for candor between us.

Cesare stepped farther into the room, shutting the door behind him.

"Have you tucked Herrera in for the night?" I asked.

A look of . . . regret? . . . flitted across his face. "He's passed out drunk, as usual. If he keeps on this way, the assassin's job will be done for him." Taking a seat on the side of the bed, he asked, "What's this I hear about you leaving me?"

Leaving him. Not Il Papa or my position in the household

or anything else. Only him. I smiled despite myself. "Are you referring to my newfound conscience, which is prompting me to contemplate retirement to a nunnery?"

"Yes, I believe I am."

"You find that plausible?"

"Not at all. The marvel is that anyone does. I take it you wanted the abbess to get close to Herrera?"

I nodded. "She offered, and I felt that I had no choice but to accept. He certainly will not let me near him."

"And you don't trust ben Eliezer to do the job?"

Cesare's notion that David might be behind the threat still lingered in the back of my mind. I did not want to give it any credence, any more than I wanted to believe that David was right about Cesare's motives. I certainly was not about to discuss either possibility.

"He may have compromised himself when he moved to stop Herrera from attacking me," I said. "Besides, a second pair of eyes is always useful."

"You think she can spot the danger to him better than, say, I could?" he asked.

Generally, I had a sensible regard for the pride of young men, particularly those raised to think of themselves as princes. But just then I answered more tartly than I usually would have.

"For once, look beyond your own vanity, I pray you. She is my best hope because no one would suspect her of being on watch for an assassin. But even with her assistance, I fear that I have little chance of success."

The admission was wrenched from me, but Cesare seemed to think little of it. "It is not like you to give up so easily."

I stared at him in mingled astonishment and fury. "Easily? You have no idea what you are talking about. No concept of what has been happening to me—"

"Of course I don't," he shot back. "You've barely told me anything. But I am not the insensitive clod you assume me to be—at least not entirely. I have enough sense to know that something is very wrong and to be worried about you."

My anger staunched, at least a little, I relented. With a sigh, I said, "I am worried about me, too."

He pulled his boots off before swinging his legs onto the bed. I had his mother to thank for that; the redoubtable Vannozza, as she was always called. He had left her roof for his father's while still a very young child, yet her influence had never weakened.

"Tell me why," he said and put an arm around my shoulders, drawing me to him.

I lay stiffly against him for a few moments, until the warmth of his body and my own need combined to drain away my resistance. Quietly, I said, "My mother didn't die when I was born, as I have always believed. She was murdered three years later by her own family, who could not bear that she had married a Jew. Just before the attack, she hid me behind a wall, but there was a hole in it. I saw everything."

"Bon déu." In his shock, Cesare lapsed into his native Catalan. Even so, I understood him well enough.

With my head against his shoulder, I added, "I've always known that there was something wrong with me. A darkness that sets me apart and threatens to consume my soul. At least now I know why it exists."

His arms tightened around me. "That is what you were running from the other night?"

"Yes, I suppose." Dimly, I remembered the shadowy figure who had seemed to be pursuing me. One of the men I had seen kill my mother? Perhaps her brother? Or an amorphous image of Death conjured by my frenzied brain?

He turned over onto his side, drawing me beneath him. Engulfed in my own concerns as I was, I remained stiff and unyielding until the slow stroking of his hand along my thigh distracted me. He was, after all, still the boy I had exchanged glances with when we were both just trembling on the edge of understanding what it was that we were. The wounded youth who had come to me the first time in pain yet still had given me such pleasure. And, too, the dark lover before whom I could drop the mask I felt compelled to maintain with all others—even Rocco, whom I refused to think about just then.

Very shortly I could not think at all. Our time apart had heightened my need for Cesare and his for me. We came together hotly, ravenous for each other. I clasped him tightly, savoring the beauty of his body and his perfectly honed strength. He groaned deeply when he entered me, and threw his head back. I arched upward, pressing my lips to the pulse beating in his throat, savoring the power of his life's blood. Moonlight, flooding through the high windows, bathed our bodies in silver. We swayed together, locked in ecstasy, until the world dissolved and we with it. Still entwined, we fell across the bed. With what little strength I had left, I pulled the covers over us both.

I was settled again in the crook of Cesare's arm, my head

against his shoulder, when he said, "Does this mean you'll forego the nunnery?"

I laughed and swatted at him lightly. We turned on our sides, spooning together. I was all but asleep when I heard—or imagined I heard—Cesare whisper: "I need you to be the woman you are, Francesca. Not whoever it is that you think you should be."

He slept then, and I did as well, soothed as I was by all that had passed between us. But hours later, in the depths of the night, I awoke, driven by the hunger for Sofia's powder that still gnawed at me. Too restless to sleep, I sat for a time beside the window, but before dawn I was up and dressed.

I stood beside the bed, looking down at Cesare. As though sensing my gaze, he opened one eye and stared back at me quizzically.

"I am going to the chapel to pray," I said in answer to his silent question.

He snorted, turned over, and buried his head in the pillow. Even so, I could just make out his reply. "Watch out for lightning bolts."

The monks had finished their prayers and were gone by the time I appeared, which suited me well enough. Contrary to Cesare's assumption, I was not going merely to be seen; I truly did mean to pray. Or, failing that, at least to try to bring my unruly mind to some semblance of order.

Clearly, the stress of protecting Borgia combined with learning of my mother's fate had undone me. Nightmares, hallucinations, visions, and now strange fears and doubts were all signals that I was closer to outright madness than I had ever been before. Perhaps I had already crossed that line and didn't realize it. Whatever the case, I had to find some way to continue functioning, and I had to do it quickly.

And so I prayed. Not well, for I was never good at doing so, but I did make a wholehearted try.

"God," I began, only to quickly correct myself. "Almighty God, Father in Heaven." Flattery never hurt with Borgia; I had to assume that it would not in this case either. "I beseech your help. Your servant, Christ's Vicar on Earth, is in mortal danger. Sustain me so that I may protect him. Do not let me be undone by delusions born of darkness but give me the light to see true danger and defeat it.

"And also, please, explain why You allow so much cruelty to exist in Your Creation. Why You leave Your children to suffer so much pain and suffering. Why You let monsters kill my mother."

As I said, I had never been any good at praying.

Nor did I expect a response, although I did wait a few minutes as a simple courtesy. The stale scent of incense hung in the air. I inhaled, coughed a little, and rose to go. Turning, I observed a priest staring at me in blank confusion. Dropping my eyes in a show of humility, I crossed myself.

The poor man stood frozen as I passed him on my way out of the chapel. He would recover quickly enough and hasten to tell what he had seen—the *strega* at prayer in God's house, apparently unscathed. Either the Almighty was proving unexpectedly lax or I was not what others claimed. Under other circumstances, I would have been amused.

As it was, my thoughts were grim as I walked through the

great hall. The nature of evil and its presence in this world weighed heavily on me. For all that Augustine's explanation was accepted Church doctrine, it appeared to be more the contrivance of an elegant mind than an insight into reality. Yet the Cathars' view—that the material world was evil by its very nature—seemed to pass over the question rather than even attempt to resolve it.

In the Mysterium Mundi, I had read sacred Cathar texts in which the sole purpose of human existence was to become *perfecti*, individuals of such spiritual enlightenment as to be able to free themselves forever from the bounds of this world. Those who could not do so in a single lifetime—the vast majority—were condemned to be reborn again and again until they at last proved their worthiness. In its time, the doctrine had attracted peasants, merchants, and even members of the nobility, all united by the conviction that there was not even the potential for good in this realm of existence.

If I were not careful, I could find myself thinking the same. I needed sunlight and fresh air, but even more I needed to be reminded that there was a world in which every thought and every breath did not hang on the will of men for whom nothing mattered except the raw exercise of power, no matter how much pain it inflicted. A world in which women cooked mutton shanks, children cut new teeth, babies were born and lived, and people were—against all odds—happy, if only briefly.

Perhaps my effort at prayer, poor though it had been, had succeeded at least in clearing my head, for I set off about my duties with renewed vigor. No one attempted to impede me, but neither did I see any sign that Mother Benedette's championing of me was having an effect. I continued to be met with hostile, hastily averted stares and cold silence.

Several hours later, as I pressed my ring into a drop of soft wax on what I hoped was the last item to be inspected that day, I glanced up and saw David, hovering just outside the kitchens. He caught my eye, then turned and walked away.

I followed. We met up around a corner of the stables. He was leaning against a wall, seeming at ease, but I sensed otherwise. The finely drawn lines around his eyes suggested that he was both tired and worried.

"Call off your nun," he said as soon as I appeared.

Taken aback, I dodged. "She's hardly 'my' nun."

"Don't prevaricate, Francesca. It's beneath you. Herrera thinks he can use her to bring you down. That's the only reason he's tolerating her."

"She had to make him believe that in order to get close to him. That business about the convent—"

David waved a hand dismissively. "I'm not talking about that. He's told his men that you're responsible for all the deaths that have occurred, starting with the kitchen boy, and that with the abbess's help, he'll be able to prove it."

"That's ridiculous. Where would he get such a notion?"

"From her? How do you know what she's told him or why? For that matter, what do you know of her?"

Anger rose in me. David was not the only one working under great strain and living in the shadow of disaster. He had no right to speak to me in such a way.

Stiffly, I said, "I know that she was my mother's friend."

"That must have been years ago. What does it matter now?"

"Because she alone told me the truth about how my mother died. Do you have any idea what that means to me?"

Holding my gaze, David said, "No, I don't, and I won't pretend otherwise. But it isn't like you to give your trust so easily."

Or to give it at all, although I would not say that to him. I worried that Borgia's meeting with the French might have been the signal David was waiting for. Yet Herrera still lived.

"Is Mother Benedette making it more difficult for you to stay close to the Spaniard?"

"She is, yes. He doesn't need a jester around when he's conspiring with a holy woman."

Was that the root of the problem, then, or was he genuinely concerned about the abbess's actions? I had no way of knowing. But I could at least try to find out.

"I will see what can be done, but in the meantime, you will have to tolerate her presence."

It was not the answer he wanted, as he made clear when, without another word, he turned and stalked away. Alone, I sagged against the wall of the stables and tried to gather my thoughts. I might even have managed it had not the world intruded yet again.

A pale, wide-eyed page approached me but stopped a good six feet away. Head down, clearly wishing himself anywhere else, he said, "Your pardon, donna. His Holiness requires your presence."

I rubbed my hands over my face, took a breath, and went.

24

Help me to understand," Borgia said. "You thought this was a good time to introduce into my household a woman whose presence prompts reflection on the sinfulness of my papacy and the need for some sort of purification. Is that right?"

"That was never my intent, nor do I believe it to be hers." At least, I most profoundly hoped that it was not. "With all respect, Your Holiness, I'm not even aware that is happening."

His face darkened. "That's because you don't have to listen to my prelates prattle on and on." In a singsong voice, he recited, "I've done too much to advance my own family at the cost of everyone else's. I should temper my ambitions, make peace with the French, be seen to say Mass more often, and—oh, yes—put La Bella aside or at least be more discreet about her. Next they'll want me in a hair shirt flagellating myself!"

The image of Borgia, who was the most worldly man I knew, behaving in any such way tempted a smile from me. With difficulty, I suppressed it and said, "Is it really fair to ascribe all that to Mother Benedette's influence?"

In fact, I knew that it was not. Borgia was listing the litany of complaints about him that had existed since the day his pontificate began. His recent advancement of Cesare and Juan had merely exacerbated matters. But if he wanted to blame the abbess, there was little I could do about it. Except, perhaps, to remind him of what he already knew.

"Mother Benedette offered her assistance and I accepted. You yourself thought having her here was a good idea."

"Because I thought the plan was to rehabilitate you so that you could get on with the job of protecting Herrera and, more important, me. Instead, you seem to have turned that task over to a nun and a jester."

"You know that David isn't—"

"All right, a nun and a troublemaking Jew. Is that better? Should I sleep more easily in my bed knowing that the two of them are looking after the man who is key to preserving my alliance with Spain?"

"At least you sleep." I spoke before I could think, and I regretted it immediately. The single decent night's rest that I had enjoyed had done little to smooth the rough edges of my temper or soothe my jangled nerves. Worse yet, the craving for Sofia's powder was greater than ever.

"I'm sorry. I shouldn't have said—"

"Sit down," Borgia ordered. When I had done so, he stared

hard at me and said, "What's wrong with you?" Before I could reply, he provided his own answer. "Do you want absolution for killing those men? You don't need it, but if it will make you feel better—"

"Can you absolve me for being able to kill them?"

He lowered himself into his chair and studied me. "So that's the problem? You don't appreciate your own nature even when it keeps you alive? Would you rather go a sheep to the slaughter?"

"As the Lamb of God did?"

Really, I seemed to have no control over my tongue. Who was I to remind Christ's Vicar of the sacrifice on the cross?

"My apologies, Your Holiness. I spoke without thought. What is it that you wish me to do?"

A great sigh escaped him, like a snort from a bull. For a moment, he looked older even than his years, weighed down by the insatiable appetite of his own ambitions. But in the next instant, he rallied, and said, "I must hold this all together. If I cannot . . ."

The results would mean disaster for *la famiglia* and all those close to Borgia. I did not need to be reminded of that.

"I will speak with Mother Benedette." After what David had told me, I had already intended to do so. As much as I did not want to send her away, if she was causing problems, however inadvertently, I would have no choice.

Cautiously, mindful of Borgia's temper, I added, "However, if you truly are as concerned as you appear to be, there is an obvious solution."

He raised an eyebrow as though daring me to continue. "Spare us both and do not suggest again that Herrera should have a convenient accident."

I took a breath, let it out slowly, and said, "I wasn't about to do so. Take him into custody. Surround him with guards, control everything and everyone that comes near him. The assassin will be unable to do his work, and you will be safe."

Borgia chuckled. It wasn't a sound that I was accustomed to hearing from him, and it took me a moment to recognize it. By the time I did, it had become a full-throated laugh.

"By God, Francesca," His Holiness exclaimed when he was able to speak again. "I had no idea that you had such a wicked sense of humor."

I was not amused. "I am not joking."

His good humor fled as quickly as it had appeared. Such mercurial behavior was unlike him. I was unsure what to make of it.

His prodigious brow drawn into furrows, he scowled at me. "But what you've just suggested is a joke, and a dangerous one at that. Juan has been arrested and is being held by the Spaniards. You want me to in effect return the favor and arrest Herrera?"

"For his own good, to keep him and yourself safe. That is altogether different."

"Their Most Catholic Majesties will not see it as such. What will I tell them? That I am powerless before one lone assassin? How long do you imagine it will take them to switch their support to whichever one of my enemies they decide is stronger?"

I could not hide my frustration. "What are we to do, then? Just let Herrera be killed and the alliance die with him?"

Abruptly, Borgia slammed his fist down on the desk. The carved silver inkwell leaped into the air, fell off the edge, and crashed to the floor, showering black droplets in all directions. Red-faced, His Holiness snarled, "Find the assassin! Kill him! Do what I keep you to do or I will be done with you, by God!"

I had seen Borgia in a fury before, but I had never seen him as I did at that moment. The ruthless prince who had clawed his way to the pinnacle of power in all of Christendom, never showing an instant's lack of certainty or confidence, was . . . afraid? Truly, genuinely frightened by events that were spiraling out of control. And perhaps by more. Borgia had what everyone recognized as the most formidable spy service in all of Christendom. It was entirely possible that he was receiving information that confirmed the danger he was in while giving no hint of its source. He—who was so accustomed to maneuvering and manipulating his way from triumph to triumph—had no real experience with defeat, but if he truly believed that he faced it now . . .

Borgia angry, greedy, ambitious, determined, caught within the irresistible force of his own will was dangerous enough. But Borgia afraid? I could scarcely imagine what he was capable of doing in such a state. More important, I had no desire to find out.

Standing on the edge of a cliff, peering into the abyss with which I was becoming all too familiar, I said, "Be assured, I will do my best."

Borgia being Borgia, he had to have the last word. I was at the door, about to leave, when he hissed under his breath, "It's your worst that I want, Francesca. Forget about the abbess redeeming you. Better that you remind men of why they feel the cold hand of terror when you pass by."

I should have brushed that off as no more than an echo of his fear, and I did try. Yet the bitter truth of it weighed on me. I left his presence hollow with sadness yet determined all the same to do what I must.

To that end, I went in search of Mother Benedette. Cesare had taken Herrera off hunting, sparing me the need to seek her among the Spaniards. I found the abbess in the garden, standing head bowed, in deep reflection. When I approached along the radiating gravel paths that ended in a sparkling fountain, she appeared startled, but she quickly smiled.

"I was just going to look for you, Francesca. Are you well?"

Though I smiled a little in turn, the effort fell short. I was too concerned about what both David and Borgia had said to pretend otherwise. "I have been better. Let us sit and talk awhile."

When we had settled on a bench nearby, I remained silent for a few moments, gathering my thoughts. Finally, I said, "I fear that I have asked too much of you."

"Dear child," Mother Benedette said, "you worry needlessly. Everything is going as we planned. Herrera finds it useful to allow my presence, which affords me the opportunity to keep watch on him. At the same time, I am doing my best to persuade him to see you in a kinder light, and I think I am making some progress in that regard."

"Are you? Yet he has decided that I am responsible for the deaths that have occurred within His Holiness's household. He thinks he is going to be able to prove that."

"Where did you get such a notion?" When I did not answer at once, her eyes narrowed. "You have someone else close to him, don't you? Someone who has fed you this nonsense."

A cuckoo swooped down to take a drink from the fountain, then darted away again. The bird is known for its subterfuge, given as it is to laying eggs in the nests of other birds, thereby tricking them into raising its young at no cost to itself. Yet for all that, it has a lovely song.

"It doesn't matter how I learned of it," I said. "My worry is that this is no place for a woman like you."

Mother Benedette sighed. Drawing her hands from inside the wide sleeves of her habit, she took hold of my own.

"Francesca, when I came here, I had no idea that I was about to encounter so remarkable a young woman. You confront the darkness that surrounds us with extraordinary courage, yet for all that, you remain trapped within it."

I could have told her that she had it wrong, that the darkness was inside me, but before I could do so she continued.

"Have you never considered that there is a better way? A truer way open to you if only you have the grace to see it?"

"That is a tempting thought, but—"

Her smooth face framed by her wimple became more animated. "It is hard, I know. But there is a means of rending the web of evil to see beyond this world. A way for the truly pure of spirit to find the path out of darkness into the light."

Was there anything that I desired more than to throw off the shackles of evil that had held me in its merciless grip since I was a tiny child and become the woman I would have been? A woman not of darkness but of the light?

"I wish I could believe you," I said.

"But you already know the truth of what I am saying," she exclaimed. "I saw it in you when we spoke of this before."

I shook my head, uncertain of what she meant. "Spoke of . . . ?"

"Of evil and the nature of this world. You mentioned Augustine, and I said there was another way of explaining the omnipresence of evil, because it is inherent in this realm of physical existence and material obsession."

She leaned back a little and studied me. "I think you recognized what I was saying and from whence it came, although I admit to being very surprised that you would have such knowledge."

Slowly, her meaning became clear. Yet even then I resisted accepting it. It did not seem possible that she could . . . "You know of the Cathar heresy?" I asked.

Her hands tightened on mine. "So-called by the very agents of the evil it defies. But how have you come to know of this? For all the promise you show, you are not one of us."

I could not have heard her correctly. The Cathars had been exterminated hundreds of years ago. Scarcely the memory of them remained except in the deepest, most hidden recesses of the Vatican, where old enemies were never forgotten.

Mother Benedette smiled. Her gaze, holding mine, was filled with excitement. "Surely there is no need for subterfuge between us any longer—and no point to it, either. I would be fascinated to learn what documents you were able to read and where you found them. Is it possible that the Church of Satan preserved our sacred texts? And if so, to what end? But unfortunately other matters must concern us."

A low buzzing filled my ears. Against it, I struggled to understand what she was telling me. Though I could hardly claim to know everything the Church had done to assure its supremacy over the long expanse of bloody centuries, I did not believe anyone had received more ruthless treatment than had the Cathars. And yet they had managed to endure despite everything?

"How—?" I began.

"How are we still here, in this world of evil?" she asked. "It is true that the Church of Satan tried to wipe out all traces of our existence in order to keep mankind enslaved in darkness forever. But the *perfecti,* the most enlightened among us, were determined to preserve the path to redemption. To that end, they sent a select group to safety even as all the others surrendered their own lives to make the Church believe that it had won. By that sacrifice, our fellows threw off the last shackles of this world and were freed from it forever. We who are still trapped in Satan's realm pray to one day follow them."

From all that I had read, the Cathars had gone to their deaths without resistance, even cheerfully, singing as the flames consumed them. Their executioners had found that deeply disturbing. Some wrote of being haunted by the spectacle, reliving it over and over until they feared they were descending into madness. Several were suspected of taking their own lives, their deaths concealed by the Church with hasty burials far from consecrated ground. In the most secret reports that I had uncovered, a few witnesses even claimed that they had seen the souls of the Cathars rise into the sky on ribbons of silver light. Generally, the Church makes a public show of executing heretics, but next to the names of those witnesses there had been only a single, singularly ominous notation: *Silenced.*

Was the Cathar faith merely a grand delusion, as, perhaps, all faith is by its very nature? Or had their rituals and practices revealed to them something that is hidden from the rest of us? The documents preserved within the Mysterium Mundi passed over the details of Cathar rites with suspiciously scant mention, as though even the act of recording them was dangerous to Holy Mother Church. Such restraint hinted that at least some in the highest reaches of the Church believed there was cause to be afraid. But why?

I tried to speak, but the muscles of my throat were oddly weak. Shock gripped me as I struggled to understand the magnitude of what the abbess was revealing. The light, fractured and jagged as it fell through the branches overhead, distracted me. There was something I needed to think about, something important. The abbess was a secret Cathar . . . there were others . . . she was here in Viterbo.

"I don't understand." My voice was weak and seemed to come from a great distance. I could scarcely hear myself, but I heard her clearly enough.

"You will, I promise. Before we are done, you will understand everything." Her grip tightened. "Do not fear what is about to be revealed to you, Francesca. Embrace the truth and be reborn into the eternal light."

My fingers were tingling, the sensation radiating up my arms. On the periphery of my vision, the world appeared to be shattering into fragments, not unlike the strange mosaic I had glimpsed in the piazza. Before it disintegrated altogether, I stared down at the hands clasping mine.

Too late, I realized why Mother Benedette was wearing gloves.

25

Poisons designed to enter the body through the skin, rather than by ingestion in food or drink, are among the most difficult to devise. Generally, they form a residue on any surface that even a person of middling sensibility will notice in time to avoid. It has taken me years to create a highly lethal contact poison for use on glass, a surface so difficult to taint as to be virtually above suspicion. Indeed, the Spanish poisoner hired to replace my father had not hesitated to touch it. He lived mere minutes after doing so.

Confronting the problem posed by contact poison, Mother Benedette had employed the time-honored solution: Do not depend on the victim touching anything but instead touch the victim. Of course, that carries certain obvious dangers for the poisoner, but sensible precautions usually suffice. The best of these is to use gloves dipped in a solution of alum and sulfate of lead to discourage the passage of liquids inward to the skin. Additionally, it is prudent to encase the hands in melted wax before donning the gloves.

To be perfectly fair, Mother Benedette had not actually poisoned me. I was merely drugged. The world was out of joint, bits of it no longer fitting together properly. I looked up and saw the branches of a tree seemingly engulfing the sky, only to shrink suddenly as I became a giantess looming above them. The gravel path curved upward like a wave about to crest, only to dissolve in a shower of light and fall back to earth. The face of the angel atop the stone fountain in the garden stood away from its body and seemed to fly straight at me. I gasped and tried to pull away, but the abbess held firm.

"We cannot stay here, Francesca," she said in a kindly manner. "People will see you and think that you truly are possessed. You know what they will do to you then, don't you?"

Flames rippled up from the ground. I opened my mouth to scream, but no sound emerged. In addition to shattering my senses, whatever I had been given had also paralyzed my vocal cords. In my disordered state, gripped by the sudden terror of burning, I could not resist the abbess as she guided me out of the garden and back toward the palazzo.

I have only scant recollection of returning with her to my quarters in the palazzo—a brief glimpse down a corridor, the murmur of Mother Benedette's voice urging care as we walked up a flight of steps, staring at the complex wood grain of a door that looked like rippling waves frozen in space and time.

And then I was lying on my bed. The abbess stood at the foot of it. At some point, she had removed her gloves and cleaned her hands. They were bare as she went about the task of removing my shoes.

I tried to resist, but the effort was futile. Despite my most desperate efforts, my mind could no longer control my body.

The abbess put her fingers to my lips. "Hush, Francesca. Don't fight this. You have no idea how fortunate you are."

Fortunate? Beneath my confusion and fear, I felt like nothing so much as like Creation's worst fool. There was a reason why the jagged mosaic appeared familiar; I had seen it before. This was not the first time Mother Benedette had drugged me; the *panetto,* the *torrone,* my mother's psalter—all had played their part. However, this time the effect was both more intense and more refined, including rendering me mute.

I tried to speak again to ask her why, but no sound emerged. She looked up in time to see the movement of my lips and frowned slightly.

"All that I have done since meeting you has been for your sake. Soon you will understand that."

As she spoke, the abbess began to bind me to the four corners of the bed with long strips of cloth.

In desperation, I struggled to jerk away, but the drug I had been given weakened me in every regard. My muscles refused to obey the frantic commands of my mind. I could only lie, compliant and helpless, as she finished securing my arms and legs.

"Don't be alarmed; this is only for your safety," she said. "The journey you are about to make is difficult and demanding. I don't want you to injure yourself. Indeed, I have gone to the greatest lengths to prevent that." Patting my arm as she might a fractious child's, she added, "They only wanted me to use you as a means of slipping into Borgia's household and arranging Herrera's death in such way that you would be blamed. But I recognized the strength in you, how you have learned to use the darkness of this world. I knew in an instant where your true destiny lies."

The sweetness of her smile belied the fierce fanaticism of her gaze. "The elixir you are about to receive is the rarest and most precious legacy of the Cathars," she said. "It was revealed to the first of us by the Angel Gabriel. Ever since, the most spiritually advanced have been able to use it to find the path to liberation from this world. But to do so takes great courage, for truly, the path to Heaven lies through Hell. Ever since we first met, I have been preparing you for this. You must not resist or hesitate; and above all, you must not retreat or you will be lost forever. Go forward, Francesca, and find the light."

With that, she drew a small vial from beneath her robe, removed the stopper from it, and held the rim to my lips. When I tried to jerk my head away, she gripped me tightly within the curve of her arm and held me immobile as she slowly dripped a pale, glistening liquid into my mouth. I tried desperately to spit it out, but again, my muscles would not obey me. To my horror, I was helpless to prevent it from slipping down my throat.

"It is done," she said when she had finished and closed the vial. "I will not leave you, and if anyone comes to inquire about you, I will say that you are in prayer and reflection and cannot be disturbed."

She would be believed. No one would think to doubt the holy woman of Anzio who stood in such stark contrast to the worldly corruption of the papal court. Only Cesare might, and he was away, hunting with Herrera. I was trapped alone with her, helpless before the power of the Cathar elixir that was taking over my body and my mind.

Never had I known such terror, or at least not since I was a child hidden behind a wall, peering out at a sea of blood and death.

Had I been able to make any sound at all, I would have screamed in horror. As it was I could do nothing as slowly but inexorably I began my descent into Hell.

To my surprise, I found myself on a street I recognized, more or less, for it was like many that run as strands of life and commerce through the thriving Campo dei Fiore, the central market in Rome. Unlike the parts of the city rebuilt by the prelates of the Church and the great merchant princes, those parts that are all travertine marble that changes hue throughout the day, the Campo is of good red brick made from Tiber mud. When the sun hits it just right, it turns to blushing gold. All around me I saw the two- and- three-story buildings that fill the neighborhood—shops and taverns on the ground floor, apartments above. The old Romans lived that way and their descendents do as well, now that the city has emerged from the chaos of the Great Schism that almost destroyed Holy Mother Church.

Baskets of autumn flowers hung from trellises, adding their aroma to the more pungent scents of manure, garbage, and offal that drifted as a low miasma along the pavement. Oddly, so I thought, the street was empty. I saw no sign of the merchants, traders, shoppers, and thieves who normally thronged the Campo. Despite their absence, I had no sense of anything being wrong, no dire circumstance that would explain why I was alone when I should have been among many.

I turned a corner and came to a street I knew only too well, Via dei Vertrarari, where the glassmakers cluster. At once, I hesitated. Rocco's shop was on that street. I had no desire to see it, much less him. Yet despite my best efforts, I was propelled forward by some force I could not resist, past a dozen other shops until I came finally to a modest timbered building half hidden between its neighbors on either side.

A woman was sitting on a bench out in front. Her head was bent so that I could not see her face. Looking more closely, I realized that she held an infant on her lap. She was singing softly. I strained to hear her.

Firefly, firefly, yellow and bright
Bridle the filly under your light,
The child of my heart is ready to ride,
Firefly, firefly, fly by her side.

As she finished, she lifted her head and looked straight at me. I gasped to see a face that appeared to be mine yet was not. The woman's expression was filled with peace and love. She seemed utterly happy. So, too, did the child she held, who looked up at her adoringly and waved its chubby little arms to embrace her.

If I had been the woman I longed to be, the woman who could have married Rocco, that would be my child. We would be sitting there, in the bright sunlight, with no shadow of darkness over us. Shortly, I would get up and go back into the shop. Little Nando would be sitting at the table, perhaps sketching as he loved to do. I was convinced that he was going to be a brilliant artist someday, not unlike his father. I would ruffle his hair as I passed, before stepping out into the courtyard in the back where Rocco had his furnace. He would be there—a tall, powerfully built man in his late twenties, his bare chest covered by the leather apron he wore when he worked at the furnace, turning globs of ordinary sand into works of surpassing beauty. He would look up and see me and our child. And he would smile with all the love that he had been ready to offer me but which I had not been worthy to receive.

But it was not Rocco I saw. It was the woman—myself. As I watched, she cried out suddenly and clasped the child more tightly to her even as blood gushed from her body to flow in a torrent that spread so quickly over the paving stones to wash up against my feet. All the while, she looked at me, her eyes dark with sorrow and pity.

I screamed and fled. As though pursued by demons, I ran with no thought to where I was going, turning corners heedlessly, racing onward, my only thought escape. I ran until, abruptly, I stopped. I was standing in front of a wall. In it there was a window comprised of small panes of leaded glass set within an elaborately carved frame. So pretty was the window that it invited any to look through it, but I refrained, knowing perfectly well what I would see on the other side. One dying mother was enough.

I ran on, coming finally to a noble piazza fronting upon a palazzo of rare elegance and beauty. A bullfight was in progress. As I watched, a massive white bull charged down a chute into an arena. The crowd, arrayed on tiers all around, cheered widely. Beneath a mulberry and gold canopy, a man I recognized as Rodrigo Borgia drew breath to speak.

I ignored him and looked instead toward the palazzo. I knew the place intimately, for I had lived there for ten years, arriving as the unnaturally quiet daughter of Borgia's newly hired poisoner and not leaving until the day Il Cardinale Rodrigo Borgia moved into the Vatican as Pope Alexander VI.

The roar of the crowd faded as the bullfight and all attending it vanished. They were of no importance, but the man coming out one of the side doors of the palace, glancing in each direction as though to make sure that he was not seen, did matter. My dead father, as he had not appeared even in my dreams, seeming so alive and real that I started at once toward him, only to stop abruptly when I realized that he could not see me. Intent on his own business, he hurried by as though I were the ghost, not he. I followed. If there was anything in my mind besides surprise, it was that I had to find a way to speak with him. But try though I did to catch up, he remained just out of my reach. Together yet apart, we sped through winding streets, along lanes, and over the Ponte Sant'Angelo, the ancient bridge that spans the Tiber. Once on the other side, in the looming shadow of the Castel Sant'Angelo, which is both prison and fortress, he did not pause but continued on toward Saint Peter's.

A heavy sense of doom descended on me. I was gripped by the conviction that I knew where he was going but was powerless to stop him. Still, I followed, for I seemed to have no choice. Not far from the basilica, my worst fears were confirmed when he turned in the direction of the charming *palazzetto* where Pope Innocent VIII had preferred to live, finding it infinitely more comfortable than the Vatican Palace.

In desperation, I cried out, "Father, no!"

My voice echoed against the walls of the houses pressing in around us. The very air seemed to crackle in warning. Yet my father showed no sign of hearing me. He continued on into the lane where I knew a man I would shortly kill in a cell under Borgia's palazzo was waiting along with several others. I would slit his throat and watch his blood drain away into the gutters carved into the stone floor of the torture chamber for just that purpose. But I would be too late. Before that happened, my father would be set upon, beaten, his skull smashed, his life left to run out in rivulets of blood washing away into the filthy Roman gutter.

Knowing all that, knowing my own helplessness, nonetheless I plunged on, entering the lane just as the men leaped on him. As though time itself had slowed to a crawl, I watched the final moments of my father's life as I had imagined them again and again in the torment of my grief. He died neither quickly nor easily, but with a valiant struggle that availed him nothing. Just at the last, before death closed his eyes forever, he looked in my direction. For an instant, he seemed to see me as I stood, convulsed with grief and shock. His hand rose, stretching out toward me, and hung suspended in the air, only to finally fall as his life left him.

I cried out, but no one heard. I tried to go to him but I could not move. Grief filled me but I could not weep. Confronted by pain and regret that had warped my life beyond all recognition of what it might have been, I was helpless.

I could only stagger on with no sense of where I was going or what I would see next until I came to a square I recognized all too well. I looked up at the Basilica di Santa Maria and trembled. In the center of the square, overlooked by the ancient church, a stake had been driven into the ground and kindling piled around it. A girl was tied to the stake.

She was very young, small, blond, and utterly terrified. I knew her only too well even though I had seen her just once months before in the city of the underworld beneath Rome. No, that was not true; I had seen her a second time. Or at least all that was left of her. The charred skin and bared bone, the flesh from which smoke still rose, after she was burned in a warning to me of what would happen if I could not defeat the evil that surrounded us all.

"No!"

Did I scream or did she? It did not matter; I could not move. The girl turned her head, staring at me with all her desperate longing to live stamped clear on her young face.

A man approached wearing the black robe of a Dominican priest. The hounds of God, they are called, because they hunt the supposedly faithless. He held a burning torch in one hand. With the other, he pulled back the hood of his habit, looked at me, and laughed. Horror filled me, the sickening revulsion of knowing what is about to happen and being utterly unable to prevent it. Without shifting his gaze to the girl he was about to condemn to a gruesome death, he touched the torch to the kindling. At once the fire caught.

It spread with fierce intensity, reaching the girl's slender feet and legs in mere moments. She screamed—oh, how she screamed!—on and on and on as I stood helpless and sobbing, unable to look away. The flames licked up her legs, over her arms; her thin white gown flared up and dissolved into her skin. Her hair caught, and for a moment, her head was wreathed in a halo of flame.

The priest threw the torch into the fire, ripped off his robe, and began to cavort, dancing round and round the screaming girl's funeral bier. In the raging glow of the fire, his great horned shadow was cast clear across the piazza to flow up and over the basilica, engulfing it in the very essence of evil.

Off in the distance, a wolf howled. The sound pierced even the intensity of my anguish. The city, the tortured girl, my own terror, all fell away, crumbling into dust. Instead of standing in the heart of Rome, I stood in the midst of a vast wasteland stretching out in all directions toward a horizon where lightning flashed and distant thunder rolled. Scattered across it, I saw the remains of what might have been great buildings or even entire cities. Nothing was left of them save for death.

A figure came toward me out of the smoky gloom. Strangely, I found that I had no further desire to flee. Until then, I had not realized how much courage can be found in despair. With seemingly nothing left to lose, and nowhere to go, I awaited what was to come with unexpected calm. What was I about to face? A demon, perhaps? Death itself? Or something beyond even the limits of my imagination?

The figure resolved into a child, a little girl of maybe six years of age. She had auburn hair that hung below her shoulders and a smattering of freckles across her nose. In appearance, she resembled me and something more. A child I might have had, perhaps? The infant I had seen in my lap in front of Rocco's shop, now grown into a beloved daughter?

"You aren't afraid," she said. "That's good."

Looking down at her, I resisted the urge to touch her hair, the curve of her cheek, to convince myself that she existed, that she was real, in some sense at least. She was not; I had to cling to the certainty of that or I would lose my reason altogether.

Yet I could not simply ignore her. "Why is it good?" I asked.

"Because that is why you have come this far. Many never make it beyond the barrier of their own regrets."

"Is that what I saw? My regrets?" Such a mild word for so much horror.

The child shrugged. "You could not save your mother or your father. The girl died in your place and you could not prevent that. You could not have the life you wanted as a wife and a mother. But you know all this already."

And did not need to be reminded of it. I answered her sharply. "Then tell me something that I do not know."

She thought for a moment, frowning, then said, "You have to cross the wilderness to reach what lies beyond."

The wasteland stalked by death and despair that I had already glimpsed. "Why would I wish to do that?"

As though surprised that I should ask, she replied, "Because of what you will find on the other side."

I looked then and saw, on the far edge of the void, a faint shimmer of light. It stretched across the entire horizon, hinting at something vast and mighty just beyond the range of my vision.

"What is that?" I asked.

The child did not respond directly but spoke carefully, as though instructing one far younger than herself. "Imagine that you are wearing a veil such as widows don to conceal their grief and despair. You have always worn it; it is all you know. You see through it, but only darkly. But now imagine that there is a tiny tear in the veil. Through it you glimpse a light unlike any you have ever perceived before. What do you do?"

"I take off the veil. Truly, I would never wear such a thing."

She smiled. "Not if you had a choice, but to see only darkly and through the veil of your own perception is the essence of the human condition. The very fact that you see even a glimmer of light makes you one among the few who glimpse what really exists."

She urged me again, "What do you do?"

I knew what she wanted me to say, yet I begrudged her the answer all the same. Rather than providing it, I asked, "Are you one of the *perfecti?*"

"Do you think I am?"

I hesitated, but the truth was too obvious to be ignored.

"Honestly, I think you are a creature conjured by my drugged mind. A figure seen in a dream, created by my own longing, who dissolves like mist upon awakening. You are no more substantial than that."

Far from being offended, she merely smiled as though amused by my attempt to cling to reality in an unreal world.

"Are you sure?" she asked.

Was I? Not entirely; a part of me longed for her to be real. I looked again into the void that seemed to stretch beyond eternity. The light was there; I could see it, and it seemed to be growing brighter. Yet the journey to it would be difficult and dangerous. Beyond the howling of the wolves, I saw horned, hunched creatures skulking across the wasteland as though in search of prey.

"What happens if I cannot reach the other side?" I asked.

"You will return to the world you know."

"The world of evil?"

"If you say so."

"But I shouldn't, should I? That is heresy."

The child dragged a toe through the dust and shrugged. "I don't know anything about that. I only know where the light is." She turned as though to go but glanced at me over her shoulder. "You can follow me if you wish." She moved a little away, and the void changed where she stepped. Near her feet, a path began to shimmer faintly.

I stared at it in unwilling fascination. How I longed to step out onto the gleaming ribbon of silver unfurling before me. To follow where it led across the void toward the light. But something held me back.

"You want to go, don't you?" the child asked as she walked out onto the path.

"Of course I do! I long to escape the darkness inside me. It has warped my life, and it is terrifying! I struggle every day to contain it, and every day I fear that I will lose."

She turned and looked at me. Staring at her, I saw for a moment not a little girl but a grown woman. A woman whose features I recognized, for I had seen them many times before, carved into stone high up on the capitals above the Basilica di Santa Maria in Rome, one more place where I had spilled blood. The face of our eternal mother.

"You fear the darkness," she said. "Yet you wouldn't expect to see the heavens in daylight, would you?"

I struggled to understand what she meant even as her voice began to fade. As though from a distance, I heard, "Fulfill your duty in the world, Francesca. Be the woman you are meant to be. The path will be here for you when you are ready."

"How can I be sure?"

I spoke to emptiness. The child, the woman, the eternal mother were all gone. I was alone except for the wind howling in that empty and abandoned place.

26

On the far edge of my awareness, someone was calling to me.

"Francesca?"

Weight pressed down on my chest. I drew air into lungs that felt starved for it, and gasped.

"You are alive!" Mother Benedette exclaimed. "I wasn't certain. For a moment, I thought—"

Slowly, I opened my eyes. I was still on the bed and still bound. The abbess was staring down at me. Her gaze was avid, her face flushed with eagerness.

"Did you see it?" she demanded. "The path. Did you see it?"

I swallowed with difficulty. My throat was very dry, an aftereffect of the elixir, I supposed. Hoarsely, I said, "Water."

Impatiently, she held a glass to my lips long enough for me

to take a few sips. My thirst was far from satisfied when she demanded again, "Did you see it?"

I looked up into her face and recognized there what I marveled that I had not understood from the beginning: the desperation of a woman who despite her greatest efforts had been denied the salvation she was convinced she deserved.

"You have never seen it, have you?" I said. "How many times have you tried?"

She flinched as though I had struck her, but she did not relent. "That doesn't matter. My faith is absolute. You saw it, didn't you?"

It occurred to me just then that there might be something wrong with Mother Benedette in addition to her fanaticism. Whatever religious significance she gave to the elixir notwithstanding, it was a powerful drug. Sofia had warned me repeatedly of what substances that merely bring sleep can do to the mind. How much more dangerous was a drug that had the ability to warp reality itself? How often could anyone take it without risking the loss of reason?

A tiny spark of pity for her stirred within me, prompting me to say, "I saw a path, but—"

At once, she clasped her hands and exclaimed, "I knew it! The One True God be praised!"

In the next instant, she turned to go.

"Wait! You can't leave me like this!"

She looked surprised, as though she had already forgotten my presence. "I really can't tarry. Herrera must be disposed of while you can still be blamed for it." She smiled as though confident of my understanding.

"I will enjoy watching Borgia's fall," she said. "So much more satisfying than just killing him outright. But what follows will be even better. Without his voracious will to subdue them, the princes of Satan's Church will have no one left to battle but each other. France, Spain, all the great families of Italy will join in. They will devour themselves alive. Don't you agree?"

I did, which made me all the more frantic. "No! You can't leave . . . we have to talk. Please." Desperately, I added, "Don't you want to know why I came back?"

But Mother Benedette shrugged that off as though it was of no interest whatsoever. "You are still mired in the physical world, trapped here by your longings—for love, vengeance, forgiveness, whatever. I was counting on that. Everything I saw in you told me that you were the one who could find the path but that you would not have the will to follow it. You would come back, and then I would finally know whether it existed or not. Praise God, you have erased all my doubts."

"Do not be so quick to say that. There were no *perfecti*. To the contrary, I saw—"

"Stop! I have no wish to hear your lies."

"I am telling you the truth! It wasn't what you think. There is good to be done in this world, and that means it cannot be a place of unrelenting evil. The Cathars were wrong."

But Mother Benedette was determined not to hear anything I had to tell her. Before I could even try to twist away, she grabbed hold of me, held the vial to my lips again, and forced more of the elixir down my throat, far more than she had given me the first time.

"The Devil has always tried to deny and destroy our beliefs," she said. "But you, who have been privileged to see the path . . . It is intolerable that you should utter his lies!" She stepped back, looking at me without pity or mercy. "You will find the path again, Francesca, and this time you will follow it. If you do not, your mind will shatter and you will be trapped in madness all the rest of your days in this evil world."

And with that she was gone, leaving me to face not my greatest regret but my greatest fear.

The moment I heard the door lock behind her, I sprang into frantic action. I could count on very little time before the elixir took effect again. If I could not free myself before then . . . I would not think of that.

Desperately, I pulled with all my strength on the bindings holding my arms to the bed. I had no hope of breaking them, but if I could only stretch one just enough to let me . . .

My shoulders were almost wrenched from their sockets before I finally succeeded. The fingers of my left hand brushed against my bodice. Burning pain surged down my arm, but I ignored it and continued until I was finally able to grasp the hilt of the knife that I always wore in the leather sheath near my heart.

Agonizing moments later, I was free of the bed. In the course of getting loose, I nicked myself several times. Blood flowed over my arms and onto the covers. For a horrible moment, the smell of it threatened to overwhelm me. Groaning, I lurched from the bed but was barely able to stand. Off in the distance, coming ever closer, I heard the wolves howling. Soon, too soon, I would be condemned to the wilderness, where my only choices would be death or the madness that had lurked deep in my mind for so long, only waiting to claim me at last.

Before it could, I found the last of my strength and managed to stagger across the room to where I had left the possessions I had brought back from the villa. In among them was the small wooden box in which I had packed a few essentials of my profession, including the substances that can, if given in time, prevent poisoning.

I will not dwell on what happened next except to say that it was both violent and unpleasant. Without knowing exactly how much of the elixir Mother Benedette had given me, except that it was a significant quantity, I could not take any chances. I purged the contents of my stomach until there was nothing left but dry heaves and a little bile.

Weak and disoriented as I was, I made to open the door, only to realize that Mother Benedette had locked it from the outside. For a moment, I considered trying to crawl out a window, but even if I were foolish enough to do so in my present state, there would be nowhere to go. I could let myself simply drop the single story to the ground below, but the distance was great enough that I was likely to be injured, possibly too much so to go on.

That left only one other possibility. Using thin metal probes from the tools I employed in my investigations, I slowly and with great difficulty managed to work the lock. By the time I had done so, I was bathed in sweat and my heart was pounding wildly. Throwing open the door at last, I hurried out.

The corridor beyond was empty—no chance of help. Still

retching, wincing with every step, I kept going until I reached the stairs. At the top of them, I stopped, terrified that I would fall. Clutching the railing tightly, I ventured down slowly, painfully, step by step until finally I reached the bottom. A guard was stationed there. By the look on his face, he had been watching my struggle with bewilderment but not with any inclination to assist me. I stared at him, straightened my shoulders, and said, "I need help."

At least that is what I think I said. My voice was little more than a rasp, and so startled was he by my appearance that I doubt he heard anything at all.

Anger flared in me, warring with despair. I would not be undone like this! By God I would not! I would be heard, I would be obeyed. I would prevail.

"I need help!"

He heard me then, for certain he did, for his face convulsed with fear. Even so, he still stood frozen.

Holy Mary and all the saints, was there no one who could aid me in this moment when all our fates hung in the balance?

"Francesca?"

I turned, scarcely daring to hope, and found myself face-to-face with Renaldo. The steward looked stunned at the sight of me.

"What has happened to you? Is that blood? Francesca?"

"Where is Herrera?"

Renaldo stared at me in bewilderment. I reached out, grabbed his robe, and held on with all my strength. "The Spaniard, where is he?"

"He and Cesare came back from hunting an hour or so ago. That's all I know. But you—"

"We must find him!" I turned, looking in all directions, trying frantically to decide what to do.

"What has happened, Francesca? What is wrong?"

"Herrera is in mortal danger. The abbess means to kill him."

Renaldo paled in shock. He grabbed my arm and stared at me as though I truly was mad. "Mother Benedette? That holy woman—"

"For pity's sake, do not doubt me now! I speak the truth! We must find him before it is too late!"

A lesser friend, one who told himself that he had only my best interests at heart, would have stopped me. Help would have been summoned, I would have been shuffled away, and ruin would have fallen upon us all. But Renaldo, that man of dry numbers and ledgers, believed in the existence of free will and even, just possibly, of the ability of a woman haunted by dire visions to change the future.

"Quickly, then," he said. Together we ran; not toward the Spaniard's apartments, for I had no hope of anyone there heeding me, but toward Cesare's. His valet opened the door. The man was a model of discretion—a necessity given his position—but even he looked surprised at the sight of me.

"Donna Francesca, is everything all right?"

"Is he here? Is he back yet?"

"Yes, but—"

Without waiting to hear more, I pushed past and hurried

through the antechamber toward Cesare's private chambers. His Eminence was lounging in his bath. Looking up from a document he was perusing, he frowned. "Is that blood on you?"

It was, but I had scarcely noticed, nor did I intend to waste any time acknowledging what could be dealt with later. "Get up. We have to find Herrera."

Under normal circumstances, I would never have been so foolish as to give Cesare orders, but exhaustion and terror combined to make me reckless. I even went so far as to grab hold of his arm and try to haul him bodily from the tub.

I didn't succeed, of course, but I did get his attention. "What's wrong?" he asked as he stood, water sluicing off him. At once, his valet darted forward with a towel.

As succinctly as possible, I said, "Mother Benedette is a Cathar. She means to kill Herrera. We have to find them."

In the midst of wrapping the towel around his waist, Cesare stopped and stared at me. "She's a what? She means to do what?"

It was not like him to be so slow, but in all fairness, I was asking him to accept in an instant what it had taken me a good deal longer to recognize.

"A Cathar," I repeated. Afraid that he would not understand, I went on hurriedly, "The Cathars were a sect that the Church deemed heretical and supposedly stamped out centuries ago, but—"

"I know who they were. Why do you think that the abbess is one of them and what do you mean, she is going to kill Herrera?"

My nerves, already shredded, were at the breaking point,

but I strove to answer as calmly as I could. "She admitted it. She has an elixir that the Cathars believe enables them to see the path to the true god. She gave it to me and—Never mind, there is no time! We must find Herrera."

"What has he to do with this?" Cesare asked as he accepted the clothes his valet held out. To my great relief, he began to dress. A taste for the habits of the war camp and the battlefield meant that he could ready himself far more swiftly than most. Even so, each moment was torture for me.

"She is the assassin sent by your father's enemies to destroy the alliance."

The danger had not come from David as I had worried, or from Cesare as I had feared. Mired in my own concerns, drugged by my own hand and hers, I had seen only a woman who claimed to be my mother's friend and mine. What had she said? People will always believe what they want to believe. Of all my sins, just then I was more ashamed of that than any other.

"Please, we must go!"

Tucking his shirt into his breeches, he looked at me closely. "You truly believe this? A Cathar assassin sent to destroy the alliance for what . . . revenge after all these centuries?"

Despair filled me. If I could not convince him . . . "More than that; to set off a battle within Christendom itself, the cardinals pitted against each other, against you, with no one strong enough to win. France, Spain, the great families of Italy all choosing sides. It will be the Great Schism all over again, only this time the Church will not survive."

When he continued to stare at me, I said, "I know that I

sound mad, and perhaps I am. But this is real, and if we don't act now . . ."

My shoulders sagged. I was asking him to trust me when the hard truth was that I could not fully trust myself.

"If we do act and you are wrong . . ." He did not finish, but there was no need. I understood full well that if I was in the grip of a delusion conjured by my drug-disordered mind, all the world was about to learn of it. The howling of the wolves would be as nothing compared to the baying of my enemies for me to be put away or worse. It did not escape my notice that I was risking everything in order to save Herrera. Truly, those whom the gods wish to amuse themselves with, they afflict with irony.

"I am not wrong," I said and prayed that it was so.

Cesare nodded once, curtly, and said, "Then we go."

Gratitude surged through me, but I had no time to contemplate it. Having made up his mind, Cesare did not tarry. I had to run to keep up with him as he strode through the corridors bustling with guards, servants, and retainers, all hastening to get out of his way, until we came to Herrera's quarters.

Cesare raised his fist and banged on the door. His summons was answered at once by a servant who, at the sight of His Eminence, bowed low. A rapid-fire conversation followed, all of it in Castilian, therefore much of it incomprehensible to me. In the course of it, a young nobleman, one of Herrera's retainers, appeared and took over. He and Cesare spoke together for several minutes. I peered around them, hoping to catch sight of David, but there was no sign of him.

By the time they were done, Cesare was frowning. "Herrera

left a short time ago after receiving a note," he told me. "He didn't say where he was going or why, and he wouldn't allow anyone to go with him. But he did appear very excited, even elated."

My stomach clenched. The Spanish emissary was not inclined to go anywhere without a retinue appropriate to his dignity. That he had suddenly done so suggested that something was very much amiss.

Cesare must have thought the same, for he turned to Renaldo, who had followed us and was listening intently.

"Find Captain Romano. Tell him that I want to speak with him."

As the steward rushed off, Cesare turned to me. "Listen to me, Francesca."

How could I not when he was speaking with all the authority of a prince who—never mind his youth—regarded himself as superbly endowed to decide all things?

"You are not well, that is obvious," he said. "Go back to your quarters, lie down, and rest. Vittoro and I will handle this. We'll find Herrera and get to the bottom of whatever is happening."

I had absolutely no intention of doing any such thing, but rather than risk trying his pride too far, I responded as meekly as I could manage. "Where will you look for him?"

Cesare hesitated. Evidently, he had not yet gotten that far in his thinking. Still, he was never at a loss for an answer. "He could be on the training field, or he could have gone off to sketch a building, or—"

"Pardon me, but didn't his man say that he was excited,

even elated? What would account for that? What is so important that he would rush off on his own without companions? When has he ever done that before?"

"I don't know."

"The note he received was from Mother Benedette; it had to be. She would never take the risk of killing him here in the palazzo. They've gone somewhere else."

"Where?"

I took the question as his way of admitting that I was not to be sent off to bed quite yet. Quickly, I said, "The abbess and I met several times at Santa Maria della Salute, on the far side of the piazza."

"Show me," Cesare ordered.

Without waiting for Vittoro or anyone else, we made haste to the church. I was breathless and gasping when we came through the heavy wooden doors into the incense-laden air. Sagging against a wall, I peered into the dim interior. To my despair, it appeared to be empty.

Cesare paced down the aisle dividing the apse, glancing into the shadows near the side altars. When he reached the main sanctuary, he called down the distance separating us.

"There is no one here."

"I realize that."

"But there will be soon for vespers. If she did draw him to this place, she would not have lingered."

As we stepped back out into the piazza, I said, "They must have gone elsewhere. If we don't find them in time . . ."

But how were we to do so? Viterbo was a small enough place compared to Rome, yet it was still a labyrinth of twisting streets and huddled buildings. We could search for hours, even days, with no hope of discovering Herrera.

But wait. If I was right and Mother Benedette did intend to destroy the alliance, she would not want to conceal Herrera's death. On the contrary, she would have to make it known.

If only I knew more about where she had gone and what she had done in the town. But one thought did occur to me. "How many convents are there in Viterbo?"

His Eminence looked at me as though I truly were mad. "How could I possibly know that?"

"She was staying at a convent before I convinced her to move into the palazzo. That might be where she took Herrera." Or it might not be; there was simply no way to tell. If I made a mistake, sent us off in the wrong direction, any opportunity we had to save the Spaniard would be gone. There would be only one chance.

The sun was lowering behind the roofs of the town; time was running out. Once darkness fell, all hope of recovering Herrera would be gone. Vittoro was coming at a run down the steps of the palazzo, flanked by a troop of men. Cesare would give orders, and the search would begin. But where? Which way? I had caused all this by trusting Mother Benedette. Whatever happened would be my fault.

Tears blinded me. Another woman would have prayed, but as I have said, I have no skill at that. Even so, just then I saw in my mind the silver path and the vast, mysterious light that lay beyond it. My tears did fall, but they washed the veil from my eyes.

"Forget the abbess," I said. "Find the fool."

27

David and I argued over Mother Benedette. He thought there was something wrong about how she was behaving, but I wouldn't listen to him. If I know him as I think I do—please God let it be so—he's been learning everything he could about her."

"Where can we find ben Eliezer?" Vittoro asked.

"There's a tavern he favors. Come, I'll show you."

Vittoro begged off, saying that he would roust out more men and prepare them to search. He arranged to meet up with us as quickly as possible.

At that hour, the proper folk of Viterbo were in their homes, preparing for their suppers and their beds. The most devout were in church to hear vespers. Which left everyone else to drink and revel in peace. David was sitting over a cup of wine and a modest meal when Cesare and I found him.

He frowned at the sight of us. "What's wrong?"

Quickly, I told him. Before I was done, he was shaking his head in dismay. "I shouldn't have left Herrera, but I thought if I could find something that would convince you that the abbess couldn't be trusted—"

"Did you learn anything?" Cesare asked.

David hesitated. "It sounds crazy, but Francesca has a friend here in town, apparently. Name of Erato. She heard I was asking about an abbess and she sent for me. She claims a nun has been renting a room in the back of a brothel not far from the market."

I stared at him in bewilderment. "That can't be right. Mother Benedette is an abbess. She has been staying at a convent in the town."

There were stories about nuns turning their convents into brothels, but they always seemed to involve sisters who dared to resist efforts by local priests and prelates to seize property left to the holy women or to otherwise assert their absolute authority over them. Though upon examination none of the tales had ever proven to be true, that was not to say there weren't many women forced to take holy vows who found chastity unbearable.

So, too, there were many actual brothels on church property. Perhaps that accounted for Erato's confusion. Although it was hard to believe that she could make such a mistake.

"I was going to visit the place," David said. "Try to find out if there was any possibility that the abbess had been there. But now—"

"She isn't an abbess." Even as I spoke, the full magnitude

of how gullible I had been almost choked me. I had imagined her a secret Cathar hidden among the clergy, as it was said certain Jews concealed themselves for safety even as they remained adherents to their faith. How readily she could have used her position of authority to pursue her own designs. But if it had all been a lie . . . She would have been taking too great a risk to try to pass among women of the cloth, who would have noticed any error in her behavior. Better to hide among the outcasts of society, who knew better than to question anyone.

"I know where they are."

Both men looked at me in surprise. "Are you sure?" Cesare asked.

I nodded. "She lured Herrera out of the palazzo by promising him evidence he can use to be rid of me."

David glanced from me to Cesare and back again. I saw the swift calculation behind his eyes. He had been in the Spaniard's company long enough to have at least a hint of how things stood between the beloved nephew and His Eminence.

Cesare did not wait. He tossed a handful of coins on the table and strode out of the taverna. David and I followed. Outside in the lane, a dank wind was blowing.

Beyond tired, stomach empty, every bone and muscle in my body aching, I stood for a moment, struggling to gather my fractured thoughts.

"Francesca?"

Belatedly, I realized that Vittoro had arrived with his men. They were all waiting for me.

"Where are we going?" Cesare asked.

Dread weighed on me, a great pall that threatened to crush all beneath it.

"To Hell," I said and showed the way.

"We can't take torches in there," Vittoro said. "A single spark and the whole place will go up like so much kindling."

We stood on Tanners Lane, looking at the ramshackle building where I had found Magdalene. In the darkness lit only by the torches the guardsmen held, it appeared like a black hole against the darkening sky. Night was almost upon us. I could make out a few shuffling, hunched figures fleeing at our approach but nothing more.

"Hooded lamps, then," Cesare said.

Several months before, as a sop to his anger at being forced to don the red skirts of a cardinal, Borgia had agreed to allow Cesare to form a military company under his own leadership. The concession, if that was what it was, merely recognized an existing reality. For several years Cesare had been ranging far and wide with a band of companions, living off the land, practicing battle maneuvers, and generally preparing for the life he really wanted to live. With the instincts of a true war leader, he had introduced several tactical innovations, including training his men for nighttime incursions. To that end, he had caused to be designed and built small portable oil lamps, each with a flame shielded by metal strips. The lamps gave only enough light to see a few yards ahead, but they had the virtue of being far less visible than even a single torch. As a side benefit, they were also far less likely to cause a fire.

Cesare's men remained in Rome, where they were watching over his interests, but apparently he had shared his thoughts on such matters with Vittoro, for the captain had equipped Borgia's own household guards with the lamps. They were produced and lit as I watched. By their dim light, I could not help but notice that the faces of the men holding them were tense and anxious. I couldn't blame them. The thought of going back into that place under any circumstances filled me with horror, but to do so in darkness . . .

"Could I have one of those?" I asked.

With a lamp in hand, I turned to look at the building. No lights shone within. Rank poverty offered its own protection against fire.

We proceeded quickly. Cesare took several men to check the shed where Magdalene's body had been found as well as other nearby structures. A larger group of guards spread out down the lane toward the tanners' shops. To a man, they had their cloaks pulled over their mouths and noses in an effort to block the stench. The occupants of the shops clearly knew of our presence; they had pulled their shutters closed and snuffed their own lights.

In near total darkness, I started toward the building. At once, Vittoro and David joined me.

"Is there any chance," the captain asked, "that I can convince you to remain outside while we search?"

"I was about to ask you the same," I replied. At his chiding look, I explained, "The more clamor we make, the likelier the abbess is to realize that we are on her trail. If Herrera is still alive, he won't be once she realizes that. I should go alone. The rest of you wait out here in case she attempts to flee."

I wasn't being entirely serious, realizing as I did that there was absolutely no chance of Vittoro's agreeing to any such thing. But I hoped he understood that there was also no possibility of my remaining outside.

The captain sighed. Not unkindly, he said, "She can kill him while we stand here arguing. Let's go."

Entering the building, I tried to remember the interior as best I could. On my previous visit, with at least some daylight seeping through the cracks in the walls, it had been difficult enough to see anything. Now, even with the help of the lamps, it was all but impossible.

Even so, I did think to warn both men. "Be careful; the ceiling is very low."

They ducked just in time to avoid cracking their heads. David, the tallest of us, had to bend so low that I feared he would end up walking on his knees. We proceeded slowly. Having some small experience with the place, I led the way. We passed stalls that appeared at a glance to be empty but where I was sure the poor creatures I had seen before were huddling deep in the shadows, praying that we would pass them by without notice.

Many others appeared to have fled entirely. Though it was difficult to be sure, I saw far fewer signs of habitation than I had before. Only the strongest and the bravest could have run off into the night. I wondered where they were hiding even as I forced myself to keep going. We came at last to the stall where I believed I had found Magdalene. It was empty; there was no sign that anyone had been there since her death.

"He isn't here," I said, unable to conceal my despair.

Vittoro leaned over, bracing his hands on his knees, and breathed through his mouth. David sat down with his back to a wall and appeared to be trying not to breathe at all. Both men, tough and experienced as they were, looked ill. I felt the same way. With each passing moment, the chances that I was wrong increased. I realized that I was straining for any sound from outside that Herrera had been found—dead or alive—and forced myself to concentrate on what was in front of me instead.

"There is much of the building we haven't searched," I said. "We should split up and cover as much ground as possible."

Vittoro looked disposed to argue, but David forestalled him. "Francesca is right. This place is a labyrinth. Our best chance is to divide it—left, right, and down the middle. Objections?"

The captain, who was accustomed to giving orders rather than taking them, hesitated; but after a moment, he nodded. "Any sign of trouble, don't keep it to yourself, all right?"

We all agreed and speedily took our leave. David went right, Vittoro went left, and I stayed where I was, resolved to work my way down every inch of the center of the building. I confess to a profound sense of unease as solitude closed in around me. The darkness, the stench, and the all-pervasive miasma of hopelessness weighed on me intolerably. I felt as though I had been buried alive.

Panic curled at the edges of my mind. I steeled myself as best I could and pressed on. In the maze of close-packed stalls, I could become disoriented all too quickly. To prevent that, and to protect myself in the event of a sudden attack,

I withdrew my knife from its sheath. By keeping the tip of the blade scrapping along the wall to my right, I left a tracing of my path.

It was a trick I had learned from Cesare when together we had penetrated the catacombs beneath Saint Peter's the previous year. On that occasion, we had stumbled across the mass skeletal remains cast aside as rubble when the Great Constantine built the basilica a thousand years ago. I had to hope that I would encounter no such reminder of omnipresent death in Tanners Lane.

Continuing on through the darkness, I looked in each stall I passed. Here and there, frightened faces peered back. Worse were the blank, empty stares of those whose minds seemed to have deserted them entirely. I picked up my pace, only to slow again as I became aware of the faint noise all around me. With such limited sight, and with my sense of smell simply overwhelmed by the stench, my hearing seemed to become more acute. A faint but growing cacophony of moans, groans, sighs, and whimpers filled the fetid air.

Horror crawled under my skin. My mouth tasted of bile. I needed every ounce of will that I possessed to keep going, and even then I almost did not manage it. Voices shouted in my head: "Turn back! He is not here! You cannot find him! Go back! Run!" Most insidiously of all, reason itself insisted that someone else could find Herrera. Someone better suited to the task. Cesare, Vittoro, David—it was best left to any or all of them. Indeed, they would be relieved if I withdrew.

Reason, it seemed, did not have much sway with me. I kept going. Deep inside the building, with nothing to guide me out again but the thin scratching of my blade, I called out softly, "Don Miguel? Are you here?"

Up until then, I had tried to refrain from making any sound so as not to alert Mother Benedette to my presence. But with time rushing past and my own fear mounting, I felt that I had no choice.

Again, I called, "Don Miguel?"

I heard a groan, not unlike all the others except for what seemed a particular note of anguish and urgency.

"Don Miguel?" I called louder as caution fell away. If it was him, he was in distress.

I heard a broken sob in a voice I thought must surely be a man's for all that it was too weak to be sure. *"Ayúdame . . . por el amor de Dios me ayúda."*

Castilian again, but close enough to Catalan that I could understand. "Help me . . . for the love of God, help me."

I surged forward, heedless of any effort to mark my trail. My knife was in one hand, the lamp in the other as I came round a corner amid the stalls and found myself face-to-face with a vision out of a nightmare. Herrera was there all right, and blessedly still alive, although it was impossible to guess how much longer he could remain that way. Mother Benedette must have drugged him as she had me. In his helpless state, she had stripped him naked. In a glance, I saw that his clothes were thrown in a nearby corner.

As for Don Miguel himself . . .

He lay on the floor, his legs crossed at the ankles, his arms flung out at right angles to his body. His hands were turned up with the palms toward the ceiling. I needed a moment to understand why there appeared to be dark stains seeping from the center of his palms across the wood slats. And from his side. And from his feet.

When I did finally grasp what I was seeing, I could only be glad that I had emptied my stomach so thoroughly a short time before. Even so, the impulse to retch was all but overwhelming. Pity and revulsion struck me with equal force as I stared at the horror before me.

Don Miguel de Lopez y Herrera, beloved nephew of Their Most Catholic Majesties, had been nailed to the floor of Hell in a crude parody of Christ's crucifixion. Left there much longer, he would most certainly bleed to death, if he did not die from shock first.

Not even the denizens of Tanners Lane would be able to conceal what had happened. In their own terror at discovering the body, word would spread and he would be found. The obvious victim of a madwoman who, I saw, had left behind a cloak by which she could be identified. My cloak, the one I had wrapped around Magdalene when I left her in the shed . . . after promising that she would be safe.

All thought of any disagreement I had ever had with Herrera fell away. Even so, I hesitated. His wounds were grievous. If I acted too hastily, I could worsen his condition beyond recovery.

I had to do something, but as I struggled to determine what that should be, a flicker of movement in the corner of my eye distracted me. For just a moment, there in the stygian darkness of the crib, I thought I saw Mother Benedette. She was standing just outside the stall, as though she had been nearby.

Her face, framed by her wimple, was startled. Clearly, she had not expected to see me.

Her reaction, more than anything else, convinced me that I was not hallucinating. For whatever reason, perhaps to make sure that he really did die, the abbess had lingered at the scene of her crime. That, I promised myself, would prove to be a fatal mistake.

With a cry, I leaped after her.

She was quicker by far than I had expected. In an instant, I lost sight of her in the darkness. But I could hear her, scrambling frantically as she sought to elude the one she had presumed to be safely dead.

I wasted neither breath nor effort calling out for her to stop. Instead, I plunged on, heedless of every other consideration. I could think of nothing other than the absolute imperative that she not escape me. The abbess, of course, had precisely the opposite intent. She ran with speed that belied what I had assumed to be her age. As I had been wrong in all else, I had to recognize that I was wrong about that as well.

Twisting, turning, racing through the maze that was Hell's crib, she managed to stay a few yards ahead of me. I held on to the lamp for dear life, for only by its faint illumination did I have any hope of keeping up with her. Perhaps because she had laid her plans so well, she seemed to know her way through the maze far better than I could ever hope to do. Too soon, before I had barely begun to tire, she ran toward a portion of wall that appeared to have collapsed outward. With a backward glance at me, she vanished into the darkness beyond.

I went after her. Without pause, without thought, I jumped

the distance to the ground and followed the shadow vanishing toward the lane. Off in the distance, I could make out the shapes of men moving amid the buildings. I thought to call out to them, but my chest was tight, my breath strained. The chances that they would hear me were faint.

Just then, the sliver of the moon moved from behind curtaining clouds, and I saw her. She was looking back over her shoulder again, directly at me. For a moment, I wondered if she had some power to see in the dark better than I could, but I dismissed the thought. It is always a temptation to ascribe unnatural powers to one's adversaries. Equally, it is always a mistake, sowing confusion and fear as it does. Far too many of my own enemies have made that error, for which I am grateful.

I ran on, feet pounding, determined to close the distance between us. What was I thinking as I did so? Of Herrera, perhaps. Of my mother, certainly. Of a world ruled by a god of evil? No, not really. And yet there is no concealing what happened. Whether because of a hump in the ground or debris of some sort, the abbess stumbled.

The moment she did so, without an instant's thought, I drew back my arm and hurled the burning lamp straight at her.

28

The lamp shattered on impact. Mother Benedette stopped, frozen in surprise, and I did the same. Truly, I have no idea what was in my mind. If I felt compelled to throw anything, it should have been my knife, but, as I have said, I have no skill with it except for close work.

For a moment, nothing happened. And then . . . I hesitate even to remember, so terrible was it. The oil in the lamp spread across the ground, lapping at the hem of her habit. A spark caught, and licks of flame raced up her skirts. The simple, undyed fabric ignited like a torch. Her white face, distorted in a scream of terror, shone from behind a sudden wall of smoke and fire.

In fact, none of that was real. True, the flame did catch and it did singe the bottom of her habit. She did react with horror, as any sensible person would, and she did make at once to stamp it out. But whether because of the lingering effects of the drugs she had given me or the darkness stirring within my mind, I saw it differently. Saw what might have been if she had been lashed to the stake as so many Cathars had been and left to burn as they had.

As I feared I would if my many enemies ever had their way.

I screamed. A wrenching, tearing sound that seemed to rend the air itself. For certain, it tore my throat, for I promptly tasted blood. Choking on it, still screaming, I ran at her.

What does it mean to seek to kill and save at the same time? I hated her; I wanted her dead. And I could not bear to see her perish in so hideous a manner. I ran straight into the flames that, in that instant, I truly believed were devouring her.

Later, I found strange patches on my arms, a sore redness almost like the beginning of a burn, as though a fire that existed only in my own mind still had the power to harm me.

She kicked, pummeling me with feet and fists, reaching with her nails for my eyes, but, driven as I was by terror, my strength was greater than her own. We fell together onto the ground and rolled, the sputtering flames snuffed out as we went. In mud and mire, in the filth of Hell, I clung to her. She was alone, and I . . . I was not. All I had to do was hold on long enough and I would win.

David got to us first. He came out of the darkness, pulling me off the abbess so that he could hold and secure her. Even then, she continued to fight, snarling at him with wild eyes and bared teeth. Her wimple came away. Dark hair tumbled loose. As it settled around her smooth face, I saw at once that she was a much younger woman than I had thought, little older than myself.

What followed was all confusion. Vittoro was there, and Cesare. I tried to explain, but really I needn't have bothered. Cesare barked orders and the abbess was surrounded by men-at-arms. My last glimpse of her as she was led away was a fierce stare and, I thought, a strangely confident smile.

I remembered Herrera.

"He is inside, badly hurt!" More explanation was needed, but I did not have it to give. Nor was there any time. Heedless of the vise gripping my chest, I grabbed up my skirts and ran with all my strength.

The others followed. Frantically, I reached out and found the thin tracing of my knife along the wall. Following it, running desperately, I came at last to the place where Herrera lay. Scarcely had I done so than I heard the strangled gasps of those behind me. Someone was vomiting; someone else could not stop moaning. I had no idea who they were, nor did I care. All that mattered was that Cesare remained in full control of himself.

Kneeling beside Herrera, he passed a hand over the other man's brow, looked deeply into his eyes, and said, "We've got you. You're safe now."

A long sigh escaped the Spaniard. He stared at Cesare a moment more before consciousness mercifully left him.

At once, I bent down beside him. Before Cesare could do anything, I said, "If we are not careful, we will make this worse."

"For pity's sake, Francesca, we have to free him!"

I heard the horror in his voice, and the anguish, but I

would not relent. Instead, I elbowed him aside and looked to David, who was right behind us.

"We have to release him slowly. If we jar the nails loose too quickly—"

"He could bleed out." Kneeling beside me, the renegade Jewish leader reached out to help the beloved nephew of the monarchs who had expelled the Jews from Spain, and who would have condemned them all to extinction had that been within their power.

"You're sure you want to do this, given who he is?" I asked, ashamed of the doubts I had harbored.

David spared me a glance, no more. "It doesn't matter," he said and with gentle strength, slowly and carefully lifted Herrera into his arms.

The moment he was free, blood did flow more freely, but not so much that I had to fear we would lose him right then and there. Cesare stepped in quickly to help David. Together, they carried Herrera outside.

I will not dwell on the journey back to the palazzo except to say that we went as slowly as we dared. By the grace of God, Herrera remained unconscious most of the way, although as we made the final push up the hill toward the papal palace, he was groaning almost constantly.

Others had run ahead with word of what had happened. Borgia was at the top of the steps, watching us come. He looked grim and worn, as though events had suddenly caught up with him. I could not help but feel the same. Somewhere in the palazzo, "Mother Benedette" was being held. I would have to talk with Borgia about her before too long, but at the moment I had to concentrate on Herrera. Even so, as we passed His Holiness, I said, "If you want to learn anything from her, leave it until I can get free."

I needn't have worried. As much as he had reason to execute her on the spot, Borgia was always able to rise above his private emotions. He merely looked at me through hooded eyes and nodded.

In Herrera's quarters, Cesare and David together moved him carefully onto the bed. At once, the black-garbed crows hovering in wait moved toward him. I grimaced at sight of the physicians and grasped Cesare's arm.

"Don't let them near him," I entreated. "They'll bleed or purge him, or both, and he will most surely die."

Turning on me, he demanded, "Can you do better? You had a hand in bringing him to such a pass, and we both know it."

I felt the color drain from my face, but I refused to back down. There would be time for me to answer for my part in what had occurred, possibly all of eternity. But not yet.

"David will help me. At the very least, we will do no worse than the physicians, and we may be able to do some good."

To send some of the most learned men of the papal court away in order to give preference to a witch and a Jew . . . few would even have considered doing so. To his everlasting credit, Cesare hesitated only a moment. He stared at Herrera, closed his eyes for an instant, and opened them to shout, "Out! All of you, out!"

Although I would never say it to him, just then he sounded uncannily like his father.

"Except you . . . and you." He pointed at David and me.

The others went amid much grumbling and backward glares. The physicians would hie themselves off to the papal secretaries, who would listen to them with sympathy, as they, too, detested me. There would be talk of appealing to Borgia directly, but it would come to nothing. His Holiness would remain apart, taking no hand in what transpired until the results were clear.

As the door shut behind them, I took a long breath and tried to decide where to begin. Herrera had yet to regain consciousness, for which I was deeply grateful, but that might be because he was about to slip into extremis. His injuries were grave, the damage extensive. I had no way of knowing how far the stab wound to his side had penetrated. If a lung had collapsed . . .

"I need items from my quarters," I said. Specifically, I needed drugs and other substances locked away in the puzzle chest that only I could open. When I explained as much, Cesare ordered the chest to be brought to Herrera's apartments, along with everything else I required. While I waited, I did my best to assess the Spaniard's injuries.

The wounds through the palms of his hands appeared to have almost stopped bleeding, but because of the swelling around them, the nails piercing the centers were tightly embedded. So, too, those in his feet. The wound to his side was jagged and deep, but when I leaned close to it, I saw no bubbling in the blood coming from it.

"All right," I said as I straightened slowly. Both men were watching me. "The wound on his side is the most immediately serious. It has to be cleaned and stitched. As for the others, we must do what we can to prevent infection and hope that in time he can recover some use of his hands and feet."

"There is nothing else to be done?" Cesare asked.

Regretfully, I shook my head. "I have no experience setting small bones. Very few do. I can try, but in all honesty, I could make the injuries worse."

As I spoke, I had a sudden memory of Herrera in the arena, his sword flashing as he moved with skill and grace that would have undone most men, just not Cesare. And I wondered at the architectural designs he drew. Would he ever be able to do either again?

"I can give you the names of several Moorish physicians," David offered. "One or more of them may have such skill."

A witch, a Jew, and a Moor . . . If Herrera did manage to survive, would he hear what God was trying to tell him?

"That is all for later," I said. "Right now, we will have a job just to keep him alive."

I was even more convinced of that after I placed my fingers, as I had seen Sofia do, on the inside of his wrist and felt the very faint stirring of his pulse there. Leaning close, I put an ear to his chest to confirm what I suspected. His heartbeat was very weak.

"He has lost a lot of blood." David and Cesare were both looking at me, waiting for me to say what should be done. I swallowed and went on. "Added to whatever drugs Mother Benedette gave him and the shock of what she did . . ."

I looked down at the Spaniard, whose face already seemed to bear the gray pallor of death. The conviction stirred in me that if I did not try something drastic, he would not see morning.

Slowly, I said, "I have substances in my possession that can be deadly but which, according to Sofia Montefiore, in smaller quantities can be used to heal."

"How would you know how much to give him?" Cesare asked. I was heartened that he did not dismiss the idea entirely, although I understood that was a measure of his desperation. But I did not have a good answer for him.

"I have a fair gauge of how much would kill him," I said. "I propose to start with a much smaller amount and see what happens."

"If he dies—?" David began, but Cesare cut him off.

"Then he dies because of what the abbess did, not because of anything Francesca did to try to save him."

My throat tightened. After everything that had happened, Cesare's willingness to trust me took me by surprise. I hurried over to the puzzle chest and worked the combination to open it. From beneath the false bottom, I removed a box containing poisons that I preferred never to use. Each time I had ended the life of a poisoner sent against Borgia, I had made a point of doing it with the very substance intended to kill His Holiness. While I was likely the only person who knew that was my practice, by doing so I retained the sense of being an instrument of justice rather than merely one of death. But I did not fool myself. At any time, I could be called upon to use a poison of my own crafting.

I was prepared to do that, or so I told myself. Yet my hands shook as I removed a vial from the box and held it up to the light, studying the contents carefully. The crumbled, dried leaves of the plant some call fairy cap and others know as foxglove were, according to Sofia, lifesavers for those with poor hearts. I knew only that they could send that organ into a rapid and erratic rhythm before stopping it entirely.

As I have said—several times, I believe—I am not much good at praying. But I said a prayer then, silently asking the God that, contrary to the Cathars, I truly did believe was good to guide my hand.

The contents of the vial were enough to kill Herrera. But in his weakened state, I suspected that half as much might also be lethal. Accordingly, I measured out only a quantity that fit on the nail of my smallest finger. Having added it to a small amount of hot water, I left the leaves to steep while I prepared to stitch up the wound in the Spaniard's side. By the time I had the equipment for that ready, I judged the tincture of foxglove to be strong enough.

Cesare lifted Herrera so that the Spaniard's head rested against his shoulder. I leaned forward and slowly, carefully dribbled the liquid into his mouth. At first I feared that he would spit it out, but such was his condition that he appeared insensible to all that was happening. To my great relief, the dosage slid unimpeded down his throat.

When it was done, I stepped back and allowed myself to breathe. But any relief I might have felt would have to wait. As Cesare lowered Herrera carefully back onto the bed, I put my fingers to his wrist once again. At first, I perceived no difference. But after several moments, his pulse seemed stronger. To be certain, I leaned close again and listened to his heart.

"I think it is working," I said as I straightened.

A great sigh escaped Cesare. He ran a hand over his face, and I realized that he looked older and wearier than I had ever seen him. But there was no time for any of us to rest.

"I must see to that wound," I said, gesturing to Herrera's side. Having managed to strengthen his heart, I feared that he might regain consciousness as I worked, but Fortune, so lately absent, smiled on us. Although he did moan several times, Cesare and David managed to hold him steady while I completed what needed to be done.

Barely had I finished than weakness threatened to overwhelm me. I only just managed to bandage the wound with clean strips of linen before I sagged where I sat.

We were all of us exhausted, but the night was far from over. Convinced that Herrera at least would not die immediately, Cesare dragged himself off for a much needed conversation with his father. David and I remained at the bedside. From time to time, I got up to check the Spaniard's pulse and make sure that he was not becoming feverish. It would be days yet before I could be certain there would be no infection, but I was beginning to believe that Herrera had at least a chance of living that long.

Considering how we had found him only a few hours before, that was remarkable. A surge of gratitude went through me for the others who had played a part in saving him: Cesare; David; Erato, who had so unexpectedly helped me; Renaldo; Vittoro; and more. Without them, the outcome would have been far different.

Sitting there in the darkness beside Herrera's bed, listening to David's soft snores, I realized that Sofia might be right in trying to persuade me to use my skills for healing, at least some of the time. Despite the darkness within me, I felt a sense of satisfaction and even a kind of happiness unlike any I had ever known before. All that might prove to be no more than a momentary reprieve if the Spaniard took a turn for the worse, but just then I was content to think only of what was, not of what might be.

Cesare came back a short time later. He stood beside the bed for a few minutes, touching his hand to Herrera's brow and looking at him. When he was satisfied that all was as it should be, he slumped down in the chair beside mine.

With a glance at David, who continued to slumber, he said, "The abbess is being held in her quarters."

I looked at him in surprise. "Not in a cell?"

He shook his head. "My father does not think it wise for people to be told that the supposedly holy woman they have been making so much of is actually a heretic assassin."

Borgia, as usual, had a point. Still, I wondered how long the secret could be kept. "What of the men who were at Tanners Lane?"

"They have been told to say nothing, but privately the word is being given that the abbess had a visitation that took her to that place, whereupon she discovered that Herrera had been the victim of a foul attack no doubt perpetrated by our enemies and Spain's. Thanks to her intervention, he was saved."

I sat up straighter in the chair and stared at him in disbelief. "*Her* intervention?"

He sighed deeply. "Tomorrow, there will be a day of prayer

during which we are all enjoined to beseech Almighty God to restore His faithful son, Don Miguel de Lopez y Herrera, to full health and strength. Unfortunately, Mother Benedette will not be able to attend. She is in seclusion, withdrawn from this world so that she may pray and fast without distraction."

I shook my head in disgust but not surprise. Borgia could not risk the truth about the "holy woman" ever becoming known. If people realized that there were surviving Cathars, if they learned anything of their beliefs . . . The threat that the Church had thought extinguished centuries ago could flare up again and set off a conflagration such as had never been seen before.

"What does he intend to do with her?" I asked.

Cesare shrugged. "First and foremost, he wants to know who sent her and why. After that, if she's still alive, she will be executed."

Perhaps I should have felt some twinge of gladness at the thought of her suffering, but none came to me. Instead, I said, "I have never been able to understand why anyone believes that information gained under torture is reliable. Won't people say anything just to make it stop?"

"So I would think," Cesare agreed. "But in this matter at least, my father apparently believes that the traditional methods are best."

I had my doubts that Borgia thought any such thing. To the contrary, the suspicion stirred in me that he was, as usual, several moves ahead of most everyone else. But not, I resolved, of me. Not this time.

Standing, my legs shaking with weariness, I said, "I will

be back as quickly as possible. If there is any change with Herrera, send word to me."

Surprised, for I surely looked too exhausted to be going anywhere, Cesare asked, "What are you doing?"

"What Il Papa wants, of course." Before I could think better of it, I hurried from the room.

29

"I have urgent business with His Holiness."

The guard in front of the papal apartments stared at me. He looked like a man torn between his duty and his desire to be anywhere but where he was, face-to-face in the middle of the night with the Pope's poisoner.

"Urgent business," I repeated.

He swallowed, managed a nod, and opened the door behind him far enough to alert a secretary. The priest who emerged was young enough to be more arrogant than able. He looked at me and frowned. "His Holiness has retired for the night."

"No," I replied with absolute certainty, "he has not." Whatever Borgia had told his servants, too much had happened for him to have sought his bed. He would be chewing events over, mulling his best moves, as only the finest insomniacs can do.

The priest shrugged. "On you, then," he said and stood aside for me to enter.

Borgia was fully dressed and seated at his desk. He looked up as I appeared.

"Ah, Francesca. I thought you might pay me a visit. Sit down." When I had done so, he asked, "How is Herrera?"

"Alive. I have given him a medication to strengthen his heart. So far it seems to be working. The wound to his side bled a great deal, but the lung is intact. I have closed the wound and we will watch for signs of infection. Cesare has sent for a Moorish physician who can deal with the injuries to the hands and feet. All in all, there is reason to be moderately optimistic."

"I am glad to hear it. What a terrible fate to befall any man. He has you to thank for saving him."

"Really? I thought the credit went to the holy Mother Benedette?"

Borgia leaned back in his chair and regarded me narrowly. "It's not like you to be petty, Francesca. What is it that you want?"

I did not hesitate but met him straight on, as I had made up my mind to do. "I know that you plan to put her to the question. I ask that you let me speak with her first."

He raised an eyebrow. "Need I point out how thoroughly she duped you?"

I winced but did not attempt to deny it. "No one knows that better than I. All I ask is a chance to redeem myself."

He considered for a moment, then spread his hands, as though granting a favor out of the pure magnanimity of his soul. "All right, but don't take too long with her. I have told the torturers to be ready at dawn."

"Do they know they will be dealing with a Cathar?"

He looked puzzled by the question. "It wouldn't make any difference if they did. Their job is to get information. They aren't required to understand it. In fact, the sooner they forget everything they hear, the better." His gaze sharpened. "Some would consider that a virtue worth acquiring."

"Whereas others believe that knowledge is the ultimate power," I countered. Borgia certainly did, judging by the pains he went to in order to acquire it.

"An excellent reason why it must be kept beyond the reach of those who would misunderstand or misuse it," he said. "Now if there is nothing else—" He flicked a hand in dismissal.

I ignored that and asked, "Did you know that the Cathars still existed?"

He hesitated long enough for me to conclude that he did not intend to answer. Finally, he said, "There have always been rumors that a remnant survived."

I thought of the secret texts preserved so carefully in the Mysterium Mundi. Against the day when a formidable enemy might rise to challenge Rome again?

"Rumors or fears?" I asked.

Christ's Vicar glared at me. "The Church does not fear, Francesca. The Church instills fear when that is necessary, in order to assure that our sheep do not stray from the one, true path into the mouths of wolves. That is why the Cathars were crushed and why they will never return."

I drew myself up, facing him directly. "With all respect, Your Holiness, we both know that they already have returned. There is no reason to believe that the 'abbess' acted alone. Who trained her to be so skilled an assassin? Who provided her with poisons and drugs more sophisticated than any I have ever encountered? If your known enemies had such capabilities, you would be long dead."

He scowled at me. "A thought that trips easily from your lips."

I brushed that aside and went on. "Yet you knew nothing of the Cathars?"

Grudgingly, he said, "Rumors . . . nothing more. And no reason to believe that there was any truth to them."

"Do any of those rumors mention Milan?"

He looked at me closely. "Not that I know of. Some remaining Cathars are said to live in England, others in France, still others in hidden places, dwelling in forests and caves. But it is all just whispers on the wind. Or at least it was."

I swallowed my disappointment and nodded. "When we return to Rome, I will scour the Mysterium Mundi for every scrap of information about the Cathars. We must be prepared to deal with them again."

I rose to go, but he forestalled me. Reaching into a drawer of his desk, he withdrew a small wooden box and held it out to me.

"This was taken from your abbess's quarters before I ordered her secured there. In light of what you have just said, I have every confidence that you will find it of interest."

Carefully, I opened the box, revealing a dozen glass vials,

all closed but several with broken seals indicating that some of their contents had been used. Among them would be the poison capable of stopping hearts between one beat and the next. Others would contain the drugs the abbess had used on me and possibly the Cathar elixir. Borgia was making a gesture of faith in entrusting them to me, but he would also expect me to investigate them thoroughly.

Girding myself for what that would involve, I inclined my head. "I will let you know what I learn."

He nodded, seemingly satisfied, and dismissed me with a wave. I secured the wooden box in my rooms before crossing to the apartment where Mother Benedette was being held. Two men-at-arms stood out in front, ostensibly to protect her from being disturbed at her prayers. I had no doubt that there were others below, in case she took it into her head to go out a window, as I had briefly considered doing.

"I have His Holiness's permission to speak with the prisoner," I said.

One of the guards unlocked the door and stood aside for me to enter. I did so with more nervousness than I cared to admit even to myself. Not only had Mother Benedette well and thoroughly duped me, as Borgia had so kindly pointed out, she had also forced me to confront my worst fears and most hellish memories. The scars from that would remain for a very long time to come.

Yet I was determined to face her calmly. Still dressed in her singed habit with the wooden rosary and cross secured around her waist, she was seated in a tall chair. Her hands were clasped in her lap and she appeared almost asleep, but she stirred as I entered. Seeing me, the woman who had plotted to destroy everything I was sworn to protect smiled as though we were the best of friends.

"Francesca. I hoped that you would come."

Staring at her, I had to wonder how I had ever believed that she was old enough to have known my mother. Without her wimple and veil, she looked only a few years my senior.

I pushed that thought aside and walked across the room and took the chair opposite her. With pride in the steadiness of my voice, I asked, "Would you care to tell me your real name?"

The question seemed to amuse her. "Do you imagine that what we are called in this world has any significance at all? Only our soul name matters, and it is not to be uttered here."

I had no intention of engaging in a discussion of Cathar beliefs. "Mother Benedette it is, then. His Holiness is determined to find out who sent you. He intends to have you tortured."

"Do you intend to watch?"

Rather than rise to the bait, I said, "We can parry questions until I accept that there is no purpose in my being here and leave. Is that what you want?"

For a moment, I thought she would not answer, but something flickered behind her eyes, perhaps a realization of just how badly things could go for her. Quietly, she said, "Why should I tell you anything?"

I took a breath, well aware that what I was about to do would add to the long list of my manifest failings where she was concerned and just might be enough to convince Borgia that he really could do without me.

Before I could reconsider, I said, "Tell me the truth and I will give you an easy death."

She looked surprised. "You would do that, against the wishes of your master?"

"I would do it for the truth."

She nodded as though I had just confirmed a deeply held conviction. "I was right about you. You have a rare spirit."

"Which did not prevent you from using me to your own ends before trying to kill me, but never mind about that. Who sent you here?"

I expected her to refuse to answer at first, to try to play for some advantage, perhaps even her own life. But she did not hesitate. "I don't know, which if I do end up being tortured is unfortunate. I can try to make up something to satisfy Borgia, but the truth is that I was hired and paid by an intermediary who gave me no indication of whom he was working for. I'm not even certain that he knew. The job could have come through layers of go-betweens."

A frustrating answer to be sure, and one Borgia was not likely to accept. Yet I knew that in the world of poisoners, what she was describing was often how such matters were handled. I could believe it was the same for assassins in general.

"So you are saying that this was not a Cathar conspiracy? That whoever hired you either knew nothing of your beliefs or simply did not care?"

"I am assuming that they knew nothing. We, the descendants of the survivors who were sent to safety, are raised to live in the world without being detected by it. We accept that we are surrounded by evil and we use it to protect ourselves."

"Don't you mean that you contribute to it by being, for example, assassins?"

"We can debate that if you like," she said. "Or you can simply accept that what I am telling you is the truth."

"You have no idea who hired you?" I asked her again.

She looked at me directly and did not waver. "I do not."

"But the intent was to kill Herrera and thereby destroy the alliance?"

"That is my understanding. In addition, you were to be blamed. Borgia would be fatally weakened by the loss of the Spaniards. And you, who had managed to thwart so many attempts on his life, would be gone. The way would be clear to destroy him."

Though I was loathe to admit it, the plan could have—even should have—worked. Yet I was far from satisfied with what she had revealed thus far.

"The gifts of food, the psalter . . . you were poisoning me?"

"Drugging you," she corrected. "The plan was to render you mad so that you would be blamed for Herrera's death. I would escape safely—always a consideration in such matters, as I am sure you understand. But when I met you, I realized that to merely use you as intended would be a terrible waste."

"Because you thought I could show you the path?"

She nodded. "Which you have done."

"I tried to tell you—"

She held up a hand, forestalling me. "I can accept that you do not fully understand what you saw."

Since I was not sure that I understood it at all, I could hardly argue with her. Instead, I turned to my greater purpose in being there. The dead cannot speak for themselves, but I could do so in their place.

"You killed the kitchen boy, the laundress, and the page?"

"I did."

"Why? What purpose did that serve?" The seemingly random pointlessness of the attacks, lives snatched away for no reason, haunted me. In my worst moments, in the grip of the darkness within, I had never done any such thing.

She looked surprised. "I did it for your sake, Francesca. Surely you understand that?"

My disbelief must have been evident, for she said, "It is true that it served my ends for people to be frightened by unexplained deaths and looking to you as the possible cause. But there was a higher purpose. I could see that you have been living in a delusion, believing that you can somehow make the world a better place through your own actions and in the process redeem yourself. It was necessary to show you that evil is everywhere. It can strike anywhere, and you are helpless before it precisely because it is the very fabric of existence. In that way, I prepared you to walk the path of light."

Bile rose in my throat. I did not doubt for a moment that she believed what she said. Lives were nothing to her, being mere encumbrances of the physical world.

"I freed them," she said, as though I would understand. "As I tried to free you."

But I had survived to confront her with her crimes. For all the lives I had taken, each and every one still counted with me.

"You also killed Herrera's servant."

"Someone had to die after I gave you the psalter. I knew how the drug embedded in it would affect you, and when I saw you leave your apartments—"

"It was you I saw? You followed me?" The shadowy figure I had glimpsed had not been Death itself, as my fevered brain imagined, but an all too real woman bent on murder.

"I must admit," the "abbess" said with a frown, "I am puzzled as to what happened to the knife. I left it to be found."

"It was. I found it the next day when I began to remember where I had gone."

She looked surprised. "You remembered? That should not have been possible. The drug expunges all memory." She thought for a moment. "Unless you've been taking something else that partly counteracted the effect."

Sofia's powder, perhaps? I still hungered for it, but after all the talk of Cathar drugs, I was determined to never take it again. Please God, I would remain strong in that conviction.

"You killed Magdalene," I said.

She shrugged. "Do not tell me that you did not consider doing so yourself. Or that you did not think about killing Herrera. We are more alike than you wish to admit, Francesca."

I looked at her, a young woman, a hired assassin who, for all of her fanaticism—or perhaps even because of it—I suspected was very good at her job. Had events worked out only slightly differently, she would have bested me. She had been shaped by an act of brutal oppression and violence that cast ripples down through the centuries into the present day and likely would continue to do so far into the future. But she would not see that. Her time was over.

Mine was not, and for that I was suddenly, overwhelmingly grateful. For all that I was not and likely never would be a normal woman, I saw the beauty of this world and I cherished it. Evil exists, it is real, but so is good. We are not alone in the dark.

"I have one more question." To which I already knew the answer, yet I had to hear it. "You made up the stories about my mother, including the manner of her death?"

She shook her head. "I have no such gift for tale spinning. The intermediary told me what to say."

That was not what I expected, yet it changed nothing. "But you have no reason to believe that any of it was true?"

"None at all." She did not sound regretful, but then I had not expected her to do so. I had come to the realization while still in Tanners Lane that she had exploited my deepest longings to her own ends. All the same, it was hard to hear. I had to force myself to go on.

"We are nothing alike," I said. "You put your faith in a vision that I will never accept. But you have kept your part of our bargain. I will keep mine."

I was reaching for the pouch in which I kept the necessities of my profession when she surprised me. Smiling, the woman I knew as Mother Benedette said, "Thanks to you, I die knowing that the path to the world beyond this place of evil does exist. I want you to know that I am truly grateful for that. Now that I have acted to redeem my soul from Satan,

I am free to follow that path at last. We will not meet again in this world, but be assured, I will look for you in the light."

Before I could reply, she snapped the string holding the wooden beads of her rosary. Most fell to the floor along with the cross, but several remained in her hand.

Still smiling, looking directly at me, she placed them in her mouth and bit down hard.

Moments later, the Cathar assassin was dead.

30

My efforts to save Mother Benedette were futile, but I made a show of trying all the same for the sake of the guards. The rosary beads, as it turned out, contained ground paternoster peas. Left intact, the peas can pass through the body without causing it distress. But once the outer covering is punctured, they release one of the deadliest toxins known to man. In all likelihood, the "abbess" was dead before she hit the floor.

I stared at her in shock, trying to understand why she had waited to speak to me before ending her own life when she had the means to do so all along. Had she nurtured some hope of escape? Believing what she did, I could not think that she truly wanted anything so much as to die and be free of this world. But for that to happen, her death had to occur in the right way . . . an act to redeem her soul. Herrera would live;

she had failed there. The Spanish alliance would remain. I would not be blamed for the deaths that had occurred and because of them be consigned to the flames. Borgia would endure.

Borgia. The answer came to me so suddenly that I cried out. She died believing that she had won and that ultimately I would know it. In her final act, she had sought to convince me of the rightness of her beliefs. And to compel me to follow the same path she had taken. Truly, she intended for us to meet again.

The full magnitude of my failure almost slammed me to my knees beside her. I only just managed to stay upright and stagger from the room, past the startled guards. I ran the distance back to Borgia's apartments, my heart pounding and my breath coming in gasps.

Bursting into his private chamber, I caught him about to raise a goblet to his lips. At once, I cried out, "Do not!"

He stared at me over the rim. Without waiting for him to act, I closed the distance between us, seized the goblet from him, and threw it to the floor, where it shattered. Panting, hardly able to speak, I said, "You cannot eat or drink anything. No one can. You must send word . . . warn them all—"

The room was beginning to spin. I feared that I was about to faint and I might have done so had not Borgia had the presence of mind to lower me into a chair, bend me over, and tuck my head firmly between my knees.

"Breathe," he ordered, holding me by the neck so that I had no choice but to obey. When he was finally satisfied that I was no longer about to lose consciousness, he allowed me to straighten up. "Stay where you are," he directed as he went to the door and had a quick word with one of his secretaries. I saw the man pale before he rushed off to do the pontiff's bidding.

"All right," Borgia said as he returned to his seat facing me. "I have just now declared a general fast in gratitude to God for sparing Herrera's life. No morsel of food or drop of drink will pass anyone's lips until I say otherwise. Now tell me what this is about."

"The Cathar is dead." Before he could react, I said, "She took poison that was in her rosary beads. Paternoster peas . . . extremely deadly."

"And?" he prompted.

"She had that rosary with her all this time, from when we first met. Don't you see? I brought her into your household, took her around with me into the kitchens, everywhere as I did my work. If I was distracted for a moment, she could have poisoned anything I had inspected and I wouldn't have realized it. I would have gone ahead and put it under seal without suspecting that anything was wrong. There could be poison lurking anywhere and none of us the wiser."

"Do you have reason to believe she actually did that?" Borgia asked.

Loathe though I was to admit it, I nodded. "It is what I would have done. A final way to destroy you and bring ruin down on the Church, in case everything else went wrong." And it would have worked if I, who so resisted the notion that the "abbess" and I were alike in any way, had not been able to realize her intent.

Borgia sat back and regarded me solemnly. "Very well; we will send to the town for such supplies as are available. That, at least, will make us popular with the townspeople. When you have recovered, you can begin re-inspecting anything that hasn't spoiled in the meantime."

"You are being remarkably calm about this," I said. "We both know that I put my need to learn about myself above my responsibility to protect you." It was the simple truth. I saw nothing to be gained by trying to evade it, nor did I expect him to allow me to do so even for a moment.

Truly, it was a night for surprises.

Borgia smiled faintly. "Yet here I am, alive and well. Why do you suppose that is?"

"Because I—"

"Told the truth just now, admitted your error. Did not try to save yourself at my expense. You could have, you know. Only you and the 'abbess' knew what took place between you. You could have claimed that she died from poison that you gave her."

The look His Holiness sent me suggested that he had suspected me of being prepared to do exactly that. He may even have counted on it to further conceal how close he had come to disaster.

And yet I had to say, "I have failed you in every way. Mother Benedette did not know who hired her. We are no closer to discovering who tried to kill you than we were before."

"That is unfortunate," Borgia said. "But I wonder, what did she tell you about your mother?"

"That doesn't matter. It was all lies."

"That she spun?"

"No, she was given a story to tell me."

"And that story was . . . ?"

Seeing that he would not relent, I related it as quickly and succinctly as I could manage. All I wanted was to put it behind me and go on with my confession, but Borgia seemed inclined to do otherwise; he listened with great care. When I finished, he said, "But that is all true. That really is what happened to your mother, and to you."

I stared at him in bewilderment. "How could you know that?"

"Did you think that I would hire your father for such a vital position in my household without investigating him thoroughly first? No, I knew what had happened, and after he had been with me for a while, we spoke of it."

My hands clasped the arms of the chair in which he had put me. I held on tightly as the world threatened once again to whirl away. "I don't understand. Who else knew the truth?"

Borgia looked pleased that I had the wit to ask the question. "Who else indeed?"

When I continued to stare at him in blank confusion, he said, "Your mother was born and raised in Milan. She died in a small village not far from that city, still well within the lands of the Duke of Milan, Ludovico Sforza. He would have had no difficulty finding out the truth."

"He is behind this? The Sforzas are?"

"Ironic, isn't it? All this time, I've been blaming della Rovere." The difficulty of giving up his justification for contriving to murder his great rival weighed heavily on him. He sighed deeply. "No wonder my esteemed son-in-law went out of his way to give such grave offense that I had no choice but to banish him from here. He must have been warned that this was not an opportune time to be in my vicinity."

"And now?" I asked. What would happen to Lucrezia and her not-quite husband? What price would Borgia exact in order to protect his papacy and his grand vision of his own immortality?

"And now," he said as his good humor returned, "thanks to you, I know who among those who call themselves my friends are in fact my enemies. That will be quite useful."

"Even so, I failed—"

"And I know something that I didn't even so much as suspect before now. The Cathars really are a threat. We will have to be alert to them in the future."

Staring at him, I saw his satisfaction in the present victory but also his avid appetite for the fight ahead. Truly, he was a man who thrived on the struggle for power in this world, no matter that it brought pain and death to others.

Slowly, I said, "The Cathars believe that you serve not God but Satan. Indeed, you are the head of his church on Earth. Killing you and setting the Church on the path to its own destruction would be the supreme act of redemption. Whoever did it would be assured of being liberated from this world forever."

Mother Benedette died smiling. I would never forget that.

"What do you believe, Francesca?"

What indeed? That if the Cathar "abbess" had succeeded in doing what she was hired to do and shattering the alliance, Borgia might have been forced to give up his grandiose vision for *la famiglia* and make peace with his rivals in order to survive? Or that he might simply have been undone and another man put in his place? In either case, war might have been averted.

It would not be now. As much as I still wanted to believe otherwise, that hard truth could not be avoided. War was coming as surely as the sun was rising behind Il Papa, a bloodred sun threatening to drown the world. And I had helped to bring it about.

That was what the abbess had wanted all along. The Church torn apart, at war with itself and with the most powerful Christian monarchs. What could hope to survive such a cataclysm?

I had time to ponder that question several days later as, His Holiness having pronounced himself satisfied with the fortifications at Viterbo, we set out to return to Rome. Cesare rode beside me along most of the route. In the hours we had spent together beside Herrera's bed, we had become closer in a way neither of us needed to speak about but which I think we both understood. He knew most, though not all, of what had happened with the Cathar "abbess," and he knew, better than any other, my fears. We disagreed on only one point.

"War," Cesare pronounced, "is not evil. Tragic, yes, especially for those who suffer because of it. But properly undertaken, it can be a force for good."

"War," I countered, "is the absence of peace, just as Augustine said that evil is the absence of good. Both are the fault of man, not God."

As I spoke, we crested the last hill. Below, Rome glinted in the sun. The rain had stopped and a fair wind was blowing, carrying the stink of the city to welcome us. The Tiber had returned to its banks and the plague had once again abated. The markets looked full, the streets bustling. Somewhere among them were dear friends, even those like Rocco with changed lives. As my own had been changed during my sojourn in the countryside. I returned to the city the same woman who had left it yet also someone else. A woman who knew her past.

Cesare gave a shout just then and surged his mount down the slope. I followed but more slowly. Over his shoulder, he called to me, "Don't worry so much about what is coming, Francesca. Seize what is now!"

Perhaps it was his smile that emboldened me. Or perhaps I simply knew that he was right. I took a breath, set my heels to the chestnut mare, and rushed to meet the endless, unfolding moment.

1. In modern terms, Francesca Giordano suffers from post-traumatic shock related to an event early in her life. Is she helped or harmed by the discovery of what really happened to her? Is the uncovering of hidden truths always beneficial or are there times when secrets should remain unspoken?

2. Do you consider Francesca to be insane? Is her willingness to kill a result of her troubled mental state or a rational response to circumstances in her world?

3. Francesca has a complex relationship with her employer, Cardinal Rodrigo Borgia. Why do you think he withheld information about her past from her? What role may he have played in the murder of her father?

4. Francesca lives at a time when both secular and religious powers are clashing for control of a rapidly changing world. How does that struggle shape this story and the challenges that she faces?

5. While she yearns for the glassmaker, Rocco, and the life she could have had with him, Francesca does not hesitate to pursue a relationship with Cesare Borgia that is sexual and more. Is she hypocritical in having feelings for both men or is she drawn to each for different reasons?

6. The Cathars believed that the material world is ruled by evil that can be escaped only by rebirth into a realm of light. Numerous followers from all classes of society were drawn to this spiritual view. What do you think influenced people to so completely reject this world and seek to escape it forever?

7. Why did the Roman Catholic Church act so brutally toward the Cathars and others considered to be heretics? Would a spirit of religious tolerance have helped conditions in Europe or would it have weakened institutions

St. Martin's Griffin

that were forces for stability, education, and overall social advancement?

8. Lucrezia Borgia is depicted very differently in this story from much of what has been written about her. Why do you think she has been portrayed in such dark terms historically? Did being a woman make her more vulnerable to exploitation by her family's enemies?

9. As Rodrigo's son, Cesare Borgia has access to great power yet he cannot use it to claim the life he truly wants. What acts might his frustration give rise to?

10. Throughout this story, poison appears as a metaphor for the stain of corruption running through the highest levels of society. Is a similar metaphor appropriate in our own time and if so, where?

11. What role do you think the corruption of the popes and other high-ranking prelates of this time played in triggering the rebellion against Catholicism that we know as the Reformation? Were there internal reforms the Catholic leadership could have taken that might have prevented the Reformation from happening?

12. If Rodrigo Borgia's dream of a papal dynasty controlled by his family had succeeded, what would have been the implications for his time? For ours?

GET A STRONG DOSE OF THE POISONER MYSTERIES

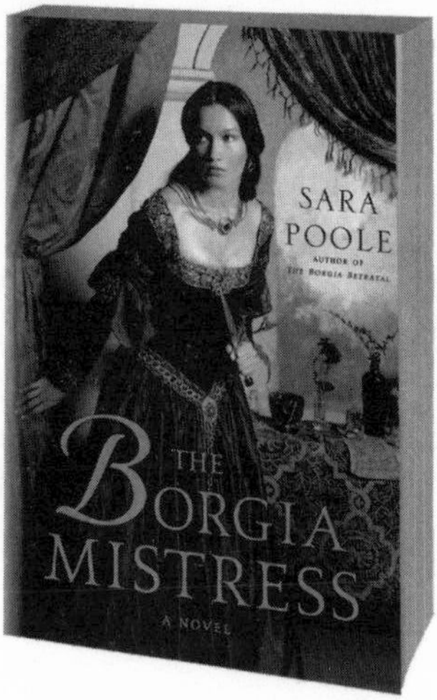

Mistress of death Francesca Giordano—court poisoner to the House of Borgia—returns to confront an ancient atrocity that threatens to plunge the world into eternal darkness.

"[An] aromatic elixir of political power plays, seductive romance, and dark derring-do."

—*PUBLISHERS WEEKLY*

"[A] stunning debut . . . deftly mixing historical fact and fiction."

—*BOOKLIST*
(STARRED REVIEW)

ST. MARTIN'S GRIFFIN
WWW.STMARTINS.COM